Reading plays: interpretation and reception

This volume of essays considers the whole concept of reading plays. Reading a play is a strange activity totally unlike the reading of any other literary text. Who reads plays and why do they read them? Among others, the readers may be actors in performance, playwrights reading to actors, directors producing a performance, or critics analysing plays. These activities and the reasons for reading a play are considered in the essays. The playwrights range from Terence, Shakespeare and Molière to Chekhov, Pinter and Peter Weiss.

READING PLAYS
interpretation and reception

Edited by
HANNA SCOLNICOV &
PETER HOLLAND

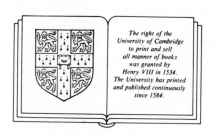

The right of the
University of Cambridge
to print and sell
all manner of books
was granted by
Henry VIII in 1534.
The University has printed
and published continuously
since 1584.

CAMBRIDGE UNIVERSITY PRESS
Cambridge
New York   Port Chester   Melbourne   Sydney

Published by the Press Syndicate of the University of Cambridge
The Pitt Building, Trumpington Street, Cambridge CB2 1RP
40 West 20th Street, New York, NY 10011, USA
10 Stamford Road, Oakleigh, Melbourne 3166, Australia

© Cambridge University Press 1991

First published 1991

Printed in Great Britain at the University Press, Cambridge

British Library cataloguing in publication data
Reading plays: interpretation and reception.
  1. Drama. Reading
  1. Scolnicov, Hanna   11. Holland, Peter, *1951–*
  808.2

Library of Congress cataloguing in publication data
Reading plays: interpretation and reception / edited by Hanna Scolnicov and
Peter Holland.
  p.   cm.
ISBN 0-521-39411-2
1. Drama.   2. Theater.   I. Scolnicov, Hanna.   II. Holland, Peter,
1951–   .
PN1655.T57   1991
801'.952–dc20   90-33172 CIP

ISBN 0 521 39411 2 hardback

SE

CONTENTS

ILLUSTRATIONS

CONTRIBUTORS

Una Chaudhuri, *New York University*
Dwora Gilula, *The Hebrew University of Jerusalem*
Herbert Grabes, *Justus Liebig Universität, Giessen*
Julian Hilton, *University of East Anglia*
Peter Holland, *Trinity Hall, University of Cambridge*
Tetsuo Kishi, *Kyoto University*
Ruth von Ledebur, *Universität Gesamthochschule, Siegen*
E.A. Levenston, *The Hebrew University of Jerusalem*
Wolfgang Matzat, *Munich University*
Manfred Pfister, *Universität Passau*
James Redmond, *Westfield College, University of London*
Hanna Scolnicov, *The Hebrew University of Jerusalem*
Maya Slater, *Westfield College, University of London*
Stanley Wells, *The Shakespeare Institute, University of
    Birmingham*

I

Introduction

HANNA SCOLNICOV

To read a play is what Shakespeare called in one of his sonnets 'to hear with eyes'. The reading of plays, which seemed to have fallen out of favour when plays became play-texts, mere scores waiting to be performed, has had an exciting comeback. The new developments in reception theory have resulted in a fresh revisionist approach to reading in general and to the reading of plays in particular.

Literary studies have made major advances in understanding the activity of reading. Theatre studies need to do the same, in their own terms; simple borrowing from literary criticism does not do justice to the specificity of theatre. Reading plays is an activity recognizably different from reading fiction or poetry. In our reading of plays we must bring to bear our knowledge of changing theatre conditions, i.e. try to relate the play to the realities of performance. Modern research has made us increasingly aware of the nature of theatrical conventions, their provenance, the constraints they impose, and their function and meaning.

The reading of plays has also become increasingly concerned with the non-verbal aspects of the text itself. Some of these aspects are described in the stage directions; others, such as gestures and voice inflexions, are only implied and need to be interpreted and justified. The expressive power of body language can be played with or against the spoken word, suggesting alternative interpretations. The spatial and temporal dimensions embedded in the play need to be understood both in scenic and conceptual terms apart from their realization in production.

In this volume of essays, theatre scholars from different countries discuss the special problems involved in reading a play in the light of present-day theories of literature and theatre. Shakespeare provides the battleground for many of the arguments, but the range of plays used as examples is wide, reflecting the different interests and disciplines of the various participants.

Some of the essays in this volume reflect on the theoretical problems concerning the reading of plays, while others demonstrate their methodologies or skills in offering their own particular readings of plays. Special cases of 'privileged' readers, such as the playwright himself reading his play to the company, one playwright incorporating his imaginative reading of another writer's play in his own drama, or the editor's authoritative control of the text, are dealt with in different papers.

A number of the papers address the issue that different readings may provide different, often mutually exclusive, interpretations, while the theatre audience is offered a particular interpretation, the choices having already been made for it. While we may accept the need for imposing a coherent interpretation on the text in production, we can still regret that our freedom of choice has been pre-empted and the crucial issues pre-judged. The question at stake is whether the production ought to be regarded as autonomous and evaluated on its own terms, or judged by criteria that refer back to the play itself, thus taking for granted a familiarity with the play-text.

Of all the readers of plays perhaps the playwright himself is the most intriguing. In the opening essay, Peter Holland traces the long history of the tradition of the playwright reading his completed play to the company of actors. From the practices of the English Renaissance companies to the systematized bureaucratic procedures of the Comédie-Française, the custom is revealed as a strange and significant moment of transition: the control over the play is symbolically transferred from writer to performers by the writer becoming himself a performer. Looking at the evidence for the event in theatre histories, genre paintings and photographs, satiric plays and anguished letters from playwrights, Holland is able to show the pervasive nature of the custom in England, France and Russia over four centuries and to suggest something of its meaning.

Amongst the many mediators between the reader and the play, arguably the most important is he who determines the text: its editor. Decrying interventionist editing and the conflation of variant texts which has bedevilled Shakespeare editions since the eighteenth century, Stanley Wells outlines his own editorial policy when working on the Oxford Shakespeare. A special problem facing a modern editor of a dramatic text is how to convey to the reader the experience of seeing the play in performance. With this aim in mind, the editor is in fact assuming some of the responsibilities of the director. Wells warns of the danger that in inserting clarifying stage directions the editor will often close interpretative options. Therefore 'both director and actor need to know how . . . to "read" the edited text in order to feel the freedom to explore it within the appropriate limits'.

Many have claimed that a play is meant to be performed and that it can only fully realize its potential when fleshed out on stage. James Redmond sets out to remind us that this was not always the case. Generations of playwrights, from Ben Jonson onwards, believed that their plays were diminished and even demeaned in production. They felt that drama is too rich and many-layered to be adequately communicated in the theatre. The bias against the vulgarity of the stage drove many critics to relegate Shakespeare's plays to 'the theatre of the mind', 'the closet theatre' or 'mental theatre'. Redmond places the reading versus performing debate within its historical context, and thinks it is being currently resolved through the coming together of professional theatre with academic teaching and research. The co-operation is transforming the traditional relationship between the dramatic text and the theatrical performance.

The traditions of reading created by critics often bear perilously little relationship to the texts they purport to describe. Dwora Gilula shows how the generalized assumptions about Terence's plots enshrined in conventional analysis do not in fact constitute an accurate assessment of the plays themselves. Her careful analysis of the action of Terence's *Andria* shows that the 'duality method' does not reflect the play at all. Critical reading here becomes misreading.

The difficulty of reading a dramatic text is analysed by Herbert

Grabes. He points to the absence of a predominant perspective and to the problem of grouping separate sentences 'allocated to the same name' into a dramatic character, and, further, the relating of different pronouncements to each other so as to discover the plot. While in performance the dialogue is supplemented by the spectacle, in reading it must be played out in 'the theatre of the mind'. Examples are drawn from different kinds of drama, in order to show the different stratagems employed by playwrights to provide helpful clues for the imagination. The ultimate example from Robert Wilson brings Grabes to the conclusion that the present-day devaluation of the spoken word in the theatre and upgrading of the spectacular element, while helping the theatre come into its own, has made the reading of plays an even more demanding activity.

The problem of making sense of printed dialogue is also taken up by Manfred Pfister. In the printed dialogue, the speakers appear to be disembodied voices, but their physical presence may nevertheless inscribe itself into the text in a variety of ways. Shakespeare's plays are so accessible to reading partly because his characters often talk directly about their own or each other's bodies. The question of body language is raised by Pfister in the context of sixteenth-century thinking. While Bacon believed that true meaning could be discovered in the discrepancy between word and gesture, Montaigne was sceptical of the conventional bodily sign as an authentic self-expression. The Elizabethan semiology of movement and gesture is shown to derive from the ancient study of rhetoric.

One distinct area in which we engage in a professional reading of plays is teaching. Ruth von Ledebur reports on an experimental seminar in which she combined close textual reading with the play-in-performance approach. The particular text studied was *The Merchant of Venice*, which challenged her German students to come to grips with its antisemitism. The students were encouraged to view the play within different historical contexts, including their own. Von Ledebur sees the achievement of the seminar as having provided its participants with the experience of the freedom of the reader while at the same time demanding of them that they assume full responsibility for their particular readings.

Malvolio's decoding of his mistress's faked letter is analysed by Julian Hilton as a paradigm of the critical process of reading a play.

In this famous episode Shakespeare has planted a clue and a warning for the reader. Like Malvolio, the reader is forever tempted to find in the text those meanings that he seeks. Malvolio is punished for taking the letter seriously; in order to avoid a similar fate, the reader of the play must adopt a double perspective, both believing the text and doubting its sincerity at one and the same time. The decisive role of the letter in Shakespeare is pursued through the analysis of the dramatic function of the letters in *Romeo and Juliet*, *Hamlet* and *Macbeth*.

The readability of Molière's plays is addressed by both Maya Slater and Wolfgang Matzat. Slater considers Molière's own bias towards performance of his plays and lack of interest in his readers. Not only are his stage directions scarce, but the little there is gives scant indication of how he envisaged the action. His printed texts record the words without providing clues for the future producer or reader, except in those rare cases when he feels the need to supply directions for the professional handling of some complicated stage business involving a number of actors. The exception which proves the rule is the text of *Le Tartuffe*; probably because it was banned from performance, the text seems designed to help the reader.

Matzat defines theatricality as that which distinguishes the art of the theatre from other art forms, the specific aesthetic possibilities of theatrical communication. Paradoxically, we must often rely on the written text to investigate the theatrical dimension of a drama because no documents of its staging remain. Matzat's reading of *Dom Juan* and *Le Bourgeois gentilhomme* discovers in them two different modes of theatricality. The theatrical structures of the two plays are related to problems of social interaction and identity inherent in seventeeth-century French society.

In her comparative study of *Hamlet* and *The Seagull*, Hanna Scolnicov analyses Chekhov's play as a special kind of reading: one playwright's reading of another. She sees *The Seagull* as a naturalistic and impressionistic reworking of structural and thematic elements used by Shakespeare. Chekhov seems to be drawn to the earlier play because of its reflexive concern with the nature of dramatic creation. Following Shakespeare, Chekhov uses the play within the play as an aesthetic sounding board which enables him to examine the conventions of the theatre and propose alternatives. Chekhov's naturalism is shown to solve the Shakespearean dilemma of how to express emotion on stage or correlate word and gesture, although Chekhov himself indicates that his solution is valid for his age, not for all time.

Edward Levenston explores the parallels between Shaw's excessive use of explanatory stage directions and fictional narrative. Shaw hoped that this supplementary material would eliminate, as far as possible, any misunderstanding of tone or intent in the dialogue. Shaw's reader is offered a much closer, privileged view of many details than the spectator can ever hope for. The elaborate stage directions are addressed to an implied reader who has not seen the plays performed. Although they are meant as a substitute for the full stage production, the stage directions in fact often exceed that function, providing moral judgement, background information or analysis.

Particular readings of modern drama are offered by Una Chaudhuri and Tetsuo Kishi. Chaudhuri sees *Marat/Sade* as a self-reflexive play dealing with the questions of the historicity of drama. In the philosophical debates between de Sade and Marat, Peter Weiss shows two different interpretations of the same events or two possible readings. De Sade's play within the play is used to demonstrate how the political statement of the play as a whole, made through the use of historical analogue, assumes paradoxical and contradictory meanings, subjective and biased interpretations.

Tetsuo Kishi's reading of *Old Times* goes beyond the surface of the text to reveal what he calls 'the much nastier subtext'. He analyses in detail a particular sequence of the Pinteresque dialogue conducted through snatches of songs from the thirties. Kishi shows how crucial the familiarity with these songs is to the understanding of what is going on in the subtext. Only thus can one detect the deliberate mistakes that are introduced by the dramatic contenders in order to score points. This paper claims that the play can only be fully appreciated by those acquainted with the quoted songs and demonstrates the complex intertextuality behind this deceptively simple-looking text.

Most of the essays included here are based on papers presented at the Jerusalem Theatre Conference 1988, which was devoted to the same topic as the present volume, *To Read a Play*. The Conference was organized by the Department of Theatre Studies in the Hebrew University of Jerusalem in association with the Israel Festival. This volume follows *The Play Out of Context* (Cambridge University Press, 1989), comprising essays from the previous Conference of 1986. I wish to thank my friends and colleagues in Israel and abroad for the help we have received in editing this book, and especially Sarah Stanton of Cambridge University Press for her continued interest and support. To work with Peter Holland has once again been a pleasure which has mitigated the labours of this volume.

2

Reading to the company

PETER HOLLAND

> Lifting my head I could see above me a frosted-glass globe full of
> light, in a glass case to one side a silver wreath of colossal
> dimensions adorned with ribbons and inscribed: 'To our beloved
> Independent Theatre from the members of the Moscow Bar . . .'
> (the final word was illegible); in front of me were rows of actors'
> faces mostly with forced smiles.[1]

That nervous awareness of other things in the room, of the look of
the members of the audience or the attempt to try to decipher an
inscription just outside our field of vision is only too familiar to all of
us who make our living by lecturing. It is a feeling that ought to
make us peculiarly sensitive to actors as they attempt to control
what Stanislavsky dubbed their 'circle of attention'. The next thing
is that a panicky awareness of something happening somewhere else
can begin to impinge on our hearing:'In the distance I was aware of
silence and occasionally something like a droning chorus which
would be interrupted by a noise like a crowd of people in a bath-
house.'[2] But the circumstances of this particular description are not
those of an ordinary lecture: the hero of Bulgakov's comic novel
Black Snow is reading his play to the assembled company of the
Independent Theatre, Bulgakov's thinly disguised version of the
Moscow Art Theatre. Bulgakov's playwright nervously reads his
play to a group of actors, theatre directors and anyone else who
claims the right to be there, friends, hangers-on, the mass of people
who accumulate on the fringes of the theatre company. Neither
lecturer nor actor, the playwright reads his own text to a bizarre
theatrical audience.

My concern in this paper is with the history and meaning of the event Bulgakov describes, an event that has always seemed to me paradoxical. Either as part of the process of getting a play accepted for production or as the opening stage of the process of rehearsal it was – and sometimes still is – the practice for the playwright, who is not an actor, to read the play to a group of actors. The professional whose skill is writing is required to take on the skills of the audience by becoming an actor for a while, demonstrating the extent to which he or she lacks precisely those skills that the play needs in performance and that are available, notionally in abundance, in this especial audience. The playwright voices the play, offering his/her voice to those whose voices will, if the reading is successful, take over the play's language with even greater success. The activity may take on other overtones; it may be an act of humiliation, of pleading, of panic, an act of teaching, dominating or defining, an act of power or, much more often, of a recognition of powerlessness. On rare occasions it may turn to the playwright's advantage. Most often it will be the moment of the loss of control over the play, the loss of privilege in the control over the text's production of meaning, a loss created by, above all, demonstrating one's inadequacies to a group all too well aware of their supreme adequacy to succeed in the ordeal the playwright is undergoing.

This event, which seems to represent a rite of passage, a transfer of control from the playwright to the company, has repeatedly acquired its own strange aura of emblematic significance. The hearing of the play has become at frequent junctures symbolic, an apparent revelation not of this lack of power for the playwright within the processes of acceptance and rehearsal within the praxis of theatrical activity but, instead, of the company's awareness of the power of the writer–creator. Reading to the company, which is nearly always a moment of the loss of power by the playwright, is surprisingly frequently emblematized as, instead, the manifestation of the especial power of the art of the dramatist, before which the actors, awestruck, can only manifest their humbled and fascinated attention.

In my survey of this event I have found no more potent vision of this moment in its paradoxes and tensions than the familiar photograph of Chekhov reading *The Seagull* to the members of the

1. Chekhov reading *The Seagull* to the Moscow Art Theatre (Novosti Press Agency; Oxford University Press)

Moscow Art Theatre in September 1898 (Plate 1). There sits the dramatist, a small, bespectacled figure, holding the notebook at arm's length behind the table, apparently dwarfed and insignificant in between the potent and emphatic presence of the actors who seem rather blatantly to perform their attentiveness, vaunting their theatricality as they act their concentration. Behind Chekhov's right shoulder Stanislavsky follows the reading, less an act of listening than of reading himself as if, for him, like the actors close enough to do so, the gaze on the words themselves is a desirable accompaniment to the aural experience. Other actors, unable even to pretend to read, still look toward not the playwright but the book, exactly framed by the photographer at the centre of the image, the book which carries the text which so enthralls them being even more important than the writer responsible for the existence of the words to which they listen.

The photograph is of course highly stylized, a posed studio piece designed as a deliberate capturing of a moment of history as the overwhelming impact of Chekhov's genius is revealed to the members of the Moscow Art Theatre apparently for the first time. I would want to emphasize 'apparently' since the powerful and talismanic sense of this reading as some sort of initiating and originating event in the company's knowledge of the play is quite simply pure fiction. The photograph seems so potent – almost as if *The Seagull* had not existed for the actors before the moment this photograph documents. But, in this traditional symbolic interpretation, the image's place in the history of the theatre company itself has not been taken into account.

The Seagull had, of course, had a disastrous first production at the Alexandrinsky Theatre in St Petersburg two years earlier but it had also had a number of other productions before Nemirovich-Danchenko persuaded Chekhov to let the fledgling Moscow Art Theatre produce the play. Indeed part of his campaign of persuasion was based on these other productions: 'So you won't give me your consent for the production? But *The Seagull* is being put on everywhere. Why not put it on in Moscow? . . . There were wonderful reviews of it in the Kharkov and Odessa papers. What are you so worried about?'[3] In May 1898 Chekhov finally agreed to the production. This photograph might then appear to have followed that agreement. Chekhov was certainly not in Moscow until September 1898 and visited the company in their temporary rehearsal rooms at the Hunting Club[4] on September 9th and 11th. It must therefore have been on one of these occasions and no earlier that the photograph was taken.

Following Chekhov's consent to the production, Nemirovich-Danchenko convinced Stanislavsky to write a full production score for the play. Stanislavsky took himself off to the countryside to prepare this *mise-en-scène* in late summer. Rehearsals began at Pushkino in August, mostly under Nemirovich's control, and he sent regular reports to Chekhov about progress. Chekhov, bemused by the sheer hard work of the Moscow Art Theatre's rehearsal method, wrote hyperbolically to a friend on 24 August, 'they seem to have had almost a hundred rehearsals, and lectures are delivered to the actors'.[5] Nemirovich-Danchenko emphasized in his letters how much he needed to talk over details of the production with Chekhov.

When Chekhov finally managed to visit the company en route from Melikhovo to the Crimea he attended two days of rehearsals, admired the seriousness of the company's work, complained about the inadequacies of some of the actors and was immensely annoyed by the full and obsessive panoply of naturalism with which Stanislavsky had covered the play. There is something pleasing about the way this photograph places Stanislavsky as a slightly malevolent presence at Chekhov's shoulder while Meyerhold, who recorded Chekhov's objections to Stanislavsky's work so delightedly, sits languidly and apparently bored on the right side of the picture. Nemirovich-Danchenko gazes on interestedly from the opposite edge.

But my point does not need such a satisfying reading of the meaning of the image. The simple and usually ignored fact is that the photograph was taken when the company was well into rehearsal, when the production's form and style were already massively determined by Stanislavsky's production book with its croaking frogs and revelatory, and distinctly unChekhovian, subtext, and when the author's influence on the production was and could only be decidedly minimal. The photograph, the emblem of the company's fascination with the words of the playwright, takes on a slightly wistful aspect; it documents a fictitious interest in Chekhov's language and in the intentions of the playwright in a production that, more than any other, might be held to symbolize the overwhelming of the writer's words by the power of the director. Yet the photograph was taken.

If by 1898 the reading of the play by the playwright to the company had acquired such enormous dignity and portentousness, at first it was no such thing. In England the earliest references to this practice of reading appear in the 1590s, in Henslowe's *Diary* and the accompanying papers. It seems to have been a normal stage, between the acceptance of proposals for a new play from one of the many regular writers used by the company and the beginnings of rehearsals, for the play to be read to the company at a tavern. In March 1598, for instance, Henslowe lent money to the company to pay Drayton, Dekker and Chettle for a play called *The Famous Wars of Henry I and the Prince of Wales* and he notes 'lent at that tyme vnto the company for to spend at the Readynge of that boocke at the sonne in new fyshstreate' the sum of five shillings.[6] Sometimes the description might seem to suggest that the company itself, rather than the playwrights, did the reading,[7] but Robert Shaa's letter to

Henslowe on 8 November 1599 demonstrates that the company often heard the playwrights read as part of their deliberations over whether to accept a play: 'we have heard their booke and lyke yt their pryce is eight pound*s*.'[8]

In the lengthy series of increasingly desperate letters from Robert Daborne to Henslowe pleading for loans as advances for a series of plays long before he had finished writing, Daborne frequently refers to his willingness to read the play whenever Henslowe wishes, either to the full company or to Henslowe and Edward Alleyn. On 16 May 1613 Daborne wrote: 'I doubt not on Tuesday night if you will appoint I will meet you and Mr Alleyn and read some, for I am unwilling to read to the general company till all be finished.'[9] A month later, with the play still unfinished, Daborne was swearing 'Before God they shall not stay one hour for me, for I . . . will that night they play their new play read this'[10] while asking for 'the other twenty shillings I desired' immediately, volunteering magnanimously to wait for the forty shillings that remains until he reads 'next week'.[11] Daborne's letters tie the reading to acceptance and payment, to the economics of Renaissance playwriting.

The evidence of Colley Cibber's autobiography suggests that the reading may have had a number of functions in the Restoration well beyond simple acceptance. He narrates for instance Dryden's reading of his play *Amphitryon*: 'I heard him give it his first Reading to the Actors, in which, though it is true, he deliver'd the plain Sense of every Period, yet the whole was in so cold, so flat, and unaffecting a manner, that I am afraid of not being believ'd, when I affirm it.'[12] It is not very likely that Dryden needed in 1690 to get a new play accepted and the reading would seem to have been part of the rehearsal process. Indeed one of Cibber's other anecdotes suggests how the brilliance of the reading might inhibit the actors. When Nathaniel Lee, himself a failed actor, read a part of his play to the actor Michael Mohun at rehearsal he was, Cibber says, 'so pathetick a Reader of his own Scenes, that . . . *Mohun*, in the Warmth of his Admiration, threw down his part, and said, Unless I were able to *play* it, as well as you *read* it, to what purpose should I undertake it?'[13]

This notion of the playwright's reading at rehearsal was formalized under Cibber's joint management of Drury Lane with Wilks and Booth. Benjamin Victor, writing in 1761 and looking back to the fine judgement of the managers in the 1720s, takes as his prime instance 'their regular, and masterly Manner of governing their Rehearsals' at which, '[If] a new Play was coming on, the first three Readings fell to the Share of the Author'[14] after which each actor was required to learn his part so that when 'he is quite perfect in the Words and Cues, he can then be instructed, and practise his proper Entrances, Emphasis, Attitudes, and Exits'.[15] This practice, of the reading of the play by the playwright to the assembled cast inaugurating the rehearsal process, is a likely reason for Cibber's description of Dryden's reading *Amphitryon* as a 'first Reading'; it was a practice that continued for a considerable time. George Bernard Shaw, for instance, read *Major Barbara* to the cast a week before rehearsals started on 6 November 1905.[16] Moynet, writing in 1873 about French rehearsal methods, states without hesitation that 'the first rehearsal is the reading the author makes of the play to the artists who are to fill the roles. At this reading are present all the crew chiefs, technicians, and designers involved'.[17] This vision of the harmony of actors, playwright and stage crew seems, despite its clarity and confidence, more than a little utopian. I would note in passing that Moynet makes no mention of the presence of the director.

At times the author's nervousness was so keen that, even at this first rehearsal reading to the company, there was no other recourse than for the playwright to nominate someone else to read for him or her. Addison, in presenting *Cato* to the company in 1712, was, as Victor notes, 'a Man of too much Bashfulness and Diffidence to assume the Author, and read his Play at their first Meeting, and therefore required Mr. *Cibber* to supply his Place; who read it so much to the Satisfaction and Delight of Mr. *Addison*, that he insisted on Cibber's performing the Part of *Cato*.'[18] Sometimes the poor author, having begun the reading, was so overcome that he had to abandon it to someone else. In 1789, William Hayley managed one act of his play *Eudora* before having to hand over to Thomas Ryder.[19]

Pierce Egan, in his *The Life of an Actor* (1824), sets out to justify the practice. He recognizes that the event may appear, perhaps, rather singular . . . when there are so many better readers attached to the theatre, persons who possess a more intimate knowledge and value of emphasis, and who likewise can express the various passions with much greater effect. But, nevertheless, it is the opinion of actors in general that, however bad as to the mode or feebleness of voice with which an author may read his piece, yet it is thought he is far more likely to convey a perfect outline of his characters in the way in which he might wish them to be represented on the stage than a disinterested individual or a mere employed reader of plays.[20]

But Egan also offers an actor's view of the event, showing a characteristic theatrical gap between theory and practice. The reading requires the playwright to have 'considerable nerve' and the event is 'no very agreeable undertaking for a novice to experience' since

In several instances it is considered not only a complete bore to the performers to attend such readings, but an encroachment upon their time; and that may in some measure account for the tiresome yawn, &c., which arises more from the ludicrous circumstances often attached to the reading of a play than anything intended to convey an insult or wound the feelings of an author.[21]

Plate 2 shows the practice Egan describes at the reading to the company organized by Peregrine Proteus, Egan's hero, for 'a new tragedy, by an elderly lady',[22] the image centred on languid actor, not playwright and play. Indeed the reading is an unimportant event, generally ignored by the company who are far more interested in taking up the opportunity for theatre gossip. Theodore Lane's caricature rams home the point in its caption:

Professional Tiresome Moments: or, assumed Gravity: The sneers, smiles, yawns, shrugs, jeers, whispers, ridicule, looks of contempt, and silent criticism, an Author is subject to in reading a play to the Performers in the Green Room.

But the activity of reading was also significant at an early stage in the campaign of acceptance as the author attempted to interest an actor or someone else with influence in the company, hoping that a full-scale reading might take place. At a later stage, the author might

2. From Pierce Egan, *The Life of an Actor* (1825): 'Professional Tiresome Moments: or, assumed Gravity' (reproduced by permission of the Cambridge University Library)

well be found reading the play in the hope that the actor might be willing to take on a particular role. Cibber, for instance, trying to secure production of his first play *Love's Last Shift*, tells how Thomas Southerne, 'having had the Patience to hear me read it, to him, happened to like it so well, that he immediately recommended it to the Patentees'.[23] Shaw was not so lucky. Having convinced William Terriss, the great actor of Victorian melodrama, that Terriss's own scenario for a play was so awful that Terriss promptly threw it in the fire, Shaw wrote *The Devil's Disciple*, tailoring the leading roles for Terriss and Jessie Millward. Shaw insisted on reading the play to Terriss, not knowing that Terriss hated listening to plays read and would rather have read it to himself. Shaw's voice, with its gentle Irish lilt, promptly put Terriss to sleep. In spite of Jessie Millward's attempts to avoid disaster, Terriss woke up and dismissed the play with 'I'm afraid it won't do. I don't like the end.' Shaw icily pointed out that he hadn't yet finished. Attempts to smooth things over by offering the teetotal Shaw a whisky compounded the problem and Shaw swept out announcing that he didn't have Terriss in mind for the role anyway.[24]

The concern with casting was crucial since the author had a substantial say in the distribution of parts. Gaining the support and interest of senior or well-suited members of the acting company was obviously vital to the play's eventual success. Cibber describes how Vanbrugh who 'had the Disposal of the Parts' for his revised version of *The Pilgrim*, 'read the Play first, with me alone, and was pleas'd to offer me my choice of what I might like best for myself, in it'.[25] David Garrick wrote to the Reverend Doctor Thomas Francklin about the latter's play *Matilda*, a dreadful work that Garrick politely thought 'not so dramatic & calculate of Success as ye Earl of Warwick', Francklin's previous play. Garrick recommended that 'Dr Franklin should read ye Play to Mrs Yates & know her thoughts upon Matilda',[26] but Francklin evidently had little success since, as the editors of Garrick's letters note laconically, 'Miss Younge, however, took the title role'.

But the problems of rehearsal and casting, even the problems of the support of powerful patrons with connections, were as nothing compared with the reading to the company or, at least, the managers. Surprisingly, given the number of plays performed in

England in the eighteenth century concerned with the horrors of rehearsals, works like *The Rehearsal, The Female Wits* and *The Critic* pay no attention to the reading of the play for acceptance. Only Fielding, in his underrated but vituperative satire *The Author's Farce*, performed in 1730, chooses to dramatize this particular moment of authorial agony. At the opening of Act 2, the unfortunate author Luckless is reading his manuscript to Marplay and Sparkish, satiric portraits of Cibber and Wilks. The scene of torture, as in Henslowe, is the tavern. Luckless reads a few lines and then has to sit in mounting fury while Marplay suggests revisions line by line:

Luckless. *No matter where, so we are blessed together.*
Marplay. In my opinion it would be better so:
  No matter where, so somewhere we're together.
  Where is the question, somewhere is the answer.
  Read on, sir.
Luckless. *With thee, the barren rocks, where not one step*
  Of human race lies printed in the snow,
  Look lovely as the smiling infant spring.
Marplay. I could alter those lines to a much better idea.
  With thee, the barren blocks (that is, trees) *where not a bit*
  Of human face is painted on the bark,
  Look green as Covent Garden in the spring.[27]

When Luckless explodes at this, Marplay advises him that the play has too many faults to please the town. Luckless takes angry issue with Marplay's critical judgement but the latter falls back on a claim of professional expertise. Left alone Marplay makes clear to Sparkish that the problem is nothing to do with the play but with the playwright's lack of influence:

Marplay. It may be a very good one for aught I know; but I know the author has no interest.
Sparkish. Give me interest, and rat the play.
Marplay. Rather rat the play which has no interest.[28]

As Sterne said, in a totally different context, 'they order . . . this matter better in France'. In France, and at the Comédie-Française in particular, the activity of the playwright's reading for acceptance has been institutionalized according to a remarkably strict set of rules. Soon after the establishment of the company in 1680 the preliminary selection of plays was placed in the hands of the *comédiens* called 'quinzaniers' or 'semainiers' who ran the company between general meetings. But the selected plays were read to all the *comédiens* (*comédiennes* were excused this onerous task) and a vote was taken with coloured lots, white for acceptance, black for rejection and multi-coloured for acceptance after corrections. By 1780 the *comité de lecture* had to include two *comédiennes*. Napoleon's decrees for the restructuring of the administration of the Comédie-Française, issued from, of all places, Moscow, reorganized the *comité de lecture* but in 1901 power for acceptance was vested in the sole hands of the theatre's administrators. The resultant outcry at the disenfranchisement of the *sociétaires* paid no attention to the feelings of the authors at all. The vote was given back to the *comédiens* in 1910. The current membership of the committee is: the administrator, the doyen of the *sociétaires*, six other performers and four people from the arts world nominated by the minister.[29] It is still the case that, after preliminary written reports on plays by writers new to the Comédie-Française, *all* new plays are read by the playwright to the *comité de lecture*, though the author may nominate an actor instead; the committee then votes by secret ballot.[30]

This institutionalization of the process of acceptance can at its best allow for a certain unexpected leakiness, a series of bureaucratic gaps in which the playwright may be enabled to establish and define his/her position *vis-à-vis* the Comédie-Française in terms of the demands that can be placed on the moment of reading or its subsequent effects. It is unimaginable, for instance, that Victor Hugo could have written as arrogantly to Baron Taylor, the *commissaire royal* at the theatre, about the reading for *Le Roi s'amuse* in 1832, any earlier in his career: 'je reviendrai à Paris exprès pour la lecture; mais comme je serai obligé de retourner à Bièvre à six heures, et qu'il y a trois heures de chemin, il faudra absolument que la lecture soit finie *à trois heures au plus tard*.'[31] (I shall be returning to Paris expressly for the reading; but as I shall be obliged to return to Bièvre by six o'clock and the journey takes three hours, it is absolutely necessary that the reading be finished by three o'clock.)

3. A painting by François-Joseph Heim, *Andrieux faisant une lecture dans le foyer de la Comédie-Française* (Bibliothèque Nationale, Paris; Comédie-Française)

The peremptory tone is that of a playwright assured of success, fully aware that the reading is a formality and that the theatre will bow to his whims. There is nothing of the cap-in-hand awkwardness that the event normally involved. Hugo's power at this stage is partly the result of his continual success at the manipulation of this reading, making it serve his own ends. After the reading of *Hernani* on 1 October 1829, for instance, the play was immediately cast, the normal step after a successful reading. In the steady build-up to the historic first night there were numerous attempts by the company to persuade Hugo to make changes in the text in an attempt to evade the looming fuss. But since *Hernani* had at its reading been received with delight, 'reçu par acclamations', Hugo was able to resist all arguments for changes since the nature of the company's approval, a white vote as it were, debarred them from any rights to demand. The actors simply had 'no right to require textual changes that had not been stipulated as a condition of acceptance'.[32] In the case of *Un Duel sous Richelieu*, a play of which Baron Taylor had doubts about the opening of Act 4 as well as worries about censorship, the Comédie-Française seems to have been hamstrung again by their initial enthusiasm. So tumultuous was the response at the reading to the *comité de lecture* that Baron Taylor announced 'il est inutile d'aller aux voix', adding 'M Hugo ne présente pas sa piece, c'est nous qui la lui demandons'.[33] Inevitably, at other times, the aesthetic opposition to Hugo's method was, though veiled, more visible. The hostility of those *sociétaires* who clung firmly to traditional neo-classical orthodoxies meant that the acceptance of *Les Burgraves* at its reading on 20 November 1839 was far less a matter of the theatre humbling itself, even rhetorically, before the innovative power of the writer's art.[34]

The structured and systematized formalization of the French system with its votes and rules lends itself to its own representation as image. Two paintings amply attest to its generalized cultural significance. The first (Plate 3), a painting by François-Joseph Heim, purports to show 'Andrieux faisant une lecture dans le foyer des artistes de la Comédie-Française'. The reader, centred as in the photograph of Chekhov reading *The Seagull*, here does not need to peer at the manuscript. Instead he declaims with his arms spread, holding the manuscript at arm's length, and his face set in a

4. Henri-Adolphe Laissement, *Une lecture au comité en 1886* (Bibliothèque Nationale, Paris; Comédie-Française)

melancholy, appropriately tragic visage, performing the play as if on the stage of the theatre itself. The playwright appears to be adopting something like the gesticulatory style of French neo-classical acting, identifying himself, in the eyes of the painter, as an actor in the presence of actors. Like the Chekhov photograph again, the painting has a certain mythifying quality: the reading of *Junius Brutus* did not take place before such a large group at all but to the few *sociétaires* constituting *le comité de lecture* in May 1828 and the playwright himself may not even have been present.[35] The painting becomes a tableau of the members of the Comédie-Française at a particular moment, each *comédien* easily identifiable in the painting. The representation of the company is thus brought together around its interest in the dramatist rather than around its own performances, and the dramatist can only effectively be represented in a painting at this moment of communication with the company, the moment of reading. In performance or rehearsal, not only is the full extent of the company unlikely to be visible but, more significantly, the playwright vanishes from view. Only in this hypothetical, mythical reading is the link of playwright to company available for the repertory of images.

The second (Plate 4), 'Une lecture au comité en 1886' by Henri-Adolphe Laissement, shows the *comité de lecture* in session, listening to Dumas *fils* reading *Francillon* on 4 November 1886. Again reality bows to the artist's desire to represent the institution, in this case the committee, rather than the event itself. Thiron, included in the picture, was not present at the reading and the archives show that two supplementary members, Prud'hon and Silvain, were.[36] As befits the dignity of Dumas *fils* he reads decorously, unlike Andrieux; once more the text is exactly centred in the image, as the elderly members of the committee pose themselves as icons of attentiveness. If Andrieux becomes an actor when painted reading, Dumas *fils* becomes a dull bureaucrat, a committee man reading to other committee men. The creative excitement is gone and a bourgeois dullness and institutionalized predictability takes over. This reading is a distinctly comfortable and uninspiring affair, more like a board meeting than a theatrical event.

Even within the rigidities of the French system the need to circumvent the restrictions of the system is richly apparent. The memoirs of Dumas *père* are filled with scenes of triumphant or abortive readings. The triumphs are predictable; the disasters less so. Demanding acceptance of *Antony* before the official reading, Dumas reads to the manager Crosnier who falls asleep. At another moment the reading of the play takes on a wonderfully erotic overtone as he reads to the great actress Marie Dorval to persuade her to play Adèle:

> I began to read, but she had not the patience to sit in her chair. She got up and leaning on my back, read over my shoulder with me. After the first act, I looked up and she kissed my forehead . . . I began the second act. In the scene between Adèle and Antony, a tear dropped on my manuscript, then a second and a third. I raised my face to kiss her.[37]

The scene ends not in bed but with Dumas sitting up all night rewriting Act 5 to suit Dorval's tastes.

If this scene is ambiguously a moment of the playwright's triumph, artistic if not amorous, Dumas also provides a wonderful description of the agonies not of the reader but of the listener. Realizing that prior to a full reading of his first play *Christine* he will need the approval of an examiner and learning that the queue of unread manuscripts stretches to more than a year, he manages to engineer an opportunity to read the play to Baron Taylor himself. He arrives to find that another author is already there.

> I went quickly into the sitting-room, where I found Taylor trapped in his bath-tub like a tiger in his den, a gentleman near him reading a tragedy called *Hecube*. He had surprised Taylor as Charlotte Corday had surprised Marat when she stabbed him in his bath; but the agony of the King's Commissary was more prolonged than that of the Tribune of the People. The tragedy was two thousand four hundred lines long! When the gentleman caught sight of me, he realised that his victim was about to escape. Clutching hold of the bath he exclaimed:
> 'There are only two more acts, monsieur – only two more!'
> Taylor gave one long moan, like a vanquished athlete, signalled me to go into his bedroom and, falling back into his bathtub, he bowed his head resignedly on his breast. The gentleman continued reading.[38]

If I have indulged myself so far with the accumulation of anecdotal history it is because even a partial history of this practice has never been brought together, as far as I know. But it is necessary that I should begin to bring the documentation together.

Initially the practice of reading to the company is premised on the simple material fact of the uniqueness of the manuscript combined with the nature of the 'foul papers'. Authors' manuscripts are rarely easily legible by anyone other than the author him or herself and the surviving example of Jacobean 'foul papers', the Melbourne manuscript supposedly by John Webster, together with the implications of Renaissance textual study, suggest the scale of the problem. It was not economically desirable to pay for the considerable cost of copying the entire manuscript prior to acceptance. There may, in addition, have been a problem of the actors' literacy. Only after acceptance would the preparation of prompt-book and actors' parts be a necessary and justifiable expense.

The fragmentary nature of the actors' perception of the whole text of the play, exemplified by the cue-scripts which are only partial witnesses even to the scenes in which an actor appears but also agreeing with what we know of rehearsal processes, suggests a further significance to the reading, both at this point and later: the reading to the company effectively constitutes the only view of the whole text that the actors will ever have, up to and probably even including performance itself. The reading is a moment of completeness, the indication of the wholeness of the drama before the fragmentation of rehearsal and performance. For the only time in the entire process of production the actors become audience at the whole play.

The materiality of the text, the unique status of the document in those dark ages before the photocopier, is the basis also for the degree of the author's possession of the text. The activity of acceptance of a play for production is also a transfer of ownership. The text, physically and economically placed in an exchange system, remains with the playwright to guarantee ownership of intellectual property through ownership of the sheets of manuscripts themselves.

But even at this stage the assumption of authorial control over meaning is glimpsed. The work of production is, in many ways, assumed to be foreseen by the playwright, embodied in his/her conception of performance, from the actor's characterization to the specific readings (note the word) appropriate for particular lines. As Victor's rehearsal description shows, the author as instructor, the author as director at rehearsal, is demonstrated initially within the compass of the playwright's own voice. Since performance is recurrently envisioned as a transfer of sound more than a transfer of sight and since the text's codification of meaning in movement seems more nearly completely expressible in the conventions of performance than the description of the generation of meaning in language can be embodied in the play-text, the result is that the playwright's own voice occupies the conventional position of author-authority. In the absence of the intervention of the director, that classic example of the consumption of authorial meaning in the assumption of authority over the performance of the text, the author's intentions, voiced in the reading or voiced as commentary at rehearsal, have an effective primacy. The inadequacies of authors as reader–actors, the strange collocation of skills underlying this procedure, are both patronized by the superior skills of the actor as writer, Cibber for example, and an implicit handicap to the acceptability of the play.

As the ramifications of the event begin to be more fully explored, both in the practice of theatrical activity and in the available documentation, so the place of the playwright in a system of patronage and influence is ever more emphatically underscored. Readings to potential actors, readings to people with influence on the organizational systems of the theatre company engage not only with aesthetic prejudices and the rhetoric of persuasiveness but also with the social encodifications of humble requests for patronage. The activity of reading seems at times like the work of a theatrical beggar. In the modification of the activity at the Comédie-Française the location of power is supposedly firmly defined, emphatically distant from the playwright, for all its evident manipulability. The playwright as client confronts the power of the theatre as state, the *comité de lecture* appointed by the minister.

Yet, if my evidence suggests a certain cynicism, that would be inadequate. The univocal reading can acquire a powerful multivocality, the playwright's voice can become a passionately animating ventriloquist. Here for instance is an account by Arnaldo Frateili of Pirandello's private reading of *Six Characters in Search of an Author* in 1921:

> As soon as Pirandello had finished writing [the play] he came to read the work in my house . . . we were shaken not only by the play but also by the passion with which Pirandello recited it . . . He entered into the part of each character and lived their passions intensely, almost painfully – their love and hate, their joy and pain, their ecstasy and irony . . . His voice heard from another room did not sound like the voice of one but of ten characters.[39]

Similarly, in the theatre, the playwright can act as instructor. The voicing of the text, even by the author as poor reader and poor relation in the praxis of theatre, is quite firmly premised on the inadequacy of the written text to demonstrate effectively its implicit ability to generate theatrical energy. Even actors can be notoriously unable to perceive the potential of a script when they themselves read it silently. If performance is a sphere of displaced intentionality in which the voice of the playwright is unheard except revoiced, reading to the company may have retained the last vestigial assertion of intention, even as the playwright, like a version of Lewis Carroll's Cheshire Cat, vanishes, leaving only the play-text behind.

In England the practice has virtually died out. Ann Jellicoe for some years invited professional playwrights to write community plays for amateur performance by the people of Dorchester. She always required the playwright to read the play to the town at the point between the end of the improvisation and workshop process and the beginning of the rehearsal of the final product. David Edgar, whose play *Entertaining Strangers* was written for this context and who underwent this ordeal by public reading, has offered a sense of the event as a wry triumph at the moment of despair when the play leaves the writer; as he says, 'It might as well be done properly once'.[40]

Notes

1. Mikhail Bulgakov, *Black Snow*, translated by Michael Glenny (London: Flamingo (1967) 1986), p. 59.
2. Ibid.

3. Letter of May 1898, quoted in S.D. Balukhaty, ed., *The Seagull produced by Stanislavsky* (London: Denis Dobson, 1952), p. 52.
4. Ibid., p. 59.
5. Ibid., p. 57.
6. R.A. Foakes and R.T. Rickert, eds., *Henslowe's Diary* (Cambridge: Cambridge University Press, 1961), p. 88.
7. See, for example, the entry for May 1602 for a loan to 'the companye when they Read the playe of Jeffa' (ibid., p. 201).
8. Ibid., p. 288.
9. G.E. Bentley, *The Profession of Dramatist in Shakespeare's Time 1590–1642* (Princeton: Princeton University Press, 1971), p. 77.
10. Ibid., p. 78
11. W.W. Greg, ed., *Henslowe Papers* (London: A.H. Bullen, 1907), p. 73.
12. B.R.S. Fone, ed., *An Apology for the Life of Colley Cibber* (Ann Arbor: University of Michigan Press, 1968), p. 67.
13. Ibid., pp. 67–8.
14. B. Victor, *The History of the Theatres of London and Dublin* (London: T. Davies *et al.*, 1761), vol. II, p. 4.
15. Ibid., vol. II, p. 5.
16. Bernard Shaw, *Major Barbara: a Facsimile of the Holograph MS*, ed. B.F. Dukore (New York: Garland, 1981), p. xiv.
17. M.J. Moynet, *French Theatrical Production in the Nineteenth Century*, ed. M.A. Carlson (New York: SUNY at Binghamtown, 1976), p. 119.
18. Victor, op. cit., vol. II, pp. 29–30.
19. C.B. Hogan *The London Stage 1776–1800: A Critical Introduction* (Carbondale: Southern Illinois University Press, 1968), p. cxlviii.
20. P. Egan, *The Life of an Actor* (London: Pickering & Chatto, 1892 (1824)), p. 248.
21. Ibid., p. 249.
22. Ibid., p. 248.
23. Fone, op. cit., p. 118.
24. George Powell, *William Terriss and Richard Prince* (London: Society for Theatre Research, 1987), pp. 53–4.
25. Fone, op. cit., pp. 148–9.
26. D.M. Little and G.M. Kahrl, *The Letters of David Garrick* (London: Oxford University Press, 1963), vol. III, p. 938.
27. Henry Fielding, *The Author's Farce*, ed. C.B. Woods (London: Edward Arnold, 1967), II.i.10–19.
28. Ibid., II.ii.3–6.
29. See Sylvie Chevalley, *La Comédie-Française hier et aujourd'hui* (Paris: Didier, 1979), pp. 73–4.
30. Ibid., p. 87.
31. Quoted in V. Hugo, *Théâtre complet* (Paris: Pléiade, 1963–4), 2 vols., I 1787.

32. W.D. Howarth, *Sublime and Grotesque* (London: Harrap, 1975), p. 149.
33. Quoted in Hugo, *Théâtre complet*, I 1755.
34. Ibid., II 1825.
35. See Sylvie Chevalley, *La Comédie-Française 1680–1962*, exhibition catalogue from the Chateau de Versailles (Versailles: Ministère des Affaires Culturelles, 1962), p. 101.
36. See P. Dux, *La Comédie-Française 1680–1980* (Paris: Bibliothèque Nationale, 1980), pp. 202–3.
37. Alexandre Dumas (*père*), *My Memoirs*, ed. A. Craig Bell (London: Peter Owen, 1961), p. 198.
38. Ibid., p. 124.
39. G. Giudice, *Pirandello: A Biography* (London: Oxford University Press, 1975), p. 115.
40. Private comment. My thanks to David Edgar, Peter Raby, Paula Backscheider and all the other friends I badgered for examples.

3
To read a play: the problem of editorial intervention

STANLEY WELLS

Many paradoxes inhere in the concept of 'reading' a 'play' – or at least of supposing that the reading experience is to any substantial degree an effective substitute for the experience of seeing a play in performance. Indeed, current critical vocabulary permits us to speak of 'reading' a play while seeing it performed, so I should specify that by reading I mean here not 'interpreting' but literally 'reading the text of' a play, an activity that is virtually essential for those who need to learn the words they are to speak on stage, and for others involved in the production process, but that might reasonably be proscribed to anyone else. For centuries people have read the texts of plays with the expectation of the same kind of pleasure as they might receive from a novel, a romance, an epic, or a narrative poem: the pleasure of following and becoming emotionally involved in a story, of encountering interesting and amusing characters, and of enjoying the writer's literary skills; and of course it is true that dramatic texts can afford these pleasures. Many dramatic texts are perceived to be of high literary value, and the period of English drama which is most highly esteemed – the period lasting for a comparatively short time, from the late 1580s to, I suppose, the early 1620s – happens to be one in which the literary and rhetorical content of plays was particularly high.

This may seem a tendentious assertion; it might be suggested that this period of English drama has been overvalued precisely because literary rather than dramatic or theatrical criteria have been applied to it, and that correspondingly, texts of other periods which offer less to the armchair-based reader have been undervalued for that reason. But it is an important factor that Elizabethan and Jacobean drama, highly poetic and rhetorical though much of it is, is also a drama of performance. It is not, like the drama of the romantic period – the plays of Keats, Wordsworth, Coleridge and Shelley – the drama of writers standing more or less wistfully outside the theatre and hoping to break in, or even, in some cases, simply using the dramatic form – as Shelley does in *Prometheus Unbound* – as a literary device, with no thoughts of practicable performance; on the contrary, the drama of Shakespeare and his contemporaries is rooted in performance, is poetic and rhetorical because this was the current theatrical mode, emerging from a period when all drama had been written in verse. The literary content of such a drama is ultimately inseparable from its dramatic power; its poetry and its prose are properly experienced only through performance.

Nevertheless, it is inevitable that such a drama should offer much pleasure to the literary-minded reader, and understandable that booksellers, and indeed writers themselves, should have sought an alternative market for dramatic texts, printing them so that they could be read both by those who had already seen the plays performed and by those who had not done so, and perhaps could not do so. To some writers this was a purely commercial matter, just a way of getting paid twice for a single product. Others were more scrupulous, and in differing ways. For instance, Thomas Heywood, in the Epistle to his play *The Rape of Lucrece* (printed 1608), claims that he is publishing it only because some of his plays have, without his knowledge or approval, 'accidentally come into the printer's hands' in a 'corrupt and mangled' form, 'copied only by the ear'; before this happened he had scorned those who 'used a double sale of their labours, first to the stage, and after to the press'. Elsewhere, too (in the Epistle to *The English Traveller*, printed 1633), Heywood disclaims the ambition 'to be in this kind voluminously read'. And John Marston, in the Epistle to *The Malcontent* (printed 1604), shows awareness that publication by printing of a work intended for performance may misrepresent it: 'only one thing afflicts me', he writes, 'to think that scenes invented merely to be spoken should be enforcively published to be read, and that the least hurt I can receive is to do myself the wrong' (in other words, if the play must be printed, at least it is better if this is done under the author's personal supervision); he asks his readers to forgive 'the unhandsome shape which this trifle in reading presents . . . for the pleasure it once afforded you when it was presented with the soul of lively action'. Other writers expressed their sense that what worked on the stage would not necessarily please the reader; so, for example, the publisher of Marlowe's *Tamburlaine*, in 1590, wrote that he had 'purposely omitted and left out some fond and frivolous gestures . . . though haply they have been of some vain conceited fondlings greatly gaped at what times they were showed upon the stage in their graced deformities', since for them 'to be mixtured in print with such matter of worth, it would prove a great disgrace to so honourable and stately a history'.

Other dramatists, rather than simply explaining that their plays were not meant to be read, attempted to mitigate the damage that might be done by this kind of publication by providing apparatus designed, with various degrees of thoroughness, to add to the printed text material that would go some way towards filling in for the reader the theatrical dimension that he would otherwise have had to imagine for himself. The most conspicuous example in Shakespeare's time is Ben Jonson, whose scholarly pretensions made him particularly sensitive to the impact that his printed texts – his 'works', as he was mocked for calling them when they were printed in folio – would make on the reading public. Thus, for example, he furnished the printed text of *Every Man Out of his Humour* (1600) with a list of the Persons in the Play along with neat little character sketches as well as providing more detailed indications of stage action than are found in most plays of the period. Jonson was particularly sensitive in his presentation of works that had been less well received in the theatre than he thought they deserved. On the title page of *The New Inn* (1631) he blazes forth his anger with both performers and spectators while indicating greater faith in his readers: it is 'a comedy, as it was never acted, but most negligently played, by some, the King's servants, and more squeamishly beheld and censured by others, the King's subjects . . . now at last set at liberty to the readers, his majesty's servants and subjects, to be judged'. A dedication 'to the reader' inveighs against the play's spectators at its single performance, and Jonson provides on their behalf a detailed summary of the action – perhaps itself a covert admission that, as some spectators found at the play's 1987 revival in Stratford-upon-Avon, the plot is by no means crystal-clear from the dialogue alone. Again, there are prose sketches of the persons of the play along, this time, with 'some short characterism of the chief actors', and the author provides not only the original epilogue but an additional one 'made for the play in the poet's defence, but the play lived not in opinion to have it spoken', rounding off with the ode to himself begotten, as he says, by 'the vulgar censure of his play by some malicious spectators'.

The care with which Jonson prepared his plays for the reading public looks forward to the ample Prefaces and highly literary stage directions of Bernard Shaw and other dramatists of the early twentieth century. Shaw – like Jonson – was a dramatist of ideas, a highly articulate and aggressive personality who liked to thrust himself between his interpreters and his public. He would have liked to act his plays single-handed; since even he admitted that this was impossible he had, as he put it in the Preface to *Plays Unpleasant* (1898), to 'fall back on his powers of literary expression, as other poets and fictionists do'. He was aware of – and slightly exaggerated – the originality of his methods, claiming that the presentation of plays as literary texts 'has hardly been seriously attempted by dramatists. Of Shakespear's plays we have not even complete prompt copies: the folio gives us hardly anything but the bare lines. What would we not give for the copy of *Hamlet* used by Shakespear at rehearsal, with the original stage "business" scrawled by the prompter's pencil? And if we had in addition the descriptive directions which the author gave on the stage: above all, the character sketches, however brief, by which he tried to convey to the actor the sort of person he meant him to incarnate' – the sort of thing, that is, that Jonson gives us in *Every Man Out of his Humour* – 'what a light they would shed, not only on the play, but on the history of the sixteenth century! Well, we should have had all this and much more if Shakespear, instead of merely writing out his lines, had prepared the plays for publication in competition with fiction as elaborate as that of Meredith.' (Apparently Shaw had not recently read Sidney's *Arcadia*.)

Shaw has, of course, a self-centred view of the dramatist in relation to his work, one which we may feel to be at the opposite pole from Shakespeare's self-effacing trust in his interpreters, but he points usefully to the fact that for centuries the dominant way of putting a play into print, and so making it available to readers (and to performers), was to hand over to a printer the script as it had already been handed over to the actors for performance, with only minimal alterations; indeed, for some dramatists, including Shakespeare, we have reason to believe that the script given to the printer was in some cases a late draft in even less finished a condition than that from which the actors would work. Such scripts lack any kind of 'presentational' material: none of Shakespeare's plays printed in his lifetime has any dedication, epistle to the reader, list of characters, scene locations, notes or act or scene divisions. These scripts use abbreviations, especially of characters' names, that may be incomprehensible to a reader; sometimes (especially in crowd scenes) they do not specify exactly who is to speak particular speeches; and they give at most a bare minimum of stage directions. On the whole, the more deeply involved an author is with the company that puts on his plays, the less specific he needs to be in the script that he provides for them. What the actors need is their lines, the words they have to speak; their cues; and, preferably, knowledge of when they should enter and leave the stage. If the author is one of them – as Shakespeare was to a greater extent than any other author of his age – then he can give them more detailed instructions on the spot, and may well leave certain decisions to be worked out during rehearsals.

The situation I have outlined has created a set of circumstances that marks a distinction in function between the editor of a dramatic text and editors of most other literary texts. Editors have in practice a wide range of functions – and, of course, the very concept of 'editing' is open to a wide range of interpretation – but most people would agree that the editor's most basic task is the establishment of a workable text by the diagnosis and removal of any corruption that may have occurred in the process of transmission. Editors of non-dramatic texts such as novels and poems may be faced with complex problems arising from, for instance, authors' revisions, alternative readings, censorship, publishers' interventions and so on, but at least they are dealing with texts in which the word is paramount. Editors of dramatic texts, on the other hand, have long seen it as part of their function to make some attempt to cope with the unwritten dimension of the dramatic script: with what happens on stage beyond the words that are spoken there. This is, however, an area of editorial responsibility which – at least so far as Shakespeare and his contemporaries are concerned – has been largely neglected by editorial theorists. Scholars such as W.W. Greg and Fredson Bowers have written voluminously about establishing the text of dramatic dialogue, but have said surprisingly little about anything other than the words spoken. They have concerned themselves, we might say, rather with the literary substance of the play than with its dramatic reality. This may be well for the most conservative types of editions, near facsimiles which are concerned primarily to reconstruct the manuscript lying behind the printed text, with no concern for the validity of this manuscript as a guide to performance – which, of course, was its initial function. But this kind of edition is of very limited utility; it is only the first stage in the preparation of a performance text; and the great majority of editors working on texts for the reading public – which during the present century has increasingly tended to mean an academic public – has acknowledged, usually tacitly, an obligation to attempt to present the text in a way that will convey the experience of seeing the play in performance more adequately than the original script would, even when that script was freed of corruption. To do this means, of course, that the editor is also preparing a text that would be more usable in the theatre than in its original state; he is taking upon himself some of the functions of the director – or at least of a theatre functionary responsible for preparing a prompt-book – in interpreting the text in theatrical terms. Let me give a few straightforward examples which will illustrate the problem.

Shakespeare's comedy *Much Ado About Nothing* was first printed from a manuscript which, all scholars agree, was in an unpolished state. The opening stage direction provides for the entry of 'Innogen', wife of the governor of Messina, and a later direction too calls for Leonato's wife. No one disputes that these directions stood in Shakespeare's manuscript. But that manuscript can have made no further mention, either implicitly or explicitly, of Innogen; she never speaks, is never addressed, and is never referred to. Anyone editing the text purely in its own right would have to retain her, because there can be no doubt that as Shakespeare wrote these directions he intended to provide a function for her in the drama. On the other hand, anyone attentive to the dramatic meaning of the text, to its function as a guide to performance, must expunge the lady, since clearly she went out of Shakespeare's head as he went on writing, and can have made no appearance in the play as performed. So she is normally written out of the edited text.

A number of the early texts obscure the points at which characters should come on to the stage. *The Winter's Tale* was first printed from a manuscript in which, in over half of the scenes, the names of the characters taking part are massed together at the opening of the scene regardless of the point at which they should enter. This is believed to have been a characteristic of a particular scribe, Ralph Crane, and is part of the evidence that the play was printed from a scribal manuscript, not from Shakespeare's own papers. It means that the editor who has in mind the play as performed must distribute the entries at points he thinks appropriate, and there may be uncertainty about where these points are. In the second scene, for instance, it is not clear how much of the conversation between the court party should be overheard by Leontes' cupbearer, Camillo. Furthermore, the fact that the stage directions have been obviously interfered with raises questions about whether indications of non-speaking roles may have been dropped. This is, in fact, a more general problem, because a playwright may have sometimes taken for granted that royal persons would be attended, and not have bothered to specify the fact. It can be quite important; in this very scene of *The Winter's Tale*, at which two kings and a queen are present, the eighteenth-century editor Theobald (himself a playwright, and thus, perhaps, particularly likely to have been influenced by the theatrical conventions of his own time) added a direction for attendants, and has been followed by most later editors; some modern directors, however, have preferred to treat the episode as a domestic scene, one that helps to establish a harmonious relationship between Leontes, Hermione and Polixenes before it is shattered by the onset of Leontes' fanatical jealousy; and textually there is no reason why they should not do so. There are many other plays – *Hamlet*, for example – where similar issues arise.

Perhaps inevitably, the way in which editors set about the task of making what we might call theatrical emendations to a text – or removing obstacles to the reader's understanding of its theatrical function – has tended to be coloured by the editor's experience of the theatre of his time. Indeed, it is doubtful whether some of the earlier editors had any concept of any other kind of theatre than their own; they may well have felt that, just as they modernized spelling and punctuation, so they should also bring the presentational aspects of the text into line with contemporary conventions. This was particularly likely to happen at a time when little was known about the staging of the Elizabethan and Jacobean period – after all, the de Witt drawing of the Swan was only discovered in 1888 – and when, also, theatrical methods were far more uniform than they are at present. During the seventeenth century, the eighteenth century and much of the nineteenth century, methods of staging were pretty uniform over a wide range of theatres. Until 1843 the two centres of English theatrical life were Drury Lane and Covent Garden, and other theatres took their pattern from them. Actors could move around the country playing star roles with local companies with little extra rehearsal. Even in this century, Professor Sprague tells the story of the old actor who, invited to play Kent in *King Lear* at, as it were, Exeter, wrote in his letter of acceptance 'Usual moves, I suppose?' Nowadays, on the other hand, editors know that productions of Shakespeare may employ an extraordinary range of theatrical techniques and may take place in widely diverse physical surroundings, and this in itself may have helped to push these editors into thinking more restrictedly of the Elizabethan theatre – a theatre of the past – as the only one that will provide a constant frame of reference, even though, of course, our knowledge of Elizabethan staging conventions is still all too imperfect. But modern editors continue to be heavily influenced by the editorial techniques of their predecessors, to accept unthinkingly stage directions that derive from, for example, eighteenth-century editors, rather than rethinking the theatrical dimension of their texts purely in terms of the theatrical conditions for which they were composed.

Let me give an example which has practical consequences for the modern editor. During what is now usually known as Act 2 Scene 5 of *As You Like It*, Amiens tells us that 'The Duke' (who is not present) 'will drink under this tree', and at the end of the scene Amiens says 'And I'll go seek the Duke; his banquet is prepared.'[1] This seems to imply that the 'banquet' has been in preparation during the later part of the scene, and is visibly ready by the end of it. But the Duke does not immediately enter; the following scene is an episode in which old Adam appears with Orlando in desperate need of food: 'O, I die for food', he exclaims, and Orlando declares, 'If this uncouth forest yield anything savage I will either be food for it or bring it for food to thee.' The Folio's opening direction for the following scene, in which the food is to be consumed, is '*Enter Duke Sen[ior]. & Lord, like Out-lawes*'. In 1709, Nicholas Rowe, the first of Shakespeare's named editors, helpfully added the direction '*A Table set out*', and this was repeated in all editions of the play until very recent years. Dover Wilson – whose directions, at least in the earlier plays in his edition, are more Shavianly helpful than those of any other editor – had directed in Scene 5 '*Some of the company prepare a meal beneath the tree*', and now on the entry of the Duke varies Rowe to '*A meal of fruit and wine set out under the tree*'. He does not direct the meal to be taken off and then brought back again, and his note reveals his thoughts on the subject: 'Where was the table prepared in Shakespeare's theatre? Not on the front stage, otherwise the next scene would be ridiculous. We must suppose, therefore, that the inner-stage was not the Duke's cave but 'this tree' (1.30), and that at the end of the scene the curtain was drawn to conceal the banquet, which was again revealed at the beginning of 2.7.'[2]

That note is marvellously revealing in two directions. First, it shows Dover Wilson working on assumptions about the past, about the Elizabethan theatre, that are no longer accepted. The very concept of the Shakespearian 'inner-stage' is now untenable, let alone the notion that it could be representative of a particular location – whether the Duke's cave or a tree – or that it would be alternately revealed and concealed by a curtain. Secondly, it shows Dover Wilson being unconsciously influenced in his concepts of the Shakespearian theatre by the conventions of his own time, when 'front scenes' such as the simple duologue between Orlando and Adam would be played on the forestage before a curtain which could be raised or drawn apart to show the full stage for the more elaborate and densely populated scene that follows.

Nearly forty years later Agnes Latham, in her new Arden edition of 1975, reverted to a variation of Rowe's direction – '*A meal set out*' instead of '*A table set out*' – and discussed the matter in an appendix, remarking on the outdatedness of Dover Wilson's concept of the inner stage and pointing out that 'The attendants might set up boards on trestles and carry them off at the end of scene v, were it not that nobody has yet sat down to the feast, which does not take place till scene vii.' Her comments make it clear that her own concepts of staging are essentially those of the naturalistic stage: 'Supposing the table is left visible at the end of scene v it must be set very far upstage, and the scene between Orlando and Adam must be played very far down. Even so there will be an awkwardness about their entrance and exit.' She is worried by the thought that the banquet 'could be concealed throughout scene vi only by being imperfectly visible in scenes v and vii', and arrives at the explanation 'that the attendants unobtrusively remove the feast as part of their comings and goings in the background at the end of scene v, and bring it on again at the beginning of scene vii'. Which leads her, understandably, to ask why Shakespeare should have been such a fool as to introduce 'the "banquet" at all at scene v', a question to which she provides no satisfactory answer.[3]

A couple of years later Richard Knowles, in his New Variorum edition, discussed the same subject, concluding 'The early setting of the table seems to me thoroughly puzzling; it is totally unnecessary, for the banquet could have been carried on, as banquets usually were, at the beginning of scene 7.'[4]

Directors, too, have been exercised by the problem. In a Stratford, Ontario, production Robin Phillips rearranged the order of the scenes so that the Orlando–Adam one preceded the other two, whilst at the Royal Shakespeare Theatre Terry Hands (like others before him) cut the reference to the banquet in Scene 5.[5]

When I came to edit the play for the Complete Oxford Shakespeare I too puzzled over the problem, coming eventually to the conclusion that it is one created by editors, a problem that exists only as a result of conditioning to naturalistic theatre practices; that for the banquet to be set up at the end of Scene 5 and to remain on stage in full view of the audience while Adam bemoans his starving condition, and while Orlando declares his determination to find food, would make a strong ironic point in a non-illusionistic theatre. Consequently I did not add a direction for the removal of the food at the end of Scene 5. Since then I have been cheered to find that Alan Dessen, in his book on *Elizabethan Stage Conventions*, makes the same point, regarding this sequence as 'a clear example of the kind of simultaneous staging often found in earlier English drama'.[6] Although the modern editor must make the point in terms of Shakespeare's theatre, the same dramatic point could be made by a director who employed entirely different conventions; even a production that introduced live rabbits into the wood and staged the banquet as a kind of Glyndebourne picnic could still have Adam and Orlando play their scene in ironic unawareness of its presence.

In the attention that editors have given to the staging of plays by Shakespeare and his contemporaries they have, to a greater or lesser degree, treated the texts as theatrical artefacts; but at the same time they have often treated them simultaneously as literary artefacts, presenting them as texts for reading rather than for performing. I mentioned that none of the texts of Shakespeare's plays printed in his lifetime – about half of his entire output – marks any divisions into either acts or scenes. The plays are printed continuously, and so far as we can tell this reflects the way they were played. Act breaks appear not to have been customary in public theatres until about 1609, towards the end of Shakespeare's career. But as early as 1623, when his plays were gathered together in the First Folio, act and scene divisions were imposed upon many of them – with, to the best of our belief, no authority from either theatre manuscripts or theatrical practice, except perhaps for the very late plays. It was part of the process of making them respectable as literary 'works', undertaken probably in emulation of the Jonson Folio of 1616. Later editors regularized and extended the practice, which was, of course, encouraged by the use of Shakespeare's texts as objects of study to which it is convenient to have a standard system of reference. It affects the typography and layout of editions, and is particularly conspicuous in the Arden Shakespeare, where every editorially created act division begins on a fresh page with capitalized headings, and each scene – even tiny and wholly artificial ones such as the brief and numerous battle episodes in the last act of *Antony and Cleopatra* – is set off from its predecessor by white space and indicated by a centred and capitalized label.

Still more 'literary' and at variance with the plays' original staging has been the provision of location markers for each scene. In the eighteenth century this may have arisen mainly out of a concern for the plays' contemporary staging, as I have hinted, but it seems to have developed rather as a result of a literary approach to the plays which saw them as fictions in which every episode had a prescribed location, a location which could sometimes be identified only by resort to the play's sources or to other external evidence. Some of these locations have passed into the plays' mythology; we easily speak, for example, of the 'heath' scenes in *King Lear*, but the word 'heath' occurs in no early text of the play, and was first introduced into the scene headings by Rowe in 1709.[7] The same is true of character lists and speech headings. In *Richard II*, for instance, Shakespeare gives no name to Richard's Queen, who nevertheless plays a part of some importance in the action. Editors, 'irritably', as Keats says, 'reaching after fact and reason', have given her the name of Richard's wife Isabel, who was married to Richard at the historical time of the events of the play, and who was not more than twelve years old when he died. In fact Isabel was Richard's second wife; the character in the play – a woman who feels more than child-like love for her husband – is closer to his first wife, Anne, to whom he had been devoted and with whose portrayal in *Woodstock* Shakespeare's Queen has much in common. Dramatically, the character should remain nameless; her function in the play is simply that of Richard's wife who is also Queen of England, and to give her a name is to slew the play in the direction of an historical fiction.

Up till, I would suggest, around 1960 (very roughly) editorial conventions seemed to be hardening. They can be seen at their most rigid in the earlier volumes of the new Arden Shakespeare, and they were the product of a period during which the division between the academy and the theatre was wide. Between the wars, performances of Shakespeare's plays still owed much to a popular theatrical tradition, still adopted traditional cuts, were only slowly responding to the semi-scholarly influence of William Poel and Granville Barker, did not even have the opportunity to use the wide range of scholarly paperback editions that are available today. It was natural then that scholars editing the plays should see little connection between their work and the practical theatre. But the post-war period saw a greatly increased emphasis in Shakespeare studies on theatrical values, encouraged by pioneers such as Allardyce Nicoll, Glynne Wickham and John Russell Brown, and by the development in England's more forward-looking universities – the provincial ones – of Departments of Drama. Slowly this emphasis came to be reflected in a rethinking of editorial conventions which is still going on (and still meeting with resistance). Editors have been able to draw on an increased amount of research into the resources and conventions of the Shakespearian stage, and have themselves taken more of an interest in the living theatre than many of their predecessors did. It is partly a matter of assumptions about readership. Editors who have in mind readers whose interest is mainly academic – who see the plays as primarily literary texts, or even as documents in social history or the history of the language – will feel little need to pay attention to theatrical values, whereas those who conceive that their editions will be read by theatre-goers, and by students who are encouraged to think of the plays in theatrical terms, and may even be used by actors, will approach their task with a different set of assumptions. Moreover, editors familiar with the contemporary theatrical scene are likely to be far more conscious of the wide range of options that Shakespeare's plays permit than those who either took no interest in the theatre or were able to see only performances that worked within a comparatively narrow range of theatrical conventions. We realize now, for example, that, so far from requiring a naturalistic setting, plays written for a non-illusionist theatre may actually gain from neutrality of setting. If Dover Wilson had seen Peter Brook's 'white box' setting for *A Midsummer Night's Dream* in 1970 he would have been unlikely to write directions such as '*A room in the cottage of Peter Quince*', or '*The palace wood, a league from Athens. A mossy stretch of broken ground, cleared of trees by wood-cutters and surrounded by thickets. Moonlight*' or '*Another part of the wood. A grassy plot before a great oak-tree; behind the tree a high bank overhung with creepers, and at one side a thorn-bush. The air is heavy with the scent of blossom.*'[8] Slowly this kind of thing has been abandoned. Early volumes of the Arden Shakespeare still include some locations, usually based on those of the eighteenth-century editors – directions such as, in *Antony and Cleopatra*, '*Athens. A room in Antony's house*'; for the next scene: '*The same. Another room*'; and for the next: '*Rome. Caesar's house*'; not as flowery as Dover Wilson's extravaganzas, but still indicative of a non-theatrical attitude to the text. More recent volumes in the Arden series, and more recent editions such as the New Penguin, the New Cambridge and the Oxford, abandon directions for location altogether. Of course, the reader of a complex play such as *Antony and Cleopatra* may be glad of guidance as to where he is in any given scene: guidance such as the theatre can provide by any number of devices, including colour-coding of sets and costumes, variations in accent, significant properties and so on; and it is reasonable for the editor to provide similar guidance where necessary in his notes; but it seems misleading to place such information in the text itself in a manner that implies naturalistic staging.

A somewhat similar situation obtains with regard to act and scene divisions. They are obtrusive even in later volumes of the Arden series, but more recent editions tend to down play them, treating them simply as a convenient means of reference and presenting the text in a manner that stresses its continuity, the fluid merging of one scene into the next, rather than breaking it up into a series of apparently self-contained units. There is a notorious example in *Romeo and Juliet*. As Benvolio leaves the stage he says

> . . . 'tis in vain
> To seek him here that means not to be found.

Romeo comes forward and completes the couplet:

> He jests at scars that never felt a wound.
>
> (2.1.42–3)

In the play as first printed – doubtless as in Shakespeare's manuscript – this is absolutely continuous. But editors have introduced a scene break at this point, with the result that the old Arden, for example, follows Benvolio's line with the direction *Exeunt*, the capitalized and centred heading SCENE II, the location '*The Same. Capulet's Orchard*', and the direction '*Romeo advances*' before Romeo breaks the suspense by completing the couplet.[9] Of course, there are some plays where the author clearly had act divisions in mind – *Henry V* is an obvious example, though there the Choruses themselves provide the markers; but for other plays the scene is a more real unit of action. When I was editing Dekker's *Shoemaker's Holiday* I searched in vain for anything approximating to an act structure and decided finally to mark only scene divisions.[10] In the Complete Oxford Shakespeare we provide act and scene references, and act markers for the plays where they are certainly appropriate: I should have been happy to abandon some of the divisions altogether, but we eventually acknowledged the need to provide a reference system.

Another editorial-cum-theatrical convention that has needed to be rethought in the light of theatrical experimentation is the aside. Early editions rarely indicate that speeches should be delivered 'aside'. Editors with expectations based on naturalistic acting frequently added the direction; more recently, in the face of stylized production methods, and also of new ideas about human behaviour, we have become more wary of doing so. Hamlet's first words – 'A little more than kin and less than kind' – were marked *aside* by Theobald and in many later editions, including the recent New Cambridge, but are not so marked in for instance the new Arden or the Oxford (1987), whose editor, G.R. Hibbard, notes: 'Most editors since Theobald (1740) have marked the speech as an *Aside*, but its barbed obscurity strongly suggests that it is intended to be heard by Claudius, to puzzle him, and to disturb him.'[11]

Clearly, then, there has been a movement away from prescriptive editing; editors are less inclined than they once were to assume the role of director. This shows itself even in quite small – but none the less significant – details of the text. Punctuation is getting lighter so that the editor, instead of trying to convey each nuance of his own interpretation of the lines, will leave them as open as possible, encouraging the reader or speaker to explore their potential range of meaning. In punctuating texts for the Oxford Shakespeare I found myself consciously trying *not* to add exclamation marks where previous editors had placed them. There is, however, a rather fine line between, on the one hand, editing in a manner that is not over-prescriptive, that leaves the director to do his own directing, and, on the other hand, measuring up to the theatrical dimension of the text so that it is genuinely presented as a theatrical rather than merely a literary text. So, although it seems right that editors should be on their guard against importing into Elizabethan texts notions derived from the theatrical practice of later ages, it does seem desirable to locate these texts within the theatres for which they were written. In the Oxford Shakespeare, for example, we have thought afresh about such matters as the use of an upper level which was certainly possible in Shakespeare's theatre even though modern designers often make no use of it, about the provision of music cues, and about the removal of bodies, especially at the ends of plays, which is necessary in an open-stage theatre without artificial lighting even though it may not be needed in theatres which make use of a front curtain or of lighting black-outs.

Editors have thought afresh, too, about symbolic gestures such as kissing, kneeling and rising. Take for example a very well-known and important episode in *Coriolanus* which as it happens is already marked by one of Shakespeare's own most eloquent stage directions. Coriolanus's womenfolk, fearful of Rome's destruction, visit him in the enemy camp, hoping to persuade him not to lead the Volscian forces against Rome. His mother, Volumnia, pleads with him in a speech that is full of implicit stage directions, though none is provided by the Folio text. As she works up to a climax, she says:

> He turns away.
> Down, ladies. Let us shame him with our knees.
> To his surname 'Coriolanus' 'longs more pride
> Than pity to our prayers. Down! An end.
> This is the last. So we will home to Rome,
> And die among our neighbours. – Nay, behold's.
> This boy, that cannot tell what he would have,
> But kneels and holds up hands for fellowship,
> Does reason our petition with more strength
> Than thou hast to deny't. – Come, let us go.
> This fellow had a Volscian to his mother.
> His wife is in Corioles, and this child
> Like him by chance. – Yet give us our dispatch.
> I am hushed until our city be afire,
> And then I'll speak a little.   (5.3.169–83)

Then comes the Folio direction '*Holds her by the hand silent*' after which Coriolanus says:

> O mother, mother!
> What have you done? Behold, the heavens do ope,
> The gods look down, and this unnatural scene
> They laugh at. (5.3.183–6)

I said that Volumnia's speech is full of implicit stage directions, so perhaps for this very reason it is not necessary to add many. There can surely be no doubt that all the supplicants must kneel soon after Volumnia has said 'Down, ladies. Let us shame him with our knees.' What is much less obvious is the point at which they should rise. Many editors provide no direction for either action. Some assume that Volumnia at least should have risen by the point at which Coriolanus '*holds her by the hand silent*'. But there is one textual indication against this which is often ignored by both editors and directors. 'The gods look down,' says Coriolanus, 'and this unnatural scene/They laugh at.' What is 'unnatural' about the scene unless, in a total reversal of expectation, the mother is kneeling to her son? And so, it seems to me, an editor who is trying to realize the theatrical dimension of the text owes it to his readers to indicate points for both kneeling and rising by means of stage directions.

The aim – not always formulated – behind directions such as these is to achieve at least one kind of purity, rather than to present hybrid texts reflecting a variety of diverse theatrical traditions, as has happened too often in the past. But even here the intervention of the editor will often be identifiable. The inadequacies, the openness to interpretation, of the original texts are such that an editor will often have to make an arbitrary decision which appears to close options even while providing a necessary clarification. There are points in the text at which the editor must add directions but where he must also exercise choice in either the precise action that he provides for, or its placing, or both. One very basic matter is the question of exits, frequently left unmarked in the original texts, presumably because, though an actor may need to be told when to get on to the stage, he can be more easily trusted to remember when to leave it. The precise point at which he does so may have interpretative consequences. For instance, in the middle of Act 4

Scene 1 of *As You Like It* Jaques bids farewell to Orlando and Rosalind with the line

> Nay then, God b'wi'you an you talk in blank verse.
>
> (4.1.29–30)

Rosalind then has the following speech:

> Farewell, Monsieur Traveller. Look you lisp, and wear strange suits; disable all the benefits of your own country; be out of love with your nativity, and almost chide God for making you that countenance you are, or I will scarce think you have swam in a gondola. Why, how now, Orlando? (4.1.31–7)

The Folio, where this play was first printed, marks no exit for Jaques, but a responsible editor must provide one as he obviously has to leave the stage. But it could be placed either after the last line he speaks, so that Rosalind says 'Farewell, Monsieur Traveller' as he leaves the stage; or after her 'Farewell, Monsieur Traveller', so that the remainder of her speech up to the point at which she addresses Orlando is a comment on him in his absence; or Jaques could stay to hear what she says about him. The Arden editor adopts and argues for the last option, commenting 'F does not mark the place at which Jaques leaves the stage. Later folios put it after *blank verse*, in consequence of the adieux exchanged then, without observing that Rosalind must have an audience for her anatomy of the returned traveller.'[12] But an actress might choose to address Jaques in his absence, so the Complete Oxford edition, while also marking Jaques' exit at this point, less prescriptively encloses it in the broken brackets that are our not entirely satisfactory means of signalling directions that are open to a variety of interpretation.

Sometimes we may doubt whether a character should be present at all, and the editor like the director will have to make a decision. For example, both early editions of *Othello* (Q, 1622. and F1, 1623) bring Cassio on with Othello in the senate scene, but as he says nothing and is not addressed, many editors since Capell in the late eighteenth century have dropped him. Yet he had earlier been sent to fetch Othello, and the fact that both early editions (which seem to be of independent origin) bring him on is a point in favour of his silent presence during the bulk of the earlier part of the scene, though the editor has to decide at what point he shall leave, since his presence is scarcely possible after the Duke's departure. So again, the editor must make arbitrary decisions. Such decisions may be intimately linked with the play's original staging. Thus, in Act 5 of *Othello*, after Iago has wounded Cassio, Othello enters and comments on the noises of the action unheard by Roderigo and Cassio; some editors mark Othello's speeches as asides; it seemed to me that in Shakespeare's theatre they were most likely to have been spoken from the upper level, and I added a conjectural direction to this effect, but I could not assert dogmatically that this is how Shakespeare intended the episode to be played, and should certainly not wish to inhibit a modern director's liberty to play it in any way that would be effective.

Stage business is often certainly required, but we may have difficulty in deciding exactly what it should be. Take for example a crucial moment in the long speech of Innogen in *Cymbeline* when she awakes over the headless body of Cloten, taking it to be that of her husband, Posthumus. The climax of the speech is:

> O,
> Give colour to my pale cheek with thy blood,
> That we the horrider may seem to those
> Which chance to find us! O my lord, my lord!
>
> (4.2.332–4)

It is obvious that at this point blood is transferred from the body to Innogen's cheek, though it is not entirely clear how it gets there. In the Complete Oxford Shakespeare we added the direction '*She smears her face with blood.*' Roger Warren, who had been involved in rehearsals of Sir Peter Hall's production with the National Theatre, objected to the phrasing of this direction, arguing that the blood should be involuntarily transferred from corpse to cheek during an embrace rather than that Innogen should deliberately smear herself with it. This indicates the difficult position that the editor is in: in the attempt to do our duty by the theatre we added a direction for necessary action where it had not been added before, but we failed to find a phrasing for this action which would leave open the full range of possibilities that the text permits.

So far I have been discussing comparatively minor areas of

editorial choice, ones which have theatrical implications but which do not individually have a significant influence on overall interpretation of the play. Recent years, however, have seen discussion of an area of editorial intervention which does indeed have such an influence. Some of Shakespeare's plays survive in variant early texts, some in Quarto, some in Folio. There are, for example, some 500 differences in wording between *Troilus and Cressida* as it was first printed in the Quarto of 1609 and the same play as printed in the Folio of 1623; the Prologue is present only in the later text. There are over 1000 verbal differences between the text of *Othello* printed in 1622 and that given in the Folio in the following year, which also adds about 160 lines, including Desdemona's willow song (4.3) and Emilia's remarkable defence of female sexual independence (4.3.85–102), whose presence or absence considerably affects the tone and content of the play. Whereas the seemingly later text of *Othello* adds lines that are not in the earlier text, the later one of *Hamlet*, printed in the Folio, omits about 230 lines – including, for example, Hamlet's last soliloquy, 'How all occasions do inform against me' – that are present in the Quarto of 1604 while also adding some 80 lines that are not in that text, and again including hundreds of verbal variants. The most radical differences are found in the two early texts of *King Lear*. The Folio has over 100 lines that are not found in the Quarto of 1608, but it also lacks close on 300 lines, including an entire scene, that are in that text; there are over 850 other differences in wording, several speeches are assigned to different speakers, and the conduct of the action differs in the two texts.

These facts have been known for a long time, and the standard explanation of them has been that each of the variant texts inadequately represents a lost original, and that the variants are the result of various forms of corruption – printers' errors, scribal misreadings, actors' interpolations and so on. On this basis, editors since the early eighteenth century – when interventionist editing made its first serious impact on the textual tradition – have conflated the variant texts, adding to one passages that are absent from the other, and choosing among the local variants those that they regarded as the more likely to be genuinely Shakespearian. In the process they have suppressed a great many readings that make perfectly good sense out of deference to a textual theory that has recently been undermined. Some of these can be crucial to interpretation.

A mixture of bibliographical and textual study undertaken during the 1970s suggests that the differences between the early texts of Shakespeare's plays are in many cases a reflection of conscious changes made by Shakespeare himself; that, for example, he first wrote *Othello* without Desdemona's willow song and Emilia's feminist outburst, and added them later; that he did a lot to streamline the text of *Hamlet*; and that he had very serious second thoughts about *King Lear*, making changes to the text as he first conceived it that amount to a radical revision. This thought is reflected for the first time in the recent Complete Works, and in the single-volume Oxford Shakespeare edition of *Hamlet*. It means, if accepted, that all other editions of certain plays by Shakespeare – editions which follow the eighteenth-century practice of conflating early texts – take intervention to the point of distortion, creating hold-all texts that have no basis in the theatre practice of Shakespeare's own time. Granville-Barker delivered an early warning against this practice in his Preface to *King Lear*, of 1927, in which he comments that 'the producer is confronted by the problem of the three hundred lines, or nearly, that the Quartos give and the Folio omits, and of the hundred given by the Folio and omitted from the Quartos. Editors, considering only, it would seem, that the more Shakespeare we get the better, bring practically the whole lot into the play we read. But a producer must ask himself whether these two versions do not come from different prompt-books, and whether the Folio does not, in both cuts and additions, sometimes represent Shakespeare's own second thoughts.' And he adds: 'Where Quarto and Folio offer alternatives, to adopt both versions may make for redundancy or confusion.'[13]

I am not so naive as to suppose that modern theatre directors, by and large, feel bound to adhere to the scripts that posterity has handed to them, nor am I so foolish as to suggest that they should be so bound. Theatre is a living art, and play scripts have a flexibility denied to poetry and the novel. Practice varies enormously. There are some very successful productions that depart substantively from the basic text, others – and sometimes by the same director – that adhere to it with remarkable fidelity. Peter Brook, for example, omitted over 650 lines from his 1955 production of *Titus Andronicus*, a landmark production which – partly because of Laurence Olivier's extraordinary interpretation of the title role – rehabilitated the play's theatrical reputation. The same director's 1970 production of *A Midsummer Night's Dream*, widely regarded as one of the most startlingly revolutionary post-war productions of Shakespeare, played the entire text with only a few minor rearrangements of dialogue. The revolutionary aspects of the production lay in what it did with the settings, costume, casting and production devices. When Peter Hall was in Stratford in the 1960s he produced *Hamlet* in a text from which about 730 lines had been cut; when he directed the same play as his opening production at the National Theatre, he used a full text. John Barton, in productions of certain of Shakespeare's history plays, has earned himself the reputation of the Colley Cibber of our times by the prodigality with which he has not merely cut and rearranged the plays but has also added to them hundreds of lines of his own composition; yet his productions of the comedies have been among the most sensitive, and textually faithful, of our time. There are some signs of a trend among recent English productions towards textual fullness. This was apparent in David Hare's National Theatre production of *King Lear* (1986) and Peter Hall's of *Antony and Cleopatra* (1987), and I understand that in rehearsal Peter Hall used complete texts of *The Winter's Tale*, *Cymbeline* and *The Tempest* for his season of the late plays, though there were some cuts in the plays as produced. The Royal Shakespeare Company, perhaps surprisingly, is less purist in general, though 1987 saw a quite exceptional production, by Deborah Warner at the Swan Theatre, of *Titus Andronicus* which – for the first time, to the best of my belief, on the English stage – used a complete text and in the process did a great deal to increase respect both for the play itself and for the audiences that made it popular in its own time.

Variations in the texts of plays are matched also by variations in the staging, a process which is made inevitable by the absence of a direct line of performance tradition from Shakespeare's time to ours. Seasoned theatre-goers are accustomed to performances in modern dress, in dress of a wide range of historical periods, in dress of no period at all, even to undress; they are accustomed to both minimalist and maximalist productions – ones that on the one hand, like the Cheek by Jowl *Macbeth* (1987), dispense with all properties, use the same performer in more than one role, and (in this case) allocate no individual performers to the roles of the Witches but present them as disembodied voices with their lines distributed among other members of the cast; on the other hand, theatre-goers know they may see productions, even in these economically distressed times, with elaborate scenery, numerous extras and complex production devices which often play a kind of fantasy on the original text, transforming it into a performance that is, for better or for worse, more expressive of the director's than of the playwright's imagination.

The fact remains, however, that even the freest of directors, even those who seem to be using the original text as little more than a quarry from which they can hew the material that suits their own imaginative concepts while rejecting or distorting anything, such as the text's obvious implications, that gets in their way – even such directors need something to start from, and what they start from will almost invariably be a text that has been subjected to editorial intervention. It is also a fact, of course, that most directors acknowledge a responsibility to the playwright's imagination, and that some are deeply concerned with the playwright's original script, whether they attempt to perform it as faithfully as modern stage conditions will permit, or to translate it into the language of modern theatre. It is desirable that such directors should be aware that an edition is not simply a glass through which the dramatist's intentions are revealed in all their original purity; that, at least for our early drama, no such return to original truth is possible; and that in every edition one layer of interpretation has already been superimposed on the original even in the attempt to free the early texts of their corruptions and indeterminacies.

It is as well, in other words, that directors should know that other options than those suggested by the edited text under their hands may well be open to them: that, to repeat a small example, Jaques might leave before, during or after Rosalind's speech about him, or, to give larger examples, omissions from the conflated texts of *Hamlet* of the Prince's last soliloquy, or of *King Lear* of the scene

(4.3 in conflated texts) in which Cordelia tells a Gentleman of the plight of her distressed, maddened father seem to be justified by the practice of Shakespeare's own company. Both directors and actors should be aware, too, that the spelling and punctuation in all the texts that they are likely to use has been modernized, that there is no consistent editorial practice of modernization, and that consequently the very form of words that the actors have to speak is open to interpretation. Some editors, for instance, are reluctant to commit themselves to a process of thorough modernization in texts which they think of as having a primarily scholarly readership, and so offer what is to me an anomalous mish-mash of old and new forms. There was a particular fashion for this in Arden editions of the '50s and '60s, which often retain archaic forms such as 'murther' (for 'murder'), 'banket' (for 'banquet'), 'accompt' (for 'account'), 'enow' (for 'enough'), 'moe' (for 'more'), 'Norweyan' (for 'Norwegian'), 'Troyan' (for 'Trojan') and so on, and I often notice actors conscientiously but misguidedly trying to convey such spellings through pronunciation. There might be some point in a thorough attempt to reconstruct the pronunciation of Shakespeare's time in a modern performance, but I see no point at all (except perhaps occasionally to preserve a rhyme) in introducing a selection of such pronunciations into a generally modernized text.

Actors might do well to realize, too, that punctuation is often more flexible than the editor can suggest. Shakespeare's own punctuation seems to have been very light. Elizabethan printers felt free to treat the punctuation of the manuscripts from which they worked according to the conventions of their own printing houses, and modern editions have too often been based on texts in which a heavily prescriptive system has been superimposed upon that of the early editions. I have heard of directors who work initially with texts from which all the punctuation has been removed, and I can see the virtue in such a procedure. Again, though this may seem a matter of insignificant minutiae, it can affect moments that are prominent in the action. Take, for example, Claudius's culminating reaction to the play scene in *Hamlet*. The words he speaks are 'Give me some light. Away' (3.2.257), and in both the good Quarto and the Folio texts the terminal punctuation is simply a full stop. Many editors have replaced this with an exclamation mark, and, as if in deference to this, actors have traditionally used the words as an opportunity for a great histrionic moment, a violent eruption of concealed guilt. Peter Hall's 1965 production showed that the moment could be equally effective if the interpolated exclamation mark was ignored. His Claudius simply stood, glared at Hamlet, and spoke the line with scornful calm, rather rebuking Hamlet for a lapse of taste than showing the depths of his own soul. In a curious way, it achieved a *coup-de-théâtre* by denying one. I am not, of course, saying that one of these ways of playing the moment is right, the other wrong. But editorial intervention should not be allowed to close the text's openness to variant interpretation, and both director and actor need to know how, as it were, to 'read' the text in order to feel the freedom to explore it within the appropriate limits.

The corollary of what I have been saying is not that editors should refrain from interpretation. They may do their best to be unobtrusive; for instance, it was directly because of the various ways in which I had seen the play scene in *Hamlet* acted that, in the Oxford Shakespeare, we did not punctuate Claudius's reaction with an exclamation mark. But, as I hope I have shown, conscientious editing is not compatible with a policy of total non-intervention. What I am suggesting is that readers, including theatre practitioners, need to learn how to use edited texts. Editors should not be deferred to; their decisions should be questioned, their interpretations greeted with proper scepticism; but this can be satisfactorily done only on the basis of an informed understanding of the nature of the original documents and of the editorial methods that have been applied to them. If such an understanding exists, then directors and actors may work with a more controlled freedom in their handling of the texts we offer them; if it does not, they had better choose their editors with care and then accept their guidance. In the past, scholars were often accused of paying too little attention to the theatre. There was much justice in the accusation. But things have changed. Many modern scholars are profoundly conscious of theatrical values, deeply aware that play scripts reach consummation only in performance. It would now not be entirely unjust, I suggest, for scholars to accuse the theatre of paying too little attention to their work, because I believe that theatre people, by becoming more aware of scholarly procedures, could learn something useful to themselves about the texts with which they work.

Notes

1. Quotations from Shakespeare are from *The Complete Oxford Shakespeare*, General Editors Stanley Wells and Gary Taylor (Oxford, 1986), unless otherwise stated.
2. *As You Like It*, ed. Sir Arthur Quiller-Couch and John Dover Wilson (Cambridge, 1926), note to 2.5.60–1.
3. *As You Like It*, ed. Agnes Latham (The Arden Shakespeare: London, 1975).
4. *As You Like It*, ed. Richard Knowles (A New Variorum Edition of Shakespeare: New York, 1977), note to line 949.
5. Alan C. Dessen, *Elizabethan Stage Conventions and Modern Interpreters* (Cambridge, 1984), pp. 101–2.
6. Ibid., p. 102, citing Bernard Beckerman, *Shakespeare at the Globe, 1599–1609* (New York, 1962), p. 159.
7. See A.H. Scouten, 'Designation of Locale in Shakespeare Texts', *Essays in Theatre* 2, 1 (Nov. 1983), 41–55, and James Ogden, 'Lear's Blasted Heath', *Durham University Journal* 81 (Dec. 1987), 19–22.
8. *A Midsummer Night's Dream*, ed. Sir Arthur Quiller-Couch and John Dover Wilson (Cambridge, 1924), stage directions to 1.2, 2.1 and 2.2.
9. *Romeo and Juliet*, ed. Edward Dowden (The Arden Shakespeare: London, 1900).
10. Thomas Dekker, *The Shoemaker's Holiday*, ed. R.L. Smallwood and Stanley Wells (Revels Plays: Manchester, 1979), pp. 63–4.
11. *Hamlet*, ed. G.R. Hibbard (The Oxford Shakespeare: Oxford, 1987), note to 1.2.65.
12. *As You Like It*, ed. Agnes Latham, note to 4.1.31.
13. H. Granville-Barker, *Prefaces to Shakespeare* (1927; two-volume edition, 1958), I, 328–9.

4

The mind's eye, the worthy scaffold, the real thing: how to read a Shakespeare play

JAMES REDMOND

Nowhere does the Deadly Theatre install itself so securely, so comfortably and so slyly as in the works of William Shakespeare . . . we find it excruciatingly boring – and in our hearts we either blame Shakespeare, or theatre as such.[1]   (Peter Brook)

Make not thy self a Page,
To that strumpet the Stage.[2]

Thou art a monument without a tomb,
And art alive still while thy book doth live
And we have wits to read and praise you.[3]   (Ben Jonson)

Heard melodies are sweet, but those unheard
     Are sweeter; therefore, ye soft pipes, play on;
Not to the sensual ear, but, more endeared,
     Pipe to the spirit ditties of no tone.[4]   (John Keats)

Behind the drama of words is the drama of action, the timbre of voice and voice, the uplifted hand or tense muscle, and the particular emotion . . . the words which we read are symbols, a shorthand, and often as in the best of Shakespeare, a very abbreviated shorthand indeed, for the acted and felt play, which is always the real thing.[5]   (T.S. Eliot)

In his verses of commemoration, Richard West praised the dramatic achievement of Ben Jonson precisely in the terms that would most have gratified the old bear. He emphasized that unlike the majority of plays, which are adequately served by the players as after-dinner confectionery, Jonson's tragedies and comedies ought to be the object of serious study when our minds are most alert; the perceptive reader will recognize that they are literature and strive to achieve a critical appreciation of their artistry.[6] Jonson himself had prepared his *Workes* for publication in 1616, devoting a great deal of earnest attention to the task. He was determined that, having been through the hurly-burly of the London playhouse, his dramas – like those of Athens and Rome – should receive attentive respect in the library. Of course there were some gentlemen in London who thought Jonson's earnestness and his choice of title were foolishly pretentious for the scripts of mere theatre pieces; and yet seven years later Heminge and Condell introduced the First Folio '*To the great Variety of Readers*' with the admonition that to understand Shakespeare's plays adequately the public must 'Reade him, therefore, and againe and againe'.[7]

It has always been central to our culture for us to read and re-read the masterpieces of dramatic literature, and most plays have been moulded by the process. Euripides read Aeschylus with great critical care, and he wrote some of his own plays in direct response. Seneca read Euripides in the same spirit. Shakespeare read Seneca, and every subsequent playwright has read Shakespeare; so that the question of how we read a Shakespeare play is at the heart of the major issue of what the functions of drama are in western culture.

Very late in his career Strindberg explained that he had never attended a production of *The Tempest* but he had seen the play in his mind's eye whenever he read it, and that was all he desired: 'there are good plays that should not be performed, that cannot bear being seen'.[8] In analysing Shakespeare's style Strindberg emphasized the complex density of the imagery.[9] Taking the help of commentators and going over the text again and again, the reader can apprehend the subtlety and strength of the language in much finer detail than is ever possible in the theatre, because the rich linguistic texture cannot be so minutely communicated through performance. In his last years Strindberg expressed his immense admiration for the beautiful profundity of Maeterlinck's plays: they won his heart as Shakespeare's did by showing an alternative to materialistic naturalism in the drama. And Strindberg's judgement was again 'that Maeterlinck is best unperformed'.[10] Eugene O'Neill followed Strindberg as his master in this as in many ways: 'I hardly ever go to the theater ... although I read all the plays I can get. I don't go to the theater because I can always do a better production in my mind.'[11] 'Is not *Hamlet*, seen in the dream theatre of the imagination as one reads, a greater play than *Hamlet* interpreted even by a perfect production?'[12]

Goethe tells us that very extensive reading of Shakespeare had determined the nature of his own dramatic writing: his mind had been so expanded by reading and re-reading Shakespeare that he rejected the temporal and technical limitations of the stage.[13] Surrendering hope that the playhouse would allow him to achieve work of the greatest substance, he intentionally in his major poetic dramas chose to create texts that are, as he put it, *theaterscheu*[14] – sensitive, to the point of stage fright. Goethe was very much aware that the influence of Shakespeare, which had been so positively formative for his own development as a poet, also had a strongly inhibiting potential. In conversation with Eckermann he expressed sympathy for the English playwrights who had the great disadvantage of following in Shakespeare's trail.[15] The daemons, as Goethe argued the point, in order to tease us mortals will set up an extraordinary figure who is so admirable that everyone tries to follow his example, and so great that no one can succeed.[16] Shakespeare has been such a treacherous paradigm for succeeding generations. The problem is not only that his genius is unmatchable: it lies above all in the fact that he seems to demonstrate the wonderful superiority of the play that is too rich, too many-layered, too complex of detail to be adequately communicated in the theatre. For many critics and dramatists Shakespeare's plays have had their only proper existence in print, there being no adequate alternative to reading Shakespeare on the page. For most writers of poetic drama it has been a matter of policy and even of pride to disdain the requirements of the playhouse, to think of drama in ideal terms, as having its being in the mind.

Coleridge expressed the central point repeatedly and with force. In a lecture in 1811 he argued that the bare simplicity of Shakespeare's stage was a blessing since it obliged him to use words alone to stimulate the imagination, rather than the vulgar stage settings and machinery of the early nineteenth century. 'If he had lived in the present day', Coleridge suggested, Shakespeare might have adapted his plays to contemporary theatre practice: 'We are grateful

. . . that he did not, since there can be no comparative pleasure between having a great man in our closet and on the stage.'[17] Coleridge went so far as to say that

> he never saw any of Shakespere's plays performed, but with a degree of pain, disgust, and indignation. He had seen Mrs Siddons as Lady, and Kemble as Macbeth:- these might be the Macbeths of the Kembles, but they were not the Macbeths of Shakespere. He was therefore not grieved at the enormous size and monopoly of the theatres . . . which drove Shakespere from the stage, to find his proper place in the heart and in the closet.[18]

Coleridge also anticipated Strindberg's view of *The Tempest*. He talks of the danger of staging the play with 'the complicated scenery and decorations of modern times':

> For the principal and only genuine excitement ought to come from within – from the moved and sympathetic imagination; whereas, where so much is addressed to the mere external senses of seeing and hearing the spiritual vision is apt to languish, and the attraction from without will withdraw the mind from the proper and only legitimate interest which is intended to spring from within.[19]

This is plerophory. The local complaint about specific theatrical behaviour is made to support a general and absolute critical conviction: Shakespeare in the mind is necessarily superior to any possible performance; whatever might be physically seen or heard will be a crude reduction of the response to the text made by 'the moved and sympathetic imagination'.

Coleridge's position may seem extreme, but in fact it is orthodox. Charles Lamb was arguing the same case vigorously at the same time. There is no connection, he tells us, between 'that absolute mastery over the heart and soul of man, which a great dramatic poet possesses' and 'those low tricks upon the eye and ear, which a player . . . can so easily compass'.[20] In an age when a small proportion of the population were literate, the great majority denied the crucial experience of reading Shakespeare in print 'are necessarily dependent upon the stage-player for all the pleasure which they can receive from the drama'. They must 'read' the plays as well as they can amid the clamour of the contemporary playhouse. To these unfortunates 'the very idea of *what an author is* cannot be made comprehensible'.[21]

We are accustomed in the twentieth century to hearing theatrical directors defend their idiosyncratic productions of Shakespeare with the argument that the mischief is really quite harmless since the published text of the play remains intact: doing *Hamlet* on roller-skates on Mars is not like firing a shotgun at the Leonardo Cartoon, they say, or like drawing a moustache on the Mona Lisa, since the printed words survive the violation. But Lamb stands firm against this defence: to have seen a Shakespeare play performed is to have had it spoiled. A performance – any performance – operates cruelly on the mind, whose free conceptions are cramped and pressed down. The reader turns with a delightful sensation of freshness 'to those plays of Shakespeare which have escaped being performed'.[22]

Lamb had probably not read the Epistle to the 'Eternall reader' that introduced one of the two states of the 1609 Quarto of *Troilus and Cressida*, but the same argument was already being put forward with similar violence. The reader is offered 'a new play, neuer stal'd with the Stage, neuer clapper-clawd with the palmes of the vulger'. We are told that the text deserves the labour of careful reading as much as the best plays of Plautus and Terence: it has not been 'sullied, with the smoaky breath of the multitude', and the discerning reader will 'thanke fortune for the scape it hath made' from the playhouse.[23] The alternative state of the same Quarto, on the other hand, introduces *Troilus and Cressida* with the recommendation that the text is 'as it was acted by the king maiestes Seruants at the Globe'.[24] The contrasting advertisements were designed to attract the attention of the two kinds of patron browsing 'at the spred Eagle in Paules Church-yeard, ouer against the great North doore' – both those who would buy a printed shadowy remembrance of the play seen in performance and those who wished to be moved only by their sympathetic, imaginative response to the poet's pregnant words; both those who loved the acted play and those who preferred the unsullied text.

John Fletcher's *The Faithful Shepherdess* had been painfully abused by the audience when it was performed in 1608, but in the verses they composed to celebrate its appearance in print Frances

Beaumont, Ben Jonson and George Chapman confidently argue that the play will be a great, enduring success as literature: it was the audience who failed so badly on the day. They speak with contempt of the illiteracy, ignorance and malice of the play-going public, and Beaumont recommends the printed book as the superior way of presenting a play of high literary excellence:

> This second publication, which may strike
> Their consciences, to see the thing they scornd,
> To be with so much wit and art adornd.
> Besides one vantage more in this I see
> Your censurers must have that quallitie
> Of reading, which I am afraid is more
> Than halfe your shrewdest judges had before.[25]

Ben Jonson delights in the fact that Fletcher's *Poeme*, foully disgraced in the playhouse, will survive in print as a 'glorified worke'. George Chapman argues that the play would not do for the stage because it is the creation of 'A scholler that's a Poet'.

> So, were your play no Poeme, but a thing
> That every Cobler to his patch might sing:
> A rout of nifles (like the multitude)
> With no one limme of any art indude:
> Like would to like, and praise you.[26]

Over the centuries it was to be a common assertion that vulgar illiterates were driving refined scholarly intellects from the playhouse into the library, and many discriminating readers welcomed the fact. Dr Johnson, for example, in his Preface to the most influential edition of Shakespeare's works denies that any actor's voice or gestures could bring new dignity or force to the text: actors add nothing positive to a play of serious merit.[27] Johnson refused to mention the name of the mighty Garrick or of any other actor in his edition: 'I would not disgrace my page with a player. Garrick has been liberally paid for mouthing Shakespeare . . . He has not made Shakespeare better known. He cannot illustrate Shakespeare. He does not understand him.' Boswell reports this blustering, and also a five-second exchange that sums up the permanent conflict: '"Now I have quitted the theatre," cries Garrick, "I will sit down and read Shakespeare." "Tis time you should," exclaimed Johnson.'[28]

William Hazlitt was our first great journalist-reviewer of plays in performance and, with Shaw as the only serious challenger, he is still the most intelligent, perceptive and persuasive. For a few years he made his living by reporting productions on the London stage, and for most of the time he did so with measured enthusiasm: 'The Stage is one great source of public amusement . . . A good play, well acted, passes away a whole evening delightfully . . . we read the account of it next morning with pleasure, and it generally furnishes one leading topic of conversation for the afternoon.²⁹ But the exception is Shakespeare: Hazlitt regarded his visits to see Shakespeare performed as very painful parts of his contractual obligation.

> The reader of the plays of Shakespeare is almost always disappointed in seeing them acted: and, for our own parts, we should never go to see them acted, if we could help it.
> . . . all that appeals to our profounder feelings, to reflection and imagination, all that affects us most deeply in our closets, and in fact constitutes the glory of Shakespeare, is little else than an interruption and a drag on the business of the stage.
> . . . in going to see the plays of Shakespeare, it would be ridiculous to suppose, that any one ever went to see Hamlet or Othello represented by Kean or Kemble; we go to see Kean or Kemble in Hamlet or Othello.³⁰
> . . . to call it representation, is indeed an abuse of language: it is travestie, caricature, any thing you please, but a representation.³¹

And Hazlitt is most emphatic with regard to the play which is his and the world's greatest darling:

> We do not like to see our author's plays acted, and least of all, HAMLET. There is no play that suffers so much in being transferred to the stage. Hamlet himself seems hardly capable of being acted . . . He is, as it were, wrapped up in his reflections and only *thinks aloud*. . . . There should be as much of the gentleman and scholar as possible infused into the part, and as little of the actor.³²

In the nineteenth century *Hamlet* held a mirror up to the nature of its readers and what many a fine reader saw was a gentleman scholar, in love with poetic drama but contemptuous of the playhouse.

Lord Byron, for example, was fascinated by *Hamlet* and preoccupied with his ambition to write plays for what he called 'the English *Closet* or *mental* theatre': 'the Stage . . . is not my object, – but a *mental theatre*'[33] with 'nothing *melo*dramatic – no surprises, no starts, nor trap-doors, nor opportunities "for tossing their heads and kicking their heels"'.[34] And Byron's effort was not fruitless, for his *Sardanapalus*, together with Browning's *Paracelsus*, is the very best of the many nineteenth-century creative responses to *Hamlet*. Browning, more than any of his contemporaries, was to persevere in the heartbreaking attempt to write literature for the nineteenth-century London stage; but when he finally gave up in defeat and despair, he was extremely bitter in his rejection of the playhouse. He would still with coolness address himself as 'Robert Browning, you writer of plays',[35] but in 1846 when he was invited to act as spokesman for the Drama at the annual speeches of the Royal Corporation of the Literary Fund, he could speak of nothing but 'the advantages of the Press over the Stage as a medium of communication of the Drama'.[36]

A milder temperament was Sir Walter Scott and, although he had theatrical failures, he suffered much less public abuse than Browning. Nevertheless, he argued the same case. In his popular 'Essay on Drama' he granted that performances were of course necessary for the illiterate and for 'the sluggish and inert fancies of the multitude; although . . . minds of a high poetic temperature may . . . receive a more lively impression from the solitary perusal of Shakespeare's plays'.[37]

In the 1898 preface to *Plays Unpleasant* George Bernard Shaw builds up an elaborate defence of the play intended for the library. 'My mind's eye,' he tells us, 'saw things differently from other people's eyes, and saw them better.'[38]

> A perfectly adequate and successful stage representation of a play requires a combination of circumstances so extraordinarily fortunate that I doubt whether it has ever occurred in the history of the world. Take the case of the most successful English dramatist of the first rank: Shakespeare . . . I . . . have seen twenty-three of his plays publicly acted. But if I had not read them as well, my impression of them would be not merely incomplete, but violently distorted and falsified . . .
>
> I have never found an acquaintance with a dramatist founded on

> the theatre alone . . . a really intimate or accurate one. The very
> originality and genius of the performers conflicts with the
> originality and genius of the author.[39]

Shaw is working towards a major proposal that would take the
argument we have looked at to its irresistible conclusion.

> What would we not give for the copy of Hamlet used by
> Shakespeare at rehearsal, with the original stage business
> scrawled by the prompter's pencil? And if we had in addition the
> descriptive directions which the author gave on the stage: above
> all, the character sketches . . . by which he tried to convey to the
> actor the sort of person he meant him to incarnate.[40]

Shaw wants the literary drama to emulate the novel: along with the
dialogue he wants a profusion of paragraphs in which the playwright can tell the reader how best to *imagine* the action. 'No doubt
one result of this will be the production . . . of . . . works that could be
read, but not acted. I have no objection.'[41] Goethe had spent more
than sixty years creating such a work on the Faust theme, and when
Thomas Hardy pondered for three decades on the 'Great Modern
Drama'[42] *his* reading of Shakespeare influenced not only much of
the local colouring but also the great expansive length of the unacted
Dynasts. At the age of twenty Alfred de Musset had such discourag-
ing dealings with Parisian actors and audiences that he chose to
write the most interesting French plays of the mid nineteenth
century for the imagination of the reader who was safely isolated in
an armchair. And Shaw himself was to compose his most seriously
philosophical dramas – 'Don Juan in Hell', *Back To Methuselah* –
with the intention that they would never be staged.

The main reason for this eagerness to escape into the library was
that the people who bought tickets for the nineteenth-century
theatre could be as offensive to the playwright and performer as the
worst Jacobean rout of nifles. To take evidence for the moment only
of patrons of the highest social standing, in the 'History of a Young
Lady's Entrance into the World' we have a fictional account of
behaviour in the best boxes, where the comic exaggeration is not in
the substance but only in the blatant directness: 'I seldom listen to
the players: one has so much to do, in looking about, and finding out
one's acquaintance, that really, one has no time to mind the stage . . .

one merely comes to meet one's friends, and show that one's alive.[43]
In 1843 one aristocratic woman describes another at a performance
of Macready's *King Lear*: 'I never saw her when she was not . . .
chattering . . . and laughing, with her shoulder turned to the stage.
. . . I heard from one who knew her and the incidents of that evening
too well to be mistaken, that the story was absolutely new to her,
inasmuch as she was not previously aware that King Lear had any
daughters.'[44] Not many people were more Victorian than Harriet
Martineau, who reported this behaviour, and no one was quite as
Victorian as the Empress into whom that unruly, ignorant young
woman in the Royal Box was to gravitate.

The busy theatrical activity of the first seven decades of the
nineteenth century has bequeathed to us very few actable plays of
literary interest, but it has passed on to us the names of some great
actors and an unprecedentedly large number of remarkable theatre
buildings. One of the most noteworthy, as quite the most handsome
theatre in the world, is La Fenice: it displays with regal pride what
can be achieved by theatrical architects when they are set free of the
requirement that patrons should be able to see and hear the
performers. Effie Ruskin has recorded her uninformed response to
the mid nineteenth-century theatre of social grandeur in Venice:

> I was very glad that Wrbna's kindness has enabled me to go for I
> never saw any thing so brilliant in Italy, every place was filled and
> the crowd in the Parterre innumerable. I was next box to the
> Governor [General Gorzkowski], and in the middle of the House
> the Emperor's box was brilliantly lighted with the Grand Duke in
> Austrian uniform [he was Colonel of an Austrian infantry
> regiment] and the Duchess, who looked very handsome in Pink
> glace with low body & short sleeves and most splendid pearls
> almost covering her neck, her hair with two large plaits on each
> side. Behind her sat Wrbna and on the other side of the box the
> other ladies and gentlemen of the suite . . .
>
> We came away before the end as it was so long. I wish they did
> not talk so much in the Theatre for it is impossible to pay any
> attention . . . for first came Nugent talking English as fast as he
> could, at the same time the Princess talking her Venetian and
> General Duodo replying – then came Falkenhayn and his
> German & Wrbna with his French making your box a sort of

5. La Fenice: 'Every place was filled and the crowd in the Parterre innumerable'

Babel, and as it would be considered quite contrary to etiquette that Ladies should ever be left alone in their box, whenever one gentleman has paid his visit of a quarter of an hour or so another arrives to take his place and you never have a chance of being alone a minute. I complained of it last night . . . and they were all against me; they said that the Theatre was [their] property and every body had a right to call upon any body that they knew, and as most people went every night for an hour it was economical as it saved them lighting their rooms at home, and that having a box . . . was the cheapest way for all to see people & society.[45]

The Fenice had been built for those who owned it, box by box, and their social requirements were dominant. The play was another thing, of occasional peripheral interest. To this day many a first-time visitor who has not been forewarned will find himself – having no more urgent claim on his attention – calculating the proportion of boxes from which he might have witnessed part of the performance. John Ruskin did not accompany his wife to the Fenice, for he was in his study dreaming of theatres that would be 'pious places'[46] with effective simplicity in performance as well as in the design of stage and auditorium. He wrote with rhetorical contempt for all ostentatious decoration – of building, of furniture, of self-regarding audience – that might take attention away from the performed work of art.[47]

Charles Dickens had similar golden hopes for the drama and a similar loathing of contemporary theatrical practices. Dickens's favourite mode, of course, was bizarre comedy and his target the opposite end of the social spectrum. He describes Sadler's Wells with characteristic exuberance.

> The play was MACBETH. It was performed amidst the usual hideous medley of fights, foul language, catcalls, shrieks, yells, oaths, blasphemy, obscenity, apples, oranges, nuts, biscuits, ginger-beer, porter, and pipes – not that there was any particular objection to the Play, but that the audience were, on the whole, in a condition of mind, generally requiring such utterance. Pipes of all lengths were at work in the gallery; several were displayed in the pit. Cans of beer, each with a pint measure to drink from (for the convenience of gentlemen who had neglected the precaution of bringing their own pots in their bundles), were carried through the dense crowd at all stages of the tragedy. Sickly children in arms were squeezed out of shape, in all parts of the house. Fish was fried at the entrance doors. Barricades of oyster-shells encumbered the pavement. Expectant half-price visitors to the gallery, howled defiant impatience up the stairs, and danced a sort of Carmagnole all round the building.[48]

The aristocracy at the Fenice, the hoi polloi at the Wells had other things to interest them than the play, and the lively conditions in each case directly echoed back the public voice. The patrons have always given the drama its laws, and so it remains today, whenever

6. 'It was performed amidst the usual hideous medley.' Plate
commissioned by Charles Dickens for Chapter 39 of *The Old Curiosity
Shop* in *Master Humphrey's Clock* (1840)

Shakespeare's plays are advertised on the posters while some other
local pastime is relished in practice. In the summer of 1988 in the
Landmark Building on Sunset Boulevard the play was again
Macbeth. It was performed in a swimming pool. The only begetter
of the event was a Hollywood 'Producer–Creator–Director', who
had deconstructed Shakespeare's text or, as they used to put it in
that neighbourhood, had left it on the cutting-room floor. Spectators were advised to relocate their folding-chairs around the pool
whenever they thought a new point of view would be a fun thing.
There were few positions from which the life of the action could be
seen clear, none where it could be seen whole, and Shakespeare's
text was utterly vanquished; but again only the uninformed would
complain, for we were really there to witness an exercise in
'Production–Creation–Direction' in which a Hollywood artiste
spent a good deal of money made in the movies in pursuit of

theatrical self-expression. Only a few kindred spirits truly appreciated the effort, but that can be taken as a guarantor of high artistry in Tinsel Town, as it was among the transpontine stews of John Fletcher's London.

The playhouse has infrequently been a place where a literary author could expect his words to be listened to with attention, even in those moments when they might be uttered and audible. In 1841 the Secretary of the Shakespeare Society delivered a lecture which emphasized the great perennial divide. He spoke of the

> universal recognition of the division of the Drama of our time, into the Acted and the Unacted . . . the Unacted Drama is now claiming the attention of the refined and the tasteful. The Press has applauded it as emanating from the efforts of genius; and the highest acted Dramatists themselves confess it is mightier in intellectual power, and stronger in true poetic excellence, than the acted . . .[49] The Unacted Dramatists proceed on entirely different principles to the Acted; have different aims in view, and desire to produce different results. They take for their model the Shakespearian drama.[50]

He offers to indicate the virtues of the unacted drama, and he does so by eulogizing *Hamlet*, which he regards as the greatest of all the superior – because unactable – plays he is familiar with, and whose protagonist is 'all that beauty could desire, or poet imagine, of princely nobility and manly love'.[51]

At this point we might give credit to the man who most encouraged the whole tradition of preferring unacted plays that delight fine sensibilities but should not be presented in public since they soar above the head of the average member of the general audience – the man who argued that the opinion of one judicious critical intelligence must outweigh the clapper-clawing of a large auditorium filled with the smokey breath of the unskilful.[52] Like Coleridge, Byron, Lamb, Hazlitt, Scott, Browning; like Goethe, Shaw, Strindberg and O'Neill he had a very strong interest in the theatre and consorted eagerly with actors. But, again like them, he most admired the kind of drama not suited for the stage. His favourite play of all had never been acted to his knowledge, and he knew for certain that if it had been performed once it had certainly not been performed twice, for it was too refined for the common palate. He told an actor that the 'excellent play' he most respected was too intricately constructed and too delicate for what Shakespeare's pen had called the 'unworthy scaffold', the 'cockpit', the 'wooden O'.[53] The poetic drama which earned his greatest admiration eschewed the bombastic noise applauded by the groundlings, and it lacked the salaciousness which would entice the quantity of barren spectators required by the public theatres. His choice of the term 'barren spectators' makes the dismissive attack on the playgoers most common from resentful theatrical poets; the majority do not come to listen to subtle language but to wait with jaded eyes for something gaudy to stare at stupidly. They are not an audience at all, they are spectators eager to gawp at a royal procession, an inexplicable dumbshow, a duel fought with surreptitiously poisoned rapier, and at lots of dead bodies wearing princely costume. They come to sate their ocular appetites on the vulgar playhouse parade

> Of carnal, bloody, and unnatural acts,
> Of accidental judgements, casual slaughters,
> Of deaths put on by cunning.[54]

This young man cultivated a reputation for hesitancy and scholarly reticence; nevertheless, he had the temerity to say all of this to the actor–manager of a touring theatre company from whom he desperately required, as a favour, the peformance of a play which would determine his own future and the future of his country. This was the gentleman scholar who most memorably argued that, with the service of the mind's eye, the only civilized thing is to read a play as words, words, words, until much of the fine language is committed to memory. Charles Lamb was speaking for the Prince of Denmark and for a great many readers in his own and other centuries when he summed up the age-old argument disparagingly: 'How much Hamlet is made another thing by being acted.'[55]

Of course it would be more accurate to say that *Hamlet*, beginning life on the unworthy scaffold, has been made another thing by being perused in the library. Two thousand years earlier, Greek tragedies had become different entities when they were made texts for academic study. Aristotle expresses low opinions of fourth-century acting and stage presentation[56], but for him it was also a matter of principle. Far from depending on performance, he argued, the crucial pattern of dramatic action can be fully appreciated through the medium of the mind's eye: 'Tragedy like Epic poetry produces its effect even without action; it reveals its power by mere reading.'[57] His convictions about the relationship between matter and form led to the proposition that *any* physical expression of an ideal must be imperfect. The play-text of *Oedipus Tyrannus* available to be read in manuscript is what he was discussing with his pupils in the Academy. He was eager to communicate to them his great respect for the literary aspect of the tragedian's art, but he had no similar praise for theatrical practitioners.[58] Aristotle set the pattern commonly followed by modern university teachers: he limited his academic approval to plays of distant generations as they were recorded for readers, as classics of dramatic literature.

A similar philosophical position and a similar distaste for the treachery of the stage led Pirandello in 1918 to argue that

> The literary work is the drama ... conceived and written by the poet: what is seen in the theatre is not and cannot be anything but a scenic translation. So many actors and so many translations, more or less faithful, more or less felicitous; but, like every translation, always and inevitably inferior to the original.[59]

Six years later T.S. Eliot was characteristically more cool and characteristically every bit as fierce:

> I know that I rebel against most performances of Shakespeare's plays because I want a direct relationship between the work of art and myself, and I want the performance to be such as will not interrupt or alter this relationship ... I object, in other words, to the interpretation, and I would have a work of art such that it needs only to be completed and cannot be altered by each interpretation.[60]

Naturally, the unalterable work of dramatic art that so many have demanded over the past two and a half millenniums can only be the text fixed on the page.

The idea that an estimable play has a superior life independent of performance has always been with us, but it is symptomatic of the poetic sensibility, and of the role of the playhouse, in the nineteenth century that the idea should have become so very dominant in the most influential educational circles. When Shakespeare's plays were introduced as set texts in the schools and then in the universities, it was certainly not with the intention that the young of the respectable middle class should be permitted – far less encouraged – to visit the theatres. Matthew Arnold was one of the very few men-of-letters who were in principle enthusiastic about plays in production, but he was very depressed about the actuality: 'We have in England everything to make us dissatisfied with the chaotic and ineffective condition into which our theatre has fallen.[61] He speaks sadly of a visit to the theatre that had fixed itself in his memory twenty years previously:

> Scattered at very distant intervals through the boxes were about half-a-dozen chance-comers like myself; there were some soldiers and their friends in the pit, and a good many riff-raff in the upper gallery. The real townspeople, the people who carried forward the business and life of Shrewsbury, and who filled its churches and chapels on Sundays, were entirely absent . . . Here one had a good example, – as I thought at the time, and as I have often thought since, – of the complete estrangement of the British middle class from the theatre.[62]

One legacy of this estrangement was the deeply ingrained contempt for plays in performance characteristic of the critical establishment that dominated the university study of Shakespeare for the first hundred years of our Schools of English. When generations of undergraduates were trying to learn how to read a Shakespeare play, the guiding voices were of one accord. Andrew Bradley was certain that in the theatre Shakespeare's greatest work

> not only refuses to reveal itself fully through the senses but seems to be almost in contradiction with their reports . . . the appeal is made not so much to dramatic perception as to a rarer and more strictly poetic kind of imagination.[63] . . . it . . . is poetry, and such poetry as cannot be transferred to the space behind the footlights, but has its being only in the imagination. Here then is Shakespeare at his very greatest, but not the mere dramatist Shakespeare.

Bradley found it not 'believable that Shakespeare . . . had the stage-performance only or chiefly in view' in writing the greatest scenes; rather he must 'have written to satisfy his own imagination'.[64] Bradley, like Shaw and many Victorians, admired the play which aspires towards the condition of the musical novel.

And when a later generation of academics announced a revolutionary coup which would utterly change the nature of Shakespeare criticism, they rejected the Victorian concern with characterization and proclaimed the new age of poetic appreciation:

> the only profitable approach to Shakespeare is a consideration of his plays as dramatic poems . . . the words on the page, which it is the main business of the critic to examine.[65] . . . We start with so many lines of verse on a printed page which we read as we should read any other poem . . . we have to allow full weight to each word, exploring its 'tentacular roots', and to determine how it controls and is controlled by the rhythmic movement of the passage in which it occurs.[66]

'A play of Shakespeare's is a precise particular experience, a poem', and the critic must bring a 'razor-edge of sensibility' to the task of reading 'the unique arrangement of words that constitute these plays'.[67] L.C. Knights, on behalf of a generation of academic legislators, went on to tell us that we must guard against 'false assumptions about the category "drama"; *Macbeth* has greater affinity with *The Waste Land* than *The Wild Duck*.'[68]

Occasionally there might be a nod in the direction of Shakespeare as a man of the theatre; for example, the 1961 British Academy lecture, entitled 'Shakespeare and the Players', began provocatively: 'Shakespeare was first and foremost a dramatist, a writer for the theatre; and, consequently . . . only in the theatre can his full impact be measured.[69] But the lecture successfully concludes with a proposition that the Fellows could applaud with enthusiasm, since they had been applauding it from the Academy's inception.

> Shakespeare's art was so much a function of his players' quality . . . what implication has this for his interpreters today? It lands them, I believe, in an intolerable dilemma. On the one hand it reinforces the conviction that Shakespeare's work can only receive full display and full appreciation in a theatrical context;

> on the other it brings home the fact that nowhere in the English
> speaking world today is it possible to find anything approaching
> the true context for which that work was designed . . .
>
> In these circumstances there is some excuse for those who claim
> that the only theatre in which Shakespeare can be adequately
> presented is the theatre of the mind.[70]

This has long been a familiar syllogism in Schools of English
Language and Literature. The plays were written for the stage, we
must admit; but the fine stage they were written for is permanently
beyond our reach; ergo, we must limit ourselves to an imaginative
response to the words on the page. We hear too much about the
original and 'true context' of the plays. The premise that the
wooden O and its barren spectators were of unrepeatable excellence
would have made Hamlet raise an ironical eyebrow and Ben Jonson
his bricklayer's heavy fist. What began in the nineteenth century as
a happy thought undarkened by much information has regularly
become a central conviction in university Schools of English: the
theatre once had an age of gold when Shakespeare's plays could be
greatly performed and generally appreciated but that age has been
lost forever.

Against all of this we now have university Schools of Drama and
Theatre Studies, many of them established, against bitter opposition from colleagues, by teachers of English who were not content
to discuss Shakespeare exclusively within the narrow anti-theatrical
orthodoxy. And in some of these Schools there has developed a new
antipodal orthodoxy eager to stand the long critical tradition on its
head by denigrating the literary text and denying it any independent
value at all.

> The script on the page is not the drama any more than a clod of
> earth is a field of corn . . . the words of *Hamlet* are merely signals
> for communication[71] . . . the text is only a plan for drama, and is
> equivalent at best to the scenario of a film or the choreography of
> a ballet, never the film or the dance itself.[72]

In many universities in Britain and the United States there is
disaffection, and frequently strife, between the teachers of Theatre
and the teachers of English; and the cause lies in these deeply
antagonistic convictions about how to read a play. There is the

historical explanation that we have seen in outline, but it is still disappointing when any one of our colleagues refuses to admit that a play has separate legitimate lives. At one extreme it can serve as a frame on which to hang an exercise in the performance arts to feed the robust theatrical appetites of designers, musicians, actors and audience; and at the other extreme it can be an autotelic poem enrapturing the individual imagination in the library. We saw the friends of John Fletcher arguing that the printed text of *The Faithful Shepherdess*, not the stage disaster, is the true work of art. John Marston one the other hand had a rich theatrical success with *The Malcontent* and he apologizes for putting the text into print, for it was written with the sole intention of its being spoken on stage and he hopes that the bare text 'may be pardoned for the pleasure it once afforded you when it was presented with the soul of lively action'.[73]

Fortunately there is a third case to be considered – the shared, fertile ground where library study and the sympathetic imagination can make the actor and the scaffold worthy of our high respect. This is the essential work to be done in our universities and in the theatre companies where our graduates and their like find scope to practise their creative skills. The best theatre practice in the later part of the twentieth century, and the best audiences, are capable of both presenting and appreciating the soul of lively action in plays which have been studied fruitfully. In this, we should clearly recognize that we have made a quantum leap beyond all other generations in the past twenty-five hundred years. The work of the best professional schools, of the universities and of the finest practitioners has transformed the relationship between dramatic text and theatrical performance. Production values in recent decades have been changed as radically as standards in medicine or technology. Hazlitt's is the most devastating condemnation of theatrical standards in the nineteenth century, but he did not set his sharp tongue loose on the contemporary state of the arts of brain surgery or of space travel. In all three fields of enterprise our great, great-grandparents could not have predicted what we have achieved. This is not to say that we would regard any performance of *Hamlet* as definitive, or suppose that many would be of the highest order. But the behaviour, on both sides of the footlights, which horrified Francis Beaumont, Dr Johnson, Coleridge, Charles Lamb and

Hamlet himself, is no longer the norm. Matthew Arnold's dream has been realized in that Shakespeare's plays are frequently performed by and for educated, cultured, perceptive and discriminating people; audiences can see the stage, hear the well-trained voices, and greatly benefit from the word being made flesh.

I work with large numbers of students of Drama, and the question of how to read a Shakespeare play is paramount every day. There is common agreement that *Hamlet* must be performed as often as circumstances will allow: no season in London will be satisfactory if a valid stage production is not available. But what of the other side of the question? What is the value of the text to be read in the library? What in the way of stage productions might compensate the educated theatre practitioner for being denied the opportunity to study the text of *Hamlet*? We have played with the idea fancifully, imagining an infinitely accommodating time-machine that would enable us to drop into any or every performance since Burbage's first night. But even then no one has accepted the implied bargain. The text of *Hamlet* is not at all like the scenario of a film or a choreographer's sketches. To read *Hamlet* is one of the most important elements of a humane education; we have been deeply altered by the experience, and will be again and again. Performing *Hamlet* is indeed another thing from studying the play; but, far from being mutually exclusive alternatives, they are complementary activities; each is necessary for the other.

Dr Johnson emphasized that there are two ways to respond to a text of Shakespeare. One is when fancy is on the wing, the mind strongly engaged with the force of the fable[74]: an excellent performance and what John Webster called 'a full and understanding Auditory'[75] make such a response to the play possible. The other way of reading the text is with a slow, patient, scholarly examination of the details where, with the help of mentors, one learns to read the poem with thorough exactness, over the years coming to a close familiarity with every nuance. Peter Brook made the same distinction with characteristic humour when he said that there 'is a place for discussion, for research, for the study of history and documents', and that there is also 'a place for roaring and howling and rolling on the floor'.[76]

Disgraceful performances and shameful audiences are outside

the argument; on the positive side, there is the text for the mind's eye, and there is also the stage as a worthy scaffold; and these two forms of publication make possible the two interdependent approaches to the question of how we should read a Shakespeare play.

Notes

1. 'The Deadly Theatre' in *The Empty Space* (Harmondsworth: Penguin Books, 1972), p. 12.
2. 'An ode. To himself' in *Ben Jonson*, ed. C.H. Herford, Percy and Evelyn Simpson (Oxford: Clarendon Press, 11 vols., 1925–52), VIII, 175.
3. 'To the memory of my beloued, The AUTHOR Mr. William Shakespeare : AND what he hath left vs' in ibid., VIII, 390.
4. 'Ode on a Grecian Urn'.
5. 'Seneca in Elizabethan Translation' in *Selected Essays* (London: Faber and Faber, 1951), p. 68.
6. 'On Mr. Ben Iohnson' in *Ben Jonson*, op. cit., XI, 468–70.
7. *Mr. William SHAKESPEARS Comedies, Histories, & Tragedies*. A facsimile edition prepared by Helge Kökeritz (New Haven: Yale University Press, 1954), A3.
8. August Strindberg, *Open Letters to the Intimate Theater*, translations and introductions by Walter Johnson (Seattle and London: University of Washington Press, 1966), p. 21.
9. Ibid., pp. 226–7.
10. Ibid., p. 300.
11. In Barrett H. Clark, *Eugene O'Neill: the Man and his Plays* (London: Constable & Co., 1947), p. 39.
12. 'The Artist of the Theatre: a Colloquy between Eugene O'Neill and Oliver M. Sayler' in *Theatre Arts* (June 1957), vol. XLI, no. 6.
13. *Dichtung und Wahrheit*, Dreizehntes Buch, in *Goethes Werke*, Hamburger Ausgabe in 14 Banden. Herausgegeben von Erich Trunz (Munich: Verlag C.H. Beck, 1981), IX, 570.
14. This was said specifically about *Torquato Tasso*, but in 1807 Goethe drafted a new version of the play that would be more suited for acting. He reduced the amount of Hamletesque introspection and increased the element of action.
15. 2 January, 1824.
16. 6 December, 1829.
17. A report of a lecture by Coleridge in *Coleridge on Shakespeare*, ed. Terence Hawkes (Harmondsworth: Penguin Books, 1969), p. 119.
18. 'Lectures on Shakespere and Milton', Lecture V, in *Lectures and Notes*

on Shakespere and Other English Poets, collected by T. Ashe (London: George Bellard Sons, 1900), p. 479.

19. *Coleridge on Shakespeare*, op. cit., p. 224.
20. Charles Lamb, 'On the Tragedies of Shakespeare, Considered with Reference to Their Fitness for Stage Representation' in *Miscellaneous Prose by Charles and Mary Lamb*, ed. E.V. Lucas (London: Methuen & Co, 1912), p. 113.
21. Ibid., p. 114.
22. Ibid., p. 115.
23. *Troilus and Cressida*, ed. Alice Walker (Cambridge: Cambridge University Press, 1969), pp. lix, lx.
24. Ibid., p. ix.
25. *The Dramatic Works in the Beaumont and Fletcher Canon*, ed. Fredson Bowers (Cambridge: Cambridge University Press, 6 vols., 1966–85), III, 491.
26. Ibid., p. 492.
27. *The Yale Edition of the Works of Samuel Johnson* (New Haven: Yale University Press, 15 vols., 1958–85), vol. VII (1968) ed. Arthur Sherbo, p. 79.
28. *Boswell's Journal of a Tour of the Hebrides*, by Frederick A. Pottle and Charles H. Bennett (London: William Heinemann, 1963), p. 207.
29. Preface to 'A View of the English Stage' in *The Complete Works of William Hazlitt*, Centenary Edition, ed. P.P. Howe (London and Toronto: J.M. Dent & Sons, 21 vols., 1930–34), V, 173.
30. Ibid., pp. 222–3.
31. Ibid., 'The Tempest', p. 234.
32. 'Hamlet' in 'Characters of Shakespeare's Plays', *The Complete Works of William Hazlitt*, IV, 237.
33. Byron, Letters of 23 August 1841 to Douglas Kinnaird and John Murray, in *Byron's Letters and Journals*, ed. Leslie A. Marchand (London: John Murray, 12 vols., 1973–82), VIII, 185, 187.
34. *Ravena Journal*, 12 January 1821, ibid., VIII, 23.
35. Robert Browning, 'A Light Woman' in 'Men and Women' in *Robert Browning: the Poems*, ed. John Pettigrew (Harmondsworth: Penguin Books, 2 vols., 1981), I, 595.
36. *Letters of Robert Browning and Elizabeth Barrett Browning*, ed. Elvan Kintner (Cambridge, Mass: The Belknapp Press of Harvard University, 1969), II, 701.
37. In *Essays on Chivalry, Romance and the Drama* (London: Frederick Warne and Co, 1888), p. 183.
38. *The Bodley Head Bernard Shaw*, ed. Dan H. Laurence (London: Max Reinhardt, 7 vols., 1970–74), I, 13.
39. Ibid., pp. 25–7.
40. Ibid., p. 28. Ben Jonson chose to supply just such a list of character

sketches for *Every Man Out of His Humour* when it was printed and offered to the young gentlemen of the Inns of Court.

41. Ibid., pp. 31–2.
42. See 'Genesis of an Epic-Drama' in Walter F. Wright, *The Shaping of the Dynasts* (Lincoln, Nebraska: University of Nebraska Press, 1967), p. 105.
43. Fanny Burney, *Evelina*, ed. Edward A. Bloom (London: Oxford University Press, 1968), vol. I, letter 20, p. 80.
44. *Harriet Martineau's Autobiography*, with memorials by Maria Weston Chapman (London: Smith, Elder & Co., 3 vols., 1877), II, 119, 120.
45. *Effie in Venice*, ed. Mary Lutyens (London: John Murray, 1965), pp. 238–9.
46. *Fors Clavigera*, VIII. *The Works of John Ruskin*, ed. E.T. Cook and A. Wedderburn (London: George Allen, 1904), XXIX, 434.
47. *Modern Painters*, V, XIX. *Works*, XXVIII, 392.
48. *The Uncollected Writings of Charles Dickens: Household Words 1850–1859*, ed. Harry Stone (London: Allen Lane, The Penguin Press, 2 vols., 1969), I, 346–7.
49. F.G. Tomlins, 'The Relative Value of the Acted and Unacted Drama' in *Monthly Magazine* (April, 1841). Reprinted by C. Mitchell, Red Lion Court, London (1841), p. 3.
50. Ibid., pp. 5, 6.
51. Ibid., p. 10.
52. See *Hamlet* 2.2 and 3.2.
53. *King Henry V*, Prologue, lines 10–13.
54. *Hamlet* 5.2. 386–8. Ben Jonson's prologues for the Stage and for the Court to his *The Staple of News* are sad indications of *his* desperate need to find an audience that would listen with attention to his words.
55. *Miscellaneous Prose*, op. cit., p. 117.
56. *Poetics*, 50b.
57. *Poetics*, 62a in *Aristotle's Theory of Poetry and Fine Art*, ed. S.H. Butcher (New York: Dover Publications, 1951), p. 109.
58. *Poetics*, 62a.
59. *Opere di Luigi Pirandello*, ed. Arnoldo Mondadori (Milan, 6 vols., 1956–60), vol. VI, *Saggi, Poesie, Scritti Varii*, 'Teatro e Letteratura', p. 989.
60. T.S. Eliot, 'Four Elizabethan Dramatists' in *Selected Essays* (London: Faber and Faber, 1951), pp. 114–15.
61. Matthew Arnold, 'The French Play in London' in *The Complete Prose Works of Matthew Arnold*, ed. R.H. Super (Ann Arbor: University of Michigan Press, 11 vols., 1960–77), IX, 83.
62. Ibid., pp. 79–80.
63. A.C. Bradley, LL.D., Litt.D., *Shakespearean Tragedy*, intro. by John Russell Brown (London: Macmillan, 1985), pp. 202–3.

64. Ibid., p. 222.
65. L.C. Knights, 'How Many Children Had Lady Macbeth?' in *'Hamlet' and other Shakespearean Essays* (Cambridge: Cambridge University Press, 1979), p. 275.
66. Ibid., p. 285.
67. Ibid., p. 286.
68. Ibid., p. 287.
69. Richard David, 'Shakespeare and the Players' in *Studies in Shakespeare*, selected and introduced by Peter Alexander (London: Oxford University Press, 1964), p. 33.
70. Ibid., pp. 53–4. But see Richard David, *Shakespeare in the Theatre* (Cambridge: Cambridge University Press, 1978), *passim* and especially pp. 1–20.
71. J.L. Styan, *Drama, Stage and Audience* (Cambridge: Cambridge University Press, 1975), pp. vii-viii.
72. Ibid., p. 65.
73. John Marston, *The Malcontent*, ed. George K. Hunter (Revels Plays: Manchester University Press, 1975), p. 6.
74. *The Yale Edition of the Works of Samuel Johnson*, VII, 111.
75. *The Complete Works of John Webster*, ed. F.L. Lucas (London: Chatto & Windus, 4 vols., 1927), I, 107.
76. 'The Immediate Theatre' in *The Empty Space*, op. cit., p. 140.

5

Plots are not stories:
the so-called 'duality method'
of Terence

DWORA GILULA

Terence was praised in antiquity for the excellence of his plot construction. Donatus deemed as praiseworthy the existence of two love affairs (*bini amores*) in all Terence's plays but the *Hecyra*, and Evanthius commended the richness of Terence's plots (*locupletiora argumenta*) constructed of double affairs (*ex duplicibus negotiis*), likewise observing that all the plays except the *Hecyra* feature two young men in love.[1] Terence's plays continued to be read, admired and even sometimes imitated in the Middle Ages, and the Renaissance comedy was modelled principally on his comedies. Herrick, who examined the leading commentaries on Terence from the fourth-century work of Donatus and on, has shown that Terence was considered a master of dramatic structure and his comedy monopolized the sixteenth-century discussion of comic theory: the 'dramatic' rules established for comedy mostly derived from the practice of Terence. On the issue of the double action, Donatus's observation was usually repeated and the double structure commended for the enriching of the action.[2] Even after the interpretation of the single action recommended by Aristotle and Horace became established, the double plot continued to be practised in the Renaissance comedy, which, as is well known, influenced comedies of later periods. It is therefore interesting to note the change of attitude among modern scholars and critics towards Terence's plots.

Legrand, for example, required the two love affairs to be of equal importance and tightly connected one with the other, using these two arbitrarily selected qualities of the double plot as a norm of evaluation. Accordingly, the *Phormio* received poor marks for having the two love affairs 'run parallel and without influence upon one another for too long a time' (i.e., they are not tightly connected), and the *Andria* was criticized, since 'one of the lovers becomes a matter of indifference to the spectators',[3] and thus fails the requirement of 'equal importance'.

These requirements are based on an Aristotelian conception of dramatic unity and transfer Aristotle's critical method and criteria from tragedy to comedy. The double plot is regarded as artistically satisfying only if it fulfils the requirements of one action which evolves according to the rules of probability and necessity. The greater the extent of the causal interaction of its two issues the nearer will the double plot be to a representation of one action, whereas their equality makes sure that neither may be regarded as a subplot. Such requirements not only demand that plots of comedies should conform with the plots of tragedies, but they also ignore, or criticize, plots with two issues of varying importance, or plots with other, not causal interconnections.

Legrand's normative approach was adopted by Norwood, who augmented it with yet another requirement. He was the first to coin the term 'the duality method', defining it as 'the method of employing two problems or complications to solve each other'.[4] Since Norwood believed in evolution and in intellectual progress, he deemed early works as immature and discerned in Terence's comedies a constant ascending line of improvement towards perfection. Thus, he proclaimed the *Andria* immature, which coincides with Legrand's view, but disagreed with Legrand's negative evaluation of the *Phormio*, which, being a later play, should reveal traits of artistic perfection. In this he was followed by Duckworth, who also canonized 'the duality method',[5] which, thanks to him, came to be taken almost for granted by others.

An amusing illustration of such a normative approach is the following criticism of the *Andria*: 'Charinus and his love for Philumena do not suit the standards for the dual plot as defined by Norwood and as practised by Terence in his later plays, particularly the Phormio'.[6] Surely it is not Terence who has to suit Norwood's, or any other scholar's, standards. Normative evaluation based on arbitrarily selected or invented *ad hoc* dramatic qualities is unhelpful. What is needed is an understanding of the actual ways in which Terence's plots are constructed, an understanding which can be achieved through an unbiased reading of the plays, without any preconceived attitudes.

For quite a long time scholars and critics of the Roman comedy were chiefly interested in establishing the degree of originality in Terence's use of his Greek models and in their speculative reconstruction, to the relative neglect of other questions. Bent on finding contradictions, inconsistencies and other proofs of Terence's inferior workmanship, scholars used a methodology borrowed from Homeric studies. This contributed a great deal no doubt to the lack of interest in characteristics specific to the dramatic genre. Plays were treated in a way similar to that used in examining epic narrative as texts to be read, not as scripts to be performed. This attitude, more than anything else, has affected the treatment of dramatic plots, either single or double.

In this paper I propose to examine the question of 'the duality method' through a reading of one play, the *Andria*, Terence's first comedy.

A typical summary of any of the Terentian double plot comedies by scholars who subscribe to 'the duality method' tells the story of the two love affairs, stressing the degree of their importance and their interconnections. Duckworth, for example, summarizes the plot of the *Andria* as follows:

> In the *Andria*, Pamphilus – passionately devoted to his mistress Glycerium – does not wish to marry Chremes' daughter, who is beloved by Charinus, and Pamphilus assures Charinus that he has nothing to fear. When Davus' plans go astray, Charinus' hopes are temporarily shattered but the recognition of Glycerium as Chremes' daughter solves the problem of both young men, and Charinus is free to marry Philumena.[7]

Factually, this is a correct summary, but it is construed of various elements of unequal dramatic standing. It tells the story of the *Andria*. But while a play has a story to tell, the story of a play does not necessarily coincide with its dramatic stage plot, namely with the words and deeds of the characters who enact before the audience the actual stage events. The dramatic stage plot differs from what the formalists call *syuzet*, which is the order and presentation of the events in a narrative. It may contain narrative elements which describe past events in a non-chronological order, but these are described in a direct discourse by one of the characters and form a part of a present tense stage event. The sum of all present tense stage events is the dramatic stage plot.

Readers of a dramatic text who wish to construct its dramatic stage plot must think in terms of performance and take into account only what the play's characters are to say and do on stage before an audience. What is narrated by the *dramatis personae* as being said and done elsewhere are narrative elements incorporated into the present tense stage event, but with a different mode of existence. In order to construct a dramatic stage plot of a play, one has to compose a short story, namely to substitute the play's dialogues with a narrative. But, since plays are not texts conceived in terms of a narrative medium, they usually defy attempts at extrapolating their plots by playing tricks on the summarizing narrator. For it is easy to narrate what is narrated, and it seems almost natural to perform the transformation of the dialogue into narrative by adulterating it with actual narrative elements picked out of the dialogue itself. The result is a story of the play not at all representative of its dramatic stage plot. Since stories are not plots, substituting one for the other leads to erroneous analyses of the plays misrepresented in such a way.

Duckworth's previously quoted summary of the *Andria*'s plot is a fine example of such a story. It not only misrepresents what actually happens on stage, but also distorts the nature of the *Andria*'s dramatic conflict, for it creates the false impression that the two love affairs are equally important and that they are the main interest of the dramatic plot, that, in fact, the *Andria* is a romantic comedy. Terence's comedies, however, are not romantic dramas, but intrigue plays in which the emphasis is not on the lovers themselves but on the persons who plan to bring them together or set them apart. The two young men are not the main protagonists of the play and the girls do not appear on stage at all. If the importance of a character is commensurate with the length of his role, the first role belongs to the slave Davus, the second to the head of the household, the *senex* Simo, and only the third to his son Pamphilus. The same conclusion is bound to be reached if the importance of a character is measured in terms of the dramatic conflict he originates or in which he is involved.[8] Even a brief glance at what actually happens in the *Andria* reveals that the action stems from a conflict between Simo and Davus.

The antecedents to the play's dramatic conflict are described by Simo in the exposition: his wealthy friend Chremes, who, impressed by Pamphilus's allegedly exemplary behaviour, had offered Simo a marriage deal, has withdrawn his generous offer after a rumour reached him of Pamphilus' affair with the *meretrix* Glycerium. Simo plans to find out the truth and test his son's obedience by pretending that the marriage is to take place as arranged. He also hopes to fool his slave Davus into believing that the marriage is real, so that his schemes against it will be wasted harmlessly. Simo's main concern is that it will be not his son but Davus who will foil his plans. He deduces his son's unwillingness to get married from Davus's fear, and it is Davus whom he orders to see to it that his son will consent to the marriage. When Simo warns Davus not to try to pull any smart tricks, it is clear that it is now Davus's turn to do exactly what he is warned not to, that is to show how clever and inventive he is.

Thus, from the onset of the play, it is obvious that the two protagonists who advance the action are Simo and Davus and not Pamphilus, the *adulescens* in love. When Pamphilus is brought on stage for the first time (Act I, Scene 5), it is not to offer a course of action but to clarify his position, which up till then has been reported by a third party. In order to appraise correctly the schemes devised on his behalf, the audience has to hear directly from him what is his attitude to Glycerium and the proposed marriage, but it is Davus, not Pamphilus, who acts. His scheme counteracts Simo's, and in spite of all its (prepared) unexpectedness it neatly parallels Simo's stratagem: it is a bluff pitted against a bluff. Davus has found Simo out, correctly guessed his aim, and consequently advised Pamphilus to agree to the pretended marriage in order to avoid disobedience and to embarrass his plotting father. Pamphilus does whatever he is advised to do.

Both Simo and Davus are prompted to action by mutual

disbelief, both constantly stand on guard and examine each other's moves. The chief comic ingredient of these situations is that each schemer, confident of his own cleverness, is led to a false assessment of events, disbelieving what is true and vice versa. Simo is, of course, only too happy to believe that his son is willing to marry Philumena. But, when Davus in his eagerness to eliminate all doubts overplays his hand with the explanation that Pamphilus's sadness is caused by Simo's close-fisted preparations for the marriage, Simo's suspicions are alerted (What is the old plotter (*veterator*) up to? 467), but his assessment of the events is false. Simo believes that the birth of Glycerium's child (his grandson) is staged in order to scare off Chremes. Not only is he led to disbelieve what is true, but, conditioned to explain events according to his expectations, he also jumps to the false conclusion that he has succeeded in fooling Davus exactly as he had planned, namely that his scheme of the pretended marriage actually helped him to uncover and to annul Davus's machinations.

Davus is quick to take advantage of Simo's mistaken conclusions and immediately proceeds to exploit his disbelief: You are right, you have detected the truth. The baby is not Glycerium's baby, she ordered it to be brought to break the marriage which is to her disadvantage but which Pamphilus now wants. Since it falls in line with his reasoning, Simo believes Davus, takes his son's promise as a firm basis for futher action, and proceeds as he initially planned. He persuades Chremes to change his mind again and to agree to the marriage (III,3). Since Davus fooled Simo into believing that he, Davus, is not fooling him at all, Simo feels free to tell him about his initial plan of the pretended marriage. Now Davus is really gloating over his success, which reaches its peak in his ironic comment: Such cleverness! I could never have guessed it (589).

Immediately, however, he learns that the situation has been reversed. Simo, although fooled and outwitted, has actually achieved his goal, whereas Davus, the arch-schemer, finds out that his cleverness, instead of averting the marriage has helped to bring it about. Thus, for Davus, the first round ends with a setback: he must devise a new manoeuvre. It is surprisingly funny and structurally ingenious that Simo himself is the source of inspiration for this second stratagem. Davus decides to use the baby to scare off

Chremes and stages an encounter with the slave-girl Mysis for him to witness (IV,4). His scheme consists of two cleverly combined and balanced parts. Davus knows that the baby is the baby of Glycerium and Pamphilus, but by pretending that he believes it was brought by a midwife to deter Chremes he hopes to evoke a strong denial from the simpleton Mysis which will convince Chremes to believe the opposite. He also hints that Glycerium is an Athenian citizen with whom a marriage can be contracted. Although this is true, Davus considers it to be false. He adds it nevertheless in order to increase the baby's potential as a deterrent.

Davus's carefully planned and executed scheme – the funniest farcical stage scene of the entire comedy – is a great success. This time, the breaking of the second marriage offer (like the second marriage offer itself) is part of the actual dramatic stage plot and not of its expository antecedent narrative. In this way, the incidents of the dramatic action, by paralleling the narrated events of the exposition, achieve a unified continuity of the entire narrated and acted out sequence of events.

By pressuring Chremes, Davus succeeds in overturning Simo's plans. According to the best tradition of comedy in the battle of wits between the master and his slave, it is the slave who has the upper hand in the end. The final virtual power, however, is in the hands of the vanquished. The victor is at the mercy of the defeated. This part of the plot is neatly rounded off by Simo's carrying out his initial threat. He arranges for a physical punishment of Davus for not taking heed of his warning.

The arrival of Crito from Andros leads to the *anagnorisis* or recognition scene. His credibility is established by Chremes, whose acquaintance he is, and the entire episode is integrated into the mainstream of the plot by Simo's attitude of disbelief. Simo's doubting of Crito's integrity and his suspecting of yet another ruse iterates his former disposition and the attitude he displayed in all the previous instances which the audience has witnessed.

From the above short analysis it is clear that the opposition with which Simo and Davus meet, impersonated for each in the person of the other (the dramatic opposing forces), causes them constantly to alter their plans up to the turning-point of the play and its resolution. It is an intrigue plot, in which the complicating factor is the outwitting of the antagonist, not a romantic comedy, in which the lover himself takes a part and forwards the action. The chief ingredients of such a comedy are lacking: there is no courtship, no chase, seduction, persuasion, capture of hearts or conquest, in a word there is a lack of the chief ingredient, the battle of the sexes.

It is no wonder that the adherents of 'the duality method', who tend to upgrade the importance of the love stories, entirely misconstrue the *Andria*'s dramatic plot structure. Norwood considers Davus a spurious character, 'a fly in the wheel', and 'a fifth wheel on the coach'. He is, also on this point, blindly followed by Duckworth, who writes: 'Davus . . . a bungler whose suggestions and schemes confuse everyone but actually accomplish little.'[9]

The secondary plot of the young Charinus and his slave Byrria is linked to the main plot, the Simo–Davus battle of wits, through causal and analogous means. Charinus is in love with Chremes' daughter Philumena, the girl whom Pamphilus, his friend, tries not to marry. This unique plot aspect of the *Andria* – in all the other double plot comedies of Terence each young man is linked with a separate young lady – is used as a causal connection of the two plot issues throughout the entire play sequence. Any fluctuation in Pamphilus's fate directly affects Charinus and repeatedly justifies his appearance on stage.[10] This causal link also serves as an analogous combining element for the tying together and delineating of the actions and reactions of the two young men and their slaves. For even more important from the point of view of the plot structure is yet another unusual feature of the Charinus–Byrria plot element, the fact that Charinus does not have a family. As the only fatherless young man in the Terentian comedies he is also the only *adulescens* who does not need to secure his father's consent to a marriage. It precludes his plot issue from developing into a traditional intrigue plot in which a schemer slave outwits a *senex* for the sake of an *adulescens* in love. Where there is no *senex*, there is no room for any plotting with his fooling or persuasion as its goal. Thus, the inertness of Byrria is not only understandable but actually necessary.

Prevented from being a schemer, Byrria is not a mirror-image of Davus but rather his antithesis. He is represented as hindered from action by contemplation and by weighing of consequences. His

cleverness, and clever he is, is not externalized in creative machinations but expressed in proverbial formulations of practical
wisdom. The relations between Charinus and Byrria, presented as
different from the relations between Davus and Pamphilus, provide
the dramatic justification for Byrria's inaction. When Byrria proposes a course of action, Charinus refuses to accept it and accuses
him of never giving him good advice. When Pamphilus urges
Charinus and Byrria to devise a way for marrying Philumena while
he will endeavour to avoid the marriage, it is immediately made
clear that nothing will be done: Charinus is represented as quite
satisfied with Pamphilus's declaration of intents (*sat habeo* 335).[11]
This is dramatized by Charinus's prompt dismissal of Byrria, which
highlights the incompatibility of the pair. Consequently the next
scene (II,2) presents the dependence of the two *adulescentes* on the
doings of one scheming slave, and ends with an analogous situation:
Davus repeats Pamphilus's advice and urges Charinus to forward
his case on his own, for no marriage for Pamphilus need not
necessarily mean a marriage for Charinus. The repetition under-
lines Charinus's future inaction and the continuing lack of initia-
tive. He is expected, as before, to be satisfied with whatever is
planned by Davus and done by Pamphilus. It is, therefore, in line
with these aroused expectations that his only line of action is to send
the passive Byrria to find out Pamphilus's whereabouts (II,5).

As a result, the causal connection between the two plot issues is
highly effective. Charinus's mistaken accusation of Pamphilus as
interested in marrying Philumena (IV, 1) has an ironic effect and
adds to Pamphilus's accumulating heap of misfortunes exactly at
the right point in plot-time, whereas Davus's promise to extricate
Pamphilus by a new stratagem from the spot into which he
'succeeded' in putting him bears hope also for Charinus. And again,
this scene's end parallels that of the previous one: Davus refuses to
act on behalf of Charinus and the latter departs conveying the
impression of continuing inaction. Finally, in the closing scene of
the play, Charinus is represented as ultimately taking the route of
action previously advised by Davus, to plead with the girl's father
through his friends. The advice itself is unusual and stems from the
unusual feature of Charinus's lack of family. Young men do not
negotiate their marriages in comedies, it is done by their fathers. But

now, once Pamphilus is found to be Chremes' son-in-law, Charinus can use his good offices for the achieving of his desire (V,5). The approval of Pamphilus's marriage to Glycerium, with its entailed huge dowry, turns him from a dependent lover into a rich *pater familias* whose authority is instrumental in bringing about a happy ending of Charinus's plot issue. Consequently, the Charinus–Byrria plot issue is intertwined into the main plot issue also through the thematic dependence of an *adulescens* on an able slave, albeit not his own, as well as by the contrasting analogy with Byrria, which enhances Davus's scheming ability and rounds off his characterization as an all-knowing, all-providing factotum with a finger in each and every pie.

As befits intrigue plots, the resolution of Charinus–Byrria's plot occupies but a tiny fraction of the play's actual stage time. The resolution of the main plot, although somewhat longer, is still far shorter and less prominent than the intrigues through which it has been achieved. Moreover, both resolutions are foreshadowed and expected. What is new and unknown are the stage situations leading to them. What Styan writes on the Restoration comedy is applicable, without much change, also to the Menandrean comedies of Terence: 'the comedies were not constructed like modern well-made plays. The outcome of each play was more or less known for the unexciting thing it was, and there were to be no surprises.'[12]

The chief requirement of Norwood and his followers for the Terentian double plot, that its two problems solve each other, is a theoretical construct of a reader, neat, clean and nice, but hardly stage-oriented. For a spectator, resolutions do not exist throughout the entire stage time devoted to the plot sequences; they merely terminate them. Obviously readers' constructs of dramatic plots have all the characteristics of an end product of a silent reading process. They resemble the constructs of plots of narrative fiction, whose readers need not consider the different essences of the plot's various component elements and the different degree of their stage prominence.

To sum up: from the above analysis of the actual stage happenings of the *Andria* it may be concluded that both the plots are plots of intrigue, each of a different quality: one based on action, the other on inaction. The secondary plot highlights by a contrasting analogy the parallel but opposite elements of intrigue in the main plot. The modern tendency to define Terentian double plots in terms of love interests and call them romantic comedies obscures the intrigue elements and shifts the focus away from the stage action as viewed by spectators.

Before Legrand and others voiced their normative requirements, Donatus and other students of Terence described the Terentian double plot structure (see above) as pleasing in its variety. Thus, for example, Gibaldi Cinthio wrote (in 1554):

> double structure . . . has made the plays of Terence succeed wonderfully. I call that plot double which has in its action diverse kinds of persons of the same station in life, as two lovers of different characters, two old men of varied nature, two servants of opposite morals, and other such things as they may be seen in the *Andria* and in the other plots of the same poet, where it is clear that these like persons of unlike habits make the knot and the solution of the play very pleasing.[13]

What enriches the dramatic plot is the addition of a second set of characters whose interests and goals multiply the original problems thus adding further angles and possibilites of comparison. Where there are two sets of lovers, fathers and slaves, with two sets of problems, their very presence on stage as part of the actual dramatic action enriches the play. But a rich plot is chiefly a plot which richly activates the spectators' minds. Interest is created and tension is increased not only when the audience's mind is occupied with what is presented on stage but also with what is not. When one plot is acted out on stage the audience does not entirely forget the other, but rather tends to think that actions of the other plot presumably take place at the same time somewhere else.[14] Thus, a double plot is *ipso facto* richer than a single issue plot. It is no wonder, then, that later comedies, and especially farcical comedies, mirrored the Terentian double plot and even multiplied it.

Notes

1. See P. Wessner, *Aeli Donati Commentum Terenti* (Lipsiae, 1902), *ad And.* 301; *Phorm. Praef.* I. 9; only the *Hecyra* is a comedy of one young man in love, a *simplex negotium*; see also *ad And.* 977, where the

structure is praised as being executed *et audacter et artificiosissime*; Evantius, *De fabula* 9.

2. See M.J. Herrick, *Comic Theory in the Sixteenth Century* (Urbana, 1964), p. 2.

3. See Ph.E. Legrand, *The New Greek Comedy*, tr. J. Loeb (London, 1917), p. 310.

4. See G. Norwood, *The Art of Terence* (Oxford, 1923), p. 146.

5. See G.E. Duckworth, *The Nature of Roman Comedy* (Princeton, 1952), pp. 184ff.; on the 'evolution' see p. 186.

6. See T. McGarrity, 'Thematic Unity in Terence's *Andria*', *TAPA*, 108 (1978), p. 111.

7. See Duckworth, *Roman Comedy*, p. 186; see also the not essentially different summary on p. 154: 'Simo wishes his son Pamphilus to marry the daughter of Chremes etc.' Thus it is no wonder that Duckworth holds the view that 'Terence, more interested in sentiment and less eager to make intrigue an end in itself, concentrates more upon character and the emotions of the youthful heroes' (pp. 237–8).

8. It is interesting to note that Donatus marked Simo as the main protagonist of the *Andria*, before Davus (second) and the other *senex* Chremes (third), although Pamphilus's role is actually greater than that of Chremes. In calculating the length of a role not only the number of lines actually spoken by a character should be taken into account, but also the number of lines directed at him and the entire time he stays on stage. Participation in a dialogue means an interaction of two or more characters, which includes also non-verbal activities such as listening. Thus the length of a role is more precisely assessed if it is calculated by the number of lines during which the character is present on stage, whether he speaks or not. As a rule speaking characters (in contrast to mute ones) are not left on stage for any length of time without being actively involved in the action, unless their silence emphasizes a dramatic point.

9. See Norwood, *The Art of Terence*, p. 33; idem, *Plautus and Terence* (New York, 1931), p . 143; Duckworth, *Roman Comedy*, p. 173.

10. But not vice versa. This is considered by Norwood and his followers as *Andria*'s main weakness of plot construction. On the second plot issue we possess a valuable piece of evidence. As appears from Donatus's commentary (*ad And.* 301, see also 325, 997), Terence added to Menander's *Andria* the figures of Charinus and Byrria. Whether he invented them or borrowed them from Menander's *Perinthia*, he is responsible for the addition and its incorporation in his *Andria*, see F.H. Sandbach, 'Donatus' use of the name Terentius and the end of Terence's *Adelphoe*', *BICS*, 25 (1978), p. 126 and p. 142, n. 13.

11. What Pamphilus actually advises is to adopt a course of action of an

intrigue plot, to invent schemes and devise stratagems (*facite, fingite, invenite, efficite*, 334). What we get is the opposite: no inventiveness and no action.

12. See J.L. Styan, *Restoration Comedy in Performance* (Cambridge, 1986), p. 210.

13. Quoted by Herrick, *Comic Theory*, pp. 112–13.

14. The intertwining of the two plots occurs not only when the characters of the two plots meet bodily on stage, are involved in a conflict, or participate in the same action. The blending may actively occur in the audience's mind, see J. Veltruský, *Drama as Literature* (Lisse, 1977), pp. 78–9. It is not, however, a part of the dramatic stage plot.

6

Staging plays in the theatre of the mind

HERBERT GRABES

I

Why is the readership of dramatic texts not nearly so wide as that of novels or stories? There are no plays ever on bestseller lists, and there are not so very many habitual readers of plays. The reason for this can be extrinsic or intrinsic, can be sought in the general reading culture or in the structure of dramatic texts. As plays are read and discussed in schools and universities, it cannot be said that people do not become acquainted with them. Yet, whilst they continue reading stories, few go on reading plays.

Those who do, more often than not, are to be found among theatregoers. They read the texts in order to prepare themselves for the viewing of a performance or are motivated by a performance to read the play. Dramatic texts in themselves apparently do not invite reading as much as novels or stories. Is the reading of plays perhaps more difficult than the reading of prose fiction?

Let us examine briefly what the process of reading involves in what we can provisionally assume the easier case, namely that of prose fiction. Here we can, at least, draw on the results of a considerable amount of research. We find that in narrative prose the predominant unit of meaning is the sentence. Novels and stories largely consist of strings of sentences, and during the process of reading we move from one synthesis of syntactic sense to the next. Thus we can always rely on the semantic unit of the sentence. We then form larger units of meaning by what phenomenologists have called 'retention' and 'protention'. We integrate the sense of the sentence we have just read into the synthesis of the meaning of all the earlier sentences and by making assumptions about the one to come.

In this activity we are guided by the predominance of a unified perspective, which is the most prominent instrument of narrative mediation. How important this guidance is becomes clear whenever this predominance is lacking, as for instance in the first chapter of Joyce's *Ulysses*. Reading narrative prose then becomes much more difficult, perhaps more difficult even than the reading of dramatic texts.

The most striking feature of these texts is their allocation of various textual quantities to functional or individual names. What we encounter there is quite varied: it ranges from a single word or a short phrase to a long string of sentences. Thus during the process of reading we cannot rely on the semantic unit of the sentence. In reading dramatic dialogue we often have to synthesize sequences of words or phrases allocated to various names in order to reach the degree of autonomy of meaning guaranteed by the sentence in narrative prose. Thus the demands on the basic synthesizing faculty of the reader are considerably greater. Nor does the reader get the benefit of guidance through a predominant perspective when trying to form larger units of meaning. It is true that the perspective for each utterance is much more clearly marked than in narrative prose, but none of the subsequently encountered perspectives can *prima facie* be considered predominant.

With each new allocation of a verbal unit to a name, the reader has to relate it to the immediately preceding allocation, and frequently to even earlier ones, in order to build a semantic unit of what is to become the larger whole of verbal action and finally plot. At the same time he has to relate this new allocation to earlier verbal groupings allocated to the same name in order to relate it to a perspective and form a semantic unit of what is to become the larger unit of a dramatic character. And on top of this he has to probe the newly established actional and figural syntheses for their contribution to a larger thematic synthesis without being guided by any narratorial mediation.

This much higher demand on the synthesizing faculty of the reader is responsible for the impression that dramatic texts read less fluently and more slowly than narrative prose, that they contain more obstacles to being quickly absorbed. And if – according to Iser[1] – the aesthetic perception of fictional prose largely depends on the need to overcome the obstacles presented by each new sentence, then it may be held that dramatic texts through their very structure enforce a more aesthetic reading than fiction does.

What we all know, of course, is that most of the difficulties I have been touching on do not arise when we experience a dramatic performance on stage. In this situation we are essentially doing what we are trained to do in everyday life: namely, to synthesize complexes of verbal and non-verbal communication. In the dramaturgical context our understanding of verbal utterances, or what we call the dramatic text, is similarly supported by a great number of iconic signs: by the stance, gesture, mien, intonation of the speaking actors as well as by the spatial arrangement, lighting and sound effects.

There are, of course, the so-called 'stage directions' for the reader to make up at least in part for what can be seen and heard in a performance. With the advent of the realistic mode in the theatre towards the end of the nineteenth century these instructions became quite extensive, and they often include information, for instance about the psyche of the characters, which cannot be transferred directly to the stage, but which helps the reader's imagination. But even a most pedantic description of a room and costume or the figure and voice of a character must fall far short in concreteness compared to a stage setting and the physical presence of an actor. And what is not given must be supplied by the reader, who endeavours to stage a play in the theatre of the mind.

II

Even though one has to admit that individual differences in the working of the imagination do exist and that these are by no means unimportant, some general and useful observations can, I believe, be made about the transformation of a dramatic text into an illusory world of people, events and places. This is particularly so when we look more closely at the effect the various dramatic modes and structures have on the reading and mental staging of plays.

I will begin with a brief note on the dramatic texts written in the rhetorical mode for which Shakespeare's plays may serve as examples. Why is it that, despite the fact that they are written in verse, they read rather well? Here is the beginning of *Hamlet*:[2]

Enter Barnardo and Francisco, two sentinels

Bar.	Who's there?
Fran.	Nay, answer me. Stand and unfold yourself.
Bar.	Long live the King!
Fran.	Barnardo?
Bar.	He.
Fran.	You come and carefully upon your hour.
Bar.	'Tis now struck twelve. Get thee to bed, Francisco.
Fran.	For this relief much thanks. 'Tis bitter cold, And I am sick at heart.
Bar.	Have you had quiet guard?
Fran.	Not a mouse stirring.

Although there is no previous description of the scene, this sequence of utterances can easily be identified as a changing of the guards at midnight. The rapid exchanges, despite their brevity, have mostly the form of full sentences, and they are linked by a logic of question and answer, even when the answers seem not (or only partially) to fulfill the demands of the questioner. Nor is it too difficult to make out what is happening, although each utterance carries several illocutionary roles and although its performative function more often than not is only implicit.[3]

As we read on, we soon encounter longer speeches which take on the character of a narrative. A good example is the beginning of Scene 2 where King Claudius in a speech of thirty-nine lines informs us of his marriage to his former sister-in-law, the military threat by Fortinbras, and his way of coping with this situation. The absence of stage directions seems unimportant, as we can gather enough important details from the main text. As soon as the Ghost has appeared, we are not only told that he looks exactly as fair and warlike as the deceased King but also that 'So frown'd he once, when in an angry parle / He smote the sledded Polacks on the ice.'[4] Nor are we left alone in our efforts to interpret this angry face. Only six lines later Horatio says: 'But in the gross and scope of my opinion, / This bodes some strange eruption to our state.'

The rhetorical mode ensures that almost everything is *in* the lines, and that we do not have to read *between* them, that the characters express verbally what they think and feel, and that the phrasing of their utterances reveals any dissimulation. It is therefore comparatively easy to stage such texts in the theatre of the mind, and this accounts for the fact that they are widely read as literature. The only difficult part is the thematic synthesis, and this is why many of these texts have invited a great variety of interpretations.

To a somewhat lesser degree this is also the case with realistic drama of the modern type, for which Eugene O'Neill's *Long Day's Journey Into Night* may serve as an example. When we start reading, we may at first hesitate about whether the title can be taken both literally and metaphorically. Yet this doubt is soon dispersed. In the dedication to his wife Carlotta, O'Neill hints at an autobiographical interpretation by calling the twelve years with her 'a Journey into Light – into love'.[5] And the literal meaning comes out when we look at the table of 'Scenes' where the four acts are differentiated by temporal divisions of one day from morning till midnight. We are also informed that the scene is set in the summer house of the Tyrone family 'on a day in August, 1912', and the list of characters shows that the *personae* are the four family members and a servant girl.

Typical of the realistic mode of dramatic writing is what comes next: a lengthy stage direction of three pages which contains not only a very detailed description of the interior and even part of the exterior of the house, but also copious information about Mary and James Tyrone, the two characters that are to appear first. The description of the parlour includes information not available to a theatre audience, such as a list of the authors and titles of the books in each of the two bookcases, which have 'the look of being read and reread'.[6] And Mary and James, who enter the front parlour via a back parlour from the dining room, where 'the family have just finished breakfast',[7] are elaborately described in the same way: first age, then height, then figure, face, hair, state of health, dress and a final overall characterization. The portraits are extended to remarks about the past (Mary's hands were 'once beautiful' before 'rheumatism has knotted the joints and warped the fingers'[8]), about the consciousness of those who see Mary's hands ('One avoids looking at them, the more so because one is conscious she is sensitive about their appearance and humiliated by her inability to control the nervousness which draws attention to them'[9]), and the significance of the past for the present inner disposition ('He is by nature and preference a simple, unpretentious man, whose inclinations are still close to his humble beginnings and his Irish farmer forbears'[10]).

The first sentence of the main text (*'Tyrone*. You're a fine armful now, Mary, with those twenty pounds you've gained'[11]) is prepared for by a stage direction indicating that his arm is around her waist when they appear, and before she retorts 'I've gotten too fat, you mean, dear. I really ought to reduce' an inserted '(*smiles affectionately*)' is meant to secure the drift of this remark.

O'Neill's text is full of such inserted stage directions, ranging from short indications such as 'teasingly', 'following her' or 'with hearty satisfaction' to more elaborate descriptions of the characters' posture and actions (for instance: 'She laughs and sits in the wicker armchair at right rear of table. He comes behind her and selects a cigar from a box on the table and cuts off the end with a little clipper. From the dining-room Jamie's and Edmund's voices are heard. Mary turns her head that way'[12]). And before James Jr. and Edmund appear they are described first in the same minuteness of detail as their parents were.

Such an abundance of additional information continually supplied by the inserted stage directions is a valuable guide to the imagination of the reader who is about to stage the text in his mind; on the other hand, the insertions, especially the long ones, are clearly so many stumbling blocks during the process of reading, because they continually divert attention from the sequence and linking of the verbal exchanges. Compared to the strings of sentences in the paragraphs of narrative prose, sentences that are styled to contain both the information contained in the main text of the play and the stage directions, the splitting up of information in a dramatic text of the modern realistic kind appears clumsy and often awkward. It slows down the reading process without creating the kind of terseness that ensures aesthetic distance.

All this holds true also for dramatic texts written in the expressionist mode, which are also full of stage directions. What is easier, though, in the reading of such plays, is the discerning of the thematic implications of the dialogue, the scenes and actions described, and the characters, who are mostly reduced to types. In

The Adding Machine by Elmer Rice, one of the few American plays written in the expressionist mode, this does not come out clearly before Scene 5, although the description of Zero's murder of his boss from the perspective of his giddily turning mind at the end of Scene 2 and the stylized appearance of the party guests in Scene 3 are typical expressionist writing. But from Scene 5 onwards the subsequent information taken in by the reader can no longer be synthesized on the realistic plane. When the guide starts describing the condemned Zero, who is placed in a large and elevated cage like an exotic animal in a zoo, the social satire and the thematic exhibition of a human animal become so direct that we must resort to an almost purely symbolic reading:

Guide.	. . . This, ladies and gentlemen, is a very in-ter-est-in' specimen; the North American murderer, Genus homo sapiens, Habitat North America (*A titter of excitement. They all crowd up around the cage.*) Don't push. There's room enough for everybody.
Tall Lady.	Oh, how interesting!
Stout Lady	(*excitedly*). Look, Charley, he's eating!
Charley	(*bored*). Yeh, I see him.
Guide	(*repeating by rote*). This specimen, ladies and gentlemen, exhibits the characteristics which are typical of his kind —
Small Boy	(*in a Little Lord Fauntleroy suit, whiningly*). Mama!
Mother.	Be quiet, Eustace, or I'll take you right home.
Guide.	He has the opposable thumbs, the large cranial capacity, and the highly developed prefrontal areas which distinguish him from all other species.
Youth	(*who has been taking notes*). What areas did you say?
Guide	(*grumpily*). Pre-front-al areas. He learns by imitation and has a language which is said by some eminent philologists to bear many striking resemblances to English.[13]

And when towards the end of this scene a character called 'The Fixer' appears who seems, like God, to have power over life and death, fixing the fate of creatures like Zero, the play has moved so far beyond realism that the reader, who has never seen an expressionist play performed, first has to search for a more comprehensive kind of illusion – one that can accommodate surprising facts like Zero's rising from his grave in Scene 6, his transposition to the paradisiacal

Elysian Fields in Scene 7, and his being prepared for another earthly existence as a mechanical slave in an extramundane training room. The synthesis on the level of story line and plot is more difficult with such a play because it has to be mediated by a previous synthesis on the symbolic level. The predominance of the symbolic level that also comes out strongly in the descriptions of the setting makes it easier for the reader to get the 'message' of the play, yet even a vivid imagining of the physical details described cannot hope to match the impression they make on the senses during the viewing of the necessarily somewhat spectacular performance such a text obviously asks for.

This should be different with dramatic texts written for what has been termed 'epic theatre'; and, indeed, the initial stage direction of Thornton Wilder's *Our Town* begins with a laconic 'No curtain. No scenery'.[14] Instead the Stage Manager places a few chairs, a table and a bench on the otherwise empty stage before he starts informing the audience about who is the author of the play, who is in the cast, and where and when the action that follows is situated. He then goes on to describe the time of day, the layout of the little town the play is about (if we trust its title), the houses of the Gibbs and Webbs families, and what happened to the Gibbses long after the events that will be subsequently shown. Then a further stage direction offers a description of what Dr Gibbs, Mrs Webb and the newspaper boy Joe Crowell are doing before they are presented through direct speeches.

As we read on, we find that there are many further directions inserted in the main text, and in general the reader is faced with the task of synthesizing the subsequent allocations of verbal groupings and names as with a text written in the realistic mode. The only difference – and this difference is significant – lies in the fact that from time to time, when the Stage Manager has the word and obviously is meant to address the audience directly, the action is disrupted and the reader gets the impression that he speaks with authority and from a superior perspective. This fact – that one perspective which encompasses all the others and lets the other perspective come to the fore only in a paradigmatic manner – is, of course, of considerable value for the thematic synthesis of what we encounter. As the text allocated to the Stage Manager is styled as a commentary on the characters and events which we are to imagine by reading the sequences of dialogue, he functions at least in part like a narrator in fiction. This is the reason why the theatre for which such a text is written has been termed 'epic', and it may well be that in a performance the repeated 'distancing' of the audience from the paradigmatic scenes that are acted out has a particular aesthetic effect, that of 'estrangement'. For the reader, however, these commentaries serve mainly as sources of additional information, as links between the dialogues, and as rather didactic statements of what the play is actually about. And the reader who tries mentally to stage a dramatic text that mixes dialogue and commentary is faced with the additional task of imagining what kind of special effect such a mixture may have on the viewer.

We also find commentary in one of the few attempts at reviving poetic drama in this century. What I am referring to is T.S. Eliot's *Murder in the Cathedral*. Whilst the title may still suggest a play full of the kind of action and suspense to be found in a detective story, the list of characters, containing as it does the name of Thomas à Becket, shifts the expectation decidedly in the direction of historical drama and, as far as Becket's fate is known, towards tragedy. Not the usual kind of tragedy, however, for Becket's is the only individual name on that list; apart from it we find only functional types: three priests of the cathedral, a messenger, four tempters, attendants and the Chorus of the women of Canterbury. And in part II the four tempters are replaced by four knights.

The initial appearance of a chorus confirms, for those who are acquainted with classical drama, the expectation of tragedy, especially since it is given the same role it possessed in Greek tragedy, which is that of introducing and concluding. The very first lines make clear that the chorus in Eliot's play represents the voice of the common people, who do not know what is going to happen: 'For us, the poor, there is no action, But only to wait and to witness.'[15] What a reading of the first text allocated to the chorus also discloses is a hypnotic tone of enchantment generated by a simple syntax and the emphatic recurrence of key words and phrases. They centre around waiting and witnessing, the cathedral, the advent of danger and the seasons of the year:

Chorus.   Here let us stand, close by the cathedral. Here let us wait.
Are we drawn by danger? Is it the knowledge of safety, that draws our feet.
Towards the cathedral? What danger can be
For us, the poor women of Canterbury?
What tribulation
With which we are not already familiar? There is no danger
For us, and there is no safety in the cathedral. Some presage of an act
Which our eyes are compelled to witness, has forced our feet
Towards the cathedral. We are forced to bear witness.[16]

Nor does the quality of style essentially change when the dialogue starts:

First Priest.   Seven years and the summer is over.
Seven years since the Archbishop left us.
Second Priest.   What does the Archbishop do, and our
Sovereign Lord the Pope
With the stubborn King and the French King
In ceaseless intrigue, combinations,
In conference, meetings accepted, meetings refused,
Meetings unended or endless
At one place or another in France.[17]

With such a text the reader's attention is inevitably drawn to formal qualities, the repetitions of phonemes, words, phrases, syntactical structures. Thus the speed of reading is slowed down, as it is in the reading of poetry; individual statements, which almost exclusively take the form of full sentences, gain greater autonomy, and the activity of synthesizing tends to be drawn in two directions: towards the establishing of a strongly contextual meaning on the one hand and a much more general, autonomous one on the other. And the concentration this requires is not disturbed by any inserted stage directions. The details of the setting and the appearance and gestures of the characters do not seem to be too important. What is all important is language, the word, the phrasing and rhythm and meaning of language.

There can be no doubt that a dramatic text written in this mode is eminently suited to reading, and it is also not too difficult to stage such a text mentally, because any appropriate staging will have to bear out the hegemony of stylized language in a ceremony of ritualized verbal action.

If poetic drama is thus a celebration of the potency of language, the reader of a dramatic text written for the theatre of the absurd must soon come to the conclusion that he is dealing with the epitome of its failure. Even in a play that still largely depends on verbal exchanges like Beckett's *Waiting for Godot*, the only function left to language is to cover up the silence, which is even harder to bear than the failure of language:

Vladimir (*sententious*). To every man his little cross. (*He sighs*)
          Till he dies. (*Afterthought*) And is forgotten.
Estragon. In the meantime let's try and converse calmly, since we're incapable of keeping silent.
Vladimir. You're right, we're inexhaustible.
Estragon. It's so we won't think.
Vladimir. We have that excuse.
Estragon. It's so we won't hear.
Vladimir. We have our reasons.
Estragon. All the dead voices.
Vladimir. They make a noise like wings.
Estragon. Like leaves.
Vladimir. Like sand.
Estragon. Like leaves.
          Silence.
Vladimir. They all speak together.
Estragon. Each one to itself.
          Silence.
Vladimir. Rather they whisper.
Estragon. They rustle.
Vladimir. They murmur.
Estragon. They rustle.
          Silence.
Vladimir. What do they say?
Estragon. They talk about their lives.
Vladimir. To have lived is not enough for them.
Estragon. They have to talk about it.
Vladimir. To be dead is not enough for them.
Estragon. It is not sufficient.
          Silence.

Vladimir. They make a noise like feathers.
Estragon. Like leaves.
Vladimir. Like ashes.
Estragon. Like leaves.
    Long silence.
Vladimir. Say something!
Estragon. I'm trying.
    Long silence.
Vladimir (*in anguish*). Say anything at all!
Estragon. What do we do now?
Vladimir. Wait for Godot?
Estragon. Ah!
    Silence.
Vladimir. This is awful!
Estragon. Sing something.
Vladimir. No, no! (*He ponders*) We could start all over again perhaps.[18]

The reader who tries to synthesize such a sequence has to take recourse to radically diminished categories. Communication is reduced to the joint endeavour to keep the language going that is always freezing into silence; reference is reduced to self-reference, to language about language; the competitive search for the right word is reduced to a parody of such a search when it doesn't really matter what is being said if only silence is warded off.

Nor is this devaluation of the verbal balanced out by non-verbal communication as it is inscribed in the text. In fact the reader has even more problems in accommodating many of the abundant stage directions, because they often enough are not supportive of the main text, but merely add something to it that is hard to integrate because gesture seems to have become autonomous:

Vladimir. Sometimes I feel it coming all the same. Then I go all queer. (*He takes off his hat, peers inside it, feels about inside it, shakes it, puts it on again.*) How shall I say? Relieved and at the same time . . . (*he searches for the word*) . . . appalled. (*With emphasis*) AP-PALLED. (*He takes off his hat again, peers inside it.*) Funny. (*He knocks on the crown as if to dislodge a foreign body, peers into it again, puts it on again.*) Nothing to be done.[19]

Just as verbal language is reduced to a mere parody of itself when nothing is to be said but something has to be uttered to avoid the threat of silence, the non-verbal language of gesture is reduced to mere clownery in order simply to do something when nothing is to be done.

A dramatic text of such a kind obviously makes great demands on the synthesizing faculty of the reader, who has to tolerate inconsistency on most of the levels of meaning where he is used to find it, and who has therefore to be continuously quite inventive in order to find a perspective from which the apparent lack of consistency seems meaningful after all and can therefore be tolerated. This continuous struggle during the reading process absorbs so much of the reader's attention that it considerably hinders a mental staging, at least during a first reading of such a text. But most probably it also takes several readings as well before one knows how to transfer this text to a real stage.

The conviction of the inadequacy of language for communication in Beckett's later work quite logically led from the presentation of pseudo-dialogue to monologue and – as in *Breath* – to mere vocal noise. In Robert Wilson's *I Was Sitting on My Patio this Guy Appeared I Thought I Was Hallucinating*[20] this inadequacy is demonstrated by what appear to be two identical collages of one man's or one woman's memories of, and participation in, various dialogues. At least this is what the reader can at best make of the long sequence of rather disconnected phrases, which can obviously be allocated to various speech situations:

> Oh hello that's just the call I was waiting for
> /oh hello that's just the call I was waiting for/
> ready aim fire
> /ready aim fire/
> aim fire
> /aim fire/
> where
> /where/
> you're here for ulterior motives
> I graduate with honors
> you're O.K.
> watch out

father
/father/
NO
NO
NO
15 years ago I remember the address it was 7 Pearl Street
I must keep that in my mind or was it 7 years ago
the reindeer are getting restless
there's a mechanical drummer
there's a mechanical soldier
there's a mechanical bird girl
she's made all of silver
the snake was used to living in a warm climate
Codie
I've been promised a vacation
she's all right Charlie
Martha
it's been a long time
it's been a long time
I don't even know what to say to you any more[21]

The detailed stage direction the reader encounters first under the name of a 'Prologue' contains an iconic clue to the provisional synthesizing of these bits and pieces of dialogue in pointing out that a spotlighted telephone keeps ringing continuously for ten minutes before the curtain. Thus the suggestion is introduced that what is given in the main text is one side of various conversations over the phone. On the other hand it says in the stage directions that the words are spoken in the first act by a man leaning forward on a couch with his words being 'punctuated by music played on an off-stage piano',[22] in the second act by a woman standing facing the audience with 'her words punctuated by music played on an off-stage harpsichord'.[23]

As the differences between the two acts with an identical verbal text must rest exclusively on the vocal shifts and the emphases supplied by accompanying gestures, and as there are no stage directions indicating such differences, the reader is left entirely alone by the author in his attempt to stage such a dramatic text in the theatre of the mind. That this is so is blatantly demonstrated by the fact that not even the main text is printed twice: all we find under the heading 'Act II' is the initial and closing lines and three lines with three dots in between. And when we read in the 'Postscript' that 'it is not necessary that the play be always cast in a similar manner. The first act could just as easily be played by a woman the second act by a man, or the cast could very well consist of two men and two women';[24] the allocation of the main text to names and thereby to fixed perspectives, which has been the constitutive principle of dramatic texts, has been given up. What remains is a text for which this allocation is intentionally left to the director of a theatrical performance.

As the possibility of synthesizing the string of textual phrases is also heavily dependent on non-verbal communication, such a text is quite unsuited for reading. It can be read successfully by someone who is well acquainted with the avant-garde trend towards using a dramatic text as a mere pre-text for a theatrical event, and it will be read by directors and critics who are professionally interested in such texts. It may even find readers among those who have attended a performance and want to know more about its verbal component, but it will not be read widely. Consequently it cannot stand much of a chance of being staged in the theatre of the mind, and even the few readers who try to do this will get very little help indeed from the text.

The fact that the verbal element has lost its predominant role in much avant-garde theatre, therefore, has grave consequences for the writing of dramatic texts, for their structure, their reading, and finally for the possibility of their mental staging. It may be that with such a development the actual theatre will come more into its own. It will clearly do so, however, at the cost of the theatre of the mind.

Notes

1. Wolfgang Iser, *Der Akt des Lesens* (Munich, 1976), pp. 183ff.
2. *Hamlet*, ed. Harold Jenkins (The Arden Shakespeare: London, 1981), I.I. I–II.
3. See Manfred Pfister's minute analysis of this passage in '"Eloquence is Action": Shakespeare und die Sprechakttheorie', *Kodikas/Code*, 8 (1985), pp. 195–216, especially pp. 207–9.
4. *Hamlet*, I.I. 65–6.

5. Eugene O'Neill, *Long Day's Journey Into Night* (London, repr. 1974), p. 5.
6. Ibid., p. 9.
7. Ibid., p. 10.
8. Ibid., p. 10.
9. Ibid., p. 10.
10. Ibid., p. 11.
11. Ibid., p. 12.
12. Ibid., p. 12.
13. Elmer Rice, *Three Plays* (New York, 1965), p. 26.
14. Thornton Wilder, *Three Plays: Our Town, The Skin of Our Teeth, The Matchmaker* (London, 1958), p. 5.
15. T.S. Eliot, *Murder in the Cathedral* (London, 1952), p. 13.
16. Ibid., p. 11.
17. Ibid., pp. 13–14.
18. Samuel Beckett, *Waiting for Godot: A tragicomedy in two acts* (London, 1956), pp. 62–3.
19. Ibid., p. 10.
20. Robert Wilson, 'I Was Sitting on My Patio this Guy Appeared I Thought I Was Hallucinating', *Performing Arts Journal* (11/12), 4 (New York, 1979), pp. 201–18.
21. Ibid., pp. 203–4.
22. Ibid., p. 202.
23. Ibid., p. 217.
24. Ibid., p. 218.

7

Reading the body: the corporeality of Shakespeare's text

MANFRED PFISTER

1. 'The play's the thing': body and text

Written discourse speaks with a disembodied voice. Although this is true of all written discourse, it applies with particular poignancy to play scripts. Here the absence of a live voice and the body from which it issues, the absence in general of the three-dimensional concreteness of objects and space that makes the images of the theatre so persuasive, so compelling, turns any reading of a play into a surrogate experience. It is for this reason that the written or printed texts of plays have – with only a few historical exceptions – always had a derivative or secondary status, either as a scenario blueprinting future productions or as a document recording previous ones.

When Ben Jonson, in 1616, published the printed texts of his plays under the proud title of his *Works*, he brought down upon himself general ridicule, and this ridicule did not only reflect the low opinion in which drama and the theatre were held at that time by the cognoscenti of literature, but also the general disdain for printed plays as literary texts. Printed plays just would not do as a token of literary authorship and could not be paraded as 'works' or 'opera'. As far as we know, Shakespeare hardly ever bothered to refer to his printed plays, let alone supervise their printing.

Even if, in the course of subsequent centuries, printed drama was to become to a certain extent autonomous from the theatre, gaining full recognition as a form of poetry or literature in its own right, the extreme claims made during Romanticism, for instance, for the superiority of the drama read in one's closet to drama performed on stage can always be related to the deplorable state of the theatrical set-up and the performing arts at that time.

We are still where we were at the beginning: the printed text of a play is disembodied, and the play itself, that is – to quote Hamlet – 'the thing', is emphatically corporeal. The line may be 'immaterial' as Lady Bracknell said; the verse spoken on stage is certainly not. And yet, the body, so poignantly absent in the written words, has inscribed itself into the text in diverse ways, in ways both obvious and unobtrusive. I shall skip the most obvious inscription, the stage directions, not only because I do not want to belabour the obvious but because my main concern is with the 'primary' and not the 'secondary text' (Roman Ingarden), that is the speeches of the characters, their dialogues and soliloquies rather than the authorial paraphernalia of the printed text.[1] The speeches of the characters have what the Swiss Anglicist Rudolf Stamm called their 'theatrical physiognomy', which is to say they are full of implied stage directions. They imply a body and its shape and movements, a voice and its articulation and inflections.[2] Take a speech like the following, from Shakespeare's *Coriolanus*:

> You common cry of curs! whose breath I hate
> As reek o'th' rotten fens, whose loves I prize
> As the dead carcasses of unburied men
> That do corrupt my air: I banish you![3]
>
> (3.3.120–3)

Here Coriolanus reacts to his banishment at the hands of the plebeians by banishing them in turn. The physical violence expressed in this speech act inscribes itself into the written text in the vehement gestural impulses of exclamations and commands; in the reduction of the plebeian body to one festering, stinking mass of rotting flesh; in the physical revulsion against, and obsession with, nauseating physiological details intensively felt and closely perceived; in the articulatory effort that the cacophonic sequence of harsh consonants and the metrical dislocations involve. This language remains, even in its abstract written form, corporeal; it implies the body that has inscribed itself into it. Reading it, we read this body in kinesthetic empathy, its nausea and revulsion, its self-absorption and obsession. Rather than describing a body, it enacts one.

We can use this brief snatch from Coriolanus's speech as a starting-point for a discussion of yet another aspect of the inscription of the body into the text. Coriolanus here, as in many other places, refers to the body figuratively, in metaphors or metonymies. Images of low and despicable animals, of curs and carcasses, point up the base animality of the plebeian body as he sees it, and the sharp focus on revolting physiological details – the stinking breath, the scabious skin – reduces the plebeians metonymically to their unappetizing bodies. His is the language of class and racial hatred, to which the animal metaphors and the metonymic reductions of human aspirations and emotions to the nauseating output of a diseased and unclean body give a shocking corporeality.

As metaphors and metonymies of the body abound in Shakespearean and Elizabethan dramatic texts, Coriolanus's deprecating figurative references to the human body can be seen as no more than a pathological perversion of widespread and ideologically sanctioned metaphorical systems that normally make the body legible in more positive ways. The metaphor of the body politic, for example, that links the human body with the commonwealth in terms of organic unity and functional hierarchy, actually strikes an important base note in the tragedy of *Coriolanus* and provides the exposition: Menenius Agrippa's fable of the belly and the members (1.1.89ff.) sets the norm against which the rebellion of the plebeians, the political manoeuvring of the patricians, and Coriolanus's overbearing attitude towards the common people and his physical aversion to them are to be measured.[4] Other, and related, metaphorical codes in the Elizabethan drama that help to read the body, or to read the state or the cosmos in the light of the body, are first of all the metaphors of the chain of being, with man in his conjunction of body and soul insecurely placed in the centre;[5] secondly the elaborate analogies between the body as microcosmos and the universe as macrocosmos;[6] and finally the notion of a ruler's charismatic body politic that transcends and gives meaning to his body natural.[7]

The most explicit inscription of the body into the text, more outspoken and less oblique than the corporeal implications of the

speeches and their figurative references to the body, occurs when
the characters talk directly about their own or each other's bodies,
when they thematize them explicitly. And this occurs more often
than one would think. There is a new physical self-awareness in
Shakespeare's characters, a new awareness of their being determined in their ideas and emotions by their bodies, a new alertness
for the physical side and bodily symptoms of their opposite
numbers on stage. Their physical peculiarities play a major role for
Othello and Shylock, for Cleopatra and Julius Caesar, for Caliban
and Falstaff, to mention only a few of the most obvious examples. In
the same way, Coriolanus's attitude towards his own and the
plebeian body and the attitudes of his family, partners and opponents towards his own body provide a dominant feature of his
characterization. At decisive points in many of the plays the body of
one of the characters is displayed like a sculpture, drawing upon
itself the comments of those standing round. As Brian Gibbons has
pointed out recently, Shakespeare's characters generally show a
remarkable degree of interest in each other's physical being, bodily
shape, size, movement, attitudes, gestures and facial expressions,
and this interest makes itself felt not only on the stage in those
'freeze-frame' moments of visual concentration on the human body,
but is inscribed into the very text and texture of the speeches.[8] In
such speeches thematizing the body, the characters decipher or read
their own and each other's bodies and we, reading these speeches,
read these bodies with them.

2. 'Read me o'er': the language of the body

My metaphor of reading the body, which presupposes a body
language to be read, may seem far-fetched and anachronistic with
reference to Elizabethan drama; but, indeed, it is not. The sixteenth
century already had a well-defined concept of body language which
derived partly from classical rhetorics and the traditional Galenic
theory of humours, and partly from a new anthropological and
physiological awareness of the body and its signs and symptoms.
After all, it was in the sixteenth century that modern medicine was
born as an empirical science of the body.[9]

During the Renaissance, one cardinal point of the reflections
upon the body, upon the 'knowledge that concerneth man's body',

to which Francis Bacon dedicated Chapter 10 of the second book of *The Advancement of Learning*, was the relationship between the body and the soul or the mind, that is the extent to which the body expresses or even determines the mind and vice versa. Michel de Montaigne, for instance, in his essay 'Of Presumption' (*Essayes*, II, xvi) no longer takes the unity of body and soul for granted nor does he agree with the traditional Christian doctrine of the superiority of the soul over the body, thus discounting the ethics of a marginalization or suppression of the body. Rather, he argues for a conscious effort to make the one consonant with, and expressive of, the other. 'The body hath a great part in our being, and therin keeps a speciall rank', he writes (in Florio's Elizabethan translation):

> Such as goe about to sunder our two principall parts, and separate them one from another, are much to blame: They ought rather to be coupled and joyned fast together. The soule must be enjoined not to retire her selfe to her quarter, nor to entertaine her selfe apart, nor to despise and leave the body (which she cannot well doe, except it be by some counterfaited, apish tricke) but ought to combine and cling fast unto him, to embrace, to cherish, assist, correct, perswade and advise him, and if he chance to swarve and stray, then to lead and direct him.[10]

Body and soul, according to Montaigne, are not simply and naturally 'joyned'; they must be consciously 'enjoined' to join up with each other. And it is to the extent that there is a natural tendency in body and soul towards congruence and that there is a conscious effort to realize this congruence, that the body becomes expressive of character, temperament, ideas and emotions and can be read in these terms.

Montaigne insists on this language of the body, and in his 'Apology of Raymond Sebond' (*Essayes*, II, xii) he uses it as an argument to level down the old hierarchical distinction between man and animal, to undermine the humanistic hubris which would set man in his rationality and power of language entirely apart from all other animals. Man, for Montaigne, is an animal amongst other animals, subjected like them to nature through his body.[11] In this context he points out that man's alleged superiority cannot be based on his power of language and communication, as animals share this power in the highly developed language of their bodies and as man also uses this body language as an important complement of speech:

> Can we have better proof to judge of man's impudence, touching beasts? . . . we manyfestly perceive, that there is a full and perfect communication amongst them, and that not onely those of one same kinde understand one another, but even such as are of different kindes . . . Do we not daily see lovers with their lookes and rowling of their eyes, plainly shew, when they are angry or pleased, and how they entreat and thank one another, assigne meetings, and express any passion? . . . What doe we with our hands? Doe we not sue and entreat, promise and performe, call men unto us and discharge them, bid them farewell and be gone, threaten, pray, beseech, deny, refuse, demand, admire, number, confesse, repent, feare, bee ashamed, doubt, instruct, command, incite, encourage, sweare, witnesse, accuse, condemne, absolve, injurie, despise, defie, despight, flatter, applaud [and so on, and so on].[12]

The intoxicating length of this list of verbs drives home one point most effectively: man's body is as eloquent as his speech, and this new and emphatic awareness of the eloquence of the body inscribes itself into the dramatic dialogues of the Renaissance in the many indications and descriptions of gesture and facial expression.

Montaigne is, however, aware of the fact that body language is, like verbal language, not entirely natural and spontaneous, but based on artificial codes and conventions, and therefore open to manipulation and distortion. What disturbs the desirable congruence of body and mind, repressing the body and falsifying its language, is society with its conventions and rituals. The word he uses for this is 'ceremony', and this concept anticipates Norbert Elias's insights into the 'Process of Civilization'. I quote Montaigne's 'Of Presumption', not Elias: 'We are nought but ceremonie; ceremonie doth transport us, and wee leave the substance of things . . . Wee have taught Ladies to blush, onely by hearing that named, which they nothing feare to doe. Wee dare not call our members by their proper names, and fear not to employ them in all kind of dissolutenesse.'[13] Montaigne perceives here to what extent shame is a social construct and he perceives, moreover, how, as a result, a certain expression of the body – blushing, in this case – may be deflected or distorted from an unpremeditated and authentic reflection of a spontaneous emotion to a coded and calculated sign. This line of reasoning anticipates, in fact, the semiotic distinction between symptoms and signs. Signs are arbitrary and conventional, which is to say they are 'artificiall' and part of that 'ceremonie' through which we present our public front. Their meaning is unambiguous, but they cannot be trusted as authentic expressions of ourselves. Montaigne mentions 'salutations, reverences, or conges' as examples and would include the well-trained female blush amongst them. On the other hand, Montaigne is struck by certain of his own gestures and movements, by a certain 'fashion in carrying of my body and gestures', which is beyond his conscious control, and can, for that very reason, denote him truly: 'Such motions many unawares and imperceptibly possesse us.'[14] There is no intention behind them and no code for them, and therefore these bodily symptoms are always open to interpretation but, at the same time, reliable as authentic inscriptions of the mind on the body. It is with reference to these symptomatic gestures that Montaigne says: 'I cannot answer for the motions of my body.'[15] They no longer constitute body language in the strict sense of a coded system of signs, but paradoxically it is here, at the very limits of body language, that the body speaks most truly.

Bacon, in the section 'Pars Physiognomiae, de gestu sive motu corporis' of his *Advancement of Learning* (II, ix), asks similar questions about the semiotics of the body and sketches out two likely areas of research for this yet neglected field. Under the heading of 'impression' he asks 'either, how and how far the humours and affects of the body do alter or work upon the mind; or, again, how and how far the passions or apprehensions of the mind do alter or work upon the body'.[16] This is a problem of symptomatics rather than of semiotics, and it is the second area, that of 'discovery', that squarely faces the problem of body language. This 'discovery' is a sort of deciphering, a reading of the signs of the body – those that are permanent, like 'physiognomy, which discovereth the disposition of the mind by the lineaments of the body', and those that change with every moment and emotion, such as movements, gestures or facial expressions. The latter are particularly important for the politician or anyone who has to find out the true motives of his partners or opponents: 'For the lineaments of the body do disclose the disposition and inclination of the mind in general; but the motions of the countenance and parts do not only so, but do further disclose the present humour and state of the mind and will.'[17] Bacon is more confident than Montaigne about this art of reading a character and his motives from his body, and he sees in it, in the discrepancy between what a person says and the signs of his or her body, 'a great discovery of dissimulations'.[18] This optimistic view disregards Montaigne's deeper insights into the language of the body, which does not always give away dissimulation, but can become a powerful medium of dissimulation in its own right. Bacon quotes in this context James I, thus paying homage to the new monarch, who wrote in his *Basilicon Doron* (1599): 'As the tongue speaketh to the ear so the gesture speaketh to the eye.'[19] This analogy is, however, more apt than suits Bacon's line of argument: body language is, indeed a language like speech – which is to say it is just as conventional, not always under full control and lends itself just as much to dissimulation as speech. The opposition between an authentic, undistorted and spontaneous language of the body and unauthentic and premeditated speech is as much in need of deconstruction as that between the spoken word and writing, between *phone* and *gramma* (Derrida).

The project of a semiology of movements and gestures envisaged by Bacon did not have to start from scratch. Important steps in this regard had already been taken within the art of rhetorics. This art was well known to all Elizabethans as it was part of the curriculum both of grammar schools and universities and of the Inns of Court. The fifth and last sub-discipline of rhetorics, *pronunciatio* and *actio*, dealt with this very subject matter of vocal inflection, movement, gesture and facial expression and it gave the speaker fairly detailed instructions as to how he could make his speech more persuasive and significant through employing non-verbal signs. Shakespeare, in the juxtaposition of the two funeral speeches of Brutus and Marc Antony in *Julius Caesar*, presents a didactically transparent model case for this: the much stronger effect of Mark Antony's speech in comparison to that of Brutus's is to no small degree due to his histrionic employment of the body. Where Brutus puts all his trust in the high pathos of his words, Mark Antony, apart from his verbal strategies of irony and dissimulation, uses grand deictic gestures, plays cleverly with objects such as Caesar's testament and gains his most persuasive effects by displaying Caesar's wounded body, thus turning his wounds into mouths, 'putting a tongue / In every wound of Caesar' (2. 230f.) – a tongue that speaks in a language more eloquent than any words. In that, he follows Cicero's advice in *De oratore* (II, 195), 'ut cicatrices ostenderem' – the showing of the wounds is more persuasive than any speech of complaint and indictment. And when Marc Antony claims to have 'neither wit, nor words, nor worth / Action nor utterance, nor power of speech / To stir men's blood' (223–5), then this is clearly another case of his all-pervasive irony. The reader of the play, as well as the audience in the theatre, clearly realizes that he is a master of both words and action (in the rhetorical sense of *actio*), that he lacks neither eloquence nor an effective body language. It is as clear to the reader, who does not see this *actio*, as it is to the spectator who does, because it is inscribed into the texture of his speech, implied in its gestural impulses and indications and spelt out in the explicit thematization of *actio* that we have just quoted.

'Action', as Thomas Wright defined this rhetorical concept in *The Passions of the Mind* (1604), 'is a certaine visible eloquence, or an eloquence of the body'.[20] The extent to which Shakespeare was aware of this 'eloquence of the body' is shown not only in the countless moments in his plays, in which certain bodily features or actions are presented as decisively significant, but also by a great number of explicit references in the dialogue to the significance of this body language. The most famous of these instances occurs in *Coriolanus*, one of the plays of Shakespeare in which movements and gestures are particularly foregrounded not only through their emphatic repetition, thus giving them the status of gestural leitmotifs (here wounding and showing one's wounds, gestures of exclusion and inclusion, towering above some and kneeling to others), but also through elaborate descriptions of, and comments upon them. It is in the context of the leitmotif of kneeling, which bridges the play from Act 2 Scene 1, where Coriolanus kneels to his mother, to Act 5 Scene 3, where mother, wife and son kneel to him, that Volumnia points out to him – and the spectator as well as the reader

– how persuasive the language of gestures can be, quoting James I and Thomas Wright succinctly and almost verbatim: 'Action is eloquence, and the eyes of th'ignorant / More learned than the ears' (III, ii, 76f.).

Some of these explicit and meta-communicational references to body language seem to share Montaigne's scepticism, that is his sceptical insights into the gap between appearance and reality, which can affect body language as much as verbal language. 'There's no art / To find the mind's construction in the face', comments Duncan upon the death of the traitor Cawdor in *Macbeth*, thus casting a spell of doubt across too simple versions of the art of physiognomy, and this doubt is deepened by the entrance of Macbeth immediately after this speech. But, true or false, the body speaks and the effectiveness of this speech is acknowledged again and again in Shakespeare's text. Two further examples, both referring to the erotic eloquence of the body, must suffice. When Claudio, in *Measure for Measure*, decides to send his sister Isabella to Angelo to plead for him he trusts as much in the persuasiveness of her youthful body's 'prone and speechless dialect' as in her 'prosperous art' of 'reason and discourse' (1.2. 173–6), and the outcome will prove him only too right. My second example is from *Troilus and Cressida*: here Cressida's erotic attractions, after having been visually staged in the round of kisses she grants to the Greek heroes, are commented upon by Ulysses in terms of a language of the body: 'There's language in her eye, her cheek, her lip – Nay her foot speaks' [4.5. 55f.]. Again, the visual enactment of the body on stage and the dialogue drawing attention to the eloquence of the body complement each other; the body's language is so emphatically inscribed into the text that its eloquence cannot be missed even in reading the play, despite the processes of corporeal abstraction that involves.

Somewhat later in the same scene there is one of those frequent comments where a character carefully scrutinizes the body of his opposite number on stage, itemizing its features with deictic gestures indicated in the text. Achilles inspects his opponent Hector as if he were some stallion or beast of chase and weighs his bodily prowess up against his own:

Achilles. Now, Hector, I have fed mine eyes on thee;
        I have with exact view perus'd thee, Hector,
        And quoted joint by joint.
Hector. Is this Achilles?
Achilles. I am Achilles.
Hector. Stand fair, I pray thee; let me look on thee.
Achilles. Behold thy fill.
Hector. Nay, I have done already.
Achilles. Thou art too brief: I will the second time,
        As I would buy thee, view thee limb by limb.
Hector. O, like a book of sport thou'lt read me o'er;
        But there is more in me than thou understand'st.
        Why dost thou so oppress me with thine eye?
Achilles. Tell me, you heavens, in which part of his body
        Shall I destroy him – whether there, or there, or there –
        That I may give the local wound a name.

                              (4.5. 230–43)

    The dialogue, even in its disembodied form of written discourse, contains the bodies that are at stake in it. Language, which in the full-bodied stage presentation serves as a comment to focus the spectators' attention on these bodies and their physical interaction, becomes, in the form of the printed dialogue, the medium in which the bodies are created and topicalized at the same time. The text here enacts the act of inspecting a body and by doing so, creates the body. This act of inspecting a body is defined by one of the characters as the 'reading o'er' of a book. We, reading a book, the script of the play, read how a character reads a body as if it were a book, reads it, in fact, as a book. The dialectic of body and text has come full circle here: the disembodied text bodies forth a body that is a text. The corporeality of Shakespeare's text and the textualization of the body depend upon each other, and this interdependence marks the precarious status of Shakespearean and Elizabethan drama in general between orality and scripturality, between scenic representation and printed text. It is due to this precarious status, or, to put it in more positive terms, to this dialectic, that the inscription of the body, the inscribed body in the Shakespearean text is still legible today, almost without the help of explicit stage directions and despite the fact that the Elizabethan conventions of *mise-en-scène* and acting, which they presuppose, are largely lost to us.

Notes

1. For the distinction between 'primary' and 'secondary text', between *Haupttext* and *Nebentext* cf. R. Ingarden, *Das literarische Kunstwerk*, 2nd edn. (Tübingen, 1960), p. 220; for the relationship between the written drama and its stage performance cf. R. Ingarden, op. cit., pp. 337–43 and my *The Theory and Analysis of Drama* (Cambridge, 1988), pp. 13–19.
2. Cf. R. Stamm, 'Die theatralische Physiognomie der Shakespearedramen', *Maske und Kothurn*, 10 (1964), pp. 263–74.
3. All Shakespeare quotations are from *The Riverside Shakespeare*, ed. G.B. Evans (Boston, 1974).
4. For the metaphor of the body politic cf. D.G. Hale, *The Body Politic: A Political Metaphor in Renaissance English Writing* (The Hague, 1971).
5. Cf. E.M.W. Tillyard, *The Elizabethan World Picture* (London, 1943).
6. Cf. L. Barkan, *Nature's Work of Art. The Human Body as Image of the World* (New Haven, 1975).
7. Cf. E. Kantorowicz, *The King's Two Bodies. A Study in Medieval Political Theology* (Princeton N.J., 1957).
8. B. Gibbons, 'The Human Body in *Titus Andronicus* and other early Shakespeare Plays', *Shakespeare Jahrbuch (West)* (1989), pp. 209–228.
9. Cf. M. Boas, *The Scientific Renaissance 1450–1630* (London, 1962), Chapters 5 and 9.
10. *The Essayes of Michael Lord of Montaigne* (London, n.d.), vol. II, p. 364.
11. This passage is indebted to a paper read by Wolfgang Weiß at the symposium on 'Body and Body Language in Shakespeare'; it will be published in the *Shakespeare Jahrbuch (West)*, 1989.
12. *The Essayes of Michael Lord of Montaigne*, vol. II, pp. 143f.
13. *The Essayes*, vol. II, pp. 355f.
14. *The Essayes*, vol II, p. 357.
15. *The Essayes*, vol. II, p. 357.
16. *The Advancement of Learning and New Atlantis*, ed. A. Johnston (Oxford, 1974), pp. 103f.
17. *The Advancement of Learning*, p. 103.
18. *The Advancement of Learning*, p. 103.
19. *The Advancement of Learning*, p. 103; Bacon quotes from *Basilicon Doron* (Edinburgh, 1599), p. 135.

20. *The Passions of the Mind* (London, 1609), p. 176. The connections between rhetorical *actio* and histrionic action/acting are worked out in full historical detail in B.L. Joseph, *Elizabethan Acting* (Oxford, 1952).

8

Reading Shakespeare's *The Merchant of Venice* with German students

RUTH VON LEDEBUR

I

The recent production of *The Merchant of Venice* at the Vienna Burgtheater[1] has highlighted the question of the relationship between the play and its stage history, the degree to which any production can hope to distance itself from previous assumptions about the play.

Its director Peter Zadek, who has, over the years, become famous for his controversial Shakespeare productions, replaced Venice by Manhattan and transformed the Elizabethan comedy into a bitter farce about our contemporary business world. There is, as such, nothing new or surprising about a modern-dress version of Shakespeare's play on the German stage. The surprise of this production stems from the crucial effect it has on the rendering of Shylock's role. In his New York broker's suit, in his speech habits and body language, he can hardly be distinguished from the Christian businessmen. As one critic put it: 'Not a lonely, hunted, spat-on Shylock enters the stage, but a winner: cheerful and sportsmanlike, he is the champion of Venice, not her adversary, unquestionably the star and godfather of the Venetian money society. Shylock is as impertinent as the Christians, but his is a spirited impudence. He is as avaricious as the others, but gracefully so.'[2] In accord with Shylock's transformation into a modern Everyman, another critic entitled his review 'A Jew like you and me'.[3] Zadek's production met with general acclaim; the critics agreed that its tendency was neither antisemitic nor philosemitic. There was even some noticeable relief that Zadek had freed Shylock 'from all the characteristics that theatrical tradition had made us accustomed to'.[4] This breaking away from the play's stage history raises a crucial issue for German audiences and readers alike. Setting aside the producer's undeniable right to stage his concept of a play, it remains an open question whether not only the theatrical antecedents of such a production should be discarded but, with them, also the inherent potential of the play that had given rise to its fateful antisemitic renderings under the Nazi regime and, vice versa, to pronounced philosemitic staging after 1945.[5] In other words, what happens to our understanding of Shylock if he is disrobed of his 'Jewishness'?

These questions appear to be arbitrary only at first sight. That there is some ground for critical doubt is revealed by other German productions of *The Merchant of Venice*, following, as it were, in the wake of Zadek's presentation of a Shylock who lacks all or most of his Jewish characteristics. After the 'apologetic' and the 'provocative' trends in rendering Shylock, dominant on the German stage in the post-war period,[6] a new trend seems to emerge at the end of the eighties, aiming at a 'neutralized' Shylock. In reviewing such a performance in Dortmund, the critic A. Rossmann voices his uneasiness at this 'lighthearted and unhistorical' presentation.[7]

To the reader of *The Merchant of Venice*, the question of perspectives is of even greater importance than to the viewer. This is partly due to the well-known differences between the rapid multisensory 'absorption' of a drama in the theatre and the slow, time-consuming reading process in the study. Whereas the audience is confronted with a text on which an 'interpretation' has been superimposed in order to engage them through their own interests, expectations or prejudices, the reader comes to a literary text which is, at least to his subjective perception, void of any such interpretative marks. His responses to the text are epistemologically and aesthetically important because they indicate his involvement in creating meaning. This activity engages his intellectual, imaginative and critical faculties. In his attempts to understand the text, he may search for past and present meanings of the same text to verify or challenge his own responses. When reading a play, he will not only stage it in 'the theatre of his mind' but may well ask himself in what ways former stagings differ from his own.

When a play is subjected to a community of readers, as is the case in the classroom, the question of eliciting responses such as those mentioned above is of primary importance. In my seminar on *The Merchant of Venice*[8] it was one of my teaching objectives to help the students reflect on their individual responses and, rather than unifying their different views, to make them aware of the conditions which give rise to a diversity of meaning. To achieve this, the students also needed to be acquainted with varying historical contexts and actualities which necessitated different readings of the play. I thus hoped to establish a link between the reading of *The Merchant of Venice* in the classroom and the history of its productions on the German stage. In addition, the students were encouraged to recognize the difficulties which confront producers, actors and audiences alike in today's productions of this play. As Professor Gershon Shaked remarked in his introductory speech at the Jerusalem Theatre Conference in 1986, the way in which *The Merchant of Venice* is today presented on the stage of any country throws light upon the political culture of that country. Taking this into account, my students should not regard this play as an isolated item of the academic curriculum, far removed from their own experiences, but as a text whose problematic 'actuality' concerns them even today.

In addition to the slow reading process in class as opposed to the immediacy of theatrical experience, I had to reckon with the 'language barrier' of Shakespeare's English, which has often been regarded as the major obstacle that faces German students when reading Shakespeare's plays.[9] I decided to make frequent use of the play-in-performance approach or workshop method, which has been tried out for Shakespeare's plays so successfully in American colleges and universities and has also been adopted by German teachers.[10] As this approach allows for a direct involvement with the dramatic and theatrical aspects of a play, it seems to mitigate the German students' initial fear of the 'foreignness' of Shakespeare's English.

II

The seminar started with a general discussion about the problems involved in producing Shakespeare's plays on a modern stage for a modern audience. This made the students aware of the complex interrelations between play and stage, actors and audience, and of the function of their own consciousness when watching a performance (or when reading a play). This initial discussion was followed by an overall view of *The Merchant of Venice*, dealing with plot, characters and dramatic structure. For their first cursory reading I had asked the students to take note of those scenes or elements which they thought to be of particular interest and also to state any points that had 'puzzled' or 'irritated' them. Students often avoid exploring irritations because they think that these irritations are mainly due to their lack of knowledge. As they do not see a meaningful function in irritating passages, it is essential to make them aware of how important it is to understand this irritation as part of their own reading and aesthetic experience.

After delineating the structure of the play, e.g. the changing of the action between Venice and Belmont, the students stated that the action in Venice was far more 'exciting' than that in Belmont, which they – in agreement with Granville-Barker – considered as 'a mere fairy-tale'. They had, accordingly, singled out for later close reading those scenes from Acts 1 to 3 that concern the development of the conflict between Antonio and Shylock. The Belmont scenes they wished to deal with in a more cursory manner. The students felt 'puzzled' by what they termed 'a lack of harmony' in the play. Compared with the 'tragic' action centred upon Shylock and the bond story, they thought the casket story 'too light'. None of the students ventured any comments on the crucial trial scene (Act 4), but quite unexpectedly a lively discussion was triggered off by a question about Jessica's conversion and her elopement with Lorenzo. Some students objected strongly to Jessica's behaviour, blaming her for her 'ruthless betrayal' of her father Shylock. These arguments necessitated a digression in which I supplied background information on the question of conversion at Shakespeare's time and on Jewish religion and ritual. This was followed by a discussion of methods: we agreed to interrupt our theatre-orientated analysis of the play whenever we were in need of any 'historical' knowledge.

From the outset, the students were thus actively involved in the choice of methods for the seminar. For their own reading strategies, they recognized the general distinction between the 'theatre student (who) will read for situation, for stage business, for audience response, (and) the literature student (who) will read for symbolic significance, for thematic strands, for intellectual nuance'. They also accepted Bernard Beckerman's premise as valid for their own process of understanding: 'What is so rewarding in having these two kinds of reading intermix is that they complement one another marvellously. One way of reading feeds the other.'[11]

Before the close examination of the play, we read a number of texts relating to the reception of *The Merchant of Venice*, mainly on the German stage. The texts included an extract from Heinrich Heine's appraisal of the play, which opens with his well-known comment on a performance at Drury Lane, where a lady left the theatre at the close of Act 4 in tears, crying, 'The poor man is wronged.'[12] Heine's text was contrasted with reviews of Nazi productions of the play, the most notorious being the one in Vienna (1943), in which Werner Krauß, a leading actor of that time, presented Shylock as 'a pathological image of the East Jewish racial type with its outer and inner impurity, emphasizing the threat in (Shylock's) humour'.[13] The reviews from the post-war period, documenting the apologetic or provocative trends of productions on the German stage,[14] were complemented by Arnold Wesker's article 'Why I fleshed out Shylock'.[15] By means of these audience responses from different ages I wished to give a historical dimension to our own reading. As these texts reveal contradictory responses to the play, and to Shylock in particular, the students could deduce from them the general tendencies of a particular performance. Thus, the overt antisemitism of the Nazi productions gave rise to the problematic question of the extent to which Shakespeare himself had given an antisemitic bias to his play and could therefore be held 'responsible' for any later antisemitic productions. (This question was to concern us again and again during our reading of the play.) Arnold Wesker's attack on Shakespeare's Shylock – 'It is a hateful, ignorant portrayal . . . nothing will make me admire [the play] nor has anyone persuaded me the holocaust is irrelevant to my responses'[16] – helped us to understand also the difficulties the German theatre faced when staging the play after 1945. Although parts of our discussion were concerned rather more with the history of Germany, antisemitism and the holocaust than with Shakespeare's play, I think it was on the whole beneficial to the students' understanding of the play. They had been made to recognize the following crucial issues:

- Every production of *The Merchant of Venice* hinges upon the way in which Shylock is presented on stage.
- Every production bears the stamp of its age.
- Present-day productions are 'tinctured' by past productions, and this concerns the German stage in particular.
- We, as present-day readers or play-goers, cannot rid ourselves of our knowledge of the past, which influences our understanding.

Thus, one of my teaching objectives had been partly achieved. The students had realized the theatrical dimensions of the play and had gained some insight into the controversy about its dramatic and thematic potential. By comparing their responses with those of other 'readers', they came to understand that the literary text not only engages their critical faculties but also arouses feelings and challenges attitudes and values. These considerations helped to pave the way for the ensuing detailed analysis of the play.

When Act 1.1–3 came under scrutiny, I suggested that we should adopt the roles of actors and producer who discuss the various parts before the first rehearsal, in order to find out what the actors should try to express by means of gestures, movements, intonation, etc. For Antonio, the students suggested slow and dignified gestures and a quiet tone, inducing respect in the other Venetians, whereas Salerio and Solanio should reveal their agitation by means of quick movements, underlining their verbosity with elaborate gestures. With Bassanio, the students immediately turned on his 'materialistic views' ('In Belmont is a lady richly left', 1.1.161ff.)[17] which they thought as disagreeable as his extravagant claims on Antonio's friendship and money. Summing up the two friends, they called Antonio 'too good to be true', and Bassanio 'too sure of himself' –'cocksure', as one student commented rather maliciously.

When applying the same method to Shylock's first appearance in 1.3, the students suggested alternative 'readings', the first pleading for a 'sympathetic' Shylock. As we had discussed the necessity of cuts before, one student suggested we should leave out Shylock's telling aside 'How like a fawning publican he looks / I hate him for he is a Christian' (1.3.41–52). If this passage is omitted (as, incidentally, has been done in various modern productions),[18] Shylock would win the sympathy of the audience, because it would appear that he is not bent on revenge from the outset but that his hatred of the Christians is occasioned by their contempt and spite and by Jessica's elopement. Shylock should act with as much distinction as Antonio; he should emphasize his religious feelings (as in the story of Laban's sheep), show superiority after Antonio's outbreak ('Why, look you, how you storm!' lines 137–42) and reveal genuine feelings in his final plea: 'And for my love I pray you wrong me not' (line 170). In the second version, Shylock was to be portrayed as a vindictive character. The above-mentioned aside was not to be cut but to be delivered emphatically, thus giving vent to the Jew's original hatred for the Christian Antonio. Shylock should act with much agitation, underlining his 'foreignness' by means of 'typical' gestures and speech habits. He should enjoy the power he holds over the Christians, chuckling about the 'merry bond' and rubbing his hands in anticipation of his revenge when the pound of flesh is mentioned. On the whole, the second reading appeared as the reverse of the first. Although the students knew that on the stage the actor of Shylock would have to make a definite choice, they did not want to do the same for our reading purposes. In summing up, one student commented: 'Our two versions show best the difficulties of the part, its inherent ambiguity.'

While we approached the development of the bond story from a theatrical point of view, we discussed the unfolding of the casket story mainly under literary aspects. With the wooings of Morocco, Arragon and Bassanio, the students were not interested in the stage business but preferred to discuss Elizabethan conventions and beliefs, and to explore imagery, verse and all questions relating to language. When I questioned the students about the shifting of their interest they argued that even during their second reading they had not discovered any dramatic tension in the Belmont scenes: 'There is no real risk in this fairy-tale; there are three caskets and three suitors, and Bassanio, as the third, is predestined to win. The characters aren't real, they don't come to life. The action is incompatible with the experience of a modern audience.' They found it particularly difficult to come to terms with Portia's obedience to her father's will and her love for Bassanio, whom they had disliked from the beginning.

Although some of the views expressed by the students seem to be naive and might stand in need of correction, I had no intention of forcing any authoritative interpretation upon them. Neither did I wish to prescribe the method of our analysis but rather to help them develop their own reading strategies. Thus we decided to apply the workshop method for the action centred upon Shylock and the more academic close-reading method for the casket scenes, although this emphasized rather than bridged the gap between the two strands of action. To a certain extent, this approach is in danger of disregarding Shakespeare's 'comic strategy', by which he combines the romantic with the realistic in *The Merchant of Venice*, and may turn it into a problem play. Many critics, among them W.H. Auden,[19] have supported this view, while others oppose it on different grounds, most noticeably Leo Salingar in his recent essay on *The Merchant of Venice*.[20] Such critical studies were also evaluated for our analysis of the Belmont scenes, and helped to clarify, if not to correct, some of the students' original notions about the play's 'lack of coherence'. As most of the sessions dealing with the Belmont scenes ran along the more traditional lines of academic classroom work, there is no need to deal with them extensively. Rather, I want to suggest that the discussion of the bond story renders a clearer view of how the students were responding to the play as a whole.

As the question of cuts and their influence on the overall interpretation of the play had intrigued the students from the beginning, it was raised again when we discussed the further development of the bond story. The students had of course noticed that Shylock's reactions to Jessica's elopement are presented twice: first in Solanio's report in 2.8 ('I never heard a passion so confus'd', lines 12–22), then in direct action in 3.1. Because of the dramatic redundancy the students first decided to leave out Solanio's report. On further consideration, however, they decided against the cut. They argued that since Solanio's biased report exposes Shylock to ridicule, especially when contrasted with Salerio's excessive praise of Antonio in the same scene ('A kinder gentleman treads not the earth', lines 35–49), the audience is thus manipulated to side with Antonio in his case against Shylock. When Shylock himself appears on stage in 3.1 he conveys a far more complex impression. He is torn between grief at the loss of his daughter and his anger at the loss of his money, and his fury is aggravated by the baiting comments of the Venetians. The outrage committed against him and the extremity of his pain gain him the understanding of the audience.

Only then did we discuss the central passage of 3.1, Shylock's plea for humanity: 'Hath not a Jew eyes? Hath not a Jew hands, organs, dimensions, senses, affections, passions?' (lines 58–73). The students saw the speech not as a famous piece of rhetoric, justifying Shylock's longing for revenge, but as the credible outcry of a human being wounded to the core. But they also pointed out the significance of the context: to Salerio's question what he would do with the pound of flesh, Shylock answers: 'To bait fish withal – if it will feed nothing else, it will feed my revenge' (lines 53–4). This opening remark struck the students as callous, even fiendish. Yet the students argued that the entire scene presents Shylock not as the personification of evil, but as a human being torn between conflicting emotions. To this discussion I added some further information about the play's German stage history, in particular about the productions in Düsseldorf and Berlin in the early fifties, in which Ernst Deutsch, the famous Jewish actor who had returned to Germany, played the part of Shylock. In his rendering of Shylock's famous speech Deutsch, who played Lessing's Nathan in the same season, brought home the 'actuality' of this scene.

When discussing the function of Launcelot, some students were of the opinion that we could dispense with most of his low comedy clowning in 3.5, as it is difficult to understand for a modern audience. With the help of the annotations they had discovered the sexual overtones in his jokes, but had not grasped the antisemitic tendencies expressed, for example, in his reference to Jessica's conversion: '. . . we were Christians enow before, e'en as many as could well live one by another. This making of Christians will raise the price of hogs' (3.5.21–6). They decided that the passage should remain as evidence of the Venetians' antisemitic bias and of the 'moral dilemma' of the play.

In this context it is of interest to recall that Launcelot and his gibes are only rarely referred to in the numerous more recent studies which debate the question of the play's antisemitic bias. Thus D.M. Cohen, to whom *The Merchant of Venice* seems 'a profoundly and crudely anti-Semitic play', devotes a whole passage to Launcelot's association of Jew and Devil in his clown's monologue in 2.2, but does not include the equally crude antisemitism in 3.5 in his charge against Launcelot.[21] On the other hand, an earlier critic, who maintains that the play is primarily neither about race nor religion, does quote the entire exchange between Jessica and Launcelot in 3.5 but only to prove that 'Shakespeare hints at the imperfection of the Venetians in ironic passages'.[22] (This problematic issue and its effects on literary criticism will be taken up again at a later stage.)

For the trial scene of Act 4, the seminar decided to apply the play-in-performance technique. We used the classroom with one door for entries and exits as our stage. The desk, in a central position served as a dais for the Duke, with Shylock on one side and Antonio, Bassanio and their followers on the other (next to the door). All the students had volunteered for their parts and were reading their lines while moving about. The acting was interrupted whenever we disagreed with some movement or the delivery of a particular speech. Apart from such elementary questions as the students' difficulties in suiting their actions to their words, they obviously enjoyed the experience of acting. An unexpected difficulty arose when Bassanio, unaware of the implications of the text, read his line: 'Why dost thou whet thy knife so earnestly?' (4.1.121). The girl-student who was reading Shylock's part, had delivered his preceding long speeches in a calm and almost dignified manner to express Shylock's unflinching resolution and his sense of superiority, matching her voice to Antonio's equally calm but resigned delivery. The student had hardly moved in her lonely position at the Duke's left side, and now looked up and didn't know what to do. It came as a shock to the entire class when I pointed out the implicit stage directions of Bassanio's words, continued in Gratiano's pun on *sole/*

soul: 'Not on thy sole, but on thy soul, harsh Jew / Thou mak'st thy knife keen' (lines 123ff.). In order to realize fully what this meant for our understanding of Shylock, we made the student go through various motions, while we discussed the following questions:

- Where does Shylock keep his knife and when does he take it out? While Antonio utters his lines of complete resignation ('I am a tainted wether of the flock / Meetest for death', lines 114–17)?
- Does he sit down on the ground to 'whet his knife' on his sole, as the text suggests?

It was the student acting Shylock who objected most strongly to the imperative of the text, and the others joined her in her arguments. For the students this was a moment of sheer bestial cruelty which they could not fit into their image of Shylock. They argued that if Shakespeare intended Shylock to be so crude and cruel, he – Shylock – fully deserved the punishment the Christians meted out to him. There was such a violent reaction against Shylock in the class that one student suggested omitting these lines because 'they would incite antisemitic feelings in the audience'. On returning to the question of acting, we pointed out the precariousness of these lines for the actor of Shylock. If the 'whetting of the knife' is overdone, it could easily incite the audience to laugh ('perhaps out of embarrassment') and this should be avoided at all costs.

This acting out of a few lines, and the discussion issuing from it, is perhaps the most rewarding example of the advantages of the play-in-performance technique. If the students had not attempted to stage these lines, they would certainly not have understood the full impact of the text. Moreover, the immediacy of the students' responses, oscillating between the rejection of Shakespeare's portrayal of Shylock and revulsion at the effects it produces, mirrors not only the moral ambiguities inherent in the role but also the dilemma that has faced the theatre as well as the critics throughout the history of the play's reception. In their initial, often sweeping reviews of past criticism of the play, most modern critics come, like Walter Cohen, to the conclusion that 'perhaps no other Shakespearean comedy at all, has excited comparable controversy'.[23] From this common vantage-point, the critics veer off into different directions.

Many of them choose the well-trodden path of historical enquiry into such topics as usury, old and new economics, Christian faith versus Judaism, biblical allusions and allegories and so forth. From these investigations, they turn to the question of how to categorize the play and, according to the trends of their analyses, decide for either of the two dominant models (romantic comedy or problem play) or leave the question undecided and thus return to the initial critical dilemma.

These summary remarks are not intended as an evaluation of the bulk of critical studies of *The Merchant of Venice*. Once again they point to the well-known critical fallacy which claims to be objective and is nevertheless biased by ideological premises and predilections. This is obvious in such studies as set out to 'rehabilitate' a Shakespearean character (Jessica) who 'has not fared well' in the criticism of *The Merchant of Venice*;[24] it is most prominent in those studies that centre upon the play's alleged antisemitism.[25] Again, there are different shades and degrees in the ways the critics weigh the pros and cons of the case, ranging from the most common academic interpretation of the Jew as (comic) stage villain (and thereby restricting the range of actual antisemitism or trying to explain it away)[26] to the outspoken verdict that Shakespeare himself was an antisemite 'under the strict interpretation of the word'.[27] What I consider to be striking is the note of personal involvement apparent in many of these studies.[28] D.M. Cohen gives a convincing explanation of this phenomenon. He suggests that often critics (many of them Jews) '*defensively* maintain that the Shakespearean subtlety of mind transcends anti-Semitism'.[29] Against these attempts to 'exonerate Shakespeare from the charge of anti-Semitism' he places the 'fear and shame that Jewish viewers and readers have always felt from the moment of Shylock's entrance to his final exit', and then goes on to find the justification for this 'intuitive response' in the play itself.[30]

The methodological advantage of Cohen's approach lies in his attempt to account for the reader's response by means of a detailed stage-orientated analysis. To a certain extent, it is similar to the approach the students adopted in my seminar when staging the first part of the trial scene. Yet again, the basic difference between extended literary criticism and the theatre or the play-in-performance method becomes obvious. Whereas the former has time and space enough to unfold an argument by showing up discrepancies and ambiguity, viewing them dispassionately from a distance, the latter demands a decision between alternatives and asks for immediate realization to elicit responses.

Even though the students may not have fully grasped the implications of this distinction, their change in method points in that direction. For the second part of the trial scene they decided against direct representation and used blackboard diagrams instead to indicate the positions and movements of the central characters, thereby reconstructing the dramatic tension of the scene. The students wished to maintain the basic triangular arrangement, so that Portia, like the Duke before her, should be positioned between Shylock and Antonio. When discussing the themes of justice and mercy and their presentation on stage, one student suggested that we should move the Duke, and Portia accordingly, from their central position to the right (where we had stationed Antonio, Bassanio and their followers). This was to indicate that the court is not impartial in its judgement on Shylock. However, such 'stage symbolism' the class considered too overt. By the central 'impartial' position of the Duke and Portia they wished to convey the idea that the Christians were sure of pronouncing a just sentence on Shylock. (Likewise, they had in a former discussion voted against presenting the Venetians as the caricature of an irresponsible *jeunesse dorée*.) They did not wish to justify the Christians but to leave room for the audience's discrimination.[31]

We analysed the final act in Belmont also in view of its presentation on the stage. As rigorous cuts have often been suggested for this act,[32] we discussed the effects of such an 'amputation'. Some students saw an advantage in this method partly because they felt uneasy about the 'ultimate justification' of the Venetians. They did not object to the idea of turning the play into a semi-tragedy by ending it with the destruction of Shylock, who would then appear to be its central character. Another group of students, however, emphasized the dramatic necessity of this act for the precarious balance between the tragic and the comic elements of the play. They also brought forth more literary arguments and saw

Act 5 as a 'summing up' of the major themes of love, friendship and harmony, which give a deeper meaning to the 'fairy-tale'.

III

From the methodological questions raised in the course of the seminar, I wish to draw the following conclusions:

– The switch between two methods of analysis – the play-in-performance technique and the literary close-reading method – proved to suit the interests of the students as well as the basic structure of this problem comedy. While the action centred upon Shylock appealed directly to the reader and called forth a theatrical response, the casket story stimulated literary, academic interest.

– The more the students became involved in the moral dilemma of the play, the more they recognized its actuality for a modern audience.

– Whereas on the stage Shylock has to be given a coherent and convincing identity that conforms to the overruling interpretation of a given performance, in the classroom alternative 'models' for Shylock can be worked out and the consequences investigated. The students made full use of this advantage of the reading process. Although they often decided in favour of one or the other 'model', they never pressed the point of making a definitive choice. This had the advantage of keeping Shylock alive while emphasizing rather than diminishing his inherent ambiguities.

– With these methods we neither achieved a balanced reading of the entire play nor did we claim to have discovered any (hypothetical) authorial intention. I do not regard this as an easy way out of the problems the play poses, but rather as an achievement. From a traditional academic point of view, the students' reading may be regarded as biased and lopsided. Although such criticism may be justified, I wish to argue that what the students achieved is of greater importance; they learned to take full responsibility for the strategies of understanding which they had developed during the seminar and thus experienced the 'freedom of the reader'.

Notes

1. During the season 1988–9.
2. Benjamin Henrichs, 'Das Messer im Koffer', *Die Zeit*, 16 December 1988.
3. Georg Hensel, 'Ein Jude wie du und ich', *Frankfurter Allgemeine Zeitung*, 12 December 1988.
4. Ibid. See also Cornelia Köster, 'Shylock, der Vernünftige', *Der Tagesspiegel* (Berlin), 14 December 1988.
5. For the German stage history of *The Merchant of Venice* see Ruth Frfr. von Ledebur, '*The Merchant of Venice*: Drama-Bühnengeschichte-Theaterrezension', *William Shakespeare: Didaktisches Handbuch*, vol. III, ed. Rüdiger Ahrens (Munich: Wilhelm Fink, 1982), pp. 851–83; Maria Verch, '*The Merchant of Venice* on the German Stage since 1945', *Theatre History Studies*, 5 (1985), pp. 84–94.
6. See Verch, '*The Merchant of Venice* on the German Stage since 1945', p. 86.
7. Andreas Rossmann, 'Unbeschwert: Shylock in Dortmund', *Frankfurter Allgemeine Zeitung*, 23 February 1989.
8. At Siegen University during the winter semester 1987–8.
9. See Eleonore Hombitzer, 'Shakespeare – Lektüre in der reformierten Oberstufe', ed. Rüdiger Ahrens, *Shakespeare im Unterricht* (Trier, 1977), pp. 77–91.
10. For a discussion of the relevant American studies see Ruth Frfr. von Ledebur, 'Teaching Shakespeare in America: Anregungen für den Shakespeare-Unterricht', *Jahrbuch 1987*, Deutsche Shakespeare-Gesellschaft West, pp. 124–33.
11. Bernard Beckerman, 'Explorations in Shakespeare's Drama', *Shakespeare Quarterly*, 29 (1978), pp. 135–45, (p. 136).
12. In 'Shakespeares Mädchen und Frauen' (1838), *Heines Sämtliche Werke*, ed. Rudolf Unger (Leipzig: Tempel, n.d.), vol. V, pp. 3–146 (pp. 97f.).
13. See reviews in Joseph Wulf, *Theater und Film im Dritten Reich* (Reinbeck, Rowohlt, 1966), pp. 280–3.
14. See text of reviews in von Ledebur, '*The Merchant of Venice*: Drama-Bühnengeschichte-Theaterrezension', pp. 874–83.
15. *The Guardian*, 29 August 1981.
16. Ibid.
17. All quotations from *The Merchant of Venice* are taken from *The Riverside Shakespeare* (Boston: Houghton Mifflin, 1974).

18. See the examples discussed by Alan C. Dessen in 'Shakespeare's Script and the Modern Director', *Shakespeare Survey*, 36 (1983), p. 61.

19. In his essay, 'Brothers and Others' (1963), *Shakespeare's Comedies*, ed. Laurence Lerner (Harmondsworth: Penguin, 1967), pp. 143–8.

20. Leo Salingar, 'Is *The Merchant of Venice* A Problem Play?' *Le Marchand de Venise et le Juif de Malte: Textes et représentations*, eds. Michèle Willems *et al.* (Rouen: Pubs de l'Univ. de Rouen, 1985), pp. 9–20.

21. D.M. Cohen, 'The Jew and Shylock', *Shakespeare Quarterly*, 31 (1980), pp. 53–63 (pp. 55f.).

22. Peter G. Phialas, *Shakespeare's Romantic Comedies* (Chapel Hill: The University of North Carolina Press, 1966), p. 164.

23. Walter Cohen, '*The Merchant of Venice* and the Possibilities of Historical Criticism', *English Literary History*, 49 (1982), pp. 765–89, (p. 767).

24. Camille Slights, 'In Defence of Jessica: The Runaway Daughter in *The Merchant of Venice*', *Shakespeare Quarterly*, 31 (1980), pp. 357–68, (p. 356).

25. Although this question, explicitly or implicitly, has never been absent from criticism of *The Merchant of Venice*, it has come more to the foreground during the last two decades. Of the numerous studies I consulted some will be referred to in the following notes. Outside the range of Shakespeare criticism, the Jew Shylock continues to be treated almost like a myth; see the chapter entitled 'Shylock' in Hans Mayer's comprehensive study *Aussenseiter* (Frankfurt: Suhrkamp, 1981); also 'The Rise of the Jew–Villain' in E. Rosenberg's *From Shylock to Svengali: Jewish Stereotypes in English Fiction* (Stanford: Stanford University Press, 1960), pp. 21–38.

26. John Russell Brown's 'Introduction' to *The Arden Edition* (London: Methuen, 1964) is often quoted as a case in point. See also B.K. Lewalski, 'Biblical Allusion and Allegory in *The Merchant of Venice*', *Twentieth Century Interpretation of The Merchant of Venice*, ed. Sylvan Barnet (Englewood Cliffs, N.J.: Prentice-Hall, 1970), pp. 33–54; R.M. Levitsky, 'Shylock as Unregenerate Man', *Shakespeare Quarterly*, 28 (1977), pp. 58–64.

27. Kenneth van Dyk, 'Was Shakespeare an Anti-Semite?', *Jewish Digest* (January 1979), pp. 55–7. In his interesting study 'Dog, Fiend and Christian, or Shylock's Conversion' (*Cahiers Elisabethains*, 26 (Oct. 1984), pp. 15–27), C.P. Laurent frequently refers to Antonio's 'racialism'.

28. Especially in R.H. Silvermann, *Suffrage is the Badge of all our Tribe: A Study of Shylock in The Merchant of Venice* (Lanham, Md.: University Press of America, 1981).

29. D.M. Cohen, 'The Jew and Shylock', p. 53, (my italics).

30. Ibid. See also D.M. Cohen's essay 'The Rage of Shylock', *Forum for Modern Language Studies*, 18 (1982), pp. 192–200.

31. The class founded their arguments on the information gained from several papers on the play's stage history, including one by Avraham Oz, 'Transformations of Authenticity: *The Merchant of Venice* in Israel 1938–1980', *Jahrbuch 1983*, Deutsche Shakespeare-Gesellschaft West, pp. 165–77, and Pinchas Blumenthal, 'Shylock, der Jude', *Jahrbuch 1965*, Deutsche Shakespeare-Gesellschaft West, pp. 279–304.

32. Perhaps the best example is the Victorian assumption that at Shylock's exit the play is virtually over; see W.M. Merchant's 'Introduction' to The New Penguin Edition of the play (1967), pp. 48f.

9
Reading letters in plays: short courses in practical epistemology?

JULIAN HILTON

Plays are among the most powerful means of storing and transmitting knowledge in human culture. Learning how to read plays, therefore, is in part a process of learning how to access and understand the knowledge they contain. Some playwrights, Shakespeare in particular, take pains to equip their readers with at least some of the techniques they will need, both for accessing and understanding complex cultural knowledge. They do so by placing their characters in the same position as their readers – struggling with the intrinsic difficulties of any epistemological concern. An example of this practice is a class of scene in which a character either writes or reads a letter. Letters fulfil a wide variety of purposes, and it is not my intention to document these thoroughly. My concern, rather, is with the way letter scenes offer practical guidance to readers about the act of reading and extracting knowledge from texts. This guidance is of more general significance, in that the plays themselves are texts and have the pseudo-status of letters to their readers.

Many of Shakespeare's plays have letter scenes, some concerned with the act of writing, others with the act of reading letters. The letters bring news, declare love, reveal secrets, mislead, betray and even kill. They tend to be taken at face value by their receivers, often erroneously. Shakespeare frequently uses letters as the principal agent in a plot development or peripeteia. He also seems convinced of the correlation between performance and reading, reading being an imaginary enactment of text, subject to similar forces to those which operate in theatrical performances as a whole.

I do not intend an exhaustive taxonomy of reading scenes, which in any case would probably fill a book. I want to concentrate on two problems: the first is the practical and technical problem for the actor of reading a text which he has learned by heart, as it were for the first time – and here I shall confine my attention principally to letters. The second is the semiotic problem for the audience of decoding the significance of a letter in a play, as a physical object or prop, as a written code system within the essentially oral medium of performance and as an epistemological agent in a complex cultural process. Shakespeare, who wrote at a time when culture itself was experiencing a major reinforcement of the status of reading through the advance of mass literacy brought about by Tudor educational reform, shows a keen interest in the nature of the relationship between epistemology and reading.

The most obvious function of reading a letter is telecommunication – to hear from a character who is not present. This has the significant value of reminding us that there are characters living and acting within the imagined time of the course of the play, whom the audience does not always see. The letter acts as a mediator between the parallel worlds of on- and off-stage action and invites the imaginative collusion of the audience in the construction of plot. In this sense, the letter scene in effect is an elliptical version of the more classical messenger scene, the letter itself eliding messenger and message. But such scenes also teach us a great deal about the reader in that invariably the reading of the letter is accompanied by comments, the nature and tone of which give us clues as to his character.

Putting a letter on stage, however, is inevitably to defamiliarize it. For an actor to 'read' something that he has in fact learned is trebly curious: first, he is not reading, secondly, he already knows the message before he has read it, thirdly, both what he reads and what he speaks have in fact been written by the playwright. Shakespeare's suggestion, however, seems to be that this epistemological paradox in which the actor is caught – knowing and not knowing the true meaning of the letter – is also true of the non-fictional letter. He observes that we tend to read letters outside the theatre as he invites us to read his plays, with the aid of our imaginations. In other words, we make the letters in our minds as we read them, reading into them as much what we want to find as what is there.

For all that plays are intended to be performed and their knowledge made in the meeting of audience and performers, there is an irreplaceable function for the written text, if only as a memory system to be mediated on some future occasion by the reading voice. Such a memory system will only function if spoken sounds are reified, cast in the form of tablets or books, standardized and capable of transmission independent of the performance tradition, which is always fragile. Indeed, the performance tradition, as an oral tradition, is in some ways the contradiction of the textual, because it is, in its focus on interpretation as well as representation, fundamentally a tradition of change. At the same time, the challenge of trying to capture the richness of a performance in a text, or to encode the possibility of reconstructing a performance tradition, if interrupted, largely from texts takes written language to its limits – the limits Shakespeare himself explored. In letter scenes, therefore, we get some inkling of what Shakespeare thought the limits of written language to be.

Reading letters: the hermeneutic conundrum

Before looking at the letter scenes themselves, such as the case of Malvolio, we need to set the problem of trying to extract meaning from letters in a double context; first, in the context of a tradition of textual exegesis, i.e. storing knowledge in and extracting knowledge from written statements, and secondly, in the context of the practical problem of acting reading.

The first problem, that of exegesis, was of particular significance at the time of Shakespeare because secular, as opposed to religious, exegesis was only just then in its infancy. It had been one of the great achievements of the fathers of the church from the fourth century AD onwards to develop a fourfold system of textual analysis which would not only, for example, yield the meanings of Jesus's parables to the faithful, but also help the fathers themselves discriminate between canonical and non-canonical texts. Consistent with the overall value shift of the Renaissance towards more human-centred approaches to knowledge and the knowable, literary criticism, as opposed to theology, underwent a slow development, partly in response to the growing tide of secular texts available widely in book form. Behind this development was a growing awareness that secular criticism entailed secular epistemology.

The classical statement of this new epistemology was Lord Bacon's in *The Advancement of Learning*, (1605), in which Bacon set out the basis of the new learning. Knowledge itself can be stored in two main ways: 'The custody or retaining of knowledge is either in writing or memory.'[1] His argument is of particular interest to theatre in that a play actually draws on both modes simultaneously, existing as a text but also in the memory of the performer. The difference is perhaps that the performer memorizes only part of the text, whereas the text represents only part of the performance as a whole. Bacon then develops further what he means by memory which has a key role in the transfer of knowledge: 'This art of memory is built upon two intentions; the one prenotion, the other emblem. Prenotion dischargeth the indefinite seeking of that we would remember, and directeth us to seek in a narrow compass, that is, somewhat that hath congruity with our place of memory. Emblem reduceth conceits to images sensible, which strike the memory more; out of which axioms may be drawn much better practique than in use.'[2] In letter scenes we see how both practices function simultaneously, the prenotion of both reader and writer determining their likely understanding of its contents and the emblem being both the letter itself – the physicalized knowledge – but also the actions consequent on the letters.

The point here, however, is not merely that physically to read is also intellectually to read. At issue is a major theme in western thought, that of the division of all forms of knowledge into two classes: what the Greeks termed *techne*, the knowledge of the craftsman, the knowledge of hand and eye, from which technology derives; and *episteme*, the knowledge of the philosopher, the professional, the knowledge of the head. These forms of knowledge are in a strict hierarchical relationship: Aristotle, for example, excludes from government the possessors of mere *techne* – the technicians, the craftsmen – because they do not, he argues, have the power of abstraction, of generalization, and hence cannot discern the basis on which laws and government are founded.[3] This is also one reason why in the *Poetics* he excludes spectacle from the necessary elements of a definition of tragic drama because those responsible for it are only technicians. When an actor reads a letter, however, he is actually drawing simultaneously on both, a technical skill in staged reading and an epistemological skill in interpretation.[4]

This duality flags a second: while the hierarchy of knowledge places *episteme* above *techne*, without the technology of writing – and later, printing – there would not have been the possibility of storing knowledge in one of the two ways Bacon defines. Not least for this reason, he challenges in *The Advancement of Learning* much of the basis on which the Greek theory of knowledge was founded. As the purpose of memory is to 'draw much better practique than that in use'[5], when an actor reads a letter therefore, what he is doing is offering his audience more experience from which to improve their own reading practice. What better practical exposition of epistemology?

In one respect, however, Shakespeare seems to go further than Bacon in his pursuit of the problem of recovering meanings from memory or texts: in his recognition that letters in plays are not real but virtual objects. While the actor behaves as if reading a real letter, it is no such thing, and while he pretends he has a text in front of him which he is reading, in fact he has memorized it. There may be no writing on the paper at all. Further, since the story is a fiction, there is no original letter of which the stage letter might be held to be an imitation. Thus an audience is made to believe that a blank piece of paper is actually an original letter with an original text. This concept of virtual existence is a profound hermeneutic conundrum and goes to the heart of Bacon's observations about memory and language: 'The custody or retaining of knowledge is either in writing or memory.' In performance, however, this division breaks down, since in letter scenes the one – memory – masquerades as the other – the written text. In Bacon's terms, in the actor's actual practice, language is turned into prenotion: one mode of memory – the emblematic nature of the letter – becomes its opposite – the actor's prenotion that the letter scene is about to occur. This has the effect of placing the question of what knowledge is firmly into the corner of what the reader believes, rather than objectively observable fact, which is where Shakespeare's epistemology appears to part company with Bacon's.

It is a commonplace of philosophy, almost what Bacon calls an axiom – a rule derived from practice – that meaning is derived first from phenomena and then from what lies behind the surface of things. St Paul tells us we see now through a glass darkly and only in the after-life face to face. But by the time we have witnessed an actor reading a letter in a theatre, which is not a letter, which is not being read, we may be much less sure that this is always the real state of affairs. The audience, confronted with this observation, is ultimately left only with the phenomenological fact of the piece of paper representing a letter, and even that starts to seem unstable. Does even the paper exist?

The second problem, of acting reading, is also tricky. It is hard enough for a performer to construct a plausible character with a plausible history from the lines written for any role, including Shakespeare's. But leaving aside the naturalistic debate over whether such a construction should occur at all, it is hard, if not perverse, to read a letter on stage as part of a dramaturgically consistent plot without attempting to display some reaction to that letter in a manner an audience may find convincingly in character. Letters are written by one discrete psychology to another and seem, therefore, to demand to be read accordingly. To achieve a plausible reading as an actor, when one's psychology is clearly not that of the addressee he plays, therefore, takes a great deal of rehearsal and mental effort.

Yet if an audience feels it is watching a rehearsed response it may feel the scene to be unconvincing for this very reason. The performer is thus faced with an acute paradox of rehearsing very hard to achieve perfect spontaneity. The most obvious cause of this dilemma is that the letter takes on something of the status of a documentary object and seems to demand of the reader the surrender of any paradoxality about the nature of acting (being and not being the role at the same time) in favour of empathy. That is, letter reading seems to demand total identification with the persona of the reader. To achieve such identification, however, requires deep sympathetic skills, i.e. skills of distanced and objective analysis. To be emphatic you must be first highly sympathetic.

The two problems, of exegesis and of rehearsed spontaneity, converge in respect of the complex nature of the knowledge any stage letter conveys both to performers and audience. This knowledge is, first, essential to the future progress of all or some of the plot, secondly, decisive in the interpretation of character and motive, thirdly, of particular formal significance in the generation of a bond between the reader and the audience (who by definition overhear what would otherwise be private and are hence necessarily complicit in a 'fourth wall' convention) and fourthly, generative of a set of ironic rules about the status of information conveyed by texts which not only condition the value placed on the letter by the audience but also, by implication, invite a similar conditionality about the acceptance of any statement made in the course of the play since it derives as a whole from a textual source – the script – which is, in effect, read out in front of the audience.

Do not believe everything you read

A classic example of both technical and semiotic aspects of the reading problem is Malvolio's scene in the box garden, when he is both tricked by others, and deludes himself, into a hermeneutic contortion which eventually costs him, briefly, his liberty and, more lengthily, his dignity. Here the price of over-enthusiastic literary detective work is a high one, his self-esteem:

Malvolio. And the end – what should that alphabetical position portend? If I could make that resemble something in me. Softly! M. O. A. I. —
Sir Toby. O, ay, make up that! He is now at a cold scent.
Fabian. Sowter will cry upon't for all this, though it be rank as a fox.
Malvolio. M – Malvolio; M – why, that begins my name ... M. O. A. I. This simulation is not as the former; and yet, to crush this a little, it would bow to me, for every one of these letters are in my name.   (*Twelfth Night*, 2.5.109–25)[6]

There are times as a critic when I feel distinctly warned: is my own epistemological searching not perhaps every bit as vain as Malvolio's?

Having convinced himself he is the addressee, the actor playing Malvolio then has to accomplish the technical feat of appearing surprised by a letter whose contents he already knows. The problem is made more complex by the fact that this letter is found apparently accidentally but actually deliberately, dropped in his way, on a path that is not a path in a box garden that is just a bare stage. Worse still, there may well be no writing at all on the piece of paper from which he is 'reading', still less the complete text that he is allegedly reading out.

In such an aesthetic context, Malvolio's use of the word 'simulation' is all the more striking, in that it suggests that Shakespeare is planting a clue for us about the nature of being a theatrical audience. In effect, watching is reflexive, is simulation. What the actor is doing in simulating an event and what the audience is doing in 'believing' in the simulation is similar as a process to the self-deception in which Malvolio engages. What is different is the epistemological perspective. The actor knows he is simulating, the audience knows Malvolio is deceived, Malvolio thinks he is extremely clever to have decoded the letter correctly. Yet is not all watching, all reading an elaborate act of self-deception in that we are always at least tempted to find the meanings that we seek?

The success of the conspirators' ruse lies in their careful definition of the epistemological context in which the hermeneutic exercise is conducted. Malvolio as reader is not permitted to entertain doubt as to the basis on which his reading is to be conducted. As a result of a shrewd analysis of his ambition, vanity and his willingness to engage in questionable semiotics (caballism?), the conspirators' desire for revenge is relatively easy to satisfy. But the trap is a double one, for not only do they catch Malvolio, they also lure the off-stage audience into highly dubious moral complicity with their trick. This complicity is premised on the common desire to see puritan Malvolio punished for his vanity and the pleasure the audience feels in a level of knowledge and understanding superior to that of at least one character on stage. This feeling of superior knowledge is in itself an epistemological trap: the audience is led into committing Malvolio's own error of certainty as to what the letter really means.

One of the ways in which epistemological certainty is reinforced is through the literal fact that the conspirators know what the contents of Malvolio's letter are. This breaches a strict social principle that it is wrong to know, without permission, the contents of other people's letters. It also introduces the concept of quotation into the reading paradigm, a concept which brings reading even closer to acting. Brecht, for example, even defined acting as a whole as a form of quotation and trained actors to deliver even personal speeches in the third person voice, 'he said'.

Malvolio himself is the first to quote in the scene in which smiling and cross-gartered he encounters Olivia:

Malvolio. 'Be not afraid of greatness.' 'Twas well writ.
Olivia. What mean'st thou by that, Malvolio?
(*Twelfth Night*, 3.4.37–8)

Olivia's question is *the* epistemological question and it introduces a brief exchange which encapsulates the whole epistemological problem. Neither Malvolio nor Olivia knows the true epistemological basis of their exchange, yet, perversely, they are the two speakers, and they are apparently determining the dialogue in which they are engaged. Malvolio explains Olivia's behaviour to himself as consistent with her desire for secrecy – why else would she have declared her love in such a roundabout way? Olivia is rapidly forced to conclude Malvolio is mad. To both on- and off-stage audience however, both are perfectly sane and their words perfectly comprehensible.

In his seminal work, *Tristes Tropiques*,[7] Claude Lévi-Strauss explains how cultures can fatally misread each other when they encounter each other for the first time. If a given event is equally meaningful to both cultures, both assume that their interpretation is shared by the other. In fact, however, they have radically different interpretations, but this only comes to light later when a course of action has been set in train by the initial assumption which is now irreversible. No person, no culture is more vulnerable to error than at such times. Of course Malvolio is not meeting Olivia for the first time, but the skill of the conspirators is in making him believe that Olivia has admitted her feelings for the first time – if she remains unable to display her true feelings in public. Worse still for him, once the first error has been made but not understood as such, the next are quite consistent. The letter starts to become the basis of its own epistemology:

Malvolio. O, ho! do you come near me now? No worse man than Sir Toby to look to me! This concurs directly with the letter. She sends him on purpose, that I may appear stubborn to him; for she incites me to that in the letter. 'Cast thy humble slough,' says she. (*Twelfth Night*, 3.4.64–9)

The trap is sprung, for the text has now been so interpreted that it is capable of justifying anything Malvolio feels it is appropriate for him to do. Love letters are not the only texts to be put to such use.

There is more than one gull to be caught in an epistemological net. Next victim is Aguecheek, who as one of the sponsors of the trick played on Malvolio should have been warned. Spurred on by Sir Toby, he has written a letter of challenge to his rival in love, Caesario. Sir Toby reads it out, with Fabian as literary critic interposing his comments on style and content:

Sir Andrew. Do but read.
Sir Toby. Give me. (*reads*) 'Youth, whatsoever thou art thou art but a scurvy fellow.'
Fabian. Good and valiant.
Sir Toby. 'Wonder not, nor admire not in thy mind, why I do call thee so, for I will show thee no reason for't.'
Fabian. A good note; that keeps you from the blow of the law.
(*Twelfth Night*, 3.4.140–6)

In performance, the comedy derives from the fact that Sir Toby reads in a bombastic manner quite irreconcilable with the character of Aguecheek himself. He thus renders the letter ridiculous. Where Malvolio's exchange with Olivia has a meaning neither of them know, Aguecheek's letter has no meaning at all, until Fabian fabricates one for it sufficient to sustain Aguecheek in his folly. Put not your trust in textual commentaries.

How to recognise identical twins

The conspirators' certainty is, however, short-lived, for even those within the play who, like Feste, think they have no doubts are soon brought to a position of utter confusion:

Feste (*unwittingly to Sebastian, whom he takes to be Caesario*). No, I do not know you; nor am I not sent to you by my lady to bid you

> come speak with her; nor your name is not Master Cesario; nor
> this is not my nose neither. Nothing that is so is so.
>
> (*Twelfth Night*, 4.1.5–9)

The device Shakespeare uses to bring even Feste and his com-
panions low is that of identical twins. This device is a perfect
semiotic and epistemological joke: two identical signs, icons,
actually signifying opposite things – male and female, lover and
beloved, knowing and ignorant. Because the significance of each
sign is assumed by the observer to be identical, the observer behaves
in a manner which reinforces this assumption. When the response
he receives is unexpected or even inexplicable, his epistemology
crumbles. Only a phenomenological explanation, the appearance of
both twins together, can resolve the problem:

Orsino. One face, one voice, one habit, and two persons! A natural
        perspective, that is and is not.   (*Twelfth Night*, 5.1.208–9)

Here, Orsino, perhaps unwittingly, in the process of unravelling the
mystery of the unreliable sign, defines the acting paradox itself, for
the actor is, in a deep sense, an identical twin of the role he plays. He
is and is not his role.

To reinforce this observation, Shakespeare next introduces the
aggrieved Malvolio, who, having so he thought received a letter
from Olivia berates her in a letter for abusing him so. It is given to
the literary critic, Fabian, to read the letter out:

Fabian. 'I have your own letter that induced me to the semblance I put
        on, with the which I doubt not but to do myself much right or you
        much shame. Think of me as you please. I leave my duty a little
        unthought of, and speak out of my injury.'
                                    (*Twelfth Night*, 5.1.295–8)

The letter is a variant of the identical twin trick, for though the
writing resembles Olivia's, the letter was not in fact written by her.
Malvolio enters and repeats, though this time in verse, his
allegations:

Malvolio. Madam, you have done me wrong,
          Notorious wrong . . .
Olivia.   Alas, Malvolio, this is not my writing,

> Though, I confess, much like the character;
> But out of question 'tis Maria's hand.
>
> $\qquad$ (*Twelfth Night*, 5.1.315–16, 332–4)

The puns on 'character' and 'hand' seal Malvolio's lesson in practical letter-reading. Do not just treat the contents with scepticism and verify their meaning, but treat even the form, the writing itself, with care. It may not be what it seems.

The implication of Malvolio's fate is a difficult one, for on the one hand he is cruelly punished for treating the text he has read as sincere, on the other hand, as Olivia admits, 'He hath been most notoriously abus'd.' The problem is that if we were all to treat every text with utter scepticism, any form of textual discourse would become rapidly impossible. So, at the end of the play, we are forced to recognize that however much we dislike Malvolio he was wronged, and in a very damaging way. For once anyone's confidence – and it could be our own – is undermined in the sincerity of texts it is very hard to rebuild. Not surprisingly perhaps for Shakespeare, the resolution of the dilemma of the sincerity of text is in performance. It is the very twinness, the doubleness of perspective, which the actor naturally has, which safeguards the reader from the Malvolio school of hard knocks – at least most of the time. For the twinness admits the possibility of two different but simultaneous types of sincere reading, complementing each other in a protective way. There is the sincere desire to believe what is written and the sincere desire to assure oneself of its legitimacy by questioning it. This apparent contradiction is resolved by making the act of reading simultaneously one of validation.

When the letter does not arrive

This issue of validation and phenomenology are central to the advice Lady Capulet offers Juliet as to how to read a text of a fine complexion, Paris's face, which conceit she builds on the metaphor of the face as book:

> Read o'er the volume of young Paris' face,
> And find delight writ there with beauty's pen;
> Examine every married lineament,
> And see how one another lends content;

> And what obscur'd in this fair volume lies
> Find written in the margent of his eyes.
> This precious book of love, this unbound lover,
> To beautify him only lacks a cover.
>
> (*Romeo and Juliet*, 1.3.82–9)

Even Lady Capulet, however, is not above some puns, 'volume', 'content', 'unbound', showing that she knows how complex signs can sometimes be. Her final pun, 'cover', is perhaps the oddest since in a sexual sense it seems to reverse the genders – for Juliet is to cover Romeo. What underlies her speech, however, is the recognition that any process of analysis, of judgement, has an element of reading to it. Reading is the mediation of phenomena and meaning.

Reading assumes that the reader is in physical possession of the text, an apparently trivial point until near the end of the play one learns that the whole tragedy might have been avoided had a letter not failed to arrive at its intended destination. The instructions Friar Lawrence sends to Romeo do not get through and the event is significant enough for Shakespeare to accord it a scene of its own:

Friar Lawrence.	This same should be the voice of Friar John.
	Welcome from Mantua! What says Romeo?
	Or, if his mind be writ, give me his letter.
Friar John.	Going to find a barefoot brother out,
	One of our order to associate me,
	Here in this city visiting the sick,
	And finding him, the searchers of the town,
	Suspecting that we both were in a house
	Where the infectious pestilence did reign,
	Seal'd up the doors, and would not let us forth,
	So that my speed to Mantua there was stay'd.
Friar Lawrence.	Who bare my letter, then, to Romeo?
Friar John.	I could not send it – here it is again –
	Nor get a messenger to bring it thee,
	So fearful were they of infection.
Friar Lawrence.	Unhappy fortune.

(*Romeo and Juliet*, 5.2.1–17)

The whole weight of the play seems to hang by the thread of Friar John's admission, 'I could not send it.' As the context tells us, however, when letters fail to arrive there is always deep cause, in this case a pestilence that speaks not only of physical malady but of the plague of feuding between neighbours. The phenomenological problem of the letter's failure to arrive is a clue to the epistemology of the play as a whole, a point reinforced by Romeo's phenomenological misreading of the nature of Juliet's 'death' – a semblance not a reality – and echoed by the late arrival of Friar Lawrence at the tomb, late arriving like his own letter. If the matter is urgent, you may be better to go in person.

When the letter is rewritten

Read in the context of *Hamlet*, Romeo may be blamed for not intervening directly in the letter-writing process himself. Hamlet is sent off to England by Claudius in the company of Rosencrantz and Guildenstern. They bear a letter to the English court instructing the king to kill Hamlet. Hamlet, an expert in the relationship between phenomenon and epistemology, has a simple but brilliantly effective expedient:

> *Hamlet.* There's a divinity that shapes our ends,
>   Rough-hew them how we will.
> *Horatio.* That is most certain.
> *Hamlet.* Up from my cabin,
>   My sea-gown scarf'd about me, in the dark
>   Grop'd I to find out them; had my desire;
>   Finger'd their packet, and in fine withdrew
>   To mine own room again, making so bold,
>   My fears forgetting manners, to unseal
>   Their grand commission; where I found, Horatio,
>   . . . an exact command . . .
>   My head should be struck off.
>   (*Hamlet*, 5.2.10–25)

His first step is to locate the incident in question within the correct epistemological context, in this case the hand of God, which intervenes on Hamlet's behalf. Then follows a narrative of events which express in phenomenological terms the problem of finding meaning in any text – like groping in the dark, in disguise, on board a ship where the very ground under one's feet is moving.

Next Hamlet, naturally enough for him, reaches for the metaphor of theatre to describe how he solved the problem, by changing the epistemology. Instead of the instruction being to kill him it is changed to refer to Rosencrantz and Guildenstern:

Hamlet. Being thus benetted round with villainies –
　　　　Ere I could make a prologue to my brains,
　　　　They had begun the play – I sat me down;
　　　　Devis'd a new commission . . .
　　　　An earnest conjuration from the King
　　　　As England was his faithful tributary . . .
　　　　He should those bearers put to sudden death,
　　　　Not shriving time allow'd.
　　　　　　　　　　　　　(*Hamlet*, 5.2.29–47)

The same technique as traps Malvolio kills the courtiers, a forgery. But there is one further problem, that of validation:

Horatio. How was this seal'd?
Hamlet. Why, even in that was heaven ordinant.
　　　　I had my father's signet in my purse.
　　　　　　　　　　　　　(*Hamlet*, 5.2.47–9)

The last sentence is the stuff of comedy (my father had a mole upon his breast . . .). It also indicates the perfect ambiguity of all epistemological speculation, which is at once the most meaningful and the most pointless of all human activities. In the end epistemological certainty is either an act of total faith, for example, in God, or of belief in contingency – 'I had my father's signet in my purse.' As the final events of the play unfold, the two even seem to merge.

By contrast with the tragic epistemology of *Romeo and Juliet*, in the comedy, *As You Like It*, Duke Senior appears to be willing in principle to read nature as a sincere text:

　　　　And this our life, exempt from public haunt
　　　　Finds tongues in trees, books in the running brooks
　　　　Sermons in stones, and good in everything.
　　　　　　　　　　　　　(*As You Like It*, 2.1.14–16)

The speech neatly combines what we would now call semiotics with a theory of benevolent immanence. That this belief in a benevolent hermeneutic system is not shared by all in Arden is, however, soon stated in the song which ends act two, 'Blow, blow thou winter wind / Thou art not so unkind / As man's ingratitude.' Here the semiotic equation of human and inanimate nature is not only disputed but if anything perceived to rest on common malevolence. As Duke Senior himself puts it at a later juncture:

> Come, shall we go and kill us venison?
> And yet it irks me the poor dappled fools,
> Being native burghers of this desert city,
> Should, in their own confines, with forked heads
> Have their round haunches gor'd.
>
> (*As You Like It*, 2.1.21–5)

If you are a hunter, or are hungry, your perspective is that to hunt and eat is good. If you are a deer, your perspective is the reverse. The Duke's wisdom is reflected in his split consciousness, his double perspective, which, far from schizophrenic or disturbed, is what establishes a balanced attitude to his surroundings. So the dialectic of opposites is resolved.

A rather different aspect of the problem of meaning is addressed in the love letters Orlando leaves on trees in the forest. At issue is whether his expressions of love are rich and compelling (Rosalind, although she denies it) or banal (Touchstone), the conclusion lying not so much in the intrinsic quality of the letters as in the manner in which they are read. Shakespeare merely juxtaposes Rosalind and Touchstone:

Enter Rosalind, reading a paper . . .

Rosalind.   'All the pictures fairest lin'd
            Are but black to Rosalinde.
            Let no face be kept in mind
            But the fair of Rosalinde.'

Touchstone. I'll ryhme you so eight years together . . . for a taste:
            If a hart do lack a hind,
            Let him seek out Rosalinde . . .
            This is the very false gallop of verses; why do you infect
            yourself with them?

Rosalind.   Peace, you dull fool! I found them on a tree.

Touchstone. Truly, the tree yields bad fruit.

(*As You Like It*, 3.2.82–106)

Touchstone's joke is an elaborate one. Poets pluck flowers, tropes, from the garden of verse. Bad poets, so Touchstone, pick bad fruit from the orchard of versification. Yet, as he himself has shown, texts may be made or marred in the reading, so it is later doubly fitting that the man who is to marry Touchstone and Audrey is called Martext.

When reading is action

In *Macbeth* we are offered perhaps the most complex of paradigms of reading. First, we see a scene in which Macbeth encounters three weird sisters and is told of his destiny. Then we hear from Lady Macbeth, reading a letter about the same incident. So we are given parallel code systems for our interpretation of the events described. The letter reads as follows:

Lady Macbeth. 'They met me in the day of success; and I have learn'd by the perfect'st report they have more in them than mortal knowledge. When I burn'd in desire to question them further, they made themselves air, into which they vanish'd. Whiles I stood rapt in the wonder of it came missives from the King, who all-hail'd me "Thane of Cawdor"; by which title, before, these weird sisters saluted me and referr'd me to the coming on of time, with "Hail, king that shalt be!" This have I thought good to deliver thee, my dearest partner of greatness, that thou mightst not lose the dues of rejoicing by being ignorant of what greatness is promis'd thee. Lay it to thy heart, and farewell.' (*Macbeth*, 1.5.1–12)

There are several puzzles even in the formal aspects of this scene. First, we may wonder that Macbeth would entrust such remarkable news to a letter at all. Secondly, we may wonder why a great dramatist would wish in effect to summarize and repeat an action, so apparently contradicting his customary principle of asking the audience to make the action of his plays in their imagination. Thirdly, no sooner has Lady Macbeth read the letter and reacted to it, than a messenger comes in to tell her of Duncan's imminent arrival at Glamis. Finally, again only a few minutes later, Macbeth himself comes in, to be welcomed by Lady Macbeth in a nice variation of the greeting of the weird sisters: 'Great Glamis! Worthy Cawdor! / Greater than both, by the all-hail hereafter'

(1.5.51–2). His entrance only reinforces the question, why use letters at all.

The key to the letter, and to the rest of the action of the play, is the invocation of a higher epistemology. So Macbeth attributes to the weird sisters the ability to see perfectly into the future, an ability beyond mortal knowledge but, oddly, not beyond the power of theatre. For on every occasion that *Macbeth* is played, the outcome is known in advance. He presents his encounter on the heath in terms of a biblical revelation, for example the annunciation of the Blessed Virgin, and the tone of the latter part of the letter is that of the Book of Common Prayer or the Letters of St Paul, in which deep and sacred knowledge is being transferred.

In principle, this is no different from Hamlet's reference to higher powers shaping our destinies, but with the one, crucial, difference, that Macbeth is on the point of deciding to give destiny a helping hand. In this context, Macbeth's writing a letter is consistent with his growing desire to intervene in history. For in having to articulate for another, his wife, his feelings about such an extraordinary moment of being he has also to interpret it; and in interpretation he sets the accent for future action. Like Malvolio, Macbeth creates a text from which his life and action will be governed. This text, as Lady Macbeth tells him, is to be misread in the book of his face:

> Your face, my thane, is as a book where men
> May read strange matters. To beguile the time,
> Look like the time; bear welcome in your eye,
> Your hand, your tongue; look like th' innocent flower
> But be the serpent under't.   (*Macbeth*, 1.5.59–63)

Duncan reads this face wrongly and dies. But other readers begin to learn new critical techniques, until finally a new epistemology is found, capable of exposing the serpent under the surface: at which point, Macbeth is deposed and killed.

In composing the letter, Macbeth makes one step towards meaning; when Lady Macbeth reads it, she makes a complementary second. Meaning emerges from the dialectic of writing and reading, both of which are halves of a hermeneutic dialectic in which that which is thought, felt, intuited is given form. So in a short space we are given a practical lesson in the relationship between hermeneutics and action. Reading the text is making the play. Reading is action. In a sense, the whole of *Macbeth* is an essay in epistemology: how are we to assess the meaning of what we have seen and heard? In this it represents a step on from the principles of uncertainty that operate in the comedies, for whereas in the comedies the audience at least knows what is going on, in *Macbeth* the audience is no more certain than the players – witness the litres of ink spilt trying to crack the code. We never know whether the weird sisters determine events, see into the future, are good at guessing or are mere hallucinations which by some freak Macbeth and Banquo share, at least at the outset. We never know whether Macbeth would have murdered his way to the throne in any case, or whether the prophecies he hears function like auto-suggestion, pushing him to action he would otherwise have rejected. There is apparently no certainty in the universe, and that, if anything is the message.

The irony of the play is that Macbeth understands this, perhaps more deeply than anyone else. 'So foul and fair a day I have not seen.' He is quite capable of seeing how deeply paradoxical experience can be. But what happens seems to mislead him, and whom would it not, into giving the weird sisters credence which perhaps they do not deserve. First, perhaps they articulate his thoughts, for as Banquo notes, his reaction is a significant one, even if we cannot determine what the significance is:

> Good sir, why do you start and seem to fear
> Things that do sound so fair? I' th' name of truth,
> Are ye fantastical, or that indeed
> Which outwardly ye show?   (*Macbeth*, 1.3.51–4)

Banquo is perhaps less subtle than Macbeth: he divides experience into reason and fantasy and wonders which he has just experienced. His question to the women, however, serves to create the distinction between the apparent and the real which Lady Macbeth later teaches Macbeth.

But what of Macbeth's behaviour and the way he reports it to his wife? He writes that he 'burn'd in desire to question them further'. In fact, his tone is more that of the commander than the feverish supplicant: 'Stay you imperfect speakers, tell me more.' But the crucial difference is in the transformation of the appellation 'imperfect speakers' in the event itself into 'the perfect'st report' in the letter. In a sense, the transformation describes the very process of writing history, of transforming imperfect (in the sense of unfinished) events into perfect (finished) narratives. But this is casuistic. What happens between the encounter and the letter writing is the arrival of the news that Macbeth is indeed Thane of Cawdor. The weird sisters have spoken the truth about this and might, perhaps must, be right about their second prophecy, that Macbeth shall be king.

The trap is a fatal one. Macbeth applies a syllogistic approach to events that in fact defy logical or probabilistic analysis. His argument is, roughly:

- All supernatural solicitings can be either good or bad.
- The weird sisters have proved to be right (good) about one such soliciting.
- Therefore they must be right about the second.

The structure of the letter reflects this logic. The encounter is approximately the first third of the letter, the empirical proof of the prophecy the second and the coded speculation on the future the third. In writing it, Macbeth has determined the text, and the hideous knowledge it contains, of the rest of his life.

Postscript

It is surely no accident that the young Schiller should begin his first great drama, *The Robbers*, with a letter scene, in which Franz von Moor, a great-nephew of Shakespeare's Richard III if ever there was one, deceives his father and destroys his brother. He achieves this because he knows his father will believe that the contents of the letter in question are true. Steeped in Shakespeare as Schiller was, he merely appropriated Shakespeare's observation that people tend to believe what they read in letters and took this observation to its logical extreme.

What perhaps lay between Schiller and Shakespeare was a quantum leap in the use of letters in European culture, principally as a means of social communication, which itself was tied up with the increase in literacy and the development of improved communication systems. Aesthetically, there also lay the success of the great epistolary novels of Samuel Richardson, *Pamela*, which started life as a slim volume on how to write letters, and *Clarissa*, another source for Schiller.

Such developments did not, however, challenge the premise of Shakespeare's analysis of reading as analogous to performance. In performance you must simultaneously believe and disbelieve what you see and hear. When you read letters you should believe and disbelieve what you read: out of this dialectic something approaching true knowledge may emerge.

Notes

1. Francis Bacon, *The Advancement of Learning and New Atlantis* (Oxford: World's Classics, 1951), p. 156.
2. Ibid., p. 156.
3. See Aristotle, *The Politics of Government or a Treatise on Government*, tr. William Ellis (London: Everyman, 1912), ch. VII pp. 11–12. I am indebted to Jon Cook for drawing this to my attention. See Jon Cook, *One Culture, Two Cultures, Three Cultures . . .* in *Dialoger*, 1989, Stockholm, forthcoming.
4. For a full discussion of Aristotle's views on spectacle see Julian Hilton, *Performance* (London, 1987), ch. 2.
5. Bacon, op. cit., p. 157.
6. All quotations from Shakespeare are taken from *William Shakespeare: The Complete Works*, ed. Peter Alexander (London, 1951).
7. Claude Lévi-Strauss, *Tristes Tropiques* (Paris, 1955), *passim*.

10

Molière and his readers

MAYA SLATER

Molière repeatedly asserted that he regarded his plays as acting texts. He maintained that seeing a performance was what counted, and that reading the play came a very poor second. In the Preface to his farcical comedy *Love, the Doctor* (*L'Amour Médecin*) he writes:

> It is well known that comedies are composed only in order to be performed, and I would recommend that this play should be read only by those people who have the eyes to see, in a reading, all the stage action.
> (On sait bien que les comédies ne sont faites que pour être jouées, et je ne conseille de lire celle-ci qu'aux personnes qui ont des yeux pour découvrir, dans la lecture, tout le jeu du théâtre.)[1]

Even when Molière is not explicitly addressing the question of performance versus reading, the assumption that performance is what counts underlies his comments. This emerges when we consider his defence of his controversial play *Le Tartuffe*. In his Preface of 1669 to this play, Molière complains that his enemies see *Le Tartuffe* as

> a play offensive to piety . . . Every syllable is impious; even the gestures are criminal; and the slightest glance, the slightest head movement, the slightest step to the right or to the left, conceal mysteries that they succeed in explaining to my disadvantage.
> (une pièce qui offense la piété . . . Toutes les syllabes en sont impies; les gestes mêmes y sont criminels; et le moindre coup d'oeil, le moindre branlement de tête, le moindre pas à droite ou à gauche, y cachent des mystères qu'ils trouvent moyen d'expliquer à mon désavantage.) (Garnier I, 628)

Molière's preoccupation here is with the injustice of the attacks on his play; nevertheless, it is interesting that he goes into more detail about the movements of the actors on stage than about the actual words of the text.

Equally significant is his standpoint elsewhere in the same Preface: he begs people 'not to condemn things before they have seen them' (not *read* them). And throughout the Preface, discussing the impact of the play on his contemporaries, he refers to them as 'les auditeurs', 'les spectateurs' and never 'les lecteurs' ('the readers'). Finally, he sums up his function as he sees it: to 'put (plays) on in the theatre' ('les monter sur le théâtre').

In a more optimistic and relaxed mood, earlier in his career, Molière responds to the success of his farcical comedy *The Ridiculous Precieuses* (*Les Précieuses ridicules*) by emphasizing the importance not of the text but of the production. The play was published, with Molière's Preface attached, in 1659. He wrote:

> Much of the charm that people have found [in this play] lies in the stage action and the way the lines are spoken. It mattered to me that it should not be deprived of these embellishments.
>
> (Comme une grand partie des grâces qu'on y a trouvées [dans la pièce] dépendent de l'action et du ton de voix, il m'importait qu'on ne les dépouillât pas de ces ornements.)
>
> (Garnier I, 193–4)

As we can see, these comments of Molière reveal a strong bias towards performance. This would explain why he was very reluctant to publish. As he wanted his plays to be seen, not read, he saw publication as more or less irrelevant. He wrote: 'I felt that the play's success in performance was a fine enough achievement to leave it at that.' ('Je trouvais que le succès qu'elles [*Les Précieuses*] avaient eu dans la représentation était assez beau pour en demeurer là.')

This reluctance to immortalize his work was very much in character. Molière seems to have placed great emphasis on being unassuming, natural and ordinary.[2] He objected strongly to pretension; and publishing or theorizing about the theatre in print for readers seems to have been associated in his mind with a kind of literary arrogance that he found obnoxious.

This attitude seems to underlie his sarcastic remarks about publication in the Preface to *Les Fâcheux*, where, probably comparing himself mischievously to Corneille, he comments that the time has not yet come for him to pontificate about his expertise as a literary theorist on the theatre:

> The time will come for me to print my comments on my plays, and one day I do not despair of demonstrating, like a great writer, that I am able to quote Aristotle and Horace. While I await my theoretical treatise, which may never get written, I am content to abide by the public's opinion.
>
> (Le temps viendra de faire imprimer mes remarques sur les pièces que j'aurai faites, et je ne désespère pas de faire voir un jour, en grand auteur, que je puis citer Aristote et Horace. En attendant cet examen, qui peut-être ne viendra point, je m'en remets assez aux décisions de la multitude.)   (Garnier I,65)

Here then he is claiming that he is not a great writer but an entertainer whose one aim is to please the public.

The above remarks must not, however, be taken too literally, for in Molière's day it was a convention that writers were reluctant to publish. Molière himself mocked at this insincere self-effacement in several of his plays. The absurd Mascarille in *The Ridiculous Precieuses*, a valet disguised as a Marquis, says he publishes reluctantly because

> It is unworthy of my position in society; but I do it purely to give the publishers who badger me a means of earning money. (Cela est au-dessous de ma condition; mais je le fais seulement pour donner à gagner aux libraires qui me persécutent.)
>
> (Sc. ix; Garnier I, 206)

Reading between the lines, we may well feel that some of Molière's own self-deprecatory comments about his lack of importance as a publishing writer may be purely conventional disclaimers. Perhaps he is not sincere when he says that his plays are ephemeral productions that should not be immortalized as published texts.

It may then be unhelpful to rely on his few prefaces, which are imbued with conventional self-deprecation, in order to discover whether the plays are performing texts or designed to be read. Instead, let us turn to the plays themselves.

Examining the written text of Molière's plays with this question in mind, we immediately notice two striking features: first, a remarkable dearth of stage directions, and secondly, a particular slant to such directions as do exist.

To take these two points in order, the lack of stage directions makes it difficult for modern students of Molière to work out how he wanted his text to be interpreted; however, it is not particularly surprising that Molière should have left us simply the bare bones of his texts. At the time he was writing, comedy, and, in particular, farce, relied heavily on improvisation. Molière would have expected a production to use a text as a basis to build on rather than as a blueprint to be followed in slavish detail. For our purposes, this is interesting because it implies that the texts were not even acting texts but something yet more schematic: improvisation texts. Molière has left the director very free. (Before Molière, in fact, it would have been the actors who were free to embroider on a text, as the director's function seems to have been minimal.)

But the dearth of stage directions is not simply a matter of contemporary convention. It also suggests that Molière's own preoccupation was with his own production, not with the printed text. This is clear from the fact that he simply published the words. As a rule, he did not make even a perfunctory attempt to give his readers, or subsequent directors, the benefit of how he wanted a role or a scene interpreted. His energies had been expended on producing a convincing rendering of a play on stage. How others might render it later was not what counted. This strong emphasis on his own production rather than the text is reinforced by his own comments, such as his remark, already quoted, that his actual production is the most important part of the experience represented by the play *The Ridiculous Precieuses*.

I said earlier that there is a second lesson to be learnt from the published texts of Molière. On the relatively rare occasions when he does give explicit stage directions, they are the directions of a professional director, not of a writer catering for a reading public. They normally consist of detailed instructions as to how to perform a complicated piece of stage business, the sort of stage action that really needs to be described, often because more than one actor is involved at one time, so that their actions have to be co-ordinated.

One could imagine that a director who left his cast relatively free to improvise would have to keep tighter control when several people were on stage. Here is an example from *The Reluctant Doctor* (*Le Médecin malgré lui*):

> Sganarelle . . . puts his bottle on the ground. Valère bends down to bow to him. Sganarelle thinks Valère wants to take away the bottle, so he puts it down on his other side. Lucas does the same thing. Sganarelle picks up the bottle and holds it against his stomach with numerous gestures which produce considerable stage action. (I, 5; Garnier II, 15)

Where comédie-ballet was concerned, a large number of performers and musicians were involved, and Molière again gives quite precise instructions. For example, here are the instructions for one of the ballets in *Le Bourgeois gentilhomme:*

> Enter four tailor's apprentices; two pull off the breeches M. Jourdain was wearing to do his exercises, two others pull off his shirt; then they dress him in his new suit; and M. Jourdain walks among them and shows them his suit, to see if they approve. The action lasts through the whole symphony. (II, 5; Garnier II, 457)

These more elaborate stage effects were very successful in Molière's day, and we have several contemporary accounts of their impact.[3] For our purposes we should note here that these more elaborate stage-directions are not geared to improving matters for the reader. The by-play with the bottle, for instance, always makes the audience laugh, but is not in the least amusing to read.

Except on rare occasions like these, Molière's stage directions are perfunctory or absent. Molière's casual attitude when consigning to paper what happens on stage may be readily accounted for; but its effects persist: certain scenes, and in particular certain roles, are enigmatic to the reader, though they would have been perfectly clear to an audience witnessing Molière's own productions. This hermetic quality, particularly striking in some famous Molière characters, has provoked much critical debate as subsequent generations attempt to remedy the inadequacies of Molière's printed text.

A notorious and complex example is Célimène in *Le Misanthrope*. This character seems opaque in the text because Molière makes her claim to be in love with her four suitors, but shows her betraying each one behind his back to the others. The unresolved problem is whether her feelings for Alceste, the hero of the play, are supposed to be more sincere than her patently hypocritical protestations to the other lovers. It is frequently argued that she does appear to be more involved with Alceste. She tells him at the end of the play that she despises her other suitors but feels guilty at having betrayed him. She certainly wants him to believe that she does have genuine feelings for him. She even offers to marry him, though she cannot bring herself to leave Paris and live alone with him in the country. Alceste takes this refusal as a gross insult: 'at this moment I hate you in my heart, / And your refusal alone is worse than everything else' (V, iv).

It is at this point that Molière leaves the reader guessing, for on hearing Alceste's insults, the stage directions simply tell us 'Célimène se retire' ('exit Célimène'). How is the reader to guess how this exit of Célimène's should be played? We are at liberty to let it remain totally enigmatic. But this is impossible in a stage production. Célimène would have to do something, demonstrate either anger or insouciance, or even amusement. Or she could be shattered by Alceste's rejection, as though, too late, she has suddenly realized how much he means to her. If she goes out unobtrusively, without expressing any particular emotion, this too has to mean something to the audience. Presumably an unemotional Célimène, who has just had her offer of marriage cast in her teeth, would be shattered and numb: the explosive emotions are to come later. Certainly it is a fact that famous Célimènes have all been strong at this moment, but in very different ways. Mlle Mars in the nineteenth century is a case in point:

> All the pride of a coquette who will never reveal her pain was expressed in her response to Alceste's last angry outburst. From the first words of this harsh dismissal, she was preparing her exit, she began a curtsey which finished with his last words. As she went out, she resumed her air of defiance, she gestured with her fan over her shoulder in an expressive manner which spoke

volumes and which made her look as though it were she who was dismissing the man who was abandoning her.[4]

It seems as though the original Célimène was more upset and less defiant than Mlle Mars. Molière's wife, Armande, created the role; and we have an eye-witness account of the first production in the 'Lettre écrite sur la comédie du *Misanthrope*' by Donneau de Visé (published with the play during Molière's lifetime). Donneau de Visé describes Armande's performance of this last scene as follows:

> The coquette seems somewhat mortified in this scene. She does not act out of character; but her surprise at finding that she has been abandoned, and her sorrow at discovering that her tricks have been discovered, make her feel secretly humiliated, and this actually shows in her face.
>
> (La coquette paroit un peu mortifiée dans cette scène. Ce n'est pas qu'elle démente son caractère; mais la surprise qu'elle a de se voir abandonnée, et le chagrin d'apprendre que son jeu est découvert, lui causent un secret dépit, qui paroit jusque sur son visage.)
>
> (GEF IV, 439)

Célimène's reaction to her final humiliation at the hands of Alceste is crucial: it could cast a retrospective light on the possible motives underlying her behaviour throughout the play. Hence it could altogether change the audience's view of the character. If she is played as though she realizes for the first time how much she loves Alceste, then we may feel retrospectively that her flirtatiousness earlier in the play was a surface mannerism, and that this has always been a heroine capable of deep feeling. If her exit is flouncing and defiant, like Mlle Mars's, the Célimène of this final scene is made consistent with the Célimène of the malicious gossip scene, and the implication is that her affections were never really engaged by Alceste or anyone else, and that she has learnt nothing from her discomfiture. Either way, a stage production must round off this character to the audience's satisfaction, whereas the reader has to make his imagination work overtime if he is not to view this exit as disappointingly non-committal.

My last point implies another crucial difference between reading and seeing a play. This is the question of hindsight. It is axiomatic that an audience is privileged *vis-à-vis* the reader in this respect. A reader comes to a text in ignorance, and his view of what is supposed to be happening may well evolve or change as the reading progresses. It becomes clear with hindsight what was meant. But the members of an audience do not need to develop a view – the text has been interpreted for them, from the start, through the eyes of a director and actors who have, of course, read the play many times. Director and actors connive to manipulate the audience, to guide their responses in a way that is appropriate to the whole text. They become, in this respect, the confederates of the author. For the reader of Molière, then, a play may seem confusing on a first reading; we may respond to what is going on in a way that will prove inappropriate in the light of later developments. An audience would not have this problem.

A case in point is *The School for Wives*. Its anguished hero, Arnolphe, is an ambiguous figure. Molière himself described him as 'a worthy man in some respects and ridiculous in others' ('honnête homme en de certaines choses et ridicule en d'autres') (*La Critique de l'ecole des femmes*, Sc. vi). Should we be viewing him as a figure of fun ('a complete madman', as one of the other characters puts it, IV, iii), or should we sympathize with his expressions of despair?

As the play moves towards its final climax, Arnolphe gets more and more frantic. He becomes aware that he loves Agnes, and realizes that he is in the process of losing her. He has several speeches in which grotesque clumsiness of expression is combined with intense and convincing anguish: the reader is left to struggle to make sense of these two extremes. When we get to the final scenes, the reader has further cause for perplexity. I should like to go into these scenes briefly to show that Molière is not thinking in terms of making concessions to the reader.

Arnolphe enters with Agnes in tow. He has brought her in to destroy her in public by making her witness the end of her love affair: the young man she loves is to be married to a girl his father has chosen. At this point we suddenly get a complete reversal: the other characters turn the tables, both on Arnolphe and on the audience. We learn, at the same time as Arnolphe learns it, that Agnes is in fact the girl in question, and that it is to Agnes that the young man is to be married. Molière introduces this news as a complete shock to the audience. Agnes, who appeared to be an orphan completely in the power of her guardian Arnolphe, has suddenly found for herself a father and a betrothed husband.

In concentrating on this information, Molière avoids any mention of Arnolphe's reaction. Arnolphe has in fact become monosyllabic. The other characters are all talking at him, but all he manages to say is 'quoi?' He remains enigmatic as the others explain the string of extraordinary circumstances that have conspired to humiliate him and make him lose control of Agnès. The other speakers go on telling him the news in a way that implies that they are quite unaware of how it is affecting him. However, Arnolphe's confidant, Chrysalde, comments to Arnolphe that he realizes how much he must be suffering. In reply, Arnolphe simply says 'oh', and exits. Even this departure remains enigmatic in the printed text. Someone turns to Chrysalde and asks in bewilderment: 'Why has he rushed away without a word?'

But at this point, as Arnolphe makes his final exit, the reader of a scholarly text learns something from the footnotes that may well cause him to rethink his attitude to Arnolphe. In the original version the part of Arnolphe was taken by Molière himself. The note to the Garnier edition, by Robert Jouanny, tells us: 'According to tradition, Molière, from the earliest performances, said not 'oh!' (elevated style) but 'ouf!' (comic style)' (Garnier I, 911).

It seems that as readers of the text we have here a real problem of interpretation with far-reaching consequences. If Molière's exit line was delivered in an uncompromisingly farcical manner, this method of delivery must have been in character with his portrayal of the role of Arnolphe up till that moment. In other words, we will have to go back over the text seeing how Molière builds up the character of Arnolphe as a farcical figure.

But the reader's problem is not a problem at all for a theatre audience. This character, like Célimène, must be performed in a particular manner, so that the silent Arnolphe at the end is compatible with the Arnolphe portrayed during the rest of the play. Molière himself, if we are to believe Donneau de Visé, played the part in a consistently ridiculous manner. Visé tells us that it was Molière's acting that made the play the success it was during his own lifetime, and comments scathingly:

> If people rush to see comedies, it is because they always find
> something to laugh at in them; sometimes the inferior and even
> the least lifelike aspects are the most diverting. Posturing helps to
> make such plays successful, and they usually owe all their success
> to the grimacing of an actor. An example is *The School for Wives*,
> in which the faces made by Arnolphe made the audience laugh.[5]

Here we are not simply concerned with the fact that the way the part
of Arnolphe is played will make the play much more amusing than it
could ever be to a reader. We have also seen that the reader may
actually have misinterpreted the whole meaning of the role, simply
because he was reading, not seeing, the play.

These arguments and examples are only a few of the many that
one could use to demonstrate that Molière is an actor–manager first,
and a publishing playwright almost as an afterthought. Is this the
case with every play, and at every stage in his career?

To answer this question I must again take up the point that
Molière's demurrers about publishing were the expressions of a
conventional attitude, and not necessarily his genuine opinion. I
believe that just one of his plays was in fact intended as a reading
text, in spite of his disclaimers. My evidence is that in this play there
are stage directions designed to help the reader specifically.

The work in question is the 'problem' play, the play with which
Molière knew he was in for trouble. This play is, of course, *Le
Tartuffe*. The historical facts surrounding the creation of the play
are important here. *Le Tartuffe* was seen as irreligious and immoral,
and banned for five years after only one performance.[6] Finally the
King was persuaded to use his influence to get it put on. Written in
1664, it was not printed till 1669. But during its period of
banishment, Molière was promoting his play in every way possible.
In particular, he was organizing and participating in play readings.
Boileau commented: 'At that time *Le Tartuffe* had been banned,
and everyone wanted to invite Molière to hear him recite it.'[7] It
seems likely then that despite Molière's remarks in the Preface
(quoted earlier) insisting that he wanted his plays performed, he
would have felt it essential in this case to produce a text adapted for
readers, since he must have had doubts about whether the play
would ever be staged.

A second point relates to the content of the play, the controversial subject-matter which caused it to be banned in the first place. Molière was not prepared to soften the remarks he made about religious hypocrites; and in his Preface to the play he justifies his material on the grounds that he was exposing a vice, but definitely not endorsing it. And yet, when the time came for the play to be published, five years after he first tried to perform it before the public, he must have felt the need to be careful: the fury of the *cabale des dévots* (the religious secret society that had great influence at court) might cause the play to be banned yet again. So he makes a particular point of apologizing, not specifically to an audience, but to the reader, for the most dubious remarks in the play. As far as we are concerned, the interesting thing is that in excusing himself he incidentally gives one a clue as to how he views the central character.

For the major problem with the play lies in the character Tartuffe. He could be seen as the embodiment of the perniciousness inherent in the whole notion of a director of conscience who lives in a family home and undermines the family from within. Tartuffe never ceases to insist on his piety: even while seducing the wife of his patron, Orgon, he continues to express his faith in God, and explains his apparently inconsistent behaviour in terms of his theological beliefs. When he usurps the rights of his patron's son, he claims that it is for reasons of virtue and religion; when he turns Orgon out of his own home and comes to take him off to prison, he insists that it is through loyalty to his God and his King.

This character-portrait emerges from the actual words he speaks. However, none of the productions I have seen has attempted to present him without interpreting his words so as to make it clear that he is a rascal, not a genuinely religious man who has squared his corrupt behaviour with a sophistical conscience. For example, in a recent production in London,[8] Anthony Sher as Tartuffe showed himself to be deliberately tricking his patron from the outset, conniving in dumb-show with his servant to make Orgon believe that he has miraculous powers.

One of the interesting things about the character Tartuffe is that despite his consistently equivocal speech, Molière insisted that his hypocrisy was obvious. Talking about Tartuffe in the Preface, he says firmly 'I have removed all ambiguity' ('je n'ai point laissé d'équivoque') despite the patent ambiguity of the words spoken by the character on stage. If Tartuffe's words never expose the scoundrel beneath the mask of hypocrisy, what are the clues that Molière gives us as to the underlying deliberate evil in the character?

Molière himself might point out that he has relied on two things: the play's title and the way he introduces the character. The original title of the play, *L'Imposteur*, does indicate how Molière viewed the character. An impostor, after all, deliberately sets out to pretend to be what he is not in order to deceive others. The second point is made by Molière himself in his Preface. He explains that the reason Tartuffe does not appear until III, ii is in order that his hypocritical nature should be the better stressed:

> I used every possible artifice, took every possible care to make a clear difference between the character of the Hypocrite and that of the genuinely devout man. To this end I took two whole acts to prepare the entrance of my scoundrel. He does not keep the audience guessing for a single moment; they recognize him at once by the marks I give him.[9]

This argument seems unconvincing. The long build-up to Tartuffe's first entrance gives him importance, and we learn how the other characters feel about him. But there is still no clear statement about Tartuffe from Molière in the text as performed on stage.

For concrete proof, we have to go back to the text, not as an audience but as readers. Our clue lies in a solitary stage direction. It is not intended as an instruction to the actor. It is a comment meant for readers of the play. When Tartuffe is presenting Elmire with his outrageous pseudo-religious arguments in favour of committing adultery, Molière interrupts the speech to make the incidental comment: 'C'est un scélérat qui parle' ('This is a scoundrel speaking') (IV, v). This addition was presumably put in by Molière to excuse the appalling immorality of Tartuffe's speeches in this scene.[10]

There are two other examples in this play of comments destined for a reader. Molière excuses the servant Dorine's comment about Tartuffe belching with the remark 'This is a servant speaking' ('C'est une servante qui parle') (I, ii). And when Tartuffe first enters, late in the play (III, ii), the written stage direction clearly implies that he is playing for effect: 'Tartuffe, noticing Dorine: Laurent, put away my hair-shirt and my scourge . . .'[11]

Le Tartuffe seems then to be a special case. Molière approached this play in a unique spirit of wholehearted involvement and determination.[12] The *Avertissement* to *Les Fâcheux* points the difference. Here he stresses the rushed process of putting on a much less controversial play: 'I believe that a comedy conceived, written, memorized and produced in fifteen days is something new.' (Garnier I, 365) A playwright who was, by his own admission, writing, producing and performing a play in a fortnight is not the sort of author to spend hours working on elaborate prefaces or polishing his texts for publication. In general, he avoided writing prefaces to his plays: we have only four prefaces for thirty-three plays. It is a matter of sheer luck that the controversy surrounding *Le Tartuffe* resulted in a highly polished text with no less than four prefatory statements by Molière.

With one notable exception, then, Molière did not write for a reading public, and his modest reluctance to publish appears to be genuine.

Notes

1. All references unless otherwise specified are to Molière, *Oeuvres Complètes*, ed. Robert Jouanny (Paris: Garnier, 1962) (Garnier). This Preface is in I, pp. 628–32. Translations are my own.
2. Contemporary accounts of his quiet social manner bear this out, as do his own remarks on acting. In *The Impromptu at Versailles* he says actors should perform 'as naturally as they can' (Garnier I, 523).
3. Donneau de Visé, for instance, in his 'Lettre sur les affaires du théâtre', singles out the complicated stage action of the lawyer scene in *The School for Wives* as having been particularly popular. Quoted in Molière, *Oeuvres*, ed. Eugène Despois and Paul Mesnard (Paris: Hachette, 1873–1900) (GEF), IV, 146.
4. An eye-witness account by the editors of GEF; see GEF V, 412.
5. 'Letter on the Theatre' ('Lettre sur les affaires du théâtre') in *Diversités galantes*, 1664. Quoted in GEF III, 146.
6. For details of the occasional semi-private performances which took place during this time, see Molière, *Le Tartuffe*, ed. H. Ashton (Oxford, 1946), pp. viii–ix.
7. See Boileau's note to Satire III, 1.25: '*Le Tartuffe* en ce temps-là avoit

été défendu, et tout le monde vouloit avoir Molière pour le lui entendre réciter.' GEF iv, 289 also quotes the Abbé de Chateauneuf. In his *Dialogue sur la musique* the Abbé tells us that Molière went to read his play to Mlle de Lenclos.

8. Directed by Bill Alexander at the Royal Shakespeare Theatre in 1983.

9. 'J'ai mis tout l'art et tous les soins qu'il m'a été possible pour bien distinguer le personnage de l'Hypocrite d'avec celui du vrai Dévot. J'ai employé pour cela deux actes entiers à préparer la venue de mon scélérat. Il ne tient pas un seul moment l'auditeur en balance; on le connaît d'abord aux marques que je lui donne.' Preface to *Le Tartuffe*, Garnier i, 629.

10. In GEF iv, 409, the editors state that the interpolation is found in all the editions published in Molière's lifetime. They comment: 'This little note which is found in all the first editions, in which notes are so rare, indicates that Molière was not too sure of the quality of this witticism.'

11. In the 1734 edition, this stage direction was expanded to make Tartuffe's hypocrisy more apparent: 'Tartuffe, talking aloud to his valet, who is offstage, as soon as he notices Dorine . . .'

12. There is, however, another example of a polemic play in which a comment for the reader could be seen as an excuse for the words in the play. In *The Impromptu at Versailles* (*L'Impromptu de Versailles*), Molière attacks the actor Montfleury, but comments in a note that he is an excellent actor (sc. i).

I I

Modes of theatricality in Molière's comedies (*Dom Juan* and *Le Bourgeois gentilhomme*)

WOLFGANG MATZAT

I

The term 'theatricality' refers to the specific aesthetic possibilities that are inherent in the theatrical communication process and distinguish the art of the theatre from other art forms. In recent work on the theatrical phenomenon we can discern two main directions. On the one hand, the process of theatre communication has been described on the basis of semiotic methods, with the chief concern of theatre semiotics being how to define the semiotic status of the theatrical media and how to describe them systematically as theatrical codes.[1] A second approach to the theatrical process takes the form of sociological, anthropological or phenomenological studies, which explore the analogy between theatrical interaction and social interaction on the basis of the old metaphor of the theatre or its recent application in role theory.[2]

One of the consequences of recent theatre research, particularly of theatre semiotics, is that the dramatic text as such is often neglected. Of course, structuralist methods have also been applied to dramatic texts, but drama analysis and theatre semiotics have in many cases been treated separately.[3] From a philological point of view this development must be considered as having decisive drawbacks, especially when compared to the traditional approach of theatre poetics, ranging from Aristotle to Brecht, where dramatic structure and theatrical function were always closely related. Particularly in the case of historical research, where no precise documents of staging are available, we must rely largely on the written text to investigate the theatrical dimension of a drama. This can only be done on the basis of a pragmatic theory of the dramatic text that allows relationships between textual structures and theatrical functions to be established.

In this chapter I shall outline some elements of such a theory. Two of Molière's comedies, *Dom Juan* and *Le Bourgeois gentilhomme*, will serve as examples. Both plays not only illustrate the theatrical quality of Molière's comedy,[4] but are also especially appropriate for distinguishing different types of theatricality. Finally, these examples will make it possible to discuss how theatrical structures can be related to historical forms of social interaction.

In the theatre the dramatic text becomes part of a complex communication process implying various levels and contexts.[5] A first level is the communication taking place between the fictional characters in the context of the situations represented on stage and in the wider context of the dramatic world that builds up in the course of the whole play. This dramatic interaction becomes part of the theatrical communication process proper, involving the different media or codes of the theatre and, above all, the interaction between actor and audience.[6] The immediate context of the theatrical communication process is the theatre as a whole, consisting of stage and auditorium. As a place governed by special conventions it forms an enclave in the overall context of the social world. We must, therefore, distinguish not only between the dramatic and the theatrical context, but also between the theatrical and the overall social context.

The interrelation of these contexts and the respective communication processes can best be described starting from the point of view of the spectator. According to the different contexts the spectator can adopt different perspectives of reception. The context of the dramatic world, allowing the spectator to assume the point of view of the fictive characters, calls forth illusion and identification. The context of the theatre, on the contrary, suggests a form of reception marked by the *as if* of the theatrical representation and by the aesthetic quality of the theatrical media. Ultimately, the spectator may relate the represented action directly to his social context, disregarding its fictive and aesthetic qualities and understanding it as a message concerning his social situation. This is the mode of reception postulated by Brecht in his theory of the epic theatre.

Normally, the spectator will be conscious of all three contexts, and thus the process of reception will be marked by the simultaneity of the different perspectives. But at the same time these contexts and perspectives are in a state of rivalry, tending to supersede each other. In the first place, the social context always tends to recede into the background during the performance. In addition, the dramatic and the theatrical contexts are to a certain degree mutually exclusive. The consciousness of watching a play is reduced by dramatic illusion, whereas the foregrounding of the theatrical representation weakens the impact of the dramatic context.

My approach to theatricality is grounded in this notion of contexts, especially in the interrelationship of the dramatic and the theatrical contexts. Although this interrelationship is, in the last instance, dependent on the way a play is staged, it is largely predetermined by the written text. Because of the references it contains to the respective contexts, the text always implies a certain mode of reception.

These assumptions make it necessary to describe the interrelationship between the dramatic and the theatrical contexts in more detail. As already stated, the dramatic context prevails when the spectator is drawn into the fictional world through the processes of illusion and identification. In order to create dramatic illusion the fictional situations must be represented in detail and they must appear as part of a coherent dramatic world that extends beyond what is visible on stage. This extension of the fictional space can be an effect of the stage setting, but it is mainly created by the references contained in the dialogue to past and future events, to places beyond the limits of the stage and to people not present in the actual situation. Identification depends largely upon the characterization of the protagonists, on the time they are present on stage, and on the knowledge the spectator has of their thoughts and feelings. A decisive factor, concerning both illusion and identification, is the construction of the plot, especially its anticipatory elements. Since dramatic tension arises from the expectations and conjectures of the audience, the dramatic impact of actions and events represented on stage depends on their appearing as part of a teleological structure.[7]

The specifically dramatic elements of the plot are therefore the intended actions of the characters as well as the obstacles and dangers they meet while trying to realize their plans.

How can the dramatic context be pushed into the background by a theatrical mode of reception? There are two basic ways: a) the reduction of the context of the dramatic world and of the possibilities of illusion and identification it contains; b) the foregrounding of the theatrical context. In the first case, here designated 'decontextualization', stage action is de-dramatized by the reduction of dramatic structures, that is by loosening its integration into a fictional context and by disrupting the plot. In the second case stage action is related to the situation of theatrical interaction as its primary context. This procedure can therefore be termed 'theatrical contextualization' or, taking into account that it involves the weakening of the fictional context, 'recontextualization'. The foregrounding of the theatrical context is explicit when the audience is directly reminded that it is watching a performance; it remains implicit when theatrical elements are introduced into the represented action. As can be seen in the typical example of the play within the play, the implicit theatricalization is marked by a very complex overlapping of contexts. Both procedures – dramatic decontextualization and theatrical recontextualization – are very often closely related. However, each of the two comedies that will now be discussed can be considered a fairly typical example of one of these forms of theatricalization: *Dom Juan* of decontextualization, *Le Bourgeois gentilhomme* of recontextualization.

II

Dom Juan departs significantly from the rules of the *doctrine classique* and its claim to coherent dramatic structure. Spatial and temporal relationships are only feebly indicated; relationships between characters, apart from the central couple Dom Juan and Sganarelle, remain just as weakly defined. As a result, the dramatic world has a decidedly fragmentary quality. Correspondingly, the structure of the action is episodic. In his version of the play Molière shows the last two days of Dom Juan. On the first day we see Dom Juan in a town where he has fled from his newly wedded wife Elvire. After meeting Elvire, who has followed him, he continues his pursuit of new amorous adventures. In the second act, later on the same day, he arrives in a peasant village near the seashore after having nearly been drowned while attempting to carry off a young bride and immediately starts courting the village girls. But he must give up this project too, because he is pursued by Elvire's brothers, and so he tries to escape into the woods. There – in the third act – he has an encounter with his pursuers and afterwards comes across the tomb of the dead Commandeur. The fourth act takes place in Dom Juan's 'appartement' on the evening of the same day, the fifth on the following day, probably somewhere in town.[8] They contain the appearances of a succession of characters, Dom Juan's father, Elvire, her brothers, Monsieur Dimanche, who have all come to remind Dom Juan of his obligations and to urge him to change his life before he meets his well deserved punishment.

As has been observed before, an important structural principle of a play's plot resides in the intentional quality of the actions assuring that – in the words of K. Elam – they can be 'understood to form coherent *sequences* governed by the overall purposes of their agents'.[9] In *Dom Juan* this principle is systematically violated. Dom Juan himself does not pursue any 'overall purposes', but only reacts to the promptings of the actual situation.[10] Neither are the actions of Dom Juan's enemies developed in a coherent sequence. Since the audience is not made aware of their plans, their appearances have an accidental quality. Thus, the actions and interactions represented on stage, Dom Juan's conversations with Sganarelle and his encounters with the representatives of society, appear as a succession of relatively independent situations that are only connected by the figure of the protagonist. This isolation of the stage situations from the context of the dramatic world has the effect of a phenomenological 'bracketing'. The ordinary meaning of situations and actions, resulting from their relation to meaning-giving contexts, is cancelled out, and therefore the structure of the interaction itself is foregrounded.

The theatrical character of interaction in *Dom Juan* has often been pointed out. J. Guicharnaud observes in his brilliant study of the play that through Dom Juan's behaviour his interlocutors are transformed into actors.[11] A brief consideration of Act 4 Scene 6 will serve to illustrate this point. Elvire comes to see Dom Juan for the last time in order to warn him that heavenly punishment is imminent:

> Je ne viens point ici pleine de ce courroux que j'ai tantôt fait éclater, et vous me voyez bien changée de ce que j'étais ce matin. Ce n'est plus cette Done Elvire qui faisait des voeux contre vous, et dont l'âme irritée ne jetait que menaces et ne respirait que vengeance. Le Ciel a banni de mon âme toutes ces indignes ardeurs que je sentais pour vous, tous ces transports tumultueux d'un attachement criminel, tous ces honteux emportements d'un amour terrestre et grossier; et il n'a laissé dans mon coeur pour vous qu'une flamme épurée de tout le commerce des sens, une tendresse toute sainte, un amour détaché de tout, qui n'agit point pour soi, et ne se met en peine que de votre intérêt.
>
> (I do not come here full of that wrath which I showed recently. You see me much changed from what I was this morning, I am not that Donna Elvire who uttered imprecations against you, whose irritated soul discharged nought but threats and breathed only revenge. Heaven has banished from my soul all that unworthy passion I had for you; all those tumultuous ravings of a criminal attachment; all those shameful outbursts of a gross and earthly love. It has left in my heart, with regard to you, only a flame refined from all sensual feelings; a perfectly holy tenderness; a love detached from everything, which is not actuated by selfishness, and which concerns itself only in your interest.)[12]

Even on its own, Elvire's speech seems like a quotation of literary and social discourses. This impression is due to the use of stock formulations, rhetorical style and corresponding rhythmical sentence patterns.

The quotation-like quality becomes still more apparent as a result of Dom Juan's reaction. He interrupts Elvire, remarking in a low voice to Sganarelle: 'Tu pleures, je pense'. This reaction is typical of Dom Juan's treatment of the representatives of society during the whole play. He counters their well-formulated speeches with silence, or with remarks that show his indifference. Thus, he violates a central rule of social interaction, which says that interlocutors have to co-operate by sustaining the other's self-image and by responding to the other's involvement in conversation with equal involvement. According to E. Goffman, violation of this rule has the effect of alienation.[13] It leads to the destruction of the 'illusion of reality'[14] that builds up in the course of social interactions. In the passage quoted, Dom Juan's attitude is underscored in the light of the reaction of Sganarelle, who has been totally taken in by Elvire's display of generous feelings. Through the contrast of these extreme reactions, the self-image implied in Elvire's speech is made visible, and, as a result, the audience takes part in the process of alienation.[15]

In this situation the analogy between social and theatrical role enactment pointed out by sociological and anthropological theatre research comes to the fore. B. Wilshire, at the beginning of his important study, states: 'Theatre is the paradigmatic mimetic art and it deals with the paradigmatically mimetic features of human life'.[16] This means that theatre is founded on the anthropological disposition towards mimetic behaviour and that it represents and brings to awareness the forms of mimetic involvement present in social life. Wilshire's definition of the theatre particularly applies to the passage at hand, because of the different kinds of mimetic involvement it contains. Elvire appears alienated in the pose of Christian charity; Sganarelle – as throughout the whole play – falls victim to his involvement in interaction; Dom Juan, on the contrary, refuses to 'take the role of the other'[17] and tries to detach himself from the mimetic bond implicit in social role enactment.[18]

Thus the theatrical role becomes the artistic model of the social role, exploiting the theatrical effect of watching actors representing situations of role enactment. But this statement does not suffice to explain the particular character of the theatricality of this scene and of the whole play. The reason is that the foregrounding of the context of performance can have quite different functions. The proposed distinction between decontextualization and recontextualization can serve to differentiate two basic possibilities. In the first case the theatrical frame merely operates as a negative context that isolates the situations of the fictive world, in the second the situations represented are positively integrated into the situation of theatrical interaction. Let us first consider more closely the case of decontextualization, the case of *Dom Juan*. Since here the foregrounding of the theatrical situation is marked by the suspension of the contextual determinations and the structures of meaning valid in the fictional world, the theatre appears as a larger and less determined context than the social situations represented, as a context that creates a perspective of aesthetic distance and irreality.[19] The more the dramatic world dissolves into this theatrical space, the more alienated and isolated the characters appear in their respective roles. In modern theatre this impression arises, for instance, when the stage is void of scenery. The theatrical context thus forms a situation of institutionalized alienation and role distance bringing into view social and existential situations of alienation.

This form of theatricality is akin to the concept of theatre as formulated by Brecht. But there is an important difference. In Brecht's epic theatre, roles are distanced in order to give the spectator the opportunity of relating them to his own social context. The dramatic world is confronted directly with the world of the audience. This means that the theatre itself does not form a specific context, but is considered an integral part of the social context.[20] Decontextualization has a specifically theatrical function only when it alienates the audience from the dramatic world *and* from the social world. Then the theatrical experience opens up a perspective that reaches farther than the dramatic world and its social counterpart. Because of its negative quality, this type of theatricality does not involve the foregrounding of acting, which would be typical of recontextualization.[21] Instead the whole stress lies on the alienated relation between the audience and the fictional character's role enactment. Roles are not made visible in relation to the here and now of the theatre, rather they point to a dimension lying behind them, that is to the problems of their subjective and existential foundation.

It is characteristic of *Dom Juan* that we cannot recognize individual persons behind the social roles of Elvire, her brothers and Dom Juan's father. Dom Juan's attempt to free himself of social roles and the norms corresponding to them is marked by a similar negativity because there is nothing he can put up against them. So he remains trapped in the alternatives of denial or hypocrisy. In addition, his attitude of denial is not consistent. He too must cooperate with others in order to satisfy his desires: with Sganarelle, the peasant girls, the poor man, Monsieur Dimanche. Dom Juan's dilemma results from the fact that there is nothing behind social roles. He can defile the costume of the Grand Seigneur, but he cannot strip it off.

III

In contrast to *Dom Juan* the theatrical context in *Le Bourgeois gentilhomme* assumes a positive function. This positive theatricality of recontextualization, however, has also as its condition that the dramatic context is dissolved. Accordingly, in *Le Bourgeois gentilhomme*, as in *Dom Juan*, the succession of stage situations is only loosely connected by a dramatic plot. In the first two acts Monsieur Jourdain previews the rehearsals of the *maître de musique* and the *maître à danser*; then he receives the fencing-master, his philosophy teacher and his tailor. Only in the third act does the conventional plot of comedy begin. Cléonte, who is in love with Jourdain's daughter Lucile, asks in vain for permission to marry her and must therefore resort to a ruse. Playing on Jourdain's aristocratic ambitions, he courts Lucile in the disguise of a Turkish prince and bestows on Jourdain the mock title of a Mamamouchi. Seen as a whole, the comedy appears less a representation of purposeful action than a succession of scenes having the function of putting Jourdain's folly on show.[22] Not only the dramatic action, but also the fictional world is marked by decontextualization. The latter is a direct outcome of Jourdain's attempt to adopt an aristocratic life style, because this attempt involves breaking the conventions of his social context, the bourgeois milieu and his family. But the violation of social norms does not only have the effect – as in *Dom Juan* – of dissolving the context of the dramatic world, but also of making way for a positive relation between the stage action and the theatrical context.

This theatrical contextualization is based on two facts. The first is that Jourdain cannot transform himself into an aristocrat, he can only imitate one. The mimetic impulse in Jourdain's behaviour is continually underscored in the concrete forms of attitude and gesture. In his attempts to learn the courtly greeting ceremony, fencing or philology, role enactment appears foremost as an exercise in body discipline. Again, as in *Dom Juan*, the result is a close analogy between the represented situation and the situation of the theatre. This analogy reaches its culmination when Covielle,

Cléonte's servant, stages the Mamamouchi ceremony like a play. Molière points explicitly to the auto-referential character of this scene by making Covielle announce the ceremony in the following way:

> Tout cela sent un peu sa comédie; mais avec lui on peut hasarder toute chose, il n'y faut point chercher tant de façons, et il est homme à y jouer son rôle à merveille, à donner aisément dans toutes les fariboles qu'on s'avisera de lui dire. J'ai les acteurs, j'ai les habits tout prêts: laissez-moi faire seulement.
>
> (All this sounds a little like a farce, but with him one can risk anything; we need not seek out-of-the-way methods, he is just the man to play his role perfectly; and he will be easily gulled by all the nonsense we tell him. I have the actors and the costumes quite ready: leave it all to me.)[23]

Secondly, Jourdain's playing an aristocrat results in theatricality because, as a consequence, the home of the bourgeois is transformed into the place of aristocratic 'divertissement'. This means that there is ample opportunity for the display of theatrical media such as music, dance and festive costumes. The first acts are filled with the rehearsal of the entertainment Jourdain wants to offer his aristocratic friends. Although Jourdain's plans are interrupted by his wife, the festivities continue to the end with the Mamamouchi ceremony, the marriage between Cléonte and Lucile and the 'ballet des nations'.

For the reasons just stated the theatrical context in *Le Bourgeois gentilhomme* is evoked in a different way from *Dom Juan*. The theatre does not appear as a place of alienation, where conventions are suspended, but as a place governed by its own conventions, a place of play, of fiction and of entertainment, realized in joyful communion between the actors and the audience. It is characteristic of the negative type of theatricality represented by *Dom Juan* that the dramatic world and the roles that form part of this world appear to be surrounded by an empty space, making this world and these roles appear unreal. In *Le Bourgeois gentilhomme* theatricalization has the opposite effect. Whereas the process of alienation in *Dom Juan* creates a context of infinite distance, Jourdain's playful appropriation of the aristocratic world implies the foregrounding of contextual limitations and of the material conditions of the theatre. Also in this respect there exists a metaphorical relation between the dramatic and the theatrical contexts. On the level of the represented action, contextual limitation is due to the fact that the great world of the aristocracy is placed into the narrow space of the bourgeois setting, and that the role of the aristocrat is enacted by a bourgeois who is totally confined to his bodily nature. This bourgeois framing of the aristocratic world is the condition for its playful representation by the comedians. This means that, on the level of performance, the reduced frame is transformed into a positive aesthetic structure. Where Jourdain fails in his role, the actor is successful, and Jourdain's acting out of his fantasy, though inappropriate in his bourgeois home, triumphs in the theatre.[24] So the reduction of the aristocratic world that results from Jourdain's playing an aristocrat is a model of theatrical modelling. Theatre too must restrict the represented world to narrow boundaries: the boundaries of the playhouse. In both cases the fictional extension of the play is contrasted with the material reduction of the context in which it takes place.[25]

Whereas in *Dom Juan* social roles are seen as mere appearances, evoking the feeling of alienation and of loss of reality, role enactment in *Le Bourgeois gentilhomme* takes on a positive value. This enhancement of value has two aspects. Firstly, role enactment appears as an opportunity for appropriating new fields of reality, and thus as a possibility to realize oneself in the act of transcending oneself.[26] In this respect, Jourdain's joy when playing the aristocrat coincides with the pleasure in theatrical enactment shared by the actors and the audience. Secondly, the role does not point primarily to a consciousness behind it – although there are some scenes where Jourdain's subjectivity comes to the fore[27] – but to the body which supports it. Thus, the role seems not to be grounded in a dimension of subjectivity, which is always marked by an element of absence, but rather in the presence of the body. This bodily presence becomes evident through the presence of the actor. So fiction is related to the concrete conditions of the theatre. The actor who plays Jourdain plays a double part that expresses the tension between the ideality of the projected role and the materiality of the body, and therefore refers directly to the conditions of theatrical enactment.

IV

The two types of theatrical interaction that have been pointed out are related to different aspects of role enactment inherent in social existence. Theatre has therefore, on the one hand, a profound anthropological significance; and, on the other hand, it points to specific historical problems attached to the enactment of social roles.[28] The latter means that the investigation of the theatrical dimension of dramatic texts leads to a historical theory of subjectivity. Space permits only a rough outline of such a historical interpretation. The social context of Molière's comedy is the mainly aristocratic society of *la cour et la ville*, the members of which formed the social elite during the reign of Louis XIV. The position of this elite, however, was unstable. The nobility in both its forms – *noblesse d'épée* and *noblesse de robe* – had lost a great part of its political function. It depended to a high degree on the favour of the king, and at the same time it felt menaced by the rising bourgeoisie. In this situation, social commerce at court and in the drawing rooms of the town became the chief occupation as well as the only way of securing one's social identity.[29] The ideal of the times was therefore the *honnête homme*, the perfect social being, who excelled in the art of modelling his behaviour according to the norms of good society. The negative side of this kind of social existence emerges in the writings of Jansenist theologians and philosophers such as Pascal and Nicole.[30] They describe social commerce as an interaction in which the participants are only intent on obtaining confirmation of their respective self-images. Behind all forms of courtesy lurks *amour-propre*, which for the Jansenists meant above all a desire for social recognition.[31] The Jansenist critique of court life brings out poignantly that the members of the society of *la cour et la ville* were totally attached to their social existence and the corresponding roles. Their identity depended entirely on social commerce, and, as Pascal describes eloquently, they were abandoned to their nothingness when alone.[32] Although Pascal's and Nicole's description of social existence is part of a metaphysically based argumentation, it gives valuable insights into the historical development of the conditions of identity. The French society of the seventeenth century finds itself in the problematic final stage of feudalism in which the individual could no longer be defined sufficiently in terms of social position. Paradoxically, however, the individual was all the more dependent on society because there was no possibility of 'private' identity outside society.[33] The mainly public life typical of the upper classes in the *société d'états* thus seemed to be a play of masks with nothing more behind it than the negative principle of *amour-propre*.

Molière's comedies deal with the difficult conditions of confirmation of identity in this society and with the resulting paradoxical strategies.[34] Together with *Le Misanthrope*, *Dom Juan* is the comedy that shows most clearly the dilemma caused by a lack of alternatives to life in society. When Dom Juan thwarts the role enactment of his interlocutors by refusing them his recognition, it becomes apparent that these roles and the corresponding social values are not based on a God-given social hierarchy, but that their validity is dependent on social interaction. The decreasing validity of social values, however, cannot yet be balanced by the concept of an autonomous subject. Dom Juan is not a romantic rebel who affirms his identity against society. Behind his social role he is nothing more than his natural impulses and restless desire.

Le Bourgeois gentilhomme has been understood as a satire on the ambitions of the rising middle class that threatened the society of *la cour et la ville*.[35] Such an interpretation does not take into account that the bourgeois is not only the butt of satire, but at the same time the central part of a play that enhances the prestige of the aristocracy. The play, particularly as seen from the point of view of the aristocracy,[36] has a marked quality of reconciliation. This reconciliation is founded in the two aspects of Jourdain's role enactment that have been pointed out. On the one hand, the aristocratic society finds confirmation of its ideal self-image in the desire of the bourgeois to imitate them. On the other hand, it is reconciled to nature as represented by the unrefined body of the bourgeois. For Jourdain's failure to take on aristocratic grace not only enhances the superiority of the aristocratic audience, but also provides a temporary release from the constraints of social role enactment. The body of the bourgeois, although exposed to ridicule, points in its obstinate naturalness to a plenitude of being that is repressed in the completely socialized body of the noble. This form of reconciliation depends entirely on the mediation of the bourgeois: on his ideal aspirations and on his naive naturalness. But the manner in which this twofold reconcilation takes place shows once more the outward dominance and the inner insecurity of the society of *la cour et la ville*.[37]

Notes

1. Cf. for example K. Elam, *The Semiotics of Theatre and Drama* (London, 1980); E. Fischer-Lichte, *Semiotik des Theaters*, 3 vols. (Tübingen, 1983); A. Helbo, *Theory of Performing Arts* (Amsterdam, 1987); T. Kowzan, *Littérature et spectacle* (The Hague, 1975); M. de Marinis, *Semiotica del teatro* (Milan, 1982); A. Ubersfeld, *Lire le théâtre* (Paris, 1978), *L'école du spectateur* (Paris, 1981).

2. Some major contributions in this field are E. Burns, *Theatricality – A Study of Convention in the Theatre and in Social Life* (London, 1972); U. Rapp, *Handeln und Zuschauen – Untersuchungen über den theatersoziologischen Aspekt in der menschlichen Interaktion* (Darmstadt, 1973); B.O. States, *Great Reckonings in Little Rooms – On the Phenomenology of Theatre* (Berkeley, 1985); B. Wilshire, *Role Playing and Identity – The Limits of Theatre as Metaphor* (Bloomington, 1982).

3. This has already been deplored by K. Elam, who gives a valuable account of both critical directions (*The Semiotics of Theatre and Drama*). For a discussion of the relationship between drama analysis and theatre semiotics see also de Marinis, *Semiotica del teatro*, pp. 24-59; E. Fischer-Lichte, ed., *Das Drama und seine Inszenierung*, (Tübingen, 1985).

4. This theatrical quality has been the main concern of the 'new Molière criticism'. See R. Bray, *Molière homme de théâtre* (Paris, 1954); J. Guicharnaud, *Molière, une aventure théâtrale* (Paris, 1963); W.G. Moore, *Molière – A New Criticism* (Oxford, 1949, 1962). However, it still needs systematic description.

5. I have developed the following model of theatrical communication more fully in *Dramenstruktur und Zuschauerrolle – Theater in der französischen Klassik* (Munich, 1982).

6. Although the description of this communication process has been the privileged field of theatre semiotics, semioticians have not been able to account satisfactorily for its central part, the actor–spectator relationship. Here concepts of sociological interaction analysis appear more appropriate, because in this theoretical framework the actor–

spectator relationship can be conceived not only as a semiotic information process, but also as a symbolic interaction where actor and audience co-operate in the creation of the role. See A. Paul, 'Theaterwissenschaft als Lehre vom theatralischen Handeln', A.v. Kesteren and H. Schmid, eds., *Moderne Dramentheorie* (Kronberg, 1975), pp. 167–92; Wilshire, *Role Playing and Identity*.

7. Cf. Elam, *Semiotics of Theatre and Drama*, pp. 120–6.

8. According to the findings of Ch. Delmas, who, on the basis of documents referring to the settings, refutes the traditional view that in the last act Dom Juan returns to the tomb of the Commandeur (see '*Dom Juan* – Pièce de machines', Delmas, *Mythologie et mythe dans le théâtre français (1650–1676)* (Geneva, 1985), pp. 105–38, particularly pp. 116f.).

9. Elam, *Semiotics of Theatre and Drama*, p. 123.

10. Cf. G. Forestier, 'Langage dramatique et langage symbolique dans le *Dom Juan* de Molière', *Mélanges pour Jacques Scherer – Dramaturgie, langages dramatiques* (Paris, 1986), pp. 293–305.

11. *Molière, une aventure théâtrale*, p. 220; cf. also J. Doolittle, 'The Humanity of Molière's *Dom Juan*', *PMLA* 68 (1953), pp. 509–34; G. Defaux, *Molière, ou les métamorphoses du comique: De la comédie morale au triomphe de la folie* (Lexington, 1980), pp. 131–56.

12. Molière, *Oeuvres complètes*, ed. G. Couton, 2 vols. (Paris, 1971), vol. II, p. 74. *The Plays of Molière*, tr. A.R. Waller (Edinburgh, 1907), vol. IV, p. 237.

13. See E. Goffman, 'Alienation from Interaction' in E. Goffman, *Interaction Ritual – Essays in Face-to-Face Behavior* (Chicago, 1967), pp. 113–36.

14. Ibid., p. 135.

15. This relationship of alienation exceeds the distance that is necessary for a comic perspective. *Dom Juan* is therefore, as has been shown by J. Guicharnaud, *Molière, une aventure théâtrale*, on the borderline of comedy.

16. Wilshire, *Role Playing and Identity*, p. 22.

17. In the terminology of G.H. Mead, cf. *Mind, Self, and Society* (Chicago, 1967), p. 73.

18. The different strategies employed by Dom Juan in order to shun every kind of social obligation are well described by N. Gross, *From Gesture to Idea: Esthetics and Ethics in Molière's Comedy* (New York, 1982), pp. 39–71.

19. On the basis of the description of the settings of *Dom Juan* given by Delmas, '*Dom Juan* – Pièce de machines', it can be assumed that in the original production of the play this sense of irreality was enhanced by the contrast between the illusionist setting of the 'pièce de machines' and the anti-illusionist structure of the play.

20. It is the aim of the 'alienation effect' to allow the spectator a critical

view of the represented action from a social point of view. ('Der
Zweck des Effekts ist, dem Zuschauer eine fruchtbare Kritik vom
gesellschaftlichen Standpunkt zu ermöglichen.' *Schriften zum Theater*,
(Frankfurt, 1957), p. 99).

21. This statement, of course, does not apply to the whole of *Dom Juan*.
Particularly the role of Sganarelle relies on the immediate effects of
comic acting.

22. This has been particularly stressed by R. Warning. Warning chooses
Le Bourgeois gentilhomme as an example for his theoretical argument
that comic situations are subject to the paradigmatic principle and are
therefore opposed to the syntagmatic progress of the plot, 'Elemente
einer Pragmasemiotik der Komödie', W. Preisendanz and R.
Warning, eds., *Das Komische* (Poetik und Hermeneutik VI) (Munich,
1976), pp. 279–333, p. 292.

23. Molière, *Oeuvres complètes*, vol. II, p. 757. *The Plays of Molière*, tr.
A.R. Waller (Edinburgh, 1907), vol. VII, p. 175.

24. Therefore J. Brody is not entirely right in his penetrating study of the
play when he affirms: 'Jourdain est avant tout esthétiquement dans
son tort', 'Esthétique et société chez Molière', *Dramaturgie et société*,
ed. J. Jacquot (Paris, 1968), p. 318. This applies only to the level of
the represented action, because the switch from social to aesthetic
norms prepares Jourdain's legitimation on the level of performance.

25. Of course, these remarks on the theatrical function of contextual
limitation constitute a very partial account of the complex matter of
spatial relationships between the fictional level and the level of
performance. In particular, the different effects of openness and
closure that can arise from the interplay of the dramatic and the
theatrical contexts need a far more detailed analysis. For some
elements of such an analysis see Ubersfeld, *L'école du spectateur*, pp.
51ff.

26. For this aspect of role playing cf. R. Warning, 'Pour une pragmatique
du discours fictionnel', *Poétique* 39 (1979), pp. 321–37.

27. For instance, when in the scene with the tailor and his apprentices
(II, 5) he shows himself aware of the way he is being manipulated.
This aspect of the play has been particularly stressed by G.A.
Goldschmidt, *Molière ou la liberté mise à nue* (Paris, 1973), pp. 146ff.

28. See D. Schwanitz, *Die Wirklichkeit der Inszenierung und die
Inszenierung der Wirklichkeit* (Meisenheim, 1977).

29. The noble's transformation from feudal warrior to courtier and the
resulting psychological impact have been brilliantly described by N.
Elias. See *Über den Prozeß der Zivilisation*, 2 vols. (Bern, 1969), vol.
II, pp. 351ff.; *Die höfische Gesellschaft* (Darmstadt, 1975) or *Court
Society* (Oxford, 1983).

30. See especially the sections on 'Misère de l'homme' in *Les Pensées*, in
Oeuvres complètes, ed. J. Chevalier (Paris, 1954), pp. 1113ff., and

Nicole's *Essais philosophiques et morales* (reprint New York and Hildesheim, 1970).

31. Nicole defines 'amour-propre' in 'De la charité et de l'amour-propre' as 'désir d'être aimé', *Essais*, p. 184.

32. *Les Pensées, Oeuvres complètes*, pp. 1137ff.

33. In his sociological study of the transition from the feudal to the bourgeois society N. Luhmann states that in the classical age only negative concepts of self-reference ('negative Fassungen von Selbstreferenz') were possible. Cf. *Gesellschaftsstruktur und Semantik – Studien zur Wissenssoziologie der modernen Gesellschaft*, vol. 1 (Frankfurt, 1980), p. 181.

34. These strategies have been studied in detail by L. Gossman, *Men and Masks – A Study of Molière* (Baltimore, 1963).

35. Cf. Brody, 'Esthétique et société chez Molière'.

36. Since the play was first performed before the court, it can be assumed that this point of view is the dominant one. Still, the reactions of Jourdain's family also offer a bourgeois audience a critical perspective of his aristocratic ambitions.

37. This insecurity is given expression in the play itself by the ambiguous role of Dorante. Contrary to the audience, Dorante indulges in the 'divertissement' offered by Jourdain for very material reasons. His role points to the fact that the playful reconciliation staged in Molière's comedy is fraught with a certain amount of shame for both parties.

12

Chekhov's reading of *Hamlet*

HANNA SCOLNICOV

That *The Seagull* is indebted to *Hamlet* in many ways has long been recognized and partially demonstrated.[1] Yet the Shakespearean play cannot be seen as a 'source' play in the ordinary sense, since it presents other characters involved in another action set within a different society. Chekhov also borrowed widely from Maupassant, Turgenev, Maeterlinck and others.[2] Stretching from verbatim citation through structural and thematic analogues all the way to parody, Chekhov's debt covers the whole gamut of possible literary links, the whole range of intertextual relations. The question of the degree of borrowing, its function and meaning, is thus raised by the play.

Chekhov's use of the *Hamlet* material can be seen as his reading of Shakespeare's play, a playwright's imaginative, dramatic, reinterpretation of the human relations and theatrical issues worked out in the earlier tragedy. Chekhov's reading is not that of a historian of drama and theatre but of a modern artist gazing at a classical model and attempting to render in his own modern idiom what he sees as its essence. His reading, one playwright's reading of another, is a truly creative reading.

In comparing *Hamlet* and *The Seagull* I wish to show how, through his dramatic recasting of *Hamlet*, Chekhov changes our reading of that play. His own play is so much concerned with the nature of dramatic art and the growth of an artist, that the focus of *Hamlet* is also necessarily shifted from the personal and political to the artistic. The young prince's dilemma about the nature of the Ghost, the ethics of revenge or his uncle's guilt, becomes redefined as the actor's dilemma about how to express emotion on the stage, how to bridge the gap between inner feeling and its communication. Chekhov's overriding interest in the theoretical questions of drama and theatre both highlights and is derived from the metatheatrical concerns in *Hamlet.*

The Seagull's borrowings from *Hamlet* are too numerous to be systematically covered. But it is the significant structural parallels which I will be concerned with here. The direct quotation from the closet scene in the conversation between Arkadina and her son Konstantin is no doubt a self-conscious attempt to draw our attention to the deliberate use of Hamletian parallels in the play. The problematic relationship between widowed mother and son, the triangle formed when they are joined by Arkadina's lover, Trigorin, who is also set up as Konstantin Treplev's professional rival, and the young man's uneasy relationship with Nina, his beloved, are carefully modelled on Hamlet's relations with Gertrude, Claudius and Ophelia.

Wherever Chekhov has introduced a deviation or a variation, this serves to accentuate the parallels, and vice versa. The question of suicide over which Hamlet agonizes, from his wish 'that the Everlasting had not fixed / His canon 'gainst self-slaughter' (1.2.131–2) to his longing for self-annihilation, 'To die, to sleep . . . and by a sleep to say we end / The heartache' (3.1.61–3), is echoed by Treplev's threat 'Soon I shall kill myself' (Act 2, p. 25), then by his attempted suicide, and finally by his committing suicide. While Hamlet only argues with himself over the advisability of suicide, Ophelia's 'death was doubtful' (5.1.217). Nina, on the other hand, though no less manipulated by the men surrounding her, survives her own ordeal, discovering that what matters 'is not fame, not glory . . . but knowing how to be patient' (Act 4, p. 57). Her reference to patience is reminiscent of Shakespeare's own phrasing of that Renaissance stoic virtue.

My discussion of the relationship between the two plays will focus on the handling of the plays within the plays. Although in terms of plot structure, there can be little to associate *The Murder of Gonzago* with the inner play in *The Seagull*, if we look beyond the content of the respective inlays to their dramatic and theatrical settings, the parallels become apparent. The reflexive quality of

Chekhov's play accentuates the Shakespearean parallel, and the play within the play becomes the central aesthetic artifact, an example of a dramatic idiom different from that used by the playwright himself.

In both cases, the playlets are offered as exclusive entertainments by the grown-up son of the family. These festive occasions are fraught with tremendous family tension, which gives vent to critical comments and sniping remarks. Both performances are broken off abruptly, creating a family scandal. The vehemence of the reactions to these 'entertainments' seems in excess of their intrinsic artistic merits, dependent rather on the relations between the artist and his audience. The extraordinary richness of these scenes is due to their multiple-exposure technique, duplicating the theatrical event on stage, making their protagonists double as viewers. Beyond this intricate web of correspondences, both amateur productions serve as a testing ground for their young producer's artistic theories.

The respective performances are heralded by a charged atmosphere. First there are the nervous last-minute preparations. Then there is tense expectation in the air, as the uneasy spectators try to relax in their seats. Arkadina tries to extricate herself from the awkwardness of the moment by assuming the role of Gertrude, thus further implicating herself. Treplev picks up the conversation from the closet scene, identifying himself with Hamlet's role.[3] It is quite natural for this theatrical Russian family to be able to quote snatches of Shakespeare at each other. Without in any way overstepping the boundaries of naturalism, Chekhov can thus underline the structural and thematic parallelism with *Hamlet*.

In this urbane interchange, mother and son air their own conflict without even alluding to it. To a certain extent, this is a parasitical scene, for without a true knowledge of its source, the son's accusation of sexual sin, too embarrassing for a naturalistic play, would be missing. But although there is no moral stigma attached, both mother and son recognize a psychological problem in the changed relationship between them because she has a lover. Even without the exceptional circumstances of death and remarriage in *Hamlet*, the psychological and practical repercussions on the young man of his mother's pursul of her own sexual life and artistic career are immense.

The bandaging scene in *The Seagull*, in which mother and son squabble over Arkadina's relationship with Trigorin, recalls the closet scene in *Hamlet*. At the height of the argument, Arkadina hurls at her son 'You are nothing but a Kiev shopman!' thus implicitly invoking his dead father, her former husband. Clearly, the triangular relationship between mother, lover and son has lost nothing of its poignancy despite the absence of the blood feud.

Chekhov's modernism has no use for royal protagonists or for a gothic plot of murder and revenge. Shakespeare himself merely manipulates these staples of his contemporary theatre so as to create the situations around which he can develop the inner character of his protagonist. But if for Shakespeare the King is still the *exemplum* of humanity, Chekhov is dealing with his peers, and the sensitive consciousness at the heart of the play is an artistic one, like his own. Chekhov represents a society of aspiring artists, competitive city people trying to relax in the country, at an old family estate in the provinces. Hamlet shares with Kostya the grudge at being forced to reside in a provincial place, away from the bubbling intellectual life of the city.

The high drama of murdering a brother and committing incest with his wife, the infringement of primeval taboos, the ritual pollution that calls for purgation by the shedding of more blood, all these are put aside by Chekhov in favour of those themes and human relationships in the play that are relevant to modern sensibility. Chekhov has no need of such outstanding events as murder and incest to justify Kostya's nervous state or Masha's mourning. The trivial and the humdrum are quite enough to trigger off the sharp response of a sufficiently delicate psyche.

With the change in sexual mores, gone is also the suggestion of carnal sin. Arkadina's affair with Trigorin seems perfectly acceptable in her milieu until the unbearable tension breaks out in Treplev's challenging of Trigorin to a duel. The tension between the two men has multiple sources: there are both sexual and professional rivalries between them. Kostya is jealous of Trigorin because, not only has he taken his mother from him and oversha-dowed him as a writer, but he has also won Nina's love and admiration. This is of course only the barest outline of Kostya's painful involvement with his mother's lover.

Trigorin is not prepared to answer Treplev's challenge, which he regards as immature (Act 2, p. 32). It is as though the great Hamletian duel has undergone a process of attrition. The possibility of ritualizing conflict in the form of fencing has been lost. In *Hamlet*, as Nigel Alexander has shown, 'the idea of duel is one of the great images which dominate the action of the play', beginning with the account of the duel between Norway and Hamlet senior.[4] Chekhov's ironic treatment of the duel highlights Shakespeare's own sophisticated employment of this theatrical convention. Hamlet's adherence to the antiquated code of honour practised by his father, which forces him to accept the challenge despite his 'gain-giving' (5.2.162), is contrasted with Claudius's *Realpolitik*, which does not scruple at using the 'play' of duel as a means of murder.

Ostensibly offered as family recreations, both inset plays are designed to be provocative. Arkadina is quick to sense this when she interprets the whole play as a direct affront to herself as an artist: 'He wanted to show us how to write and what to act. This is getting tiresome! These continual sallies at my expense – these continual pin-pricks would put anyone out of patience' (Act 1, p. 13). By contrast, Claudius's suspicion is aroused relatively late, when he enquires 'Is there no offence in't?' (3.2.219). He has sat through the motions of the dumb-show, apparently unperturbed, and makes his enquiry only when Hamlet converses with his mother during a scene change. Despite their different messages, both inset plays contain direct attacks, which, however, are only clear to their addressees.

Arkadina is engaged in light social conversation when her thoughts suddenly return to her son's amateurish theatrical production: 'But my conscience is beginning to trouble me. Why did I hurt my poor boy's feelings? I feel worried' (Act 1, p. 14). This momentary awakening of motherly instinct is one of those supreme naturalistic touches which Chekhov manages to charge with drama. It is a startling psychological disclosure of the inner discomposure and unease of Arkadina beneath the assumed appearance of perfect composure and ease.

Arkadina's conscience has been stirred by what has just happened at the performance; she feels guilty about the way she has treated her son Konstantin and is worried about what his hurt reaction might be. But beyond the naturalistic twist of thought allowing us a fleeting glimpse into the complex psychological make-up of the actress, society woman and mother, there is the symbolic weighting of the moment through its literary association with Hamlet's plan to 'catch the conscience of the King'.

The parallel is only partial, for while Treplev catches his mother's conscience, Hamlet catches his uncle's. Chekhov has picked out elements from *Hamlet*, rearranging them into new patterns. In this case, he may have felt intuitively what Richard Proudfoot and others have shown, that Hamlet may be suspicious of his mother being an accomplice to the murder and wishes, perhaps subliminally, to catch her conscience as well.[5]

While imitating the circumstances of the *Mousetrap* performance, Chekhov places his own inner play at the beginning of *The Seagull*, rather than in its middle. Its performance sets the whole plot in motion. Treplev's playlet lacks a name, but presumably it too should be called *The Seagull*. The figure of Nina sitting on a big stone, all dressed in white, representing the lonely world-soul, evokes that image, and in the framing play, as Nina becomes increasingly disturbed, she accepts her identification with the seagull, first suggested by Trigorin, and internalizes it. The inset and frame plays are associated with each other through their common central symbol, without however establishing any material relation, or any parallel structure, as in *Hamlet*.

Treplev attacks the conventionality of modern theatre where 'When the curtain goes up, and by artificial light, in a room with three walls, these great geniuses, the devotees of holy art, represent how people eat, drink, love, move about, and wear their jackets' (Act I, p. 6). He strikes an avant-garde pose, calling for 'new forms of expression'. Chekhov challenges us to view his own play in relation to Treplev's production and views on theatre. But Treplev is merely a character in Chekhov's play, a dramatic means of introducing the debate on the aesthetics of theatre. From the wealth of uses to which Shakespeare has put his play within the play, Chekhov has chosen to focus on the metatheatrical implications. By making the inset a futuristic piece compared with its more conventional frame, he has inverted the old versus new relationship between inset and frame established in *Hamlet*.

The Seagull as a whole may be seen as an impressionistic reworking of *Hamlet*. It was Tolstoy who reputedly first suggested that 'Chekhov has his own manner, like the Impressionists.'[6] This observation captures, according to Ernest Simmons, Chekhov's unique contribution to traditional Russian realism, and also surely differentiates between him and traditional realists like Tolstoy and Dostoevsky. Tolstoy himself was not apparently sure whether he liked or disliked this innovation, and on one occasion told Chekhov, 'But I still can't stand your plays. Shakespeare's are terrible, but yours are even worse!'[7]

The impressionist style is apparent not only in the seemingly random flow of conversation but also in the general tone and colour of the play. The French Impressionist painters often went back to famous paintings, both old and contemporary, in order to show what was new in their own approach and technique. Chekhov put *Hamlet* to a similar use, changing the *chiaroscuro* of the older play into an iridescent picture with softer contours. The gloomy medieval Danish castle he transformed into a Russian country house. The political problems, the questions of state, the threatening wars, all these darker shades at the back give place to a much brighter setting.

Hamlet's 'nighted colour' also undergoes in *The Seagull* an interesting displacement. Not having recently lost a father, Treplev has no cause for wearing black; this affectation is transferred instead to another character, to Masha. But Chekhov insists on the *Hamlet* allusion by evoking it in the opening line of the play. To Medvedenko's question: 'Why do you always wear black?' Masha replies: 'I am mourning for my life. I am unhappy.' Unlike the older master, the modern one no longer feels the need to supply a motive for mourning. Masha is not in mourning for a dead father but for herself, for her own unfulfilled life. This example demonstrates Chekhov's impressionist approach to his source play in two ways: (1) He chooses to keep the black spot on stage, but transfers it from his protagonist to another character, and (2) he refuses to provide a precise motivation for the character's behaviour. Chekhov does not even need to keep melancholy as a distinctive feature of his protagonist; it is enough that his canvas contains this daub of colour. It surely shows a measure of insensitivity to dress all the characters save Nina in black, as was done in Alexander Tairov's 1944 production.[8]

By lifting the black-clothes motif out of its original context, Chekhov directs our attention to it as an issue of intrinsic interest, not just as subservient to the plot. The question is brought to the fore of the colour scheme, the design and the costumes as non-verbal communicative systems in both the theatre and real life. The wearing of black is, in western civilization, a prime example of a conventional sign. From among Hamlet's various external signs of melancholy, Chekhov singles out the one that is most prominent, and places it before us as an object for contemplation by choosing to open his play with it. But he presents it from an ironic angle, with Masha's mock-romantic mourning over herself, assuming the classical 'Hamletian' pose.

If Masha's clothes reflect her state of mind and her feelings, so do Hamlet's. Shakespeare makes the most of Hamlet's sombre appearance in the midst of the colourful court by insisting on its inadequacy as a means of expressing his psychological condition. The body language of sighing, crying, wearing a 'dejected havior of the visage' and black clothes, all these are 'actions that a man might play', but they do not 'denote me truly'. In this, his very first long speech in the play (1.2.77–87), Hamlet is already transcending the immediate dramatic situation to direct our attention to the question which will later engross him in relation to the play within the play: how to suit the action to the word and the word to the action. The search for an artistic vehicle which will be capable of conveying the emotion or 'passion' becomes an end in itself, beyond the immediate exigencies of the plot. Anticipating Hamlet's interest in co-ordinating word and action, Shakespeare is searching here for a way of superseding conventional behaviour both in everyday life and in its theatrical representation. He employs the Elizabethan stage convention of the melancholic young man, but makes Hamlet defy that stereotype. Shakespeare is attempting to go beyond the visible appearance, the 'trappings and the suits of woe' to an expression of the inner self, 'that within that passes show'.

But theatre must show. The situation is paradoxical: in order to be communicative, body language, as all language, must be conventionalized, but as it is conventional it cannot convey particular ideas and emotions. From the vantage point of Chekhov's own time, the way to escape this paradox is by a whole-hearted commitment to introspective naturalistic acting of the kind developed by Stanislavsky. While Hamlet can have nothing like this in mind, he does seem to advocate in his advice to the players a greater degree of naturalism in acting.

However, the question of naturalism is forever a relative one. The ability to convey meaning through movement and expression is dependent on the search for naturalism, rather than on its attainment.[9] Hamlet's demand for a freer style of acting is grounded on his understanding of the mimetic nature of the theatre. The players should not 'o'erstep . . . the modesty of nature', because the 'end' of playing is 'to hold as 'twere the mirror up to nature' (3.2.16–19). Hamlet endorses the familiar Renaissance emblem of art as a mirror, but then qualifies the mirrored 'nature' as having a distinctly ethical bias: 'to show virtue her own feature, scorn her own image, and the very age and body of the time his form and pressure' (3.2.19–20).

In *Hamlet* the purely aesthetic and theoretical considerations are subordinated to the plot and to the moral issues and intertwined with them. But the play within the play provides an opportunity for reflecting on the nature of theatre as an art. On stage is reproduced the theatrical performance with all its paraphernalia: the preparations, the producer's intentions, the social occasion, the audience reaction. The very act of performance itself, as distinguished from the contents of the play performed, becomes an object of mimetic representation.

How to perform and what to perform are the issues picked up by Chekhov from his model as the questions to be explored in Treplev's experimental play. Because Chekhov is much less encumbered with a plot, his delineation of the purely aesthetic, forever dangerously close to the decadent, is much more pronounced.

'Decadent' is indeed Arkadina's immediate judgement of her son's theatrical experiment, and 'decadent' was also, strangely enough, the reaction of many of the first reviewers of *The Seagull*.[10] Our own response to Treplev's play is complicated by the wide range of critical opinions provided by Chekhov, from Arkadina's condemnation to Dorn's admiration. Is Chekhov trying to baffle us? To warn us against a simplistic response? Whose opionion are we to adopt? Are we meant to regard Treplev's play as a parody or as an artistic experiment? Does Chekhov support the avant-garde, or the older, more conservative, generation? Does he endorse Treplev's search for new forms or Trigorin's well-oiled naturalistic technique? The evaluation of the inset *Seagull* is crucial, for at stake is our understanding of Chekhov's own artistic aims and achievements.

Though Treplev's spoken text is highly rhetorical and slightly ridiculous, his theatrical invention is none the less inspired. When the curtain rises on the makeshift stage-on-stage, 'the view of the lake is revealed; the moon is above the horizon, its reflection in the water' (Act 1, p. 11). Konstantin has previously calculated the effect: 'Here is our theatre. The curtain, then the first wing, then the second, and beyond that – open space. No scenery of any sort. There is an open view of the lake and the horizon. We shall raise the curtain at exactly half-past eight, when the moon rises . . . If Nina is late it will spoil the whole effect' (Act 1, p. 5). Surely we must agree with Sorin that this is 'magnificent'. Konstantin has hit on the brilliant idea of using not a naturalistic setting but framing nature itself for his most unnaturalistic play. The view of the lake is itself so breathtaking that it creates the strongest possible theatrical effect. This is a play created for a particular performance, hence the hour of performance can be set so as to show the moon rising behind the lake, thus enhancing the spellbinding beauty and at the same time providing theatrical lighting.

But the purity of this artistic conception is undermined when we realize that this 'natural' effect is in its turn created artificially on Chekhov's stage. The moon and lake are in fact not real but part of the scenography. Ultimately what we get is yet another naturalistic effect, not a window opening out on nature.

Chekhov may be taking here a side-glance at another Shakespearean *locus classicus* of theatrical technique. The question of how best to represent the moon in the theatre was already taken up by the artisans in *A Midsummer Night's Dream*. After consulting the almanach, Bottom suggests leaving 'a casement of the great chamber window, where we play, open, and the moon may shine in at the casement' (3.1.43–5). Perhaps a naive solution to the problem of bringing moonlight into the chamber for Pyramus and Thisbe to meet by moonlight, but certainly a very effective one, and not too far from Treplev's symbolist usage of the rising moon. The alternative solution, proposed by Quince, to have an actor representing Moonshine come in with a bush of thorns and lantern, is no less naive, but its artificiality and stylization contrast with Bottom's 'natural' setting.[11]

Chekhov's sophisticated superimposing of Treplev's 'natural' scenery onto his own naturalistic scenery forces us to consider the central problem of theatrical aesthetics: How can reality be represented on the stage? What is the nature of the mimetic relationship? Treplev himself abandons the mimetic concept of theatre, repudiating Hamlet's notion of holding the mirror up to nature, and prefers to use nature as a backdrop, investing it with symbolist overtones. His experimentalism purports to represent lofty futuristic ideas rather than life as we know it. His art is abstract, beyond life and experience. He is a true harbinger of post-realistic art.

Chekhov's practice and theory direct our attention to Shakespeare's grappling with similar problems, though in a less rigorous and more scattered manner. *The Seagull* draws together the theoretical references in the two plays most concerned with theatrical presentation, *Hamlet* and *A Midsummer Night's Dream*. From Chekhov's point of view, Hamlet's Ciceronian definition of the basic mimetic nature and ethical function of the theatre is supplemented by the yokels' more pressing staging problems.

That Chekhov rejects this radical path there can be little doubt, for his own play has living people in it and romance, so that even Nina, who decries the lack of these in Konstantin's play, could enjoy it. But although the inset is a gentle parody, the young man's experiment is portrayed with much sympathy and his ideas deserve serious consideration. Treplev is shown as a young man with an artistic vocation, and there is a measure of admiration for his serious-mindedness. At the same time, his excessive seriousness is portrayed with gentle humour, as an aspect of his emotional immaturity.

The Seagull can be seen as devoted to discovering why Treplev's potential talent has not found its right outlet, why society cannot accept his work as legitimate art, and why he has failed in his bid for love. Like other distinctive Chekhovian features, the theme of the blighted life of a young man is already present in Shakespeare, even if it is overshadowed by the direct dramatic appeal of the plot.

The Seagull uses *Hamlet* as its 'classical' frame of reference. Shakespeare's play lends its shape to Chekhov's naturalistic material, and provides it with a sense of direction and purpose. For Chekhov, as for many writers, *Hamlet* had assumed the same importance that classical antiquity had had for Shakespeare. 'I am more an antique Roman than a Dane' (5.2.294) is how Horatio sees himself. In asking to hear the speech about Priam's murder from Aeneas' tale to Dido, Hamlet implicitly compares himself to Pyrrhus avenging his father Achilles' death. Looking back to the heroic literature of the Homeric age, he sees himself as miscast in the avenger's role. He is not the only one who cannot measure up to his classical precursor: the late King 'was to this / Hyperion to a satyr' (1.2.140), and Gertrude's grief falls far short of Hecuba's or Niobe's.

Hamlet may see himself as a mere 'rogue and peasant slave' (2.2.538) compared to the epic figure of Greek mythology, but, from the perspective of *The Seagull*, he in his turn becomes a figure of heroic stature. Placed beside Chekhov's anti-hero, Hamlet assumes a 'classical' dignity. To our own latter-day anti-heroism Treplev himself might seem a larger-than-life romantic hero in his attitude to both art and love and in his courage to commit suicide in the face of failure. The dramatic image we have of ourselves is probably closer to that of the Beckettian protagonist, so impotent that he cannot even take his own life.

With one well-aimed shot at the seagull, Treplev topples Hamlet's belief in the special Providence in the fall of a sparrow (5.2.166–7). Shakespeare's universe still retains, though tenuously, this metaphysical dimension of man's life. Treplev shoots first the seagull and then himself, because for him there is nothing beyond his own needs and his own life. The theatrical clashing of swords in which Hamlet both kills and is killed gives way to Treplev's off-stage, very minor-key suicide. Chekhov's subdued ending makes us question the 'heroic' ending of *Hamlet*, the military funeral procession accompanied by '*a peal of ordnance*' (5.2.356 stage direction), and return to Hamlet's own words of exit: 'The rest is silence' (5.2.311).

Finally, Chekhov used *Hamlet* as his classical model, imaginatively transposing both its form and artistic concerns into a modern idiom, moving towards a greater degree of naturalism, a more immediate and direct expression of thought and feeling. But if, to a certain extent, he thereby solved the riddle of suiting word and action to each other, he also indicated ironically, through Kostya's bumbling experimentation, that his own solution was only temporary and that the artistic equilibrium achieved was unstable.[12]

Notes

The texts used are as follows: *Hamlet*, ed. G.R. Hibbard (Oxford: Oxford University Press, 1987); *A Midsummer Night's Dream*, ed. R.A. Foakes (Cambridge: Cambridge University Press, 1984); *The Plays of Anton Tchekov*, tr. Constance Garnett (New York: Modern Library, (1929)).

1. Eleanor Rowe, *Hamlet: A Window on Russia* (New York: New York University Press, 1976). David Magarschak, *Chekhov*, p. 146; quoted in Rowe, p. 110. Thomas G. Winner, 'Chekhov's *Seagull* and Shakespeare's *Hamlet*: a Study of a Dramatic Device', *American Slavic and East European Review* 15:1 (1956), pp. 103–11. T.A. Stroud, '*Hamlet* and *The Seagull*', *Shakespeare Quarterly* 9:3 (1958), pp. 367–72. Robert Porter, '*Hamlet* and *The Seagull*', *Journal of Russian Studies* 41 (1981), pp. 23–32.
2. On *The Seagull*'s indebtedness to Maupassant's *Sur l'eau*, which is read by Arkadina in Act 2, see Richard Peirce, *Chekhov: A Study of Four Major Plays* (New Haven: Yale University Press, 1983), pp. 23–8, and Jerome H. Katsell, 'Chekhov's *The Seagull* and Maupassant's *Sur l'eau*', *Chekhov's Great Plays: A Critical Anthology*, ed. Jean-Pierre Barricelli, pp. 18–33. For Turgenev's influence on Chekhov, see Eleanor Rowe, p. 109, and Marc Slonim, *From Chekhov to the Revolution* (New York: Oxford University Press, 1962), p. 72. On

Chekhov's interest in Maeterlinck and especially on the close connection between Trofimov's play and Maeterlinck's drama see Laurence Senelick, 'Chekhov's Drama, Maeterlinck, and the Russian Symbolists', in Barricelli, pp. 161–80, and J.L. Styan, *Chekhov in Performance* (Cambridge: Cambridge University Press, 1971), p. 17.

3. For a discussion of which translation of these lines Chekhov was using, see Winner, pp. 106–7, n.

4. Nigel Alexander, *Poison, Play, and Duel: a Study in Hamlet* (London: Routledge, 1971), p. 25.

5. Richard Proudfoot, '"The Play's the Thing": Hamlet and the Conscience of the Queen', *'Fanned and Winnowed Opinions': Shakespearean essays presented to Harold Jenkins*, ed. J.W. Mahom and T.A. Pendleton (London: Methuen, 1987), pp. 160–5.

6. Ilya Ehrenburg, *Chekhov, Stendhal, etc.*, ed. Harrison E. Salisbury (New York: Knopf, 1963), p. 58; quoted in Ernest J. Simmons, *Introduction to Russian Realism* (Bloomington: Indiana University Press, 1965). Cf. also Slonim, *From Chekhov to the Revolution*, p. 74.

7. Harvey Pitcher, *The Chekhov Play* (Berkeley: University of California Press, 1973), p. 1.

8. Vera Gottlieb, *Chekhov in Performance in Russia and Soviet Russia* (Cambridge: Chadwyck-Healey, 1984), p. 50.

9. On Shakespeare's criticism of the older, more rhetorical style of Alleyn's acting, see Peter Holland, *'Hamlet and the Art of Acting'* in *Drama and the Actor*, ed. James Redmond, *Themes in Drama*, vol. XI (Cambridge: Cambridge University Press, 1984), pp. 39–61. The difficult question of Shakespeare's views on acting is taken up by Ekbert Faas, *Shakespeare's Poetics* (Cambridge: Cambridge University Press, 1986), pp. 39–42. He thinks Shakespeare has made his hero 'the mouthpiece of a theory of drama . . . out of tune with his actual practice', a neo-classical, didactic and elitist theory akin to Ben Jonson's.

10. Gottlieb, *Chekhov in Performance*, no. 1.

11. Cf. Styan, *Chekhov in Performance*, p. 26: 'The scene is to be lit by the real moon, a plan which only Bully Bottom could otherwise have conceived, and the backdrop is to be the mysterious lake itself, the ultimate scenic realism. He goes over the plans with a breathless fervour, as if to justify his concept of theatre.'

12. An earlier version of this paper was read at the Shakespeare Institute in Stratford-upon-Avon in 1989.

13
Shaw's stage directions

E.A. LEVENSTON

The shrewdest assessment of the purpose of Shaw's stage directions comes, naturally enough, from Shaw himself – and right at the beginning of his career as a dramatist. In 1898, in the preface to *Plays Unpleasant*, the first of the many prefaces he was to write to accompany the published versions of his plays, he is quite explicit about the need for a 'serious effort to convey their full content to the reader'.[1] For want of adequate stage directions Shakespeare, he tells us, left no intellectually coherent drama.[2] Ibsen, too, by giving the reading public very little more than the 'technical memoranda required by the carpenter, the electrician and the prompter' gains mysteriousness of effect at the cost of intellectual obscurity.[3] By contrast, the readers of Shaw's plays, if they 'do their fair share of the work' will understand nearly as much of the plays as the author himself.[4]

What Shaw sought above all else was intellectual clarity. As far as possible, any misunderstanding of the tone and intent of dialogue must be eliminated. So the reader – and the actor – must be given not only a precise description of the character's emotions, but even an understanding of his political and religious convictions: 'The Reverend James Mavor Morrell is a Christian Socialist clergyman of the Church of England, and an active member of the Guild of St Matthew and the Christian Social Union.'[5] And the reader – and the producer – is told not only what furniture and lighting effects must be provided on-stage but also, when relevant, what has been happening off-stage: 'Caesar, fresh from the bath . . . comes in.'[6]

The physical appearance of the characters, the contents of their bookshelves, the view from their windows – everything must be spelt out, sometimes in quite startling detail: 'restless blue eyes, just the thirty-secondth of an inch too wide open'.[7]

Shaw was well aware what such extravagant concern for the reader might lead to: the production of works 'part narrative, part homily, part description, part dialogue and (possibly) part drama: works that could be read but not acted. I have no objection to such works; but my own aim has been that of the practical dramatist: if anything my eye has been too much on the stage. At all events, I have tried to put down nothing that is irrelevant to the actor's performance, and, through it, to the audience's comprehension of the play.'[8]

Such at least is his claim in this early preface to *Plays Unpleasant*, though later the notion of relevance sometimes has to be stretched to breaking-point. It is possible surely to understand a play about Napoleon without the Irishman's barbed comment: 'it is even now impossible to live in England without sometimes feeling how much that country lost in not being conquered by him'.[9] In one respect, however, the concern to put down nothing that is irrelevant to the *audience's* comprehension of the play leads him to treat the reader even more like a member of the audience than was customary in printed plays. In Elizabethan play-texts, for instance, it was standard practice to identify by name all the characters that came on stage and precede all speeches by the speaker's names. So the reader of *King Lear*, peopling the stage of his imagination, is immediately able to recognize Edgar when he enters 'disguised as a madman'.[10] By contrast, there is no knowing at what point the spectator in the theatre will succeed in identifying Poor Tom, who keeps up his pose of madness till the end of the scene.

Shaw's practice is quite different. He prefers not to give a name to his characters until the dialogue itself has revealed their precise identity. So of the crowd sheltering from the rain under the portico of St Paul's Church at the beginning of *Pygmalion* only Freddie is addressed by name and so identified; the others remain the flower-girl, the mother, the daughter, the gentleman, the notetaker. Only at the end of the scene do Pickering and Higgins find out who they are talking to, and the labels to their speeches shift accordingly:

> *The Gentleman.*   I am Colonel Pickering. Who are you?
> *The Note Taker.*   Henry Higgins, author of Higgins Universal Alphabet.
> *Pickering*   (*with enthusiasm*). I came from India to meet you.
> *Higgins.*   I was going to India to meet you.[11]

If we regard the dramatic text as a variety of fictional narrative, then in this respect it is clearly told from the point of view of the spectator. And the reader of the text experiences the events on the stage, comes gradually to understand their significance, in the same way and at the same speed as the spectator in the audience.

But this is not always the case. In other respects the dramatic narrative is told by an omniscient narrator who knows his characters' innermost secrets, judges them severely – and shares his judgement with the reader. When we first meet Sir Ralph Bloomfield Bonnington in *The Doctor's Dilemma*, we read:

> Even broken bones, it is said, have been known to unite at the sound of his voice; he is a born healer, as independent of more treatment and skill as any Christian Scientist . . . He is known in the medical world as B.B.; and the envy roused by his success in practice is softened by the conviction that he is, scientifically considered, a colossal humbug.[12]

This final judgement can only be made by the theatre audience as the play develops. The personality projected by the actor and the subsequent development of the plot will, or should, eventually combine to establish humbuggery. But the reader knows immediately. And reading the play is definably different from seeing it on the stage; as the stage directions increase in scope, so the distinction between play and novel begins to blur.

In *John Bull's Other Island*, Shaw even gives the reader a broad hint about the way the plot is going to develop. When Nora Reilly first comes down the hill, a slight weak woman in a pretty muslin print gown (her best), we are immediately informed how she strikes the two visitors from England: 'For Tom Broadbent . . . an attractive woman, whom he would even call ethereal. To Larry Doyle, an everyday woman fit only for the eighteenth century, helpless, useless, almost sexless, an invalid without the excuse of disease, an incarnation of everything in Ireland that drove him out of it.'[13] It comes therefore as less of a surprise to the reader than to the spectator when Tom proposes to Nora and Larry rejects her so cruelly. Here again reading the play-text is a different experience from seeing it on the stage, at least as far as the degree of suspense is concerned.

Shaw's narrative omniscience also allows him to share background information with the reader that most spectators will certainly lack. When Patsy Farrell in *John Bull's Other Island* is asked why he was in such a hurry to deliver a message, he explains: 'I was afeerd o forgetn it; and then may be he'd a sent the grasshopper or the little dark looker into me at night to remind me of it.' The spectator then hears Cornelius expostulate, 'Yah, you great gaum, you! Widjer grasshoppers and dark lookers!' but is himself left in the dark as to what they are talking about. The reader has already been informed that 'the dark looker is the common grey lizard, who is supposed to walk down the throats of incautious sleepers and cause them to perish in a slow decline'.[14]

Most of the examples discussed so far bear out Shaw's view that works would be produced 'part narrative . . . part description . . . and (possibly) part drama'. But what about the other element he foresaw: part homily? In *Caesar and Cleopatra*, the second of the three *Plays for Puritans*, he takes pains to let his readers know how far the Romans, though they lived nineteen and a half centuries ago, were our superiors: 'The palace . . . is not so ugly as Buckingham Palace; and the officers in the courtyard are more highly civilized than modern English officers: for example, they do not dig up the corpses of their dead enemies and mutilate them, as we dug up Cromwell and the Mahdi.'[15]

This is the kind of comment on the theme and ideas of a play that seems more appropriate in a preface than in the stage directions – but Shaw did not always bother to keep them apart. Why does Mrs Dudgeon in *The Devil's Disciple*, the first of the three *Plays for Puritans*, stand 'inept, crushed by the weight of the law on women, accepting it, as she had been trained to accept all monstrous calamities, as proofs of the greatness of the power that inflicts them, and of her own wormlike insignificance'! The spectator in the theatre can rely only on his own historical awareness for an understanding of her apathy. The reader of the text is given a sharp nudge by the author: 'at this time, remember, Mary Wollstonecraft is as yet only a girl of eighteen, and her Vindication of the Rights of Women is still fourteen years off'.[16] It is probably in historical plays that such homiletic intrusions are most evident. Shaw could not be sure that his audience would share his view of history, but he leaves his reader in no doubt where he stands.

Even when Shaw is clearly presenting the action and dialogues from the point of view of the spectator, without historical judgements of Roman civilization or encyclopaedic footnotes about Irish superstition, it is hardly the point of view of a spectator in the audience, the other side of the footlights, possibly in the back row of the stalls. In *The Philanderer*, for example, the reader as spectator is close enough to make out precisely what the members of the Ibsen club are reading: 'Cuthbertson is seated in the easy chair ... reading the Daily Graphic. Dr Paramore is on the divan . . . reading the British Medical Journal . . . Sylvia Craven is sitting in the middle of the settee before the fire, reading a volume of Ibsen, only the back of her head being visible from the middle of the room.'[17] Note that since the fire is explicitly situated stage centre, at the back, and the settee is facing it, no real-life spectator, even with the most powerful of opera-glasses, would be able to make out what she is reading with such absorption – and there is no discussion of the subject in the dialogue. Similarly, in *Man and Superman* the spectator is close enough to identify the busts, portraits and photographs that decorate Roebuck Romsden's study as those of John Bright, Herbert Spencer, Richard Cobden, Martineau, Huxley and George Eliot[18] – assuming, that is, that he can recognize them when he sees them. Shaw soon came to realize that he was not exactly describing the scene as it appeared to the audience; in fact at the beginning of *John Bull's Other Island*, he explicitly states: 'Let me describe it briefly from the point of view of a sparrow on the window sill.'[19] Such close proximity to the scene has another advantage for the sparrow – or the spectator whose point of view is shared by the reader: it enables him to smell the room as well as see it: 'It is a room which no woman would tolerate, smelling of tobacco.'[20] This is a detail which may add intellectual clarity for the reader, but presents quite a challenge to the producer.

The actors in Shaw's plays also face some remarkable challenges. If they are to remain faithful to his stage directions, they must be able to control their bodily reactions to a degree that would daunt the most adept of yogis. Mrs Dudgeon in *The Devil's Disciple* turns white with intense rage.[21] Lentulus in *Androcles and the Lion* 'becomes white with terror; and a shade of green flickers in his cheek for a moment.'[22] Probably the most demanding part in all Shaw's plays, from this point of view, is that of the strange lady in *The Man of Destiny*:

> As she recognizes him, she becomes deadly pale. There is no mistaking her expression: a revelation of some fatal error, utterly unexpected, has suddenly appalled her in the midst of tranquillity, security and victory. The next moment a wave of angry colour rushes up from beneath the creamy fichu and drowns her whole face. One can see that she is blushing all over her body.[23]

Shaw himself realized that this was asking too much. In fact, he parodies such physiological excesses in a deservedly little-known play, *Passion, Poison and Petrifaction: or the Fatal Gazogene. A brief tragedy for barns and booths*: '*Lady Magnesia (waking and sitting up).* My husband, (*all the colours of the rainbow chase one another up his face with ghastly brillancy*) why do you change colour?' Shortly afterwards, for reasons too tedious to explain, occurs the stage direction '(his face is again strangely variegated)', whereupon Lady Magnesia remarks, 'Your complexion is really going to pieces.'[24]

Change of colour is the extreme example of Shaw's constant concern to help his reader grasp both the physical appearance and the personality of his *dramatis personae*. They come on stage for the first time to the accompaniment, in the written text, of a thumbnail description which for the reader serves the same purpose as the physical encounter for the spectator. For Shaw – and his reader – this initial confrontation is often the occasion for a moral judgement. Sometimes, as we have seen in the case of Sir Ralph Bloomfield Bonnington, this is a matter of common knowledge. Sometimes the judgement is derived from the physical appearance itself: 'He has a thick silly lip, an eager credulous eye, an obstinate nose and a loud confident voice. A young man without fear, without reverence, without imagination, without sense . . .'[25]

And sometimes the initial judgement turns out to be wrong: 'Lady Utterwood, a blonde, is very handsome, very well dressed, and so precipitate in speech and action that the first impression (erroneous) is one of comic silliness.'[26] A similar kind of misjudgement is liable to occur later in *Heartbreak House* when Lady Utterwood's husband, Randall, comes on stage: 'He has an engaging air of being young and unmarried, but on close inspection is found to be at least over forty.'[27]

Again, it is the reader whose intellectual grasp of the relationships between the characters is facilitated by this anticipation of possible misjudgement. At what point, if at all, the spectator will correct his erroneous first impressions, if indeed he forms them, presents yet another problem for the actor and the producer.

Shaw's early claim, then, that he 'tried to put down nothing irrelevant to the actor's performance' should not be taken too seriously. Many years later, recalling his association with Granville-Barker and his first steps as a playwright, Shaw gives a simpler account of his purpose in writing the way he did: 'I had, therefore, not only to publish my plays but to make plays readable . . . I substituted readable descriptions for technical stage directions, and showed how to make the volumes as attractive in appearance as novels.'[28]

Intellectual clarity is one indispensable facet of readability. It is also concern for the reader that leads Shaw to abandon the desperate attempt to render Eliza's dialect without a phonetic alphabet as unintelligible outside London. And it is the reader that Shaw is out to entertain when, in *John Bull's Other Island*, he allows the blarney of his Irish characters to spill over into the stage directions: 'The mutilated remnant of a huge plaster statue, nearly dissolved by the rains of a century, and vaguely resembling a majestic female in Roman draperies, with a wreath in her hand, stands neglected amid the laurels. Such statues, though apparently works of art, grow naturally in Irish gardens.[29]

All these features of the text can best be summarized by using another concept from the theory of fiction – the implied reader. Shaw's implied reader is an intelligent, educated layman with a sense of humour. He has no special knowledge of London dialect or Irish superstition and no professional concern with the theatre. In fact, it is because he has not even had the pleasure of visiting the theatre that Shaw provides him with the next best thing: a text that gives all the details of a fully staged production.

By contrast, for most other playwrights, both before and after Shaw, the implied reader is the producer of the play. It is the producer who can make do with the barest minimum of information about entrances, exits and stage business. Everything else – the actor's age and appearance, the details of the stage setting, the lighting effects – depends on the producer, or the resources of his theatre and his company. Sometimes the instructions to the producer are quite explicitly embodied in the printed text, as when Noel Coward adds to Act 2 of *Hay Fever* the note: 'The following scene should be played with great speed',[30] or when Feydeau, near the end of the first scene of *Une puce à l'oreille*, suddenly remembers to add: 'En réalité, et dans tout le courant de l'acte, il doit parler d'une façon absolument inintelligible . . . en ne prononçant, mais bien nettement, que les voyelles, comme les gens qui ont le palais perforé.'[31]

The most interesting playwright from this point of view is Oscar Wilde. In *Salome*, *A Woman of No Importance*, *Lady Windermere's Fan* and *The Importance of Being Earnest* he keeps to the old tradition of writing for the producer, and gives us no information whatever about his characters; all the force of Lady Bracknell's personality derives from her utterances, not Wilde's description. But in *An Ideal Husband*, first published in 1899, one year after the appearance of *Plays Unpleasant*, the descriptions of the characters are positively Shavian, though with a Wildean touch of art for art's sake: 'Mrs Marchmont and Lady Basildon, two very pretty women . . . They are types of exquisite fragility. Their affectation of manner has a delicate charm. Watteau would have loved to paint them.'[32]

Could it be that Wilde was the first to learn from his fellow-Irishman the secret of making plays readable? The only trouble with this suggestion is that *The Importance of Being Earnest* was, I think, written and published after *An Ideal Husband* (though published in the same year); perhaps only *An Ideal Husband* was revised for publication.

My suggestion that plays can be written with one of two implied readers in mind, either a producer or an intelligent layman, is of course an oversimplification. Actually, this conceptualization covers two end-points of a scale; a playwright may have more or less consideration for the needs of the non-professional reader. Shaw was not the first to add comments to the text that could mean nothing to the audience in the theatre, nor am I the first to make the point. Max Dessair, in his *Aesthetik und allgemeine Kunstwissenschaft* (Stuttgart, 1908) quotes the stage direction from Hauptmann's naturalist drama *Before Sunrise*: 'It is the farmer Krause who, as usual, has left the inn last of all' and comments 'this note by the poet, put in parenthesis, only looks like a stage direction'. In fact, Jiri Veltrusky, from whose *Drama as Literature* this reference to Dessair is taken, prefers the term 'author's notes' to 'stage directions', seeing the relationship between author and reader as more important than that between author and producer.

The first moves away from the bare minimum required by a producer seem to have occurred at least as early as the end of the eighteenth century; Sheridan in *The Rivals* marks some speeches with such comments as 'peevishly', 'sullenly' and 'softening'. Pinero, whose early plays were published before *Widowers' Houses*, even adds brief descriptions of his characters: 'Dunstan Renshaw enters. He is a handsome young man with a buoyant self-possessed manner, looking not more than thirty, but with the signs of a dissolute life in his face.'[33]

It is Shaw, however, who first realized the need to make plays readable and changed the face of the printed play. His successors have varied in the degree to which they have been prepared to follow his example. Brecht and Pinter, for instance, still write primarily for the producer. O'Neill and Authur Miller are among those who have used Shaw's techniques for introducing their characters: 'His face is well-formed, good-looking, but its expression is resentful and defensive. His defiant dark eyes remind one of a wild animal in captivity. Each day is a cage in which he finds himself trapped but inwardly unsubdued. There is a fierce, repressed vitality about him.'[34]

But Shaw's prophecy of the direction in which playwriting might develop was never actually realized. In fact, no one has ever gone quite so far as Shaw himself. If there are any plays of which the description 'part narrative, part homily, part description, part dialogue' is even partly true, it is those of George Bernard Shaw.

Notes

1. Bernard Shaw, *Plays Unpleasant* (Harmondsworth: Penguin Books, 1946), p. xxiii.
2. Ibid., p. xx.
3. Ibid., p. xxii.
4. Ibid., p. xxiii.
5. Bernard Shaw, *The Complete Plays* (London: Constable and Co. Ltd., 1931), p. 124 (*Candida*).
6. Ibid., p. 285 (*Caesar and Cleopatra*).
7. Ibid., p. 335 (*Man and Superman*).
8. Preface to *Plays Unpleasant*, p. xxiii.
9. *The Complete Plays*, p. 153 (*The Man of Destiny*).
10. See *King Lear*, Act 3, Scene 4.
11. Shaw, *Complete Plays*, op. cit., p. 720 (*Pygmalion*).
12. Ibid., p. 510 (*The Devil's Disciple*).
13. Ibid., pp. 418–9 (*John Bull's Other Island*).
14. Ibid., p. 421 (*John Bull's Other Island*).
15. Ibid., p. 252 (*Caesar and Cleopatra*).
16. Ibid., p. 227 (*The Devil's Disciple*).
17. Ibid., p. 39 (*The Philanderer*).
18. Ibid., p. 332 (*Man and Superman*).
19. Ibid., p. 405 (*John Bull's Other Island*).
20. Ibid., p. 405 (*John Bull's Other Island*).
21. Ibid., p. 221 (*The Devil's Disciple*).
22. Ibid., p. 691 (*Androcles and the Lion*).
23. Ibid., p. 158 (*The Man of Destiny*).
24. Ibid., p. 1114 (*Passion, Poison and Petrifaction: or, The Fatal Gazogene*).
25. Ibid., p. 156 (*The Man of Destiny*).
26. Ibid., p. 760 (*Heartbreak House*).
27. Ibid., p. 769 (*Heartbreak House*).
28. Bernard Shaw, 'Granville-Barker: Some Particulars', *Drama*, New Series No. 3, Winter, 1946, p. 7.
29. Shaw, *Complete Plays*, op. cit., p. 424 (*John Bull's Other Island*).
30. Noel Coward, *Hay Fever* in *Plays: One* (London: Eyre Metheun, 1979), p. 44.
31. Georges Feydeau, *La Puce à l'oreille*, in *Théâtre complet de Georges Feydeau IV* (Paris: Le Bèlier, 1950), p. 126
32. Oscar Wilde, *An Ideal Husband* (London: Methuen, 1899), p. 4.
33. Arthur W. Pinero, *The Profligate* (London: Heinemann, 1891), p. 9.
34. Eugene O'Neill, *Desire under the Elms*, in *The Complete Works of Eugene O'Neill*, vol. II (New York: Boni and Liveright, 1924), p. 149.

14

Marat/Sade and the politics of interpretation

UNA CHAUDHURI

Peter Weiss's *Marat/Sade* is perhaps the pre-eminent example since Pirandello of that most theoretically productive of dramatic devices, the play-within-the-play. But, unlike his predecessor, Weiss explicitly links metatheatricality to politics, so that the central question raised by his use of this familiar structure moves away from Pirandello's philosophical problematic and can perhaps best be framed in terms of affect. Quite simply, we can ask: is *Marat/Sade* a truly frightening play, an urgent reflection on political horrors, or does its complicated structure work to domesticate its danger, to tame its political power?

Needless to say, such a question quickly overflows the text at hand: it can be asked of much politically oriented avant-garde drama, including Brecht's, in which structural and stylistic experimentation threatens to neutralize revolutionary analysis and convert it into a purely aesthetic experience. Yet *Marat/Sade* remains a privileged site for such an interrogation, for the reason that it fully internalizes and theorizes the issue of drama and politics. Furthermore, the play produces a model for a resolution of this issue, a model characterized by a profound and pervasive historicity. At its most basic level, the play is a demonstration of the idea that both historical knowledge and dramatic representation are suffused with temporality. The play's structure first highlights the acknowledged temporality of our relationship to the past, stressing, as it were, the pastness of the past, its quality of being disjunct from the present. It then gradually transfers that recognition to the theatrical experience of its spectator, ultimately making of that experience a matter not simply of imbibing history but of inserting oneself into history. This process, by which play-watching is transmuted into history-writing, is hardly a simple one, but it is, as I hope to show here, precisely structured into the play's text.

In *Marat/Sade* we do not simply see history in the making, we participate in making it, and our first instrument for doing this is metatheatre. *Marat/Sade* is not only a play-within-a-play, but also, quite explicitly, a play-about-the-play, a play about play-making and play-watching. Thus to read *Marat/Sade* is inevitably to theorize the topic, 'to read a play'.

Weiss's play begins by raising a question that has been in the forefront of much contemporary drama theory (especially semiotic theory), namely: what is a play? In the theory, this question is articulated as a textual choice, a choice between play-text and performance-text,[1] with the result that the original question is transformed: not *what* is the play, but *where* is the play – on the page or on the stage? Can we read a play independently of its performance? Or is the performance already a reading?

The structure of *Marat/Sade* offers, if not a solution to the problem of dramatic identity, at least a valuable reformulation of it, and it does so by recasting the original spatial and textual terms of the debate into temporal and processive ones. The play seems to suggest that the appropriate question is not 'where is the play?' but 'when is the play?'

Marat/Sade is written as a play in the making, a play under construction. Its self-consciousness, which, of course, it shares with many other modern plays, and indeed with modern art in general, is special because here it is totally focused on the idea of process, and at two levels, that of history (the process of moving from one time period to another) and that of theatrical experience (the process of moving from text to performance). That is to say, multiplicity is not merely a fact of this play's stage history[2] (as it is of most others), or even of its textual history[3] (as it is of many others); rather it is a property of the play's meaning, structured into its text in the form of a complex system of historical and psychological layering.

What appears as the complex historicity of *Marat/Sade* is actually a doubling and problematizing of the normal temporal model of drama. In most traditional plays, dramatic communication and meaning are produced by an initial process of mapping a presumed absent reality, be it historical or fictional, onto the theatrical present. A 'there and then' is rendered as a 'here and now'. In a play there is no mediating narrator. Everything occurs in the present tense, before our eyes.[4] It is not, as the popular television formula had it, that 'you are there', but rather 'it is here'.

In *Marat/Sade*, the first such mapping of absence onto the theatrical present produces the 'frame play', the play we watch, the play called *Marat/Sade*, the play toward which we expect to suspend our disbelief. The time is the year 1808, and the place is the lunatic asylum of Charenton in France. However, the process of mapping 1808 onto 1964 (when the play received its first production), or 1989, or any future date, is more complicated than usual, for it involves the presentation, the rendering present, of an absence that is already (and pointedly) divided between fact and fiction. According to the frame play, the Marquis de Sade is (as indeed he actually was) one of the inmates at Charenton. Tonight, he is staging a play (as indeed, amazingly, he sometimes actually did) in which the roles are played by the other inmates (as indeed they actually were). De Sade's play itself, however, is fictional, in the sense that the historical Marquis never staged a play about the death of Marat; yet it is also 'historical', in the sense that it dramatizes events that did indeed occur.

In this way the first (and already fissured) mapping of absence onto presence opens into a second one, the play-within-the-play, the play we watch others watching, the play entitled, in nineteenth-century titular fashion, *The Persecution and Assassination of Jean-Paul Marat as Performed by the Inmates of the Asylum of Charenton Under the Direction of the Marquis de Sade*. This inner play, of which the events and the representation are separated by only fifteen years, holds out the promise of a less complicated mapping, for it claims to present only certain historical facts of 1793: how Charlotte Corday came to Paris, purchased a knife, went three times to the home of Jean-Paul Marat, was finally admitted, and assassinated Marat as he lay in his bathtub.

Two things, however, keep this inner play from functioning as the stable 'core drama', the rich, meaning-laden mother-lode that a play-within-the-play often is.[5] First, it quickly becomes apparent that this core historical drama is itself only a pretext for its author, de Sade, who repeatedly enters it, not as a character but in his own person, to engage its protagonist, Marat, in an extended debate. This debate, which pits Marat's revolutionary conviction against de Sade's naturalistic despair, gradually displaces the inner play from the centre of dramatic interest, tempting spectators and readers to base their responses to and interpretations of *Marat/Sade* at this level of the play.

Indeed, the great debate between Marat and de Sade is so powerful, so rich in intellectual content, as to be a kind of paradigm of dramatic meaning-production, obeying all the conventions that traditionally govern it, including the layering of an *agon* with multiple philosophical meanings. The debate between Marat and de Sade can quite easily be read as an archetypal conflict between reason and passion, idealism and cynicism, mind and body, history and myth, progress and repetition, time's arrow and the wheel of time.

There is even a theatrological dimension to be found in the conflict, a boon to those critics and pedagogues who value the play chiefly for its encyclopaedic use of twentieth-century experimental theatre techniques. Almost everyone, including the author himself[6] as well as the play's various directors[7] and certainly its critics, has been guilty of kicking the play back and forth between Brecht and Artaud, as though the two were opposing goalposts on the field of theatre practice. For, like Brecht, Marat believes that conscious, collective action can produce social change; while de Sade antici- pates Artaud in claiming to have learnt that this world is a world of individual bodies. To him, human history is a nightmarish cycle of rebellions against the horrible indifference of Nature, and 'All movements,' he says, 'move in vicious circles'.[8] Marat, refusing to accept the grotesque evidence even of his own body's domination (he is confined to a bathtub by the agonizing skin disease he acquired while hiding in sewers before the revolution), keeps trying to dictate his call to action, for, he says, 'Against Nature's silence I use action / In the vast indifference I invent a meaning / I don't watch unmoved I intervene / And say that this and this are wrong / And I work to alter them and to improve them' (26–7).

However, as loaded with archetypes as this debate may be, its status within the play is not unambiguous. For, just as the debate intervenes and ruptures the historical play-within-the-play, it is itself under constant attack by the frame play. The agent of this attack is Coulmier, the 'director', as he is called, of the asylum. The censorship he exerts on the other director, de Sade, provides a vivid illustration of the ideological constraints on dramatic representation.

But it is not simply that both the inner play and the debate are controlled by the keeper of the madhouse; the keeper himself is an unconscious battleground for the very same philosophical conflict being articulated within the debate. In Coulmier's case, the battle rages around the status of madness, and its terms exactly match those by which, after the Enlightenment, the category of madness was gradually transformed into that of mental illness. Weiss's depiction of Charenton makes it an early model of the modern mental health facility, a place designed for socio-medical intervention into madness.[9] Yet it also retains strong traces of an earlier view of insanity, which was, precisely, a *view*, an objectifying gaze that confirmed the onlooker in his normalcy while leaving its object intact in his lunacy.

In Weiss's play, Charenton is poised between these two definitions of madness; madness as a spectacle, a wholly objectified otherness, versus madness as a deviation, an area ripe for coercive social intervention. This schizophrenic attitude is revealed in Coulmier's opening remarks to the audience, telling them that the play they are about to witness has been produced 'for your delectation / And for our patients' rehabilitation' (4). Thus the ancient Horatian formula is split between the occupants of the stage and those of the auditorium; the play will profit the former, delight the latter. There will be drama therapy for the sick, dramatic pleasure for the hale.

That this double standard is perfectly untenable is made clear by the paradox generated when, with almost touching naiveté, Coulmier hands over control of his progressive social mission, which is that of introducing rationality into the discourse of madness, to one who has been incarcerated precisely for his anti-social, anti-progressivist critique of reason.

What is the result of this misdelegated authority? Does the

yoking of theatre to rational social change, with madness as the third, 'wild' term, imply the inevitable failure of de Sade's play – both as mechanism of social change and as instrument of individual knowledge? Of course, the question applies not only to de Sade's play but also, by transitivity, to Weiss's, with regard to which it takes a starker form: are theatre and revolution antithetical to each other? This formulation recalls another famous coupling of meta-theatre and politics, Genet's *The Balcony*. Genet's 'third term' is not madness but sexuality, and his response to the question of theatre and revolution is unequivocally negative. Weiss, however, does not answer the question as it is: rather, he causes it to be reframed, introducing into it the problematic of our access to the real.

The incessant interruptions of the play-within-the-play by both the debate and the frame play make of this structure a process, an oscillation between different temporalities as well as different intentionalities. The play seems to occur neither in 1793 nor in 1808, but in the projection of the former onto the latter, in the process of dramatic mapping itself. Its subject becomes not history, but the representation and reading of history, and the motives of those who are performing the reading. Against de Sade's representation of the past as a mirror, Coulmier opposes his representation of the past as difference; against de Sade's allegory, Coulmier asserts anti-allegory. Needless to say, this opposition does not remain restricted to the inner play that *they* are watching, but gradually adheres to the frame play we watch, implicating us in a choice about our relationship to history. Is post-revolutionary France a blood-soaked mirror for the twentieth century, or do we, as Coulmier insists, live in less barbaric, more hygienic times? Or, more broadly: is history a cycle of repetitions, of differences without distinctions, or does the sameness of its surface conceal an undercurrent of alterity? Does revolutionary violence always already harbour brutal counter-revolution, or does the move into a new temporality open a space of genuine difference, for a new political history?

Weiss's obvious association of post-revolutionary France with post-Nazi Germany would seem to suggest the former stance, were it not for the intervention of metatheatricality into his political allegory. Here it is spectacle that produces the gap of difference by which the sameness of history may be breached. And spectacle, in *Marat/Sade*, is madness: a radically non-psychological coding of human experience in terms not of ideology but of physical symptoms and institutional repression. In *Marat/Sade* dramatic meaning is *absorbed* by the spectacle of madness, a spectacle from which all the traditional means of conveying dramatic information, such as psychologically motivated characters, have been systematically removed.

That de Sade and Coulmier are able to draw diametrically opposed conclusions from the inner history play is one way that *Marat/Sade* thoeorizes the topic 'reading a play', by reintroducing into it a contextuality that its original form had repressed. One cannot talk of reading a play, it suggests, without asking who is reading a play, when is she reading the play, why is she reading the play?

Most importantly, it also suggests that reading is a two-way street, a mutually constructive transaction between reader and read. The contextualized reader produces the play, but the play itself is one of the contexts operating on the reader, producing her. A model of the play as process also involves a model of the self as process. As the historical structure of *Marat/Sade* gives us, its readers and spectators, an oscillating double vision of the past, its psychological structure sharpens that ambivalence by problematizing the issue of character identification.

Marat/Sade contains several versions of the actor-role formula, alternative models of dramatic subjectivity, ranging from the most traditional to the most experimental. The traditional version, in which the relationship between actor and character is one-to-one, stable and fixed, is embodied, appropriately, in Coulmier, who always speaks for himself. He is the dramatic character as speaking subject, the formula most amenable to spectator identification. Yet Coulmier is also so obviously the spoken subject of an oppressive ideology as to make us feel utterly unsympathetic to him. In contrast, Marat, along with the other characters in the inner play, is a character in process, entering and exiting from his fictional identity before our eyes. He is the character as spoken subject, a creature and instrument of his author, yet endowed with such ideological and rhetorical powers as to make spectators deeply sympathize, if not actually empathize, with him. In between these two extremes we find the figure of de Sade, both speaking subject and (within the debate) spoken subject, neither an actor-as-character (like Coulmier) nor a character-as-actor (like Marat) but somehow both, a being, as it were, in quotation marks. He is not only, as he says, a stranger to himself, but also, and radically, a stranger to us.

De Sade, as author both of himself and of his antagonist Marat, would indeed seem to be holding all the cards in the debate, but the debate itself is, as we have seen, contextualized within Coulmier's ideological-therapeutic programme. The situation recalls an amazing fact noted by Weiss in his postscript to the published play, namely, that it was de Sade who spoke the memorial address at Marat's funeral. But, Weiss adds, 'Even in this speech his real attitude towards Marat is questionable, since he made the speech primarily to save his own skin' (106).

Thus de Sade's political vulnerability and Coulmier's ideological servility direct their readings and writings of the inner play. That play does not so much proceed as lurch forward, revealing snatches of intentionality that are immediately occluded by Coulmier's official interventions. Yet, paradoxically, the pattern of these interventions gradually outlines a homology between the inner play and its representation. The madmen slowly come to occupy the same position *vis-à-vis* authority as the French populace they play in the inner drama. Like the latter, they experience betrayal at the hands of those who claim to serve their best interests. Thus de Sade's play provides them with an *experiential* version of the political thesis articulated by Marat, the need to keep the revolution ongoing. If they are rehabilitated, it is not in the sense that Coulmier desires, that is, towards a docile acceptance of their stigmatization and incarceration as lunatics, but in the sense that they begin to challenge the ideological structure within which their alleged lunacy is established.

While the debate between Marat and de Sade seems to totalize a specific political conflict into an archetypal opposition, the acts of the madmen, and the response of their jailers to these acts, seem not merely to represent but to *recreate* the political situation that gave rise to the debate. The role of madness in the play now comes into view. It is precisely as spectacle, as objectified otherness, that madness can physically realize itself as oppression. Rational argument and individual psychology have nothing to do with it. The political debate that matters is inscribed on the bodies of the mad actors by the clubs of their guards. Ideas about violence become violent gestures and movements, talk of revolution becomes active rebellion, and a mythologized, dehistoricized past regains a new particularity.

It is significant that the conclusion of *Marat/Sade* has frequently been altered by the play's directors. Each choice, however, is a response to, a reading of, the play's gradual transfer of the image of revolution from a historical past to the theatrical present. But whether the final rebellion of the madmen is rendered politically, philosophically or theatrically[10] by directors, there is no denying that, in the play's final moments, the assassinated Marat's spirit has entered the theatre/lunatic asylum to lead a new revolution, in response to a new oppression.

In the published play, Coulmier brings the curtain down at the height of the madmen's rebellion. It is a final act of censorship,[11] but its victims are the spectators, fictional and real, not the madmen. For them, it is a liberation from one of the kinds of violence they have been subjected too, that of theatrical representation. Now the spectacle of madness is over. Now, beyond representation, its political history can begin. De Sade's play of double temporality has done its revolutionary work; Peter Weiss's play, which will always exist in relation to a third temporality, that of contemporary politics, has set itself the same work to do.

Notes

1. See Keir Elam, *The Semiotics of Theatre and Drama* (London, 1980), pp. 208–9.
2. See, for example, Sidney F. Parnham, '*Marat/Sade*: The Politics of Experience, or the Experience of Politics?', *Modern Drama*, 20 (1977), pp. 235–50; also, for an excellent theoretical discussion of the play's performance history, see Darko Suvin, 'Weiss's *Marat/Sade* and its Three Main Performance Versions', *Modern Drama*, 31 (1988), pp. 395–419.

3. Wesley V. Blomster and Leon J. Gilbert, 'Textual Revisions in Peter Weiss's *Marat/Sade*', *Symposium*, 25 (1971), pp. 5–26.

4. In Thornton Wilder's memorable formulation, 'On the stage it is always now.' Quoted in Manfred Pfister, *The Theory and Analysis of Drama* (Cambridge, 1988), p. 275. An excellent, though debatable, summary of the theoretical implications of this feature of dramatic signification is Peter Szondi's: 'Because the Drama is always primary, its internal time is always the present. That in no way means that the Drama is static, only that time passes in a particular manner: the present passes and becomes the past, and as such, can no longer be present on stage. As the present passes away, it produces change, a new present springs from its antithesis. In the Drama, time unfolds as an absolute, linear sequence in the present.' *Theory of the Modern Drama* (Minneapolis, 1987), p. 9.

5. Suvin helpfully distinguishes between illusionist and non-illusionist uses of the play-within-the-play device. The former, he says, privilege one or other level of the play (frame play or inner play), the latter do not, because 'they deal frankly with epistemology and not ontology' (p. 398).

6. In 1963, Weiss noted of the contemporary political state of affairs: 'In the one case, a constructive critique of the age is pertinent [i.e. Brecht] in another Antonin Artaud's thesis.' Quoted in Suvin, p. 399.

7. See Roger Ellis, *Peter Weiss in Exile* (Ann Arbor, 1987), pp. 32–41.

8. Peter Weiss, *The Persecution and Assassination of Jean-Paul Marat as Performed by the Inmates of the Asylum of Charenton Under the Direction of the Marquis de Sade*, trans. Geoffrey Skelton (New York, 1965), p. 41. Hereafter all page references to this text appear in parenthesis after the quotations.

9. In his chapter 'The Birth of the Asylum', Foucault writes: 'The asylum no longer punished the madman's guilt . . . it organized that guilt; it organized it for the madman as a consciousness of himself, and as a non-reciprocal relation to the keeper; it organized it for the man of reason as an awareness of the other, a therapeutic intervention in the madman's existence.' And, a few pages later: 'Until the end of the eighteenth century, the world of madmen was peopled only by the abstract, faceless power that kept them confined; within these limits, it was empty, empty of all that was not madness itself; the guards were often recruited among the inmates themselves. Tuke established, on the contrary, a mediating element between guards and patients, between reason and madness. The space reserved by society for insanity would now be haunted by those who were "from the other side" and who represented both the prestige of the authority that confines and the rigor of the reason that judges.' Michel Foucault, *Madness and Civilization* (New York, 1965), pp. 247 and 251.

10. As it was by Swinarski, Perten and Brook, respectively. See Parnham.
11. I have discussed a similarly complex use of the curtain in Genet's *The Blacks*: see Una Chaudhuri, *No Man's Stage: A Semiotic Study of Jean Genet's Major Plays* (Michigan, 1986), pp. 77–108.

15

'They don't make them like that any more': intertextuality in *Old Times*

TETSUO KISHI

Old Times is Harold Pinter's 'intertextual' play *par excellence*. For its effect it depends very heavily – much more so than his other works in a similar vein such as *No Man's Land* and *Betrayal* – on references to existing texts and the audience's familiarity with them. The existing texts in this case are a group of popular songs, most of them dating from the 1930s (and the film *Odd Man Out* which I will not discuss here). These songs eventually became 'standards' and were widely sung during the 1940s and 1950s. This makes the play peculiarly 'historical', which is quite unusual in the Pinter canon. To put it another way, the three characters of the play, who, according to the author, are 'all in their early forties', are supposed to be at that particular age in 1971, the year of the play's first production. This would mean that they were born around 1930, and one hardly needs to mention that Pinter himself was born in that year.

What I am concerned with is the way one reads a text for performance which has assimilated other texts, also meant for performance, and the way this reading might affect both acting and audience responses. *Old Times* offers an extremely intriguing case.

The scene in Act 1 of the play where Deeley and Anna sing fragments of popular songs represents a climax of their territorial struggle, the territory being the quiet and enigmatic Kate herself. Of course it makes perfect sense to understand the scene as yet another example of a couple of middle-aged people reminiscing about their youth, and it would be wrong to ignore this more obvious aspect, but this after all is only the surface of the text, and a much nastier subtext emerges only after we analyse in detail the way the two characters quote and sometimes *mis*quote apparently innocent bits of popular culture.

The scene follows a short exchange between Anna and Deeley in which Anna says that Kate was a 'delightful' person. To this Deeley answers, 'Lovely to look at, delightful to know'. This line is a quotation from the opening passage of the refrain of 'Lovely to Look At' (words by Dorothy Fields and Jimmy McHugh; music by Jerome Kern; first performed in the film *Roberta* released in 1935). Then the two characters talk about old songs (and Kate's response to them), but Kate interrupts the conversation, which leads to the following exchange:

Kate   (*to Anna*). I don't know that song. Did we have it?
Deeley   (*singing, to Kate*). You're lovely to look at, delightful to know . . .
Anna   Oh we did. Yes, of course. We had them all.
Deeley   (*singing*). Blue moon, I see you standing alone . . .
Anna   (*singing*). The way you comb your hair . . .
Deeley   (*singing*). Oh no they can't take that away from me . . .
Anna   (*singing*). Oh but you're lovely, with your smile so warm . . .
Deeley   (*singing*). I've got a woman crazy for me. She's funny that way.
           Slight pause
Anna   (*singing*). You are the promised kiss of springtime . . .
Deeley   (*singing*). And someday I'll know that moment divine,
           When all the things you are, are mine!
           Slight pause
Anna   (*singing*). I get no kick from champagne,
           Mere alcohol doesn't thrill me at all,
           So tell me why should it be true —
Deeley   (*singing*). That I get a kick out of you?
           Pause
Anna   (*singing*). They asked me how I knew
           My true love was true,
           I of course replied,
           Something here inside
           Cannot be denied.
Deeley   (*singing*). When a lovely flame dies . . .
Anna   (*singing*). Smoke gets in your eyes.
           Pause

Deeley   (*singing*). The sigh of midnight trains in empty stations . . .
            Pause
Anna   (*singing*). The park at evening when the bell has sounded . . .
            Pause
Deeley   (*singing*). The smile of Garbo and the scent of roses . . .
Anna   (*singing*). The waiters whistling as the last bar closes . . .
Deeley   (*singing*). Oh, how the ghost of you clings . . .
            Pause
            They don't make them like that any more.
            Silence[1]

Deeley, as if to renew Kate's memory, sings a line from the song, but what he is up to is far more complicated than this. 'Lovely to Look At' is, to put it simply, a homage to feminine beauty, and Deeley by indirectly praising her charm is trying to draw her attention to him. The stage direction 'to Kate' makes this clear. In other words, he is responding somewhat challengingly to Kate, who had interrupted the exchange between him and Anna a moment before and spoken 'to Anna'. But Anna is far from content with being a passive bystander. It is because she simply cannot stand Kate directing her attention towards Deeley and also because she has to deny categorically Kate's doubt about her own knowledge of the old song and their possession of the record, which in this context clearly conjures up their intimacy of twenty years ago. Thus Anna ignores Deeley's speech (or rather singing) and before Kate can respond to Deeley, answers Kate's question with a strong affirmation. The timing of these speeches is precisely calculated, and the actors are expected to play the scene with this in mind.

Undaunted, Deeley attempts once again to draw his wife's attention to him, singing what sounds like the opening line of the refrain of 'Blue Moon' (words by Lorenz Hart; music by Richard Rodgers; published in 1934 as an independent song). Interestingly enough, and although the published text of the play contains an acknowledgement about 'reproducing' an extract from the song, the line is not from 'Blue Moon' at all. This sentimental song has to do with the plight of a man with no girlfriend (or a woman with no boyfriend, depending on the gender of the singer) and his (or her) joy at finding a true love. The moon which is, so to speak, an objective correlative of the singer's feeling used to look blue but has turned to gold, and the correct version of the opening line of the refrain is 'Blue Moon, you saw me standing alone'. Deeley has changed both the two personal pronouns and the tense of the verb. But Deeley's version simply does not make sense. How on earth can the moon 'stand alone'? This incongruity may not be evident if we do not know the song itself. But to those members of the audience who know it by heart – and many will – it is too gross a mistake to overlook. There are perhaps three different explanations for this. The first is that Pinter remembered the song inaccurately. This is highly unlikely because to accept it implies that not only Pinter but everybody who was involved with the production did not recognize the mistake. The second explanation is that although Pinter remembers it correctly, Deeley does not. This might prove interesting, since one of the central themes of *Old Times* is the unreliability of memory. But if Pinter had indeed intended the line to be interpreted this way, he could have made the point more explicitly. As it is, there is nothing to indicate Deeley's poor memory. The third and most plausible explanation is that Deeley changed the line on purpose. He is trying to call Kate 'Blue moon' even though it does not quite make sense, as he wants to see her as a lonely and loveless woman and is subtly trying to persuade her to accept a closer relation with him, which would help her overcome her loneliness. This implication is clear to those people who are familiar with the entire lyric of the song.

There is no doubt that Anna is meant to be one such person. She has to challenge Deeley more directly, that is, she too has to join the game and start singing 1930s songs. The first line of her song sounds like a line from 'They Can't Take That Away from Me' (words by Ira Gershwin; music by George Gershwin; first performed in the film *Shall We Dance* released in 1937). Significantly enough, this too is bogus. In the film, Fred Astaire who is about to lose Ginger Rogers – they are eventually reunited of course – tells her that although they may never meet again, he will always keep the memory of the various features of her behaviour, and counts them up repeating the phrase 'the way you . . .' But the line 'The way you comb your hair' never appears in the film. It does not appear in the definitive collection of Ira Gershwin's songs either. Poetically this line is an extremely banal one. Pinter quotes 'They Can't Take That Away from Me' at length (and accurately) in Act 2 of the play – he knows the song very well after all – and there we get such lines as 'The way you wear your hat', 'The way you sip your tea' and 'The way you hold your knife'. These 'ways' can be mannered but the way one combs one's hair cannot, which leads to only one conclusion. Anna notices the distortion Deeley has made to the lyric of 'Blue Moon', and answers that distortion with another of her own. She is virtually saying, 'You can't trick me so easily. It's wrong if you think you can take her away from me.' At the same time it must be noted that Anna's line sounds more physical and intimate than any line in the original version where the line 'The way you sip your tea' is probably the most sensual. Anna's distortion eloquently expresses her feeling towards Kate. Deeley quickly recognizes this, and snatches from Anna the chance to sing the concluding line of the song, which in this context means 'No, *you* can't take *her* away from *me*.' In performance Deeley's singing would have to begin immediately after Anna's line. Otherwise he would look too insensitive.

Anna, still undaunted, then quotes from 'The Way You Look Tonight' (words by Dorothy Fields; music by Jerome Kern; first performed in the film *Swing Time* released in 1936). The gist of the song is that when the singer is lonely, he (or she) will think of the lover and the way she (or he) looked that night. Needless to say, Anna sings it with Kate in mind. Deeley, cutting in, sings a line from 'She's Funny That Way' (words by Richard A. Whiting; music by Neil Morét; first published in 1928 as an independent song), which is a song of a modest man who claims that although he himself is no good, his girlfriend is 'crazy' for him. This particular line occurs several times in the refrain of the song. What Deeley does is perhaps a little too much for Anna. Hence 'slight pause'. It is Deeley who wins the first round of this 'lyrical' boxing match.

Anna feels the pause was long enough to prepare her for a new round, and tries to attack Deeley with the opening line of the refrain of 'All the Things You Are' (words by Oscar Hammerstein II; music by Jerome Kern; first performed in the stage musical *Very Warm for May* in 1939) which is intended as praise for Kate. Deeley knows the song, accepts the challenge at once, skips six lines (or twenty-four bars), and sings the last two lines of the refrain. Again Anna feels beaten, and once more there is a slight pause.

The subtlety of the exchange is sufficient to convince any reader of Pinter's remarkable artistry. What is even more striking is that this essentially antagonistic exchange can be interpreted at the same time as perfectly friendly party conversation in which one joins the other ('Yes, I know that one'). The whole passage works on at least two levels.

The next three lines of Anna's are the opening passage of the refrain of 'I Get a Kick Out of You' (words and music by Cole Porter; first performed in the stage musical *Anything Goes* in 1934). The point the song is trying to make would be clear from these three lines and the fourth line sung by Deeley, and of course the first three lines are merely a preliminary to making 'the punch line' sound more memorable. Again Deeley sings it before Anna has time to get there. Though there is no stage direction, if the actor playing Deeley allows himself to pause even one tenth of a second, it will destroy the sequence. Anna is beaten more drastically than before. Hence 'pause' rather than 'slight pause'. If properly performed, the scene could be greeted with a roar of laughter.

Anna then sings the opening lines of 'Smoke Gets in Your Eyes' (words by Otto Harbach; music by Jerome Kern; first performed in the stage musical *Roberta* in 1933. 'Lovely to Look At' which I have already referred to was added to the film version). This song, unlike previous ones, directly deals with disappointment in love. The singer used to trust his (or her) 'true love' ignoring other people's warnings, and would not accept that all who love tend to be blind because when one's heart is 'on fire', smoke gets in one's eyes. Eventually the singer is betrayed, but refuses to admit the truth of the warning and insists that the tears are caused not by sorrow but by the smoke after the death of 'a lovely flame'. (Here is a rather intricate use of a metaphor.) Deeley pretends that he is not going to interfere – Anna can go on singing for as many as five lines this time – but then abruptly skips thirteen lines and jumps to the conclusion, implying that Anna is going to be the loser. This time, however, Anna is quicker and throws back the last line at Deeley, suggesting that it is Deeley that is the loser. The actress playing Anna could emphasize 'your', but doing so might result in a loss of the subtlety and seeming pleasantness of the whole exchange.

In any case 'pause' rather than 'slight pause' is necessary for Deeley to recover from the blow. He then sings a line from 'These Foolish Things' (words by Eric Maschwitz; music by Jack Strachey; first performed in the revue *Spread It Abroad* in 1936. This is the only British song in the sequence.) This again tells of disappointment in love and the singer lists various 'foolish things' which remind him (or her) of the ex-lover. (Incidentally it is, like 'They Can't Take That Away from Me', one of those 'laundry list' songs which popular songwriters used to produce regularly. The master of the genre was, of course, Cole Porter, the prime example being 'You're the Top'.) After the initial line Deeley waits to see if Anna is going to join in. Anna does join in, but only after a 'pause', and stops abruptly after her line. Deeley tries again. This time Anna answers immediately, which misleads Deeley, and he, believing (wrongly) that Anna is sympathetic, sings 'Oh, how the ghost of you clings'. If Anna is indeed being co-operative, she will sing the next line of the song 'These foolish things remind me of you', or so he assumes. She does not, because singing this particular line would mean an open admission of her defeat. The only thing Deeley can do is to declare the end of the battle, and it is followed for the first time in this exchange by 'silence' rather than 'pause' or 'slight pause'. Deeley tries to treat the songs – and by implication the whole exchange as well – as something irrevocably belonging to the past ('They don't make them like that any more', which being a cliché is itself a form of quotation) and retreats briefly to prepare a new aggression with the story of his first encounter with Kate in a cinema showing *Odd Man Out*.

The text of *Old Times* contains this intricately constructed subtext, appreciable only by an audience who has a sufficient amount of knowledge about the songs which have been assimilated. Perhaps such exclusiveness is true with any literary work, but as the existing texts in this case belong to a clearly defined group, the distinction between the audience in the know and the audience who is not will be more than usually wide. (Of course the majority of the audience would belong to the first group, since the songs are well-known.) One can go further and overlap for instance the context of the film *Roberta* in which 'Lovely to Look At' is sung with that of *Old Times*, but perhaps this is going too far. In any case, some members of the audience will fail to understand why certain moments of the exchange are so uproariously funny. Unless one knows the correct version of 'Blue Moon', one cannot recognize the distortion. Unless one remembers that the line 'Oh, how the ghost of you clings' is followed by 'These foolish things remind me of you' (which is not quoted), one will miss the emotional tension between the two characters. In this exchange what is not quoted is just as important as, or more important than, what is. In some cases, omission itself is what matters.

But the intertextuality in this play is perhaps more distinctive than that in *Rosencrantz and Guildenstern are Dead* for instance. The existing texts *Old Times* relies on are not plays but songs, with more strictly defined notation than literary texts. Of course the actors can deviate from the way the songs are supposed to be sung, but if their performance is to be properly appreciated, the audience's knowledge of the music is an absolute necessity. In other words, a knowledgeable audience can enjoy the difference between the original versions of the lyric and Pinter's versions with their distortions and omissions as well as the difference between the original music and the way the performers may or may not 'distort' it beyond what a singer would normally be allowed to do. The intertextuality in this play is not simply verbal but also musical.

As a matter of fact, there is not much room for performers' freedom of interpretation. Though Pinter does not incorporate extremely detailed stage directions in the way Shaw and O'Neill do, a careful reading of his plays will reveal precise directions as to timing, rhythm, intonation and so forth. But what is impressive about Pinter's text is that it has successfully incorporated what will presumably be a proper audience response. The pauses are necessary not only to the actors but to the audience as well. They are there not only to heighten dramatic tension but to provide the audience with time to laugh to its heart's content. An inexperienced playwright all too often writes a speech containing crucial information immediately after 'a laugh line' and an incompetent actor who cannot 'control' audience response all too often speaks before the laughter dies. This is unlikely to happen in *Old Times*. The analysis of its intertextuality can help us contemplate more objectively and convincingly the question of audience response. It is true that audience response is supposed to be inherent in a text. But an interpretative approach to a text will contribute little to a clarification of such responses, which are much more physical and cursory than many scholars may believe. Of this Pinter's plays will remain a constant reminder.

Note

1. Harold Pinter, *Old Times* (London: Eyre Methuen, 1971), pp. 27–9.

INDEX

Index